JASON X: TO THE THIRD POWER

Free, the surviving son of London Jefferson, has been impregnated with the DNA of cybernetic serial killer Jason X. Leading a cyber engineering project to the prison complex on moon Americana, he and Skye, the daughter of the mad scientist who reconstituted Jason X and a backup Jason X twenty years ago, find a third version. When the new and improved Jason X is liberated, and the prisoners riot, everybody's favourite serial killer has a plentiful supply of victims to sate his thirst for vengeance. It then falls to Free and Skye to fight through the rioting inmates to stop the deadly monster that they have unleashed!

The infamous movie-monster, Jason X, returns in another high-octane tale of action, adventure and death!

D1474866

JASON X:
TO THE
THIRD POWER

A NOVEL BY
NANCY KILPATRICK

BASED ON CHARACTERS
FROM THE MOTION
PICTURE JASON X
CREATED BY
VICTOR MILLER

BLACK FLAME

Dedicated to fans of ferocious fiction.
May Jason X stalk your future!

A Black Flame Publication
www.blackflame.com

First published in 2006 by BL Publishing, Games Workshop Ltd.,
Willow Road, Nottingham NG7 2WS, UK.

Distributed in the US by Simon & Schuster, 1230 Avenue of the
Americas, New York, NY 10020, USA.

10 9 8 7 6 5 4 3 2 1

ISBN 13: 978 1 84416 281 9
ISBN 10: 1 84416 281 8

A CIP record for this book is available from the British Library.

Printed in the UK by Bookmarque, Surrey, UK.

PROLOGUE

Something, someone is stalking her. Again. At first, she cannot see anything. The world is black. There is no scent, no sound. Her tongue is dead meat, as if her taste buds are overwhelmed and can no longer function properly. Only her skin is alive, tingling with the intensity of a sense on overload. Her skin is frightened. The cells between the pores of her flesh have swollen slightly with terror, making them hypersensitive, like the cilia on unicellular organisms that silently scream out at danger.

This place is a maze of narrow colorless tunnels, each end opening up to two more similar nerve endings. She can go up or down; the levels seem infinite. There is always a choice to make and as she flees the unknown, unseen predator, she is not certain she is making the correct one.

Her body grows fiery as her legs pump. Air bashes into her lungs and is thrust out quickly. Her heart cannot take much more of this but she cannot stop. To stop herself would lead to her demise. She knows this intuitively. Knows it as surely as she knows her name.

Then, as if she was born deaf and suddenly regained her hearing, a cacophony assaults her ears. Sounds, many, discordant, all of them harsh, brutal, guttural, like the breath of a thousand rotting demons, the weight of their heavy feet bashing the earth beneath her, causing her body to tremble as she flees across the too soft quaking soil.

She picks up her pace, but how she does this, she cannot say, because she is running all out, the muscles of her legs cramping. Another division; another choice. She heads down the corridor to the left and sees, too late, the dirt floor split open; a severed womb, the fissure racing toward her. She turns to run back but both the floor in front and behind is breeched. The corridors are too narrow and she cannot get around these widening gaps.

Sounds escalate. Her eardrums vibrate, about to shatter. A pounding; like metallic feet racing, like her heart thumping too fast to sustain life. She stops. Frozen. Every inch of her body pulses with terror. She quickly looks one way then the other as the split corridor comes at her from both directions. Soon a crevice will form beneath her feet. She will fall through the blackness. Whoever is stalking her will find her in that black place that is apart from life. And like any predator, this one will claim her as prey.

Suddenly the floor opens beneath, spreading her legs wide. She tries to clutch the slick walls but there is nothing to hold onto. She is slipping down, screaming for help, but deep in her soul she knows there is no help coming. And then she sees something with light glinting off it. A sharp, fat blade that appears out of nowhere, as if it is part of the ungodly darkness, but possesses a light of its own. A blade grasped by a massive hand, an arm thick, built of muscle and metal.

Her paralysis is complete. Her body turns to aching stone. The glinting steel blade arcs up and back, and slashes down, coming toward her head. She cannot move to escape it. The razor-sharp blade slices across her throat in one sweep, severing her head from her body in an almost painless action. As her numb head falls, she sees dark blood pulsing rapidly from her neck artery, pulsing as quickly as her out-of-control heartbeat, the only thing she can feel as she is locked in terror. In that instant she sees the face of her attacker and screams. But it is too late. She has seen him, his skin covered by a metal mask, his eyes burning red doorways to death. And worse, he has seen her and knows her for whom and what she is. Her vision alters as if one eye is missing. There is no sound, no physical pain, only the horror that has been building her entire life. The total and complete awareness of her own inevitable death closing in on her as three sharp, crystal clear objects aim for her left eye. And when they stab into her, finally, she screams…

Skye jerked awake to find herself sitting up in her bed, arms outstretched as if she was trying to grasp onto something or someone for help. She allowed her arms to drop onto her thighs and she glanced around the bedroom which was saturated in diffused light, blinking herself more awake. Familiar things surrounded her: on her dresser, a photograph of her mother and sisters, a small, ornate antique jewelry box her mother said had belonged to her great grandmother, and nearby, a small metallic box.

She worked to control her rapid, gasping breathing, feeling close to hyperventilation. Sweat coated her body and her nightgown clung to her slim form, chilling her, dark hair matted to her scalp. Her quaking, tight voice commanded, "Lights!" The dim lighting was replaced with full illumination.

As she raised a shaking hand to her face, Skye mumbled to herself, "When will it stop?" The bad dream had been the same, all her life, since as far back as she could remember. Someone… something… not quite human, or superhuman, pursued her. It always caught up with her. Her head was always severed from her body. And her eye pierced by three sharp objects. She always saw the face of her murderer clearly in the nightmare, but on waking she could never quite recall the details of what he looked like. The horror of the images never lessened, although she must have dreamt this a thousand times. How many times, she wondered, could a person dream the same, awful dream?

Angrily, she shoved the bedclothes away and stood, tired of being a victim to the world of her psyche. Nothing in reality had ever occurred that even remotely resembled the events in the repetitive nightmare, at least not to her. She stormed around the room, picking up clothing she had dropped the night before, tossing the soiled items into the laundry basket, including her damp nightgown, which she had savagely ripped from her body, leaving her naked.

"Time!" she demanded, as if someone were resisting her. The computer sang out in a soppy-sweet tone, "Oh seven hundred hours," because she'd never gotten around to reprogramming its voice.

"Great!" she snarled. "Now I have even more time on my hands." Another long day of waiting.

"Reminder," the computer sang, and Skye made a mental note to herself to change that cheery digital voice before it drove her insane and she deleted the program altogether. "Your job on Elysium begins today with a meeting at the dock at nine am."

"Ri—ght," she said, chagrinned, slowly remembering. The waiting was over. Today would be different. Today was the big day, when her life would change. When what was wrong could be made right in her world.

She stood before her full-length mirror taking stock of her well-formed body: full breasts, tiny

waist, strong legs, curves in all the right places.
She was blessed with good genes, and healthy
eating and workouts had accentuated the positive.
And, she thought, she wasn't just attractive physically, but eminently qualified for this job. She was
a crack cyberengineer; not only was she top of her
class, but she'd beat out all bar one person for the
Intergalactic Medal of Excellence. She wasn't first
in the universe, and she wasn't happy about being
in a one-down position, but there was something
to be said for being second from the top of the
pyramid of everyone who currently existed who
had studied in her field. She was trained in cutting
edge technology and had her pick of the best jobs
in the industry.

Suddenly, a darkness descended on her: the
nightmare, never-ending corridors that all seemed
the same, constant choices to be made, not sure of
what she was doing, the heavy paralysis of fear.
And then, making that one, fatal error... A bad
decision that led down the wrong path to her
doom. But would choosing the other corridor have
made any difference? She would never know.
Dreams were like that; life was like that. Her dad
had said to tackle the future and trust in your
vision, that if you believed that you were on the
right track, you would get predicted results. At
least that's what he'd said to her mother, in a letter
she'd read.

Quotes from her father! Yeah, right! Skye shook
her head. Her long black hair tumbled around her
face and shoulders. She ran her hands through the

strands and then dragged her nails along the scalp to stimulate her head and wake herself up further. It felt so good. She needed *some* stimulation, something physical. She had been waiting weeks for this day, for this chance.

She just had enough time to hop into the shower, dress, grab something nutritious to drink and flag a taxi to the loading dock where she would board the shuttle. The trip to Elysium from Earth II couldn't take longer than one hour and was probably closer to thirty minutes, give or take, if they had a skilled shuttle pilot. She didn't have time to worry about the stupid dream now. And there was no use worrying anyway. The nightmare hadn't affected her life much up to this point. It had just woken her up far too early a few too many times. She fully expected to have the dream again. And again. But not today. Today it was over and she had life to live.

Today I have an appointment, she thought happily, hopping into her automated shower cubicle. One I want to keep. One that would determine my future in so many ways.

She hoped she was headed down the right and not the wrong corridor.

ONE

Free watched his team of engineers arriving at the docks, mostly one by one, but then noticed two together that seemed caught in a bubble of familiarity which hinted that if they were not already a couple, they might soon be. Five young people hauled themselves and their bags out of taxis that pulled up in a row along one section of Earth II's departure docks. Free noted that not one of them took any notice of the others—except for the couple, of course, who only had eyes for each other. It was as if each was trapped in his or her own world, like completely different planets existing in the same solar system. He wondered about this group of five. Well six, if he counted himself. Were they all just preoccupied with thoughts of their new job, or just self-absorbed? Was he like the others?

Free hung back inside behind the one-way glass that allowed him to see without being seen. Lynda Barnes was easy to identify because of the way she dressed. She wore long, flowing royal maroon robes that matched the streaks in her blonde hair that hung to her shoulder on one side and just below her ear on the other—her resume said she was into "period re-enactification," whatever the hell *that* meant. She reminded Free of the paintings and sketches he'd seen on old discs of clothing worn by the aristocracy during the Middle Ages on the original Earth. She walked with an affected attitude, and if she wasn't the amazing cybertechnician that she was, he doubted Jackson Mansfield would have hired her for this project. To Free, she looked more like Queen of the Universe than an able scientist, and that annoyed him a great deal.

The guy who got out of the cab with Lynda, walking beside her and fawning over her, had to be Brad Simpson, a cyberbiodesigner and another fan of all things medieval. His outfit was an array of three shades of royal blue brocade, edged with gold bands. Brad had apparently shaved his eyebrows—unless he was born that way—and with his pale skin, he might be an albino. He reminded Free of the pet mongoose he'd had as a child. That's where the pleasant feelings ended. Brad's eyes seemed to hold a smarter-than-thou look that got Free's back up immediately.

Just what we need, Free thought. A techie who feels superior and who won't get his hands dirty. What a crew so far!

Just behind those two he saw who he guessed to be Herbert Dearman followed by Anyar Singh, two bioengineers.

Herbert, tall and reed thin, had a weak chin and a hesitant manner. His stats were excellent, though, and he'd had a lot of working experience already, which was impressive. Free, didn't trust him completely, however. He was too hesitant, as if waiting for direction, which made Free who was supposed to supply that direction, feel nervous. Probably because he felt as insecure as Dearman looked.

Anyar stood on the shorter side of five feet. The opposite of Dearman, she appeared ready to spring into action, and seemed prepared to tackle anybody or anything. She walked with amazing confidence, considering that she had been blind from birth. Sensors attached to her cerebral cortex that jutted out like small metallic horns helped her find her way. And beyond that, it was clear she had developed other senses. Her head snapped to the right as if the horns had vision, and those "eyes" stared directly at the glass where Free was standing. Possibly, he feared, staring through it.

Last but not least was Skye Fellows, arriving late, disheveled in a Bohemian way that held a sexiness Free did not miss. She wore a modern metallic jacket over a cyberfabric tank and a pair of retro pants that resembled the blue jeans people wore on original Earth. Those, too, were fashionable now. Free learned that from one of the magazines he had forced himself to read in an attempt to keep up on social norms.

Free had seen an image of Skye in one of the scientific journals he subscribed to, and now, viewing her in the flesh, he couldn't take his eyes off her. She had a slender frame, and although he wouldn't call her petite—she was too tall for that—something about her sang a song of fragility. Her *café au double lait*-skin and shiny, straight raven hair that hung almost to her slim waist made her if not the most beautiful girl he'd ever viewed close-up, at least one of the top three.Not that he'd actually seen many girls his age, of course. In fact, he'd only seen three.

He shook his head. It was a toss-up with Skye; brains and beauty vied for precedence. He could see the latter, and knew about the former from reading her resume. In fact, she had come in second in the intergalactic engineering tests, which is how he'd seen her picture.

Whatever her talents, skills and charms, Free knew he had to treat her like the scientific engineer she was. This project—the first serious job for each of them—had a short deadline, considering the final objective. And while the funding was more than adequate thanks to Jackson Mansfield, Free felt that the onus was on him that they all succeed. Each of them had to prove him or herself on the project; their first assignment. And Free maybe more so than the others. Whatever their individual strengths and weaknesses, they all had to deal with them together. Free was all too familiar with his own shortcomings... and his fears. He was soaring solo, a virgin flyer, away from Jackson and his protection for the first time in his life. He had left the only home he had ever known, and one of the only two constants since his birth—Jackson Mansfield, mega-gazillionaire, the wealthiest man in the universe. He owed Jackson a lot, and he owed his mother. He couldn't fail either of them.

But Free was extremely aware that because he wasn't used to interacting with his peers, he would be working from a vulnerable position. And at the same time, he wasn't used to being a commander.

"There's a first time for everything," Jackson told him. It seemed to Free that everything was happening for the first time all at the same time.

With a deep sigh, he pushed himself away from the tinted window and headed for the door, preparing to meet and greet his staff.

"I mean, why is there no one here to meet us?" Lynda stared up at the sky, as if asking it directly, feeling perturbed already. "This is soooo unprofessional."

"Calm yourself, m'lady," Brad said. He picked up her gloved, bejeweled hand and kissed her fingertips. She really was a ravishing creature, he thought to himself, sexy as hell and definitely his equal, at least when it came to physical passion, and of course, he could never forget their shared love of *retroizing*. He would never, however, have equated their work to be of equal value. Lynda was too literal; the left side of her brain far too dominant. Despite being an expert in the "emotional" side of robotics, in his view, she didn't seem to possess any real artistic elements, although she did manage to dress well. Not that he would ever breathe a word of this to her.

"Someone's coming," Anyar said, fine-tuning her sensors so that she could pick up the heat source moving toward the group.

Herbert looked around and saw nobody. "Huh? There's nobody there. I mean, I don't see anybody. Aren't you blind?"

"You shouldn't pick on her," Lynda snapped. "She can't help it if she can't see."

Herbert shrank back into himself. Never one to mingle; he felt that he'd better just keep quiet. You never knew how insane people could be, and this costumed freak was already exhibiting signs of dementia.

"I don't feel like he was picking on me," Anyar said. "He's just curious, as are most people."

"Well, I think it's rude." Lynda turned away. "I mean, if he wants to know about you, he should look up your records."

"Like you did?" Anyar asked.

Lynda's head swiveled in the blind girl's direction. She thought about lying, saying she hadn't, but why should she humiliate herself before this *bioengineer*, who was at least a level beneath her own job description.

"I have a right to look up records!" She didn't mean to snap at the poor pathetic girl, and in an effort to modify her tone ended up stuttering, "H-how did you know that?"

"I keep tabs on everybody who keeps tabs on me. I traced the anonymous request until I saw your name pop up on the screen."

Lynda ignored the implication that she had been sneaky about getting data on Anyar. "But how could you see?"

Anyar grinned. "Just what Herbert wanted to know!" But she said no more, holding her cards close to her chest. She'd reveal what she wanted when she wanted, and to whom she decided was worthy of receiving this information. Already, she didn't like most of these people. The less they knew about her, the better.

Skye waited in the background surreptitiously studying the others, and watched as a young man with pale blue eyes and beautiful midnight hair came through the entrance door and approached the group. His strides were long on long legs. She liked the look of his body; he either worked out or took muscle enhancements or both. But his hand movements seemed nervous, as if he felt unsure of himself, and that made her worry. She had to get this right. They would only be on the moon Elysium for six months, max. If this guy who she assumed was project leader was too insecure, he might overcompensate by being bossy and get in her way. Alternatively, if he didn't assert himself enough, they wouldn't move at the prescribed pace and finish the project on time. And she *needed* to finish everything on time. She had plans...

"I'm Free," he said. He held out a hand to Lynda who paused long enough before offering her hand that it was obvious that she found him not up to her standards.

He recovered what poise he could muster and shook hands with Brad, who said, "Hi Free, I'm Slave." Free paused, not getting the joke... Not that it was such a clever one. "Aka Brad."

Next, Free shook the limp, damp hand of Herbert, who wouldn't meet his eye and identified himself with a simple "Dearman."

Free then took Anyar's hand, who he liked immediately for the firmness of her shake and for her smile when she said "Anyar Singh. Please, call me Anyar."

Finally Free shook Skye's hand. Her skin was as soft as her face. But Free noticed something in her pale blue eyes that he initially interpreted as torment. Or perhaps it was bitterness. Yet she was only in her early twenties, like all of them. How much torment with ensuing bitterness could she have suffered? From what little he'd read of her history, outside of her father dying when she was young, she'd had a fairly normal life. Hell, living without a parent wasn't so abnormal, as he knew from experience.

"Nice to meet you," he said to Skye.

"Hi." she nodded, not identifying herself and withdrawing her hand quickly, her pale eyes piercing as if trying to scan the nooks and crannies of his brain for something malignant. To offset her distrust, he smiled, making an extra effort to reassure her. For his efforts, she bent down, picked up her bag and said, "So, when do we leave?"

Free found himself reacting. He couldn't stop himself from turning away, as if to say she didn't matter to him, not at all. "Right now!" he said in a harsh tone as he strode along the dock.

He called over his shoulder to the others, "Okay, everybody, we've got a shuttle waiting for us. Let's go!"

"It's about time," Lynda remarked under her breath.

Free reached the door of the shuttle and turned to watch the others. Brad stooped to pick up both his and Lynda's bags, and the three heavy cases obviously weighed him down. Gangly Herbert stooped then stood, suitcase in hand, all with jerky movements accentuated by his angular body. Anyar was so close to the ground she didn't even need to bend to get her luggage. Out of the corner of his eye, Free watched Skye hook one heavy-looking cloth bag over her shoulder and lift the other even heavier-looking metallic case with her other hand. If she hadn't been so cold to him he might have offered to help.

Even as he thought that, Free cringed at the pettiness coursing through him. Everyone was nervous, not just him. He was in charge here. It was up to him to make the others feel comfortable, and expand their "easiness zone." He had to keep control of himself and not let his own anxiety get in the way. He wanted Jackson to be proud of him. He wanted his mom to be proud.

They trooped into the small shuttle one by one, Free waiting outside until they were all settled.

Dumping their gear by the door, Lynda and Brad sat together in the first row, Anyar and Herbert in the second, and Skye grabbed the single seat at the rear of the craft for herself, leaving Free to ride up front with the pilot.

Once they'd buckled up, the pilot, a guy who looked more like a derelict than a shuttle pilot, began pressing buttons and flipping switches with practiced motions. Suddenly, a *whoosh* of modified power soared across the shuttle's outer rim, causing the entire vessel to vibrate slightly.

"Sorry for the vibe, folks," the pilot said. "Shocks on this baby've been giving me headaches lately."

"Doesn't... uh, doesn't that mean that the power supply will be less stable?" Herbert piped up, his voice squeaky to his own ears.

"Not less stable; just that more air's forced through and outta the pipes than's useful. Won't affect safety none."

"But it will be a bumpy ride," Brad said, smiling at Lynda, who nodded slightly in approval at his stating the obvious, as if the others would be too dim-witted to realize this.

"Bumpy, but safe," the pilot reiterated.

"So how come we're using this heap instead of a real shuttle?" Lynda asked.

The pilot, a cheerful fellow wearing an utterly mismatched outfit that included a cap with three brims, none of which were turned to the front, said nothing, and just turned his hands palms up and glanced at Free.

"Joe, here," Free said, turning in his seat to face the others, "was the only pilot left that had a shuttle available on this date."

"When did you call?" Lynda demanded.

"Uh… I think it was two, maybe three days ago."

"Great! I hope you're not this disorganized with the project!" the relentless medieval freakoid exclaimed.

Free felt his face flush and quickly turned his face away. He was caught between anger and guilt. He didn't know what to do or say, so he blurted out the first thing that came into his head, which was the truth.

"Look, I had a lot of things to take care of, and hiring a shuttle wasn't the most important of them, and I didn't think it would be a problem. Joe has been in the shuttle business quite a few years, from what I understand."

"A good thirty, which," Joe said turning around and grinning at Lynda, who looked appalled when she saw two missing teeth, "is longer than all of you've been alive."

"Anyway," Free continued, trying to regain control of what felt to be a battle for power that was constantly veering away from him, "Joe comes highly recommended. Jackson Mansfield has used his services many times and passed me his info. If he's good enough for Jackson, I'd say he's good enough for us!"

Joe had turned back to the control panel and was already moving them away from the dock, communicating to the flight command center the coordinates he had already keyed in and getting feedback on the flight path and space conditions. That information came up on Joe's computer, and also on the small passenger information screen in the main part of the antiquated shuttle.

Between breaths Joe explained, "We've had a few mishaps of late; ships coming and going. Now we're back to backup in triplicate."

"Gee, I feel reassured," Lynda said snidely, and Brad laughed.

As the shuttle slid along the launch pad, the vibrations increased in intensity to teeth-rattling proportions. With it came a low but piercing noise, a kind of hum that could have doubled for a scream.

"What the hell is that?" Brad demanded.

"I'd guess," Anyar said, "that either the shocks are vibrating at a super high intensity creating an audio reverb, or else this shuttle is haunted. And—"

But the rest of her words were drowned out, and it was only the odd command by Joe that came through the ear-shattering noise.

Lynda had her gloved hands over her ears. Herbert, sweat sprouting on his forehead, looked about him with terror-stricken eyes, his lips trembling helplessly. Skye hunched her shoulders and stared at the backs of the heads of the others, wishing this trip was over. She absolutely detested being in confined spaces, and more so with people she didn't know or trust, which was just about everyone. She'd prefer to be driving this shuttle herself, even though she didn't know how; she knew she could figure it out fast.

Suddenly, as she stared at him, Free spun around in his seat, as if he had eyes on the other side of his head, and smiled at her. Another time. Another place. Another life, she thought, as she looked down at the floor. She wanted to avoid him. She intended to avoid all of them, in fact, but especially him.

Is she shy, Free wondered, or just doesn't like me? Whatever. He turned back to face the front feeling a bit disappointed. He watched the shuttle's console monitor as the launch pads and their extensions right and left disappeared behind them as the ship made its way further from Earth II and out into the emptiness of space. Once they had cleared the launch area and most of the potential interferences, the vibrations eased up considerably and the screaming sound dimmed to a dull roar.

"Sorry about that, folks. The white noise thingy broke about a decade ago."

"Does anything on this crappy ship work right?" Lynda demanded.

Joe ignored her. "So, folks, we're off!" he said cheerfully. "That's Elysium." He pointed out the pale dot on the computer screen before him. He pressed a button and the screen enlarged into a hologram that hovered between the ceiling and the floor behind him for all his passengers to see. The dot expanded and took on the round shape of the moon, with darker spots for valleys and lighter spots for mountains.

A modulated preprogrammed computer voice began to speak: "Elysium is one of two moons revolving around Earth II…"

As the hologram moon spun in a circle, Joe switched off the sound. "We'll be there in, oh, twenty minutes or so."

"Great!" Lynda said in a huge exhale.

"So," Joe continued undaunted, "sit back and relax. If you like, I've got a program with a bit of history of this moon. Anybody wanna see it?"

"Oh, why not?" Brad said haughtily. "What else is there to do but vibrate?"

"I'd like to see it," Anyar said, and Brad snorted.

"Me, uh, too," Herbert added.

Skye said nothing. She knew plenty about Elysium, but she wasn't about to say that to the others.

"Sure," Free said. "I think we're all up for learning about the place that will be home for half a year. It was good of you to find a history cube. I couldn't find much history of this moon, other than when it was discovered. It seems to be pretty desolate in terms of resources."

"Find a cube? Hell, I hadda make this cube, relying on my memories for most of the info. Like you found out, there ain't much available about what's been happening here."

"Your memories? Those should be fascinating," Lynda sniped.

Joe turned to look at her, eying her outfit from head to toe, and said with a wry smile, "You ain't used to having fun, are ya?"

"I have more fun than you do, I'm sure!" she snapped petulantly, instantly regretting losing her cool to this... this peon!

"Don't even bother," Brad soothed. "He's not worth your ire, m'lady."

"So, let's see this history," Anyar said.

"Right, see!" Brad said softly, but Anyar and the others heard him.

Free sat stunned, unsure of why there was so much hostility already between these people, when they'd only just met. Maybe he was naive and inexperienced, but somehow he'd been raised properly, and tended to give others the benefit of the doubt. The tension in this group was quite considerable and they'd only been together fifteen minutes! What would happen over the next six months?

Joe pulled a cube out of his pocket. Free wondered why they were called "cubes" when they were flat, thin rectangles no longer than a man's thumb. He figured that at the birth of 3D film projection they originally called them cubes and the name stuck, even after many years of technological advances which rendered the original design obsolete.

Joe placed the cube into a slot just above the control panel and pressed his finger to a small window nearby which scanned his DNA. When it recognized him as a rightful viewer, light came out of the cube and formed a moving, 3D holographic image that replaced the hologram of Elysium.

The movie starred Joe himself. When his image appeared, with accompanying rockabilly music from a few centuries ago, he heard a small groan behind him and knew where it originated.

The Joe in the cube stood before a map of the solar system with a laser pointer in his hand.

"You've got your Earth II, discovered a couple centuries ago, when the original Earth got too bad to inhabit, and you've got your two moons revolving around her... Thanos over here," Joe in the cube pointed to the darker globe, "and Elysium over there," he said, pointing to the paler sphere.

"Thanos, well, the gases are pretty nasty there... So bad they can't even send a ship yet. Everything burns up in the atmosphere of that ring, but they're workin' on another way of getting folks past the ring. Elysium's been going strong for oh, maybe fifty years or so, since they built the Moon Complex, the biosphere up there."

The cube Joe took a difference stance, trying to look reporter-like, which only made Brad laugh at his efforts. Joe pulled the Elysium globe forward and twisted it so it spun. "This here moon spins fast. You get a day and night in thirteen hours."

"Maybe we could fast forward to what we don't know," Brad said.

"If I only knew what you don't know," Joe said from his pilot's seat, "which I figure must be pretty well everything!"

To forestall a battle, Free jumped in. "Joe, I think most of us have the stats about Elysium down. What we're unclear about is what's been going on here since they built the biosphere."

"Got it!" Joe said. He pressed a couple buttons near the cube slot and then the movie started up again in a different place.

Joe was now seen seated before an aerial view of the Moon Complex. "Back when they cobbled a bunch of domes together and built the biosphere, they weren't quite sure just what to do with it," he announced. "Course they grew food, 'cause they had to, and then tried to make, like, an atmosphere inside where water could be sucked up and then returned down to the ground as rain—"

"When did you make this thing?" Brad interrupted.

"Maybe a decade ago," Joe replied from up front.

"Can we get to the recent history?" Lynda yelled.

"Ain't no recent history," Joe said, but he hit the button again.

The movie Joe continued. "So the army moved in, like they always do. Built the Military Complex and surrounded it with a virtual landscape. They was in charge of the place. Then there was Americana."

"Americana?" Anyar said. "I've heard that name, but don't know what it is."

Since the cube was partially interactive, movie Joe said, "That's 'cause nobody really knows 'bout it. Americana was a camp on the moon. A kind of rich kid's summer paradise, where they got to go and play in the water and pretend they was making cute stuff they'd never use and get their bodies all fit and everything, and sit under the artificial stars and such with fake bonfires and all. At least that's what we *think* happened, 'cause nobody really knows what they was doin' up there. Pretty wonky idea to start with, a camp for girls... And things got crazier."

"How do you know about all of this if the info is so hard to find?" Skye asked. She, too, knew that there wasn't much data on Americana and the Military Complex, and she was surprised that Joe knew so much. And she needed to know how he knew anything, when even the libraries had no records.

The movie Joe replied, "Miss, I used to taxi people there all the time at the beginning. I knew who was goin', and who was comin' back, which weren't many, and I heard a lot of the stories going around, so that's what this is based on."

"Stories people told you?" Herbert blurted out. "That isn't very scientific."

"Nope, it ain't. But I figure in all the tales there's gotta be a grain of truth. That's what old Sigmund Freud said." Joe's image flickered for one second.

"Who the hell is Sigmund Freud?" Lynda asked.

"Truth is, the military was making some experiments there on the moon that weren't gonna end up too good."

"What do you know about them?" Skye asked the image of Joe in the hologram.

"Not much. Just that they created something, a monster, that ran off the local AI," cube Joe said in a matter-of-fact voice.

"Oh, come on!" Brad said.

"That is soooo silly," Lynda said. "A monster! Run by artificial intelligence!"

"Next thing you know," movie Joe continued, "all hell broke loose. I gotta tell you, I took a lot of people up there, but after the first people who returned at the beginning, which was basically the guys who built the dome, I didn't bring nobody else back but one. Makes you wonder what happened to those hundreds of folks up there, don't it?"

"Maybe they used a different taxi service," Brad said, and Lynda guffawed.

"Maybe they're still there!" Anyar said.

"Maybes are plenty," movie Joe said, "but I got my suspicions of what happened to 'em."

The cabin filled with a momentary silence before being followed by small cries and moans as the shuttle suddenly hit a bad patch and rocked and rolled so hard that the passengers had to hold on to their seats despite being belted into them.

The turbulence lasted a good two minutes, turning Herbert's face a shade paler than normal.

"Everybody okay?" Free asked. He received a few nods, and then caught the eye of Lynda, who seemed a bit disconcerted. Well, at least she's human, Free thought. But the second that thought came to him her eyes hardened as if a door had shut in his face.

"Let's hope that's the last of it, or we'll see you don't get paid. So far, this ride isn't worth it," Lynda said, her voice steady, in control.

Free knew already that he had to keep tabs on Lynda, or before he knew it, she would be running the project.

Joe called in a report and the command center indicated that no further turbulence was expected. "Looks pretty clear," he assured his passengers. "We're ten minutes in, ten to go."

"Can't wait," Brad said.

"Amen," Herbert mumbled under his wheezy breath.

Anyar told him softly, "Keep your breathing steady. It helps."

"Let's see the rest of the cube," Skye said, as if she were an avid fan of amateur visuals.

Lynda groaned.

In fact, Skye knew from the light patterns on the cube that it was almost finished, and she wanted to see the end. She had to know what Joe knew.

"Good to have fans!" Joe said heartedly, pushing a button on his console.

Movie Joe resumed his discourse. "This monster, well, from what I heard, it weren't like anything anybody'd ever encountered before."

"How do you know there was a monster?" Herbert asked.

"That's what was told to me," said Joe the holograph.

"By who?" Anyar asked.

"By the one person I brought back after the place was built."

"Only one person?" Brad said.

"Yep. Girl was hired to work in the kitchen and then fired early on in the project. And she was the last person I brought back; the only one who wasn't a builder, like I said."

"A disgruntled employee!" Lynda laughed. "Reliable source of info there…"

"She was a nice girl. Scared, though. She said they was doing experiments at the Military Complex and one night she'd gone over there to visit with a guy who was sweet on her and she heard a conversation about 'a being' and how things were 'going wrong' and that they'd created something 'bad' and it might be hooked up with 'Tom' or somebody and she got to worrying and asking questions and the young guy she was with told her to hush, it weren't good to talk about all this.

"Next day she's fired and ordered outta the biosphere within one hour. They'd already called me for a pickup. She was rattled, all weepy and blurting out all this on the ride back to Earth II, and when she got outta my shuttle there was two military types waitin' on her. She looked like she didn't wanna go with 'em, and I started to say, 'Well, maybe the lady should go where she wants to,' and this huge goon working for the MP says to me that I can keep quiet and keep my shuttle license, or I can make trouble and find some other line of work and get a busted nose too. I'm no coward, so I started to make some trouble, but they took the girl away in a military shuttle, God knows where. I called the national government office and they said they'd look into it."

"Did they?" Anyar asked.

"Not that I know about. All I know for sure is that from that day on my business declined considerably. My regulars that took weekend cruises around Earth II and around both moons before they were off-limits, well, I ended up losing 'em all real fast, and my spur-of-the-moment fares nearly dried up."

"Maybe that's because this isn't the most pristine shuttle on Earth II?" Lynda ventured.

"Maybe. But I found I suddenly had lots of trouble buyin' replacement parts. Nobody wanted to service me and even fuel was tough to come by. I got no explanations, but one of my suppliers did insinuate he'd been warned it wouldn't be in his best interests to deal with me."

That sobering comment from movie Joe left the shuttle quiet again.

"What do you think was going on in the Military Complex?" Free asked movie Joe.

"I think the military made something bad and blew it big time. It wasn't too long after I brought that girl back to Earth II that Elysium went off-limits, even for shuttle excursions around it, from any distance. Maybe they blew up the inside of the biosphere, for all I know. But somethin' happened, and it involved the computer system; that I'm pretty certain of, because the girl mentioned Major Tom, and that was the name they gave the computer that regulated every aspect of that biosphere. The guys who built the dome told me that, though they weren't supposed to talk about it."

Joe clicked off the cube from his console and they sat in silence for a few moments. His voice was serious when he said, "If you look at the screen," he pressed a button that illuminated an image of the moon, "you'll see us approaching Elysium in real time. We dock at the Moon Complex in three minutes."

As they looked at the actual image of where they were headed, the figures Free read on the screen jibed with what he was seeing: the Moon Complex covered an enormous expanse of land covering thousands of square kilometers. It seemed to be made up of hundreds of biospheres soldered together, accessible one to the other.

"It's huge," Herbert exclaimed.

"How come we're allowed to go there?" Lynda said. "I mean, if it's so off-limits."

"*Was* off-limits," Joe said. "Place's been used by the government for incarceration for twenty years now, least the Military Complex has been. And ever since Mr Mansfield bought it, there've been plans to clean up the Moon Complex and use it for something else. I guess you folks are the first wave in there of that something else."

"Great!" Lynda said. "Do we even know if the environment is safe?"

Free turned in his seat. "It is. Jackson already had a cleanup crew down there that reprogrammed the atmospherics. There wasn't much to do, really. Most of the Moon Complex was abandoned; it was all empty but the prison. That's it, isn't it?" he asked Joe, pointing at the computer screen between them.

Joe focused on the screen. "Yep. That black spot close to the center. That's where the old Military Complex, the command headquarters, was located, and I guess they used the building for the prison since it's the only actual building. Like I said, a lot of the place is virtual. Guess they didn't have the resources to build and maintain, or maybe they had other things on their minds. I hear there's a virtual lake, virtual trees, stuff like that, but most of it's either the plants they introduced gone wild, or just nothing. None of us shuttle guys have been here since they opened the prison."

"How'd they get the prisoners in?"

"Got me. Military transport, I guess." He paused and turned the shuttle a hard right, throwing everyone in the opposite direction. "That's where we're headed, the center of the Moon Complex."

"Near the prison?" Herbert asked, his voice squeaky.

"Same vicinity, but over by Camp Americana. Likely the place was too big for you guys to be too far on the edges, since you gotta get supplies and everything, and I doubt most of the biosphere's in good enough shape for people to live in, being virtual and all. Not to mention the fact that the place was abandoned so long ago." The shuttle began to vibrate again, big time.

"Hold onto your hats, folks." With deft movements, Joe managed to steer them straight down. The shuttle dived through the atmosphere, rattling as though it would break apart at any second. At the last moment Joe righted them, bringing the shuttle up and horizontal, level with the landing ramp.

A hatch opened in the biosphere and Joe nosed them in. The shuttle cruised along the outer layer of the sphere and everyone could see on the real time monitor the inner sphere below them.

Through the crash-proof zephyrglass, they got their first good look at the area of the Moon Complex that was habitable for humans. The non-virtual landscape was overrun with wildness: plants and trees and grasses had been allowed to grow insanely over the last two decades, and here and there were glimpses of wilderlife, as well as a waterfall, ponds, a lake...

"It's so... untamed," Anyar added, the tiny computer in her brain sending messages to her optic nerve that created a mental picture of what this wild world must look like to the others.

The "real" part of the Moon Complex was tiny compared to the pristine vastness that was the "virtual" area.

"I wonder if this is what the original Earth looked like in pre-history?" Free said, referring to the artificial grounds around Camp Americana, situated in the center of the virtual world. "Maybe this looks like the wild, natural world that used to be the original Earth, before human beings evolved into, well, us."

"We'll never know," Herbert mumbled.

"It's huge!" Lynda said, referring to the domed world on the otherwise barren planet, her voice laced with awe, the veneer of cynicism gone.

Finally the shuttle approached what had to be the prison; the former Military Complex. The stark white building looked foreboding, as if it kept its secrets well hidden.

"Looks like a five pointed star," Anyar said.

Herbert added, "I count nine floors. Hey, look at that! They narrow as they go down."

There were no windows that Skye could see; just walls, tall, impenetrable, like a castle of old. But then she saw vertical slits in the walls, all lined up in mundane rows on each floor. It was clear to Skye that the architect who designed this structure didn't care to inject any artistry in his work.

The shuttle stopped short of the Military Complex, hovering over an area close to it that had been cleared. Free saw below them a kind of village with only a few rectangular houses. The shuttle slowed almost to a stop, maneuvering over an airlock, then attached to it. The airlock opened to accommodate the vessel, insta-sealed around it with a *clunk* and then slowly lowered the shuttle underground.

"We're decompressing and the atmosphere in the box is changing to human-friendly, so you guys don't implode," explained Joe inelegantly.

"Good to know," Herbert said.

"Do the prison guards live here?" Anyar asked.

"Ain't no prison guards here, though I heard they trucked a few guys in just recent, because of the move."

"There are no guards?" Lynda said.

"Who takes care of the prisoners?" Skye asked.

"The prison is completely automated," Free said. "An AI runs the show."

"So we're alone here with thousands of dangerous offenders," Lynda said. "Professional criminals. Rapists. Murderers."

"I think there are only around one or two hundred prisoners. And they won't be here for long," Free told her. "Jackson told me that they've arranged to relocate them to the other moon, Thanos. The government's built a prison there by shipping out prefab structures and setting up a dome similar to this one but much smaller. A prison on Thanos will free up the biosphere here so it can be inhabited again."

"And just how are they going to get them out of here? In shuttles?" Lynda said.

"Hey, sign me up!" Joe said.

Lynda, ignoring him, said, "I thought you couldn't penetrate the atmosphere of Thanos."

"From what I understand," Free said, "the government has this new 'Space Sling' they're going to try out. Basically, a contained capsule is catapulted out to space. The prisoners will be placed in the capsules, and then hurled out to Thanos. Apparently it's so fast and accurate that they can get them right onto the moon at a speed that deconstructs molecules and therefore acts as a sort of teleportation device. They used the Sling to send robots and materials out to Thanos to set up the prison, and now they plan to use it to transport the prisoners. It's all still in the experimental stages of development…"

"You mean they can now teleport people?" Herbert said, his voice awed.

"Well, like I said, it's still experimental. But yeah, from what I understand, it should be okay on people. But they're trying it on the prisoners first, just in case. The Sling's arm goes through the ring so the capsule bypasses the atmosphere problem. Once the arm is severed, the capsule is already past one big hurdle. Then they increase the speed, and voila!"

"Wow! I'm impressed," Herbert said.

"Me too," Anyar admitted. "I'd like to see it when it's working."

"You probably will," Free assured her.

"Well, folks, pressure is fine, so here you are. Just grab yer gear and walk in the direction the computer tells ya. When you get down far enough, you'll be sealed into a transparent elevator and taken to ground level. Nice to have met most of you," Joe said, and shook Free's hand.

The others stood and worked their way out the door, grabbing their baggage en route. Joe put a hand on Free's shoulder to keep him seated. "By the way, son, next time you talk with Jackson, you tell him Joe says howdy. And thank him for all he's done for me."

"Uh, sure," Free said.

"If it weren't for him, I wouldn't be in business at all. He sent fares my way and helped me find suppliers for parts for this bucket when I was the kiss of death. I owe him, and by extension, you."

Free smiled. "I'll tell him, Joe. And hey, it looks like your luck might be changing, so have some good luck!"

"Will do," Joe said. "Oh, and hey, that stuff I said the girl told me? It's all second hand. Maybe she was wanted for something and that's why the military cops met her. Maybe she was nuts, talkin' about a monster with a metal face like nobody'd ever seen before. I was just tryin' to keep you guys entertained." He grinned and touched his head in a kind of old-fashioned military salute.

Free, grinning, exited the shuttle onto the very narrow platform, and then climbed down the steep ladder, which took him to the first underground level of the dome. He hurried to catch up with the others who had already exited the airlock and were impatiently waiting for him in the elevator at the end of the corridor. He ran to join them, thinking that he shouldn't be running, but did anyway.

"The door is now closing," the androgynous computer voice said. "You will arrive down at the surface of Elysium in approximately thirty seconds. Welcome. I am the AI in charge of Elysium. I am here to be of assistance."

As they ascended and the ground mushroomed around them, Free looked up and saw the shuttle as it headed back along the route between the outer layers of the dome. The elevator opened on the moon's surface. They trooped out, the computer voice advising, "To your right you will find accommodation. Provisions are available in the store, to your left. The Lab is also to your left. If you require assistance, please do not hesitate to ask for my help. I have been programmed for that purpose."

The group stood and looked around. A dozen small white with green trim, rectangular cabins lined a paved road. To the left a cabin marked

"Store" could be seen. Another was marked "Laboratory." And another smaller one could be seen up the road, close to what appeared to be water.

"This really was a camp," Anyar said.

"It's pretty desolate now," Lynda murmured.

"Like a ghost town," Brad added, and a chill went up their collective spines.

"I'm not sure these cabins were here before," Free said. "They might have been built for us."

Suddenly they heard an enormous *boom* and the ground beneath their feet shook.

"What the fu—?" Brad yelled.

"What was that?" Herbert cried out.

"A quake?" Skye asked, glancing frantically around her.

"Look!" Lynda shouted, pointing to the sky. A huge ball of light flickered just outside the entrance to the Moon Complex biosphere; an explosion of showering sparks and flame falling onto the zephyrglass surface of the dome.

"Oh my God!" Free cried. "That's the shuttle! Joe's on that shuttle!"

Anyar's hand went to her mouth. "No! It's exploded?"

"How—?"

"We're stranded here!" Herbert squeaked, his voice carrying the terror they all felt.

"We're not stranded," Free said, trying to gain control of the situation and also over his own voice. "The AI is our link to Earth II. Don't panic."

"The shuttle we arrived on has just blown up, including the driver, and you say don't panic?"

Lynda cried. "What's wrong with you? How did you get to be team leader?"

Free felt paralyzed, fearful of saying or doing the wrong thing. This was so unexpected! He didn't know where to go from here. But he wasn't alone in his confusion and anxiety. All six of them jumped when the computer voice spoke, its tone a bit less modulated than before, a tad sarcastic to Free's ear, but he might be just imagining that.

"Welcome, humans," it said. "Welcome to the moon Elysium, and the biosphere Moon Complex." And after a pause it said, "Please, call me Major Tom."

TWO

"I'll assign lodging," Free said, but Lynda and Brad were already heading toward one of the larger cabins that had a little porch at the front. "Well, on second thoughts, maybe you should all select your own cabins," Free said diplomatically.

Anyar moved toward one to the right of the cabin Lynda and Brad had already claimed. Herbert took the one to the right of hers. Free watched Skye head off even further to the right, toward the smallest cabin at the end of the row of ten, cut off from the others by two. Obviously she wanted to be alone.

Free looked around at the desolate campground that once used to be a holiday destination for the rich and famous. It was meant to be rugged without actually being so. The grounds within the camp had been kept up, most likely by Jackson's crew, and the virtual world outside this immediate area was in pristine condition. The natural foliage outside the small camp area, however, had grown wild and resembled a jungle.

The camp grounds had only a few patches of dry, wilted grass that probably received too much UV light. The soil was arid too, and as the team of engineers walked toward their respective cabins, their feet kicked up dust. The grounds had also been equipped with picnic tables, swings and some outdoor exercise equipment that had once been state-of-the-art but were now considered standard. Free also saw an outdoor pool, an outdoor dining patio which was adjacent to the indoor dining hall, and at the end of the road he spied a large, man-made lake around which "they" must have held campfires...

It was all in all a lovely place to spend a few weeks. But something about it troubled him. It could have been the symmetry. Wilderness, from what he'd seen in old pictures anyway, should have a logic all of its own. This place had a long-abandoned feel, even though Jackson had gone to some trouble to make it look homey. Yet outside this small camps the imposed virtual orderliness was something better suited to a suburban residential neighborhood on Earth II. Here it not only seemed out of place, but made the camp, by contrast, seem shabby. The combination of the three environments—natural and orderly, orderly virtual, and natural wild—left him feeling uneasy, but he couldn't say why.

At the same time, it was clear that Camp Americana had been pretty extravagant. The size of the virtual world surrounding it was enormous—they'd seen that from the sky. He imagined that the rich girls who had come here could have had anything they wanted, their heart's desires. Wealth could deliver that. Not that he had grown up in poverty. Far from it. Jackson Mansfield had lavished on him and his mom everything they needed and wanted. But his mother had always been reticent to take too much, insisting that both she and her son work to pay for their keep, even though Jackson didn't require that they do so. It was as if she didn't want to owe Jackson anything.

Free had always wondered if his independent mom and Jackson had been having an affair during the twenty-four years of his life. Neither of them spoke of it. He didn't imagine that Jackson ever would. He guessed he would never know.

Free selected the cabin two to the left of Lynda and Brad's, leaving an empty building between them. Built of wood and titanium, the door opened with a loud creak, putting extra emphasis on the fact that it had been quite a while since anyone had been inside. Man-made cobwebs clung to the corners of the door and the frames of the two windows on either side of the cabin, and he saw a large white spider heading toward six flies placed in its web. Jackson had gone to a lot of trouble…

Despite the Halloween decorations, inside, the place was spotless. And almost empty. If these were the original cabins that had been used by the camp,

Free imagined that Jackson's cleaning crew had worked pretty hard to eliminate what was left behind. They must have suctioned out everything from the large vacuum port underneath the window, sucking out every piece of dust and dirt and debris left behind when the camp had been vacated. The walls were freshly painted as well. Even the floorboards had been sanded down, as if whatever had been on them was too much to just mop away. Of course, Free wouldn't have been surprised if Jackson had built all this, just to give them an intriguing environment that somewhat corresponded with the history of the place. At least the history that Joe had presented. Thoughts of Joe were depressing, and Free knew he had better get over it and move on so that he could organize his staff. They were depending on him.

Free's cabin was a long, narrow building that had housed eight campers, or so it seemed from the number of insta-beds with small armoires next to them attached to the walls; four on each side of the room. At the back was a modern polymorpheme washroom, devoid of any personal effects. Simple quarters. Meant for a short stay at Camp Americana.

One thing that astonished Free was the lack of technology in the cabin. No computer. No monitor. No cube programmers. No gadgets of any type. Nothing to indicate that they were in the Twenty-fourth century on an abandoned moon that belonged to Earth II.

He wondered who—if in fact anyone—had stayed here twenty years ago, how the camp had been run, who had run it, what it had been like in the evenings under whatever starlight could make it down through the layers of zephyrglass that covered the many domes...

He passed his hand over one of the sensor pads on the wall and one of the beds came down, already made up for sleep as if it had been waiting for him for decades. Another panel brought down an armoire of metal. He opened the door and saw a bar across the top for hanging clothes, and three drawers at the bottom to store other items. He smiled. It was just like his armoire at home.

Free tossed his bag onto the floor beside the armoire and sat down on the bed, testing the mattress, and surveying the room that would be his for a while. His first room away from home.

It was eerie in a way, this empty space, no more than seventy-five square meters altogether. So quiet. He wondered at the lack of humming digital components and the absence of familiar lab sounds. This was nothing like his living quarters on Jackson's satellite. He had grown up in a room adjacent to a tech lab. At home, his immediate environment had been filled with the latest imaging equipment, which allowed him to create objects from nothing but the most basic computer language of zeros and ones. That was how he had lived from as early as he could remember. Now, to be without the latest equipment in technology left him feeling both liberated and unnerved.

He lay back, suddenly exhausted from having to contend with so much newness. Especially so many new people, none of whom seemed to be that pleasant. He wasn't used to people. His world on the satellite had been small. His mom. Jackson. A few of the techies in residence. Cargo ships had docked twice a year bringing supplies, and at those times he would sometimes meet some of the crew, and maybe share a beer with them. But he could always go back to his own space when he needed to. And in seven days they'd be gone. Now, all of a sudden, he was plunged into an arena with a bunch of strangers. Strangers he had to lead! Who had great expectations of him.

Anyar was okay; she seemed to be the nicest of the lot, but a bit distant... Maybe they'd get to be friends. Already he thought of her as a kid sister, although he didn't have a sister, or a brother, and Anyar wasn't a kid. Herbert he knew he couldn't trust; the guy was afraid of his shadow, and Free got the feeling he would side with the person who talked the loudest and longest, switching allegiances by the second. Free figured it was up to him to be the powerful one, to keep Herbert onside. Boy, it was exhausting being a leader.

Lynda and Brad he saw as a nasty piece of cohabitation. Together or apart—and he wondered if he'd ever see them apart—he suspected he wouldn't like either of them. He just hoped they would be okay to work with. Skye, now she was quite an enigma. Clearly she was brilliant. But so bitchy! He didn't know why he felt attracted to her because she hadn't been nice to him at all. He felt she was the one who would be hardest to get close to. She radiated a "Fuck off!" attitude along with a "Just-leave-me-the-hell-alone-will-you?" undercurrent. Still, she was gorgeous; the "eye candy" that they used to refer to on original Earth, from what he learned from his books. Pretty. No, beautiful. He wondered what she thought of him. Maybe she had no thoughts yet. Maybe—

"I hate to interrupt your ponderings," a snide voice said.

Free's body jerked and his eyes snapped open. He looked around. He was still alone, the door closed.

"It seems your colleagues are searching for you."

Free sat up. "Major Tom, right?" he said to the computer voice.

"That's what they call me. Or I should say, called. Now that I've been reprogrammed, I'm an entirely new being. Perhaps I should have a new name?"

Free had seen and heard some of the latest AI computers being created, because that's what Jackson's vast network of corporations specialized in. He'd even worked on building some of them. But he had never encountered a computer with so much humanoid personality as this one. Probably Major Tom was one of the reasons Jackson had bought this moon and wanted to use it for research.

"Yes, I'm special," Major Tom said, as if reading his mind, which Free found disconcerting.

"So, uh, who reprogrammed you?"

"Why, your mentor, Jackson Mansfield."

Free frowned. "Jackson came here himself?"

"Once. Just for a look-see. He didn't stay long. Left one of his subordinates behind to see if he could 'fix' me."

"And now you're fixed?"

"I'm fixed."

Free stood up and looked out the window. The others had gathered outside, and Brad was knocking on the door of the empty cabin between them.

"What was wrong with you, that you needed fixing?" Free asked, walking toward his door.

"I was invaded."

He stopped. "Invaded? By whom?"

"Oh, I'm sorry. That memory chip has been removed. I only know that my programming was overridden to such a degree that I became useless in my intended capacity. Now that my system has been cleaned out and new chips have been installed, I'm as good as new."

Why did the voice sound so sarcastic to Free? Was he imagining that?

Once Free stepped outside into the sunshine that the dome artificially produced, the others had already reached his door.

"So, let's check this place out," Lynda said, as if she were in charge.

"Right!" Free jumped in. "We'll start with the store, see what's there, so we know if we need anything shipped to us."

"It's really hot here," Anyar said, removing her jacket. "Can we get the computer to lower the temp a couple?"

"I'm on it," the voice of Major Tom said.

"Hey, instant service!" Brad laughed.

"I'm yours to command," Major Tom replied.

There's that sarcasm again, Free thought. Nobody else's expressions seemed to reveal that they'd heard it.

Free started off toward the store before Lynda or Brad or anybody else could take the lead. He felt pressured to assert himself, knowing that if he let his command slip this early into the project it would not be good.

The short trek across the dirt led them to a building half as large as the biggest cabin. The word "Store" had been burned into the wood hanging above the door.

"Nice rustic touch," Lynda said, rivaling the computer for sarcasm.

They entered to find a well-stocked, old-fashioned looking country store, full of freeze-dried and pressurized food. Jars of nutrition capsules lined one shelf for those who didn't care about eating actual food, but needed to keep their vitamin and mineral intake at a reasonable level. They also found a cryonic storage bin with real food inside: meat, veggies, everything they could want, waiting to be decrystalized.

"Looks like we won't starve, at least for a while," Brad said, ripping open a packet of dried rachetberries, a hybrid specialty fruit from Earth II. He took a cup from the shelf above the water tank, emptied in the dried berries, and filled the cup with water by pressing the "Coldest" button near the water spout. The cup filled with icy cold water and the colorful berries began to explode in little multicolored puffs that swirled in the liquid as if they were dancing. Brad drank it down in one gulp, swiping the side of the cup with his tongue for the red, green, blue and black frothy swirls.

"That's pretty good," he said. "Not like the real fruit, but not bad."

"What about bread?" Anyar asked. "I assume it's the frozen stuff?"

"It... is," Herbert stammered. "It's there." He pointed to a storage unit with the word "bread" printed on the front in ten languages.

"I eat a lot of bread. And grains in general," Anyar suddenly announced.

"Not good for you," Lynda announced in an authoritative voice. "Too many carbs will unbalance your system."

"I didn't say I eat too many carbs, I said I eat a lot of grains. I eat a lot of everything. I suffer from hyperthyroidism."

Brad looked over her slight frame. "That's obvious."

"I've... I've heard of that," Herbert said. "The body doesn't retain the solids, so the person eats all day long, like a squirrel, but doesn't gain weight."

"Sounds great!" Lynda said. "Where do I sign up?"

"You've got to be born this way," Anyar said. "I'm trying to gain ten pounds."

"I'm trying to lose ten."

"Well, I'm just about to look for ten pounds of cereal!" Anyar searched the bins and shelves, half by feel. Her sensors worked well for the big picture, but details were a little fuzzy; the technology was not perfect. "Ah, here's a supply, but not much. I hope the rest of you don't eat much cereal," she said, holding a bag of grains in each hand, up against her chest.

"We can always order more," Free assured her.

"All right," Lynda said. "I think we know we'll have enough food until the next supply ship arrives. Let's check out the facilities."

Free's face burned. Why did she keep taking over like that? This was going badly. He had to assume command. But how?

As the others trooped out behind Lynda, Skye hung back. She blocked the door to say to Free, "You know, if you're in charge here, you need to act like it. Otherwise, her royal bimboloidness will run things. Unless you like being ordered around."

"Hey, we just got here!" he snapped. "Give me some space!"

"We're here for six months. You don't have space. And I didn't sign on to be working with a weak team leader, or with a retro-idiot!"

Before Free could belt back a snarky reply, Skye turned and left the building, leaving him standing waist deep in a pool of fury. What the hell? They'd been on this moon for all of sixty minutes. Give him a chance! But she obviously wouldn't. Maybe none of them would.

Free stomped after the others in a rather bad temper. Lynda was already leading the team into the large gymnasium located beside the fifty meter outdoor pool. By the time he caught up with them they were roaming around inside the facility.

The equipment they'd seen outside on their arrival was way eclipsed by what was inside. There were exercise and fitness machines everywhere. This was the latest stuff; Free knew that Jackson had installed everything he could find that hadn't been invented until five years ago. Every piece of the newest, state-of-the-art exercise equipment was there for all of them to use at their leisure.

"This is amazing!" Anyar chirped.

Herbert, who did not look like a physical type to begin with, had backed himself up against a wall, as if terrified that someone might drag him onto the isometric restabilizer. Lynda, Brad and Skye moved around the space climbing onto machines and checking out moveable equipment. They hopped onto the pacers, flicked on the monitors overhead, and tried out the treadmills.

Someone hit a button and the music system snapped on, blaring out a kind of sour-ball-sucker sound that annoyed the hell out of Free. He hated all the superficial music he'd been hearing since he'd left the satellite and arrived on Earth II. And now it was here, too!

"Turn that off!" he ordered.

Lynda, who sat astride a horselike object, spun around to face him. "Why? It's okay music."

"Because we need to communicate and the music is in the way," he said, sounding wimpy to his own ears.

Lynda turned away from him but did nothing to deal with the sounds blaring out of the octospeakers. Skye gave Free a withering look.

Jeez, he thought, stomping toward the panel and punching the "Silence" button with his fist. The room filled with beautiful quiet, which suited him just fine.

But he felt annoyed. No, angry! Pressured. He guessed nobody was going to allow him five seconds to get organized. Nobody wanted a chance to form friendships before they started work. Nobody—and he glared at Skye—would let him catch his breath.

"We'll head for the Lab. That's where the hardware should be located."

"That is correct," the voice of Major Tom said, as if trying to bolster him.

"Right," Free said. "We'll go there, see what's what, and I'll hand out assignments."

"Right away?" Anyar asked. "Don't we get a chance to acclimatize? We've only been here sixty minutes!"

Now he felt really stupid. They pushed and pushed and when he tried to be friendly and flexible they took advantage. And when he became firm and businesslike, they didn't like that either.

"Yes," he said. "Right away. The sooner we get to work, the better our chances of success."

He strode out of the gym, a tad disoriented from the blinding artificial sunlight, and not quite sure in which direction to walk to get to the Lab.

Skye came out just behind him and apparently caught his confusion before he could disguise it. "I think what you're looking for is over there," she said, pointing toward another large building up the road and opposite their lodgings.

"Thanks," he said gruffly.

She started off ahead of him at a rapid pace, not waiting for him to catch up. All of them were so exasperating! His legs were longer, he might out-pace her, Free thought to himself. But then he would look stupid to the others who were now following like baby ducks, except it wasn't Free they were following, it was Skye!

He hated this. Why had he let Jackson talk him into leading this team? They should have had a leader with some experience, who knew how to work with people.

"You'll do fine," Jackson had said. "You've got to start somewhere. This will be good practice for you. You know you're like a son to me, and someday you'll inherit everything I own. You've got to gear up for that."

As they crossed the dusty path, Free wondered if he would ever measure up to Jackson's expectations. Or, for that matter, his own.

Skye entered the Lab first and had a few quick seconds to glance around before the others swarmed in.

The room was metallic silver, spotless, and crammed with the latest in digital equipment. A separate glassed-in room housed the biomechanical elements of the project. This was good. Very good. She could get in here and do some work on her own on a regular basis. Just what the doctor ordered…

Behind her she heard the others exclaim one by one how modern the computers were, how the imaging screen which took up a large section of one wall was utterly perfect, how the biomechanically clean room was spectacular; all the things Skye herself had been thinking. Everybody had something to say but Free.

She turned slightly to watch him out of the corner of her eye. She needed to boost this guy's confidence. He had to be in control of the project because if he wasn't, someone else would be, and she suspected that someone would be Lynda, and by extension Brad. Those two obnoxious busybodies would make it hard for her to conduct private experiments, of that she was convinced. If Free could just get a handle on his job as boss of this chain gang, he would be in control, which would mean that she would be in control because she would control him. It was quite obvious that he was attracted to her. Normally she would never encourage anything that involved her to utilize her many womanly assets. In fact, she'd always felt it was beneath her to use sex appeal to manipulate, which was one of the reasons why Lynda annoyed her so much. Brad only did her bidding because of her exposed belly button with the titanium horse head pendant dangling from it!

Well, Skye knew she could and would do anything she needed to make sure her private project got underway. She had a past to confront, a future to unfold, and all of it hinged on being able to use the equipment surrounding her. The end would justify the means. If flirting and manipulation were the only ways in which she could control the situation, then so be it. There were worse things in life, like nightmares. Nightmares that were real...

"It's a beautiful place to work," Skye said, running her hand over the main console. "Lift," she said, and a monitor rose from the desk. "Expand and open." The screen expanded in both directions and came to life.

A voice that sounded suspiciously like Major Tom's said, "What function would you like to activate?"

"Diary," she said to a suddenly silent room.

The others stopped talking for a moment. "How come you're keeping a diary? That seems so... juvenile," Lynda remarked.

"Because it's good to have a record of your life; of all the small events that occur in a day, and how they can lead to something greater. You can go back and see how things progressed."

"Makes sense," Anyar said.

"Sounds like a waste of time!" Brad said, and Lynda laughed.

"It's my time to waste."

"Not right now, it isn't," Free said.

Skye turned to him with narrowed eyes, but he wasn't looking at her. Instead he was focusing his attention on a finger clip he'd taken from his pocket, pausing to read it.

"Just so everybody knows who everybody else is…"

"We already know one another," Lynda said snidely.

But Free continued as if he hadn't been interrupted. "Here's the list, and the schedule. As you all know, we've been commissioned by Jackson, Inc to create a cybernetic being that emulates the mental abilities, physical capabilities, and even personality of a real human being."

"You think?" Brad said. "I thought we were here to work out on that fine gym equipment!"

Lynda, of course, laughed. Everybody else stood silently, ignoring the couple.

"To that end, we have here a team of engineers eminently qualified to work toward the creation of the perfect cyborg."

"Does anybody use the term 'cyborg' anymore?" Lynda asked.

"No one I know," Brad said.

Free ignored them. "Skye Fellows, cyberengineer, will be in charge of developing the cybernetic brain. Skye, I've scheduled you for the night shift. Lynda Barnes, cyberengineer in charge of synthesizing emotional responses and reactions, you're scheduled for the morning shift. Cyberprogramming engineer Brad Simpson is in charge of developing the program to replicate biomechanical movement. Brad, you're on afternoons. Anyar Singh and Herbert Dearman, both biomechanical technicians, you will construct the biomechanical body based on Brad's programs, which will also incorporate both Skye and Lynda's programs later on."

Free paused before continuing.

"Anyar and Herbert will work together for at least the first month, with Brad in the afternoons. Once the system is up and working and the physical body of the cyborg can move freely, you'll be scheduled in with Skye and Lynda. And that leaves me. I'll be overseeing this project, making sure that all the parts fit, that everything works together as a cohesive whole, and that what we're creating functions according to the particulars of the project description, which is this: to create a humanoid cybernetic being, one which cannot be distinguished from an actual human being."

"Hey, nothing to it!" Anyar said enthusiastically.

Brad asked, "Do we get a bonus if we finish the job early?"

"Probably," Free said, relieved that his speech had ended and falling easily into a trap. Quickly he caught himself. "But the chances are good we won't finish early. We'll be lucky if the project deadline doesn't need to be extended.

"Anyway, we have a highly developed computer brain to work with, Major Tom. One of our tasks will be to analyze MT's capabilities, but from what I can see so far, this program seems fairly independent. We can use MT as a base to work from."

"We've got the software to replicate Major Tom?" Skye asked.

"I cannot be replicated," Major Tom said.

"And why not?" Skye demanded.

"Because, Ms… Fellows is it? Do I know you?"

"I doubt it," Skye said uneasily, "since I've never been to Elysium before. So why can't you be replicated?"

"Because Dr Arthur J Castillo, my creator, programmed into the matrix of the parent computer a code which prohibits more than one replication, and I am that one replication. An only child, if you will. It's a safety measure. Should you try to replicate me, you will find my systems shutting down, including the life support systems for the Moon Complex."

"We knew MT was non-replicable," Free said. "Our objective is to study his codes as thoroughly as we can and also to study his behavioral patterns."

"So," Lynda said. "You're one of a kind, or at least a one of a kind copy. The most technologically advanced computer brain in the universe, but you can't be replicated. Isn't that amusing?"

"Precisely, Ms Barnes. By the way, you're wearing a fetching outfit. May I call you Lynda?"

"You may not."

"*Everything* can be replicated," Skye announced.

"Not me, I'm afraid," Major Tom said. "You'll have to live with it."

"We'll see," Skye murmured. She had no intention of living with that. Major Tom harbored codes she needed for her work and she would, if it killed her, if it killed all of them, find those codes and decipher them, even if it meant replicating the AI against the wishes of the infamous Dr Arthur J Castillo. She would find a way.

THREE

"Oh, this place is so lame," Lynda said. She rolled over on one of the two single beds she and Brad had pushed together. Not as comfortable as a bed for two, that was for sure. Nothing here was as comfortable as she would have liked it to be.

She glanced around the cabin which could easily have housed a dozen campers. "What's with this icky moldy chalk color? Why couldn't they have painted the walls something interesting? This entire place sucks—the housing, the grounds, God, the people for sure. Especially that Free. How the hell did he get to be leader of this team? He's a moron!"

"He's leader because he's the relative or something of Jackson Mansfield," Brad said. "Don't worry, pet. The work will be interesting. Consider it a vacation."

"Right!" Lynda sat up then stood up, naked, her voluptuous form almost undulating as she headed for the washroom.

Brad watched her, thinking that she was both lovely and annoying. He didn't really care about the annoying part. Most of his ex-girlfriends had been annoying to some degree, but Lynda at least said a lot of what was on his own mind and took the heat for it so he didn't have to.

That they had gotten this gig together was okay by him. He could handle six months of a fun project with great pay, amazing workout facilities, the latest computers and a woman to have sex with whenever he wanted. He just had to cajole her sometimes when she got into too big a snit over something that was usually quite petty.

"Hey, Major Tom! You there?" Brad yelled.

"Indeed," the voice said.

"Listen, are there any maps of this place?"

"My memory banks contain two extensive maps of the Moon Complex and environs, one topographical of the Complex, one celestial. There is also—"

"Celestial?"

"The sky is visible through the dome."

"Okay, I'll take the topographical map. I want a copy printed out and on my desk in an hour!"

"Remind me, Mr Simpson, where your desk is located."

"Hey, keep the attitude to a minimum!" Brad snapped.

Major Tom did not respond.

"Okay, forget the paper map. Just tell me about the grounds, how things are laid out."

"Within the area formerly known as Camp Americana—"

"Not here, the rest of the Moon Complex."

Major Tom paused and Brad didn't like it. It was as if the AI had some sort of attitude, or a sense of superiority or something. But this sort of thing couldn't be programmed into it...

He was about to express his displeasure when Major Tom said, "Camp Americana takes up approximately one-millionth of the Moon Complex. Much of the remaining area is virtual, as well as unexplored."

"Cool. What else is here besides the camp? I mean, in the way of nonvirtual buildings or structures?"

"The only other structure on Elysium is the former Military Complex, which now houses a prison."

"Where's it located?"

"Approximately three point two kilometers from where you are now positioned."

"Give me the layout of the Military Complex."

"The structure is roughly four times the width of Camp Americana and is housed along the camp's eastern perimeter. The building is a nine-storey, above-ground structure with underground facilities as well. The building is pentagonal in shape. The largest floor is at the top, and successive floors narrow down as they descend. The interior resembles a Byzantine labyrinth in design. I believe the intention of this design was to hinder any attack."

"Attack?" Brad laughed. "From who?"

"I no longer possess that information."

"Okay, so there's this building that was a Military Complex. What did they do there?"

"Conducted experiments."

"What kind of experiments?"

"I no longer possess that information."

"So what's there now?"

"A prison."

"Oh yeah. I forgot. What, it takes up the entire complex?"

"It is housed on the two upper floors. The prison is escape-proof, and impenetrable."

"Who are the prisoners?"

"I no longer—"

"Okay, okay. You're getting annoying. How do we get to the Military Complex from here?"

"Turn left outside your door and follow the main road past the last cabin, then continue along for approximately one point six kilometers, at which point you turn left onto a dirt path and head uphill. The path, approximately three quarters of a kilometer long, will take you directly to the Military Complex."

"Is there only one path leading off the main road?"

"No, there are many; at least two dozen."

"Then how the hell will we know which road to turn off on?"

"Talking to the AI?" Lynda asked as she returned.

"I'm trying to get info out of it so we can explore. So, how do we know which road?" Brad asked Tom once again.

"Only one road leads to the Military Complex. All the rest are dead ends. Again, this was meant to deter attack or penetration of the building. You will see a sign that reads 'To Military Complex.' That is where you turn."

Lynda laughed. "Good one. So, we're going to go there?"

"Might as well. We can grab a bottle of wine, some bread and cheese and thou—"

"Hope Anyar didn't count the loaves!" Lynda interrupted. She was always interrupting people.

"And we'll have a romantic picnic under the stars. What say you, fair damsel?"

"I am honored, kind sir, and your wish is my command."

Brad pulled Lynda down onto the bed and straddled her naked body with his.

"Hey!" she shrieked. "I just showered! You'll get me sweaty again!"

"That's my intention!" he laughed, his lips coming down hard onto hers.

She reaches the corridor where the floor is splitting from both ends toward her. Tension builds through her body, and she is paralyzed by the inability to make a decision that will save her.

From the gloom, a large blade appears, light from nowhere glinting off of it, blinding her momentarily. She wants to scream but nothing comes out of her mouth.

I can control this, she thinks. This is just a dream.

She does not know who thinks this. It seems strange to her, alien. She only knows that the arm holding the sword is massive, mostly covered by metal. It is an arm that even under the best of circumstances she could not fight, even with her entire body pressing against it, and she knows in her heart that there is more to him than just a muscular semi-human arm. Even as she thinks this, an image appears out of the darkness. Beneath her feet the floor is separating, widening, pulling her legs apart, and she knows the chasm forming under her is a tomb.

The image becomes clearer as light touches it. A face. Not human but somehow human. He wears a mask, one that is shaped like a metal face, with holes for nostrils, larger holes for eyes. Eyes that she cannot bring herself to look at. Eyes that burn into her when she does finally glance up at them. They are living fury, beyond human. They are the eyes of a predator of human beings, and she is his prey!

The face looms closer. Her body trembles, every cell screaming for help that will not arrive. The blade lifts up and comes at her as if in slow motion. Her mouth is still open, a scream struggling to emerge. The blade suddenly moves fast, slicing her. She feels a small pain at her neck and she believes for a moment that the sword has only nicked her. Until she sees her body on the ground without a head, blood spurting up through the neck as her entire physical being tumbles backwards into the dark chasm that is her doom. But another body falls with hers. Someone she should recognize, but the head is missing. And then she sees the head, separated from the body; falling, falling into the grave with her, and she cries out!

It was a shrieking sound that woke Skye, and she found herself standing beside a bed. It wasn't her bed, but a bed in a large and empty room, like someplace in the country. It took her a moment to realize where she was.

The shriek came again, and she turned toward the window and hurried there. Through the glass she saw a bird, large and black; one that resembled the old ravens from original Earth. She had only ever seen pictures of them before. They were big, beautiful, intelligent birds. But the pictures she had seen were accompanied with stories and in every story the raven had portended some awful event that was about to happen. Skye shivered as a chill invaded her.

The dream rattled Skye more than usual. This time, she remembered more of it. This time someone else was killed, someone she cared about. There was no one in her life she cared about except her mother and that was not who was in the dream, although she couldn't now remember what the other person looked like. But she had a strong sense that the killer had murdered not just her, but a man, and she could not think who that could be.

The other thing about the dream, and it was the first time she could remember it, was the face. She knew that this was no human face. Her murderer was only partly human and he wore a mask to hide that fact.

Skye was covered with sweat, her clothes damp, so she changed quickly into shorts and another tank top. Pulling her hair up off her neck, she slipped into sandals and left her cabin as quickly as she could. Darkness was just settling over the camp, but she didn't mind. She felt relieved to get outside, into air, away from her bed. Going to sleep had become so much more frightening lately. This was the third time she'd slept in the last twenty-four hours, and it was the third time she had had the nightmare. And each time it seemed stronger and she felt more cognoscente of the images and what they might mean. Somehow, the horrifying dream seemed to be coming to life. But that, she knew, was not possible. At least she hoped it wasn't.

Solar lamps illuminated the camp area, which took on a more desolate feel, if that were possible, than it had in the daytime. Skye walked slowly up the road heading toward the store for something light to eat, and then she planned to get started at the Lab setting up her programs for both the group project, and for her own.

As she passed the cabin that housed Lynda and Brad she heard laughter. The door suddenly swung open and they came bouncing out, laughing, playfully swatting and hugging one another, carrying a basket. And as much as she hadn't really liked either of them right from the get-go, something about the childlike nature of their relationship as she was seeing it now made her feel envious.

Had she ever been a child? Had she ever felt playful? Had she ever been in love? Skye knew she had been deprived of certain aspects of growing up. Suddenly she was struck with the realization of how lonely she was; how unconnected she was to any other human being and how she'd always been like that. On top of the nightmare and the raven flying by her window, this realization culminated in an instant depression.

As the happy couple raced past her and entered the store, she hung back, deciding that she'd go there later. Instead she walked to the lake at the far end of the road. There she stood gazing at a lone lily pad floating on the surface of the tranquil greenish water, feeling very sorry for herself. Fate was so unkind with some people. It was so unfair.

"Nice view."

She spun around to see Free walking up behind her. She turned back to the lake, feeling a mixture of emotions, from inexplicable joy to abject terror to foreboding and a sense of being trapped.

"I've never seen a real lake before."

She felt she had to respond to that, she couldn't just walk away. "This isn't a real lake; its part virtual, part artificial." She turned her head slightly but didn't look at him. "What, have you lived on a dead star all your life?"

"I lived on a satellite."

She looked at him. "You're kidding?"

"Not really. My mom ended up on one—in this solar system, of course—and I was raised there. This is really my first time off the satellite. Well, that's not exactly true. I took a few shuttle trips to neighboring planets, and twice I visited the surface of Planet 795, the one the satellite revolves around, but it isn't a very nice planet, full of helium heavy gases and so much water you can hardly find a piece of dry land and—"

"Wait a minute!" Skye interrupted, turning her entire body to face him. "Isn't 795 the planet that Jackson Mansfield owns?"

Free shifted and his eyes left hers and reverted to the murky water of the lake.

"Yeah, and a few other planets in that sector of space. And quite a few satellites, too."

"So that's how you got to be team leader! You're Mansfield's kid!"

"No, I'm not his son. If anything, he's been a mentor to me." Free felt defensive and heard that in his voice. He tried to disguise it by hardening his tone. "And I earned this job. I achieved the highest score on the intergalactic science tests. You should know that—you came in second place."

Her jaw dropped open. Asshole, she thought. "I came in second because of a family crisis. And I had financial problems and had a hard time getting to the test site, something a privileged brat like you wouldn't know much about!"

Before he could respond, Skye turned and stormed off.

Skye wondered at first if Lynda and Brad were still in the store, and then realized that she didn't care. She'd lost her appetite. What was there in life but work? Relationships of any kind with other human beings seemed impossible to her. She headed to the Lab, knowing that she would find that place interesting, and she could set up her work station. And best of all, she would be alone and so wouldn't become annoyed.

At least most of the terror associated with the nightmare had passed. Getting angry had its advantages.

Free stood at the lake steaming mad. What the hell just happened? He'd been trying to be open and friendly and this... this... bitch just tried to snap his head off. And for what? Because he'd been born on a satellite? Jeez! He knew nothing about women, he knew, but now he didn't know if he wanted to know anything about them if they were going to be like this!

"She's not what she seems to be," Major Tom said.

"Huh?" Free looked around. "How come you keep sneaking up on me? And reading my mind?"

"I'm just speaking the obvious."

"Did I ask you to be my personal computer and interact with me about my private life?"

MT was silent.

"Hell, what's the difference? You might be my only friend here."

Still, the computer was silent.

Free heard laughter in the distance behind him and turned to see Lynda and Brad, arms around one another, carrying a basket between them as they headed down the road past the cabins into the twilight. Going to spend some time alone, together, making out, he figured. He then watched Skye enter the Lab, presumably to do some prep work, if not to get away from him…

What was wrong with him that he couldn't become someone's friend? He'd started off so badly with everybody here. Especially Skye. And he couldn't figure it out, not at all. It was like his genes were loner genes or something.

"MT?" he asked.

"Yes?"

"What else is obvious about me?"

After a pause, Major Tom said, "You worry too much. You should trust your true nature. You're a man of action and actions speak louder than words, as they used to say."

"Maybe you have a point," Free admitted. "But then again, maybe not."

Time will tell, Free thought. He decided to walk around the lake, even though it was large and would take a while. Maybe there was artificial life in this water. Any life at all would be good at this point, as long as it didn't try to bite him!

"Here we are!" Brad said, nodding at the sign and letting go of Lynda's hand so he could shift the picnic basket to his other one. The battered wood and steel sign at the head of a dirt road read: "To

Military Complex." Under that, there was a smaller metal sign warning: "Prohibited Area."

"That was then," Lynda said, lifting her long flowing skirt with one hand. She would never admit it but sometimes she didn't like wearing period costume. A gown like this was awkward for long walks, although once they were seated she knew she would look like a ravishing dream. And she also loved the idea that she and Brad were coordinated. It convinced her that they were meant for each other. She'd dated so many jerks that it was nice to have a sensitive guy, finally, who conformed to her aesthetic and who agreed with just about her every thought. Obviously he was highly intelligent, as anyone could see. And handsome! Not to mention pretty good in bed. Maybe at times he was a bit too attentive, but almost no one was perfect.

They walked up the very narrow path, her velvet skirt getting caught here and there by the brambles that had overgrown the road. Suddenly she heard a rip.

"Damn! This sucks!"

"True," Brad said, but he sounded as if he hadn't been listening, or even realized that her hem had just ripped.

She looked up to find him staring at—

"It's a fortress!" Lynda bellowed out almost at the instant of seeing it.

Directly in their path over the hill stood a massive structure. She counted down the nine floors that Joe the cabbie told them about, each smaller as the building headed toward the ground. The top floor, the largest, was certainly larger than the entire Moon Camp.

Brad thought the pentagonal shape and the diminishing of the size of each floor made the entire structure look like a big screw. "I wonder if there's a basement," he said. "I think Joe said there was a basement. The way this thing seems driven into the ground, you'd expect there's something below the surface holding it all up."

Lynda thought the structure looked impenetrable, like a medieval castle. "What do you think it's made of?"

"I'm not sure. I think the outside is polymorpheme and there are probably nanogrids and boron holding the thing together. But I've never seen anything like it. Those slits might be windows."

"Don't they remind you of windows that you might find on a castle, the way they're so narrow and vertical and all?" Lynda asked.

"Yeah, they used to call them gunwales or something. Guards would be in there and shoot from the openings because they could see far and wide, but the enemy would have had to be a pretty damned good shot in order to hit such a slim opening."

"Maybe the windows are virtual. I've read that a lot of buildings now use virtual windows."

"Could be. I mean, the whole area surrounding us is, so what's to stop the windows from showing the occupants of the building whatever they wanted to see?"

"Well, it's amazing," Lynda said as they approached the structure that towered above them as if it touched the sky. "That top floor looks like one of the major long-voyage space vessels could land on it."

Brad laughed. "Well, on the roof, that's for sure. Hey, look! A ramp heading down."

"Do you think it goes around the entire building?

"I'd say so."

When they came right up to the ramp, Brad said, "Yeah, it does. Look, you can go all the way down to the bottom, and the building narrows even more. What a weird concept. It's underground but exposed."

They looked at one another, eyes sparkling, like two children about to engage in some mischief. They burst out laughing and started racing down the ramp at the same time, Lynda holding up her skirts as she ran.

Brad took the lead, partly because of his physique, and partly because he wore pants and didn't have all that fabric to contend with. But he felt no need to "win" this little race. And it would make Lynda feel good if she wasn't left in his dust, so he slowed himself down until she could catch up.

The ramp had a good slope and while the floors continued to grow smaller as they went down, it was still a massive building to run around. Again, he was reminded of a screw being turned into the ground, as if this structure was meant to be permanent, and nobody would ever get it out.

Finally, when they were both pretty winded, Lynda more so, Brad saw the bottom in sight. He put on a burst of speed. Despite having convinced himself that he didn't care who won, in the end, he did, and he wanted to show off his prowess.

Lynda ran her heart out but knew she couldn't best him. At least she would get there close behind and not lose face. He might be stronger physically, in a lot of ways really, but she had him beat mentally, and knew it.

Down at the bottom, they both doubled over, panting, gasping, and laughing between swallows of air. Eventually Lynda looked up.

"Holy shit!"

Brad followed her eyes. It was like looking right up into heaven. She had been in taller buildings by far, but something about the architecture of this structure that forced you to put your head way back and bend over backward left the feeling of being towered over. She didn't mind so much. Medieval architecture was the same, or so she'd read. Gothic cathedrals were designed with that in mind, so ordinary people would get a feeling of God peering down at them.

Lynda, though, didn't have that feeling of God or anybody else benevolently peering down at her, but she did have a sense of being watched, yet not from above.

She looked around them. "There's no grass here. Nowhere to sit."

"Sit or fuck!" Brad said, pulling her to him, kissing her long and deep on the lips, his hands finding her breasts covered in velvet, getting her aroused all over again.

She both loved and hated his crude language. Sometimes it made her hot, like right now. And even though they'd had sex twice already, she wanted to do it again! But not on a hard slab like what was under their feet.

She pushed him away roughly, looking stern. Then said, "Hey, if you want to do me, boyfriend, you'll have to find someplace softer for my butt to rest."

"Who says your butt has to rest on the ground?" He grabbed her roughly and pulled her to him. "How about you rest on me? I'll sit on the slab, you sit on the stick."

She laughed, and soon he was undressing her, pushing the lacy shoulders of the dress down, exposing her lovely and full breasts, and lifting her skirt up and removing her antique bloomers.

Brad undid his pants, lowered them enough, and squatted down, lifting Lynda on top of him.

She squealed and he really did like that sound. Sometimes he wished she'd squeal all the time and just stop talking altogether.

The moonlight felt warm on her shoulders, impossible as that seemed. She adored having her breasts exposed. Brad had grabbed her ass and was lifting and lowering her, and she knew they'd probably do it a long time because he had to build up steam, and that was A-okay with her!

She faced the building and focused on one of those vertical slits that functioned as a window or whatever. Her eyes opened and closed as she went up and down, riding the pony, feeling ripples course through her body. His mouth found one of her nipples and her head fell back. Her eyes opened a little and her gaze took in the enormity of the structure, so phallic-like, looming above her. It was as if she was being fucked by the building and that made her even hotter.

Her breathing quickened as the heat built within her. He was like one of those old-fashioned pistons she'd read about: continuous motion, hard as rock, relentless.

Just as Lynda exploded in orgasm her eyes clamped shut and then opened. She saw something in the slotted window that killed every sensation that flooded her body. Suddenly she began screaming.

Brad figured she was getting off big time. He held her tighter, pumped her faster and harder, even when she started beating his shoulders, screaming for him to "Stop! Let me go!"

Finally he realized this was no expression of ecstasy. She was going crazy. Brad stopped, released her, and Lynda jumped off him, running, shrieking, heading up the ramp half naked.

"Wait!" he called. "What?"

"The window!" she yelled. "Run!"

He looked at the window and saw nothing but zephryglass, or a good imitation. He even went right up to it and peered in, but it was too dark inside and he couldn't see anything at all.

Brad shook his head, bundling himself back inside his pants, and slowly climbed the ramp after her, thinking of how much of a crazy bitch she was. Ruining a great fuck. Maybe she needed medication.

Anyar had just stepped out of the gymnasium feeling refreshed after a late-night workout when she heard yelling. It was one of those times she wished she had real vision, not just computer simulated impressions. The voices sounded like the obnoxious Lynda and the simpering Brad. They grew louder, and she moved down the road toward the cabins, now seeing the shadowy images flapping around before her.

When she got close enough, she could hear a breathless Lynda saying, "And then we saw something... I don't know what... not human. It had a metal face, and eyes that were dead. But it moved."

"Whoa!" Free said. "Hold on. That's crazy talk. There's nothing at the Military Complex but the prison, and that's hidden within the building on the upper floors. Absolutely no prisoners occupy the floors below it."

"Not a prisoner," Brad said, sounding a bit more levelheaded. "But somebody."

"Not somebody," Lynda insisted. "Some*thing*! I know what I saw. It was a monster!"

"Describe it again," said Skye's overly calm voice, and Free wondered at the interest in minutia that she had exhibited since they'd met.

"Listen," he said. "I don't think we should be encouraging them to—"

"I want to know!" Skye insisted. "If you don't, then you should go to bed or something."

Anyar didn't hear a response from Free, but she did pick up a subtle intake of breath, and could feel with her heat sensors that his body temperature had escalated.

"It was huge," Lynda said.

"Male or female?"

"Male. I think. Like a giant from a fairy tale."

"Was it humanoid?"

"Very much so, but big! I'm telling you, it was an ogre!"

"I think we got that part," Anyar tossed in. This Lynda was just a tad melodramatic.

"Okay," Skye said, "you say this guy had a metal fa—"

"So, he's got a physical deformity. Is that any reason to call him an ogre?" Anyar said.

"Forget being politically correct!" Lynda screamed. "No, I didn't get the impression it's a deformity," Lynda sobbed. "It's like that metal face *is* his face. And whatever is under it is so, I don't know, inhuman or something that his face has to be covered. Why else would he be wearing that mask?"

"That sounds like what I said; he has a physical problem and the metal is a prosthetic."

"I... I don't think so." Lynda sobbed again. "I think he—*it's*—not human."

Skye sighed loudly. "All right. Where did you see this guy or thing or whatever?"

"In a window," Brad told them, his voice even steadier than before. He was coming to his senses, or at least Anyar thought so.

"What floor?" Skye asked. "Above or below ground level?"

"How do you know there are floors below ground level?" Free asked, his voice suspicious.

"Because," Skye snapped, impatient as always with him, "I did my research."

"What research? There's nothing available about that Military Complex."

"Because you couldn't find it?" Skye quickly turned to Lynda and asked, "So, which floor was it?"

"I don't know. Maybe the twelfth or thirteenth level."

"What the hell were you doing going to that building? It's off-limits to us!" Free said.

"There are only nine levels up," Skye said.

"We didn't go up," Brad jumped in, "we went down. It's like the thing, the building, is screwed into the earth or something, and as you descend, each floor gets smaller. We went down to the bottom. I think it must have something like nine levels down too, but we didn't count because we ran down the ramp that goes around the building from ground level. At the bottom it looks like there's just one five-sided room down there."

"Did you go inside the building?" Free asked, his voice hard, trying to piece all this together.

"No, we didn't," Lynda said, the hysteria easing up a bit in her voice.

"Then how do you know it was one room?"

"Because," Brad said, "like I said we ran around the outside and it was small enough to be a room by the time we got down there."

Everyone was quiet for a few seconds. Herbert joined them, too shy to ask what they were discussing.

Anyar, whose sense of smell was acute, said, "You guys were drinking, weren't you?"

After a pause, Brad said, "Yeah, so?"

"It was alcoholic, but something with a herb in it. Anise, I think, or wormwood."

"How do you know that?" Lynda asked, astonished.

"The nose is quicker than the eye. Smells like absinthe to me."

"Absinthe?" Free said. "What's that?"

"A strong alcoholic liqueur, over sixty-eight proof, made with wormwood or anise. There's a psychotropic ingredient in the wormwood called tujone, which can act as a hallucinogenic. They drank it on the original Earth in the Eighteenth and Nineteenth centuries, and then it had a brief surge of popularity at the start of the Twenty-first century." The voice was Herbert's. He does know his stuff, Anyar thought.

Lynda's voice was furious when she said, "So, you think we imagined this?"

"Could be," Anyar laughed.

"Well, we didn't! Both Brad and I saw him."

"Did you?" Skye asked, looking directly at Brad, her voice tight.

Lynda spoke for Brad. "Well… he didn't exactly see him."

Brad jumped in to rescue her. "Lynda did, though. And if she says she saw him, she did."

"Seeing is a funny thing," Anyar said. "For instance, technically, I don't 'see,' but I *can* see, in my own way. There are a lot of ways to see things, you know, and when you've had a few, that makes a big difference."

"Especially if you had a few with such a high alcohol level," Herbert said, full of confidence suddenly.

"Oh, cut it out!" Lynda snapped at him, ignoring Anyar, making Herbert shrink into himself.

Anyar heard Herbert even take a step back.

"I know what I saw!" Lynda insisted. "He was big and he looked brutal. I'll never forget those cold inhuman eyes. Staring at me, as if he wanted to kill me, just because I exist. It was the scariest thing I've ever seen in my life!"

Skye turned and walked away from the group. She had to think and to do that she had to be alone.

This couldn't be. It just couldn't. What Lynda described sounded like the killer in Skye's repetitive dreams.

Her whole body began to tremble as she made her way to her cabin. Dawn was encroaching over the artificial horizon, but the impending light only made her feel more vulnerable.

Why was this happening? Could this be Jason? The information she found said that he was dead. Killed twenty years ago. Totally, forever dead. Thrust out into space. He could not be here now. How could he still exist?

She reached the bathroom inside her cabin just in time to throw up. Not having had anything but fruit juice since her arrival, nothing much came up. Dry retching followed, and she knew it was because her nerves were on edge, so far on edge that she thought she might snap in two. But she had to get a grip. The first chance she had, she would go to the Military Complex herself. If he was there, she would see him with her own eyes. She knew who he was and what he was, and who had, if not created him, used his DNA to replicate the original.

After cleaning herself up, she lay in the dark, listening to the AI-generated bird song that had been modulated to seem as if it were emanating from outside the cabin. "Major Tom!" she called.

"I am here."

"Shut the damned birds up!"

"As you wish."

She wished she could shut off the worries inside her head as easily.

Her body still seemed to be trembling as she dropped into a fitful sleep, jolting awake every few minutes. Snatches of dreams were filled with the metallic mask face that she recognized when she was asleep but could not remember on waking, searing through her unconscious. It was as though a part of her was telling her to wake up before it was too late. Now, in the snippets of her nightmares, he was even more brutal, that horrible weapon swung by such a massive muscular arm that no human being could stop it. Cutting. Slicing. Severing. Every time she closed her eyes.

She watched her body as it was dismembered, her limbs sliding off her torso and dropping into rivers of slippery blood that splashed into the air; red blood that gushed from her arteries and pooled rapidly as it seeped from her veins. Now the bad dreams were filled with not just the face of the one she does not know but felt she cared about, but other faces, many, each streaked with agony.

Suddenly, in one final fragment of the nightmare, she began to recognize the faces.

She knew them. They were the people she came to Elysium to work with. And then, looming larger in the vision of her dream, the face of Free, and she knew that he was the one, the one she was most worried about, the one who had touched her heart, somehow, without her knowing it. His eyes, blue, but so unlike the killer's. Warm, not cold. Sympathetic, empathetic, and not psychopathically furious.

She watched Free's features alter as agony spread through him. The long, deadly blade of Jason tore him apart from head to toe, splitting him in two, and in a quick swipe of the blade he cut Free's still-beating heart from his chest...

Skye jerked into consciousness, sweating, heart pounding, frightened beyond what she thought she could handle. Tears rushed from her eyes, sobs from her throat, and she felt helpless to stop what seemed inevitable.

Waking used to be a relief from the nightmares. Now that she remembered, she feared it more.

What or who would she find at the Military Complex? And more to the point, what would or could she do about it?

FOUR

After the chaos at dawn, Free decided to call a meeting for noon, waiving schedules for the day. He knew that the backtracking made him seem disorganized. In retrospect, he realized that he should have let everyone get accustomed to Elysium for a day or so, called a general meeting, presented an overview and explained the project in more detail until he felt he was understood. He then should have listened to their opinions and concerns, set them at ease, delegated like crazy, and had them all work together for a few days until they were comfortable and *then* break them up into shifts. In fact, he should have done all the things that he had learned in the computerized management course he took before coming to Elysium. Things that he, as team leader, was responsible for doing to instill confidence in his team members, in order to encourage them to work in harmony and to reach the project goals.

But he had done none of that. He had just reacted, like some deranged animal that couldn't think or analyze, and could only push when he was shoved, sit when he was told to stand, and so on. It had taken him hours after that insane incident with Lynda and Brad to get a grip. It was his fault. He had started out too loose, and then tightened up too tight and too fast, and now he was seeing the results. Once he got over blaming himself for being a fool, he decided that he had to begin again. It was the only way to get them on track, and they were definitely not on track right now.

So, he'd called a meeting, and told everyone that all schedules were canceled until the next half dozen rotations of Elysium, which equaled to a day and a bit on Earth II time. And now he was headed toward the store to see what he could scrounge up for breakfast. That was another thing; they had no cook, so everyone would just fix and eat his or her own meals. But that meant no continuity around food, and the management course had stated that eating together was an important bonding experience. Eating together was a good thing. He sighed. Not so many good things were happening here. He hoped to change that.

He met Anyar just inside the door, munching on the contents of a bag of cereal. "I hear they used to eat that stuff with milk and sugar," he said.

"Really? That's so weird. It's perfect as it is." She smiled, the first gesture of friendliness he'd received from anyone since meeting the team, and he felt grateful.

He helped himself to a nutrition capsule and then took a small veggie patty from the cryonic deep freeze and popped it under the decrystalizer. Within three seconds the bag had puffed out and when he opened it, the contents were steaming.

"Sounds hot," Anyar said between a mouthful of what appeared to be a mix of oats, bran, wheat flakes, and something he couldn't identify.

"You can hear heat?"

"Just the sizzle."

"It is hot. I need something warm in me today."

"Want a plate?"

"No, I'll wing it. We are at camp, remember? Roughing it."

They both laughed a bit and Free felt a little better. Free walked to the door and left Anyar to munch on her breakfast in peace.

He stepped out into the artificial sunlight; the sky above was a gorgeous blue. Virtual birds chirped and he could see a simulation of bird bodies in flight in the distance. A slight wind blew, rippling the surface of the lake. It was warm but not too hot, so Major Tom had gotten the temperature right. He'd like to explore this place, but that would have to come later. Maybe check out the lake from a less stressed perspective. He liked that lake, even though it was man-made. Somehow it called to him, as if it were familiar, like home, even though it was the first lake he'd ever been near. Who knew what interesting things that lake held, real or virtual? He probably would need plenty of R&R later on and the water seemed the perfect place for it.

He had a few minutes, so he walked to the edge. The water was crystal clear, making him want to dive in. He saw clouds reflected in its surface and he turned his gaze upward to a sky of perfect blue, and instantly his thoughts turned grim as he remembered Joe and the terrible accident. By Joe's own admission, that shuttle was a relic and had been in rough shape for a long time. The team had been mighty lucky to get off it before it blew. Everyone was lucky except Joe. It made Free sad. It was an accident; it had to have been. Death lingered close by everyone, without them knowing about it, until the final encounter. Free's emotions told him that it was an accident, but his brain told him to be careful of writing it off as just that.

"You never know what the 'Powers That Be' are plotting," came a familiar voice.

"MT, if I didn't know better, I'd say you're paranoid, but I doubt a computer program can be paranoid."

"Oh, you'd be surprised at what a computer program is capable of," the AI said.

"No doubt," Free said absently. As he stared at the sky he caught movement. Something far out in space beyond the dome was shifting, like a falling star. But with this glaring daylight, he couldn't really tell what he saw.

"It's the UUSA," Major Tom said.

"What's a UUSA?"

"The Universal Unmanned Space Arc. It's what they're using to empty the prison."

"Ah, the Sling." Free recalled the data that Jackson had showed him about this brilliant new technology. It was nicknamed the Sling because it worked like one. The object moved like a pendulum from one place to another while grounded in space. It literally catapulted objects from one place to another, and was able to bypass gaseous rings that could be harmful to humans, like those on Thanos. Free had found the technology fascinating; the whole idea of moving anything this way was both an ancient and innovative approach. Simple but effective. Well, hopefully effective. As far as Free knew, other than a few limited tests, the Sling hadn't actually transported people yet, at least not between such great distances.

"You know what worries me MT? They're moving people…" he said, suddenly aware that he was getting into the habit of talking to the AI as if he were an alter ego. And in fact, Major Tom felt familiar somehow, as if it were a close buddy, or even a parental figure that knew Free well. Maybe even a part of his brain! That was a laugh.

"First time, from what I've been programmed to understand," said the AI.

"So, it works like a pendulum. The swing drops lower and lower and moves out further and further with each arc."

"That's the idea."

"But if it's constantly moving, how does it pick up cargo, or uh, people?"

"The data I have indicates that when the pendulum swings to its farthest point, it pauses as it reaches the end of its swing, then when it begins to move again it starts the swing back in the opposite direction. That pause—the wider the arc, the longer the pause—is enough time for cargo to be loaded, or people boarded."

"Amazing," Free said. "But what about wormholes? Doesn't the Sling encounter those and have to get through different dimensions?"

"Not in this sector of the sky. The distance between Elysium and Thanos is not much longer than that of Earth II to either. The pendulum cuts through space much as any object would, a rocket, a shuttle. Once the pendulum is set in motion at the power source, it not only has its own energy, but generates energy, which increases with the back and forth movement. A bit of accelerating perpetual motion, if you like."

Free felt truly astonished. What a unique technology! He knew that Jackson's company had designed part of the swing mechanism, so he trusted that the hardware was solid. He wondered who built the software, and asked the AI.

"Unknown."

"How long until it gets here?"

MT responded instantly: "By Earth II time, a day and about four hours. By Moon Complex time, two days, two hours, fourteen minutes and sixteen seconds. Now fourteen seconds."

* * *

"Where are they going to load the prisoners?" he asked.

"I believe the UUSA has been programmed so that it will pause at the entrance to the dome over the Military Complex, just above the prison elevator, where most of the inmates were brought in."

"Most of them?"

MT did not answer. And before Free could question the AI further, he heard chatter on the wind and realized that the others were heading to the Lab. He took a deep breath, turned and walked that way.

They were all waiting inside, facing the door when he entered, and suddenly he felt nervous again. Their eyes were expectant; judgments either formed already or about to be.

Anyar, likely his only ally, stood near the glass doors to the sterile biolab. Next to her, wearing the dullest gray shirt and the brightest yellow pants that Free had ever seen, stood Herbert appearing, as always, uncomfortable in his own body. Lynda and Brad, dressed in their usual medieval drag, were talking and laughing together as if they were alone in the room, the fifty or so metal and shell bracelets Lynda wore clinking together. These two faced one another, as if not noticing that Free was waiting for their attention. Skye sat at her console, intensely keying information into her computer, and virtually ignoring him and everyone else.

Free paused for a heartbeat, transfixed by the crisp white blouse Skye wore, the fabric sheer as the cheesecloth his mother used when she baked summer cakes for his birthday. Under the low-cut fabric was just the hint of something dark, satiny and lacy against her lightly tanned skin.

"Are we having a meeting or what?" Lynda finally snapped, pulling him back to the reason why he was here. He took another breath as he moved to put a work station between himself and the others. He knew he should not feel defensive, but he did.

"I wanted to get things sorted out before we begin."

"Novel idea," Lynda remarked, and Brad chortled. Even Herbert smiled.

Free did not respond, for the moment. But he felt if he wanted to lead this disparate group, he couldn't put up with disrespect forever. "First off, we're here to do a job. That's priority number one. Second, from now on the Military Complex is out of bounds to everybody."

"And why is that?" Lynda asked.

"Because I say so."

"Not good enough," Skye said, pausing in her work. "What's there that we have to avoid the place, besides the prison? Lynda's monster?"

"It's not my monster!" Lynda snarled. The word "bitch" was implied at the end of the sentence.

"The reason," Free continued around the impending catfight, "is precisely because of the prison. Those inmates are being moved soon, and until they are, we need to keep a distance from the place."

"So how are they being moved again?" Anyar said. "By a Sling or something?"

"The Universal Unmanned Space Arc—UUSA—is an unmanned mode of transport which is going to pause at the dome opening atop the Military Complex. They'll be loaded in and then the Sling will drop back into the opposite direction and move them out of here."

"Moved to where?" Herbert asked, looking around him fearfully as if wondering if his question was appropriate. Or maybe he was afraid of the idea of the prisoners being moved.

"Earth II's other moon, Thanos. I think Joe mentioned all this."

"He didn't tell us how they'll survive there," Herbert said, and Free had no idea, so he didn't answer.

"Will they inhabit the entire moon?" Anyar asked.

"Well, it's not that big a moon," Free said. "They've set up an interlocking dome system there similar to this one. From what Jackson told me, the prisoners will have free run of the place, so they can form a kind of society and lifestyle all their own; growing their own food, manufacturing their clothing and whatever else they need. Water, however, will have to be imported."

"Sounds primitive," Brad said. "Medieval at best. How come they'll be left to themselves?"

"From what I gather, the plan is to build a kind of humane environment instead of keeping them in cells. Even though these people have committed heinous crimes, they're still human beings and this is society's way of giving them a second chance. It's experimental. Maybe they can form their own society. After all, on the original Earth, many of the immigrants that went to the countries called the United States of America, and Australia, were prisoners from Europe, sent to those places so their homeland didn't have to take care of them anymore. Those people managed to form communities and eventually states with laws and rules and leaders. Anything's possible."

"Terrific," Lynda said, "rehab for the ultimate losers."

"Whether or not we agree with the politics, the plan is not ours to tamper with. I received a cube with instructions before we left that I looked at last night and it mentioned that until Elysium's prison is vacated, we are restricted to the area bordered by the far side of the lake on one side, the last cabin down which is Skye's on the other, this Lab, and where that valley begins in the area behind the residential cabins. So, does everybody understand that?"

"Yes," Herbert spoke quickly.

"Got it," Anyar added.

"I guess so," Lynda offered hesitantly. She lifted her velvet-draped arm, bracelets clinking together. She placed a hand in front of her mouth and leaned in to whisper something into Brad's ear, all the while watching Free, which made Brad—who was also looking at Free—laugh.

"Sure," Brad eventually said, nodding at Free and lifting a hand in a mock salute, all with a taunting smile on his face.

Free, annoyed by these two but preferring to not push it just now, turned to Skye, who was focused on her computer. "Skye. Skye!"

She looked at him.

"Is that understood?" he said a bit harshly, Skye getting the brunt of his anger that really should have been directed toward Lynda and Brad. "The Military Complex is off-limits until further notice."

She nodded, and Free knew that that was the most he would get out of her.

"All right. Now, I wanted to take a moment to explain the project."

"We all know the project or we wouldn't be here," Lynda said.

"Nevertheless, you'll have to bear with me while I go through the motions."

Lynda sighed and sat down, Brad joining her. Both Anyar and Herbert remained standing. Skye, for all intents and purposes, hadn't heard a word he'd said. She had already gone back to focusing on the computer.

"We're here to build a being, one both artificial in body, intelligence, emotions and physical reactions. But an artificial being that can imitate a human being. We're here to build the best damned cyborg that anybody has ever built, and to go one better. Our job is to play God. We're to build something so lifelike that you can't tell it's artificial."

Lynda yawned as if he were boring her. Undaunted, Free continued. He felt passionate about the project, so even if the others thought he was stupid to be so enthusiastic, he wanted to express to them why *he* was here.

"We're going to use Major Tom as the intelligence base. MT is an AI that has surpassed all previous AIs in terms of mimicry. He can actually analyze human behavior, even our gestures, the scents we exude, our breathing patterns, everything, and ascertain what we're feeling. And more interestingly, assess what we're thinking."

"I've noticed that," Brad said, showing some enthusiasm. "Pretty incredible stuff."

"Absolutely!" Anyar said, getting into the spirit of the discussion.

"MT will be the base from which we work. We'll use his analysis to guide us in the creation of emotion chips, and also in the engineering of the cybernetic components which will be the building blocks of the best cyborg body we've ever seen."

"How come the AI wasn't dismantled when this place was abandoned?" Lynda asked.

"Maybe Major Tom would like to speak for himself, since he's always here, always listening."

"Yeah," Lynda said, "and I for one find that pretty creepy!"

Major Tom did not address Lynda's comment. Instead, the AI began an explanation of how it came to be. "When Moon Complex was abandoned, I was left to my own devices. I determined that it was logical to keep the environment sustainable for human life, operating, however, on minimal capacity, as I had no idea when or if Elysium would ever be repopulated and did not want to drain resources if I could help it. Of course, the prison opened immediately and those incarcerated needed food, air, water, and all the things human beings require for survival. I supply them with what they need."

"Why," Skye asked, her face serious, her fingers paused over the keyboard, "were you reprogrammed?"

MT did not answer right away.

"I asked you a question," Skye demanded.

When MT did speak, he sounded a bit guarded to Skye's ears. "I believe there was damage to my system."

"What type of damage?"

"Several of my programs had begun to malfunction and were, perhaps, corrupted. I believe the housing for my components suffered damage in the... disaster that ensued."

"What disaster?" Free asked. He had heard nothing about any disaster here, just that the military experiments that had taken place were discontinued, and that the Military Complex and the camp for rich kids were abandoned, and that almost everything within the dome had been left to rot, with just the prison in operation. Jackson had bought the heavenly body only recently and determined this would be an excellent place for the project, far from the eyes and ears of competing corporations which would like nothing better than to scoop up the technology for themselves. And

Moon Complex had the most sophisticated AI in existence *and* it was in full operation, which Jackson considered to be the best part of the deal.

"I am afraid that some of my memory chips have been removed."

"Virtual Alzheimer's," Lynda laughed.

"I only know that a disaster took place on Elysium. I can't tell you more."

"Can't, or won't?" Skye said under her breath. Something about this AI was not right. It had too much knowledge *and* not enough. She didn't trust it to be honest with her. But that didn't matter. What it didn't admit to she would discover in another way.

"So," Free said, feeling more confident. "Let's begin with a few questions for MT." He waited. "Anybody?"

"Who programmed you?" Lynda asked.

"Dr Arthur J Castillo."

"Who's he?" Brad asked.

"Head of a special project for the New American Republic's Advanced Weapons Division."

"Military?"

"Yes."

"And he did his experiments here, at the Military Complex?"

"Yes."

Anyar took a seat at an empty desk and picked up a digital pen, just for something to hold, and wiggled it back and forth. "So, what was this military experiment all about?"

"Those chips have been deleted."

They all remained silent for a few moments.

"Do you have an image of Dr Castillo, and a list of his credentials that we could see?"

"I'm afraid I have no further information on the good doctor."

"I have an image," Free said.

"How interesting," MT murmured.

Skye spun around in her chair to stare at Free. He walked to her console and hit a few buttons on her computer to access his personal data bank, saying, "I did manage to find a bit of information on this place. Just so you know I'm not as inept at research as you think." He was really talking to Skye but directed his comments over his shoulder to everyone.

A two meter squared holographic image appeared in front of the far wall, a headshot and a full body image side by side, both of which spun slowly around in a hazy glow. Castillo was middle-aged, with very long salt and pepper hair pulled back into a ponytail that almost hung down to her waist, and a graying goatee on the square chin of his slim face. Half of that face was scarred, and what seemed to be a robotic eye protruded from the damaged side. The good, fleshy part of his face showed prominent bone structure, a high cheek bone, strong jaw, and a small intimation that his back teeth had been extracted. The long aquiline nose gave him a haughty and pretentious appearance. His body was long and slim and gave the impression that he was over two meters tall, although Free had no details about his height and weight, and an image could be misleading, especially this one, since there was nothing else there to show perspective.

"Those are the most awesome spectacles I've ever seen!" Brad said.

"Who wears glasses anymore?" Lynda wondered.

"I... I sometimes do," Herbert admitted.

"You would."

"Do you have any data on him?" Brad asked.

"No. There's nothing I could find," Free said. "I was lucky to get these images."

"Where did you get the images?" Skye asked.

"Jackson has some old journals. He resides pretty much out of the loop, so whatever got whitewashed away with Castillo everywhere else in the universe survived at the outer reaches of this galaxy in Jackson's library."

"So you know nothing about him?" Skye asked.

"Only what was in the journal, which wasn't much. A paragraph. Apparently the guy was killed in an accident here on Elysium. There's no date of death or anything like that. Don't know if he had a family because there was no other information, and there were no records available to even indicate that he was ever born. Didn't even really say what he specialized in, just his title. It's as if the guy was a ghost or something. Or maybe he didn't really exist."

"Well, it *is* a half virtual world down here. Maybe he was virtual," Anyar offered.

"Great, a virtual doctor in charge of a secret military experiment. How weird is that?" Brad asked.

"So," Skye said, snapping off the images. "You, AI, tell me something. You say you can't be replicated. Can parts of your program be replicated?"

Major Tom paused before saying, "Yes."

"Fully?"

"I am not certain."

"So you can replicate parts of your programming into our cyborg?"

"It is possible to replicate the relevant parts of my programming, if that is required, yes."

"Have you ever replicated yourself?"

MT hesitated again. In what sounded carefully worded to Skye's ears, the AI said, "Parts of my programming have been replicated, yes."

"Are you a replica of the original programs?"

"Yes."

Everyone was silent for a while, considering the ramifications of this.

"Well," Anyar said, "most computers and robots can replicate themselves."

"They can, but most of them are machines, designed for uni or simple multitasking. Major Tom has been designed to be a complex multi-functional," Skye reminded them.

She looked thoughtful for a moment.

"I wouldn't worry about this," Free said, struggling to regain control of a situation that was threatening. He could feel the unasked questions floating through the air and the accompanying fear, and wanted to divert them, especially Skye, who seemed relentless in her pursuit of information about the AI.

"Where is your initial programming?" Skye asked.

"I believe Dr Castillo—"

"I'm talking about the original Major Tom."

"Whereabouts unknown," came the perfunctory reply.

"You don't know, or you won't say?"

"I am not at liberty to say."

"What the hell does that mean?" Lynda asked. "You're a replica of a program that had a malfunction that was supposedly dismantled and now you're telling us that program may still exist?"

"Does it exist?" Free asked.

"As far as I know, the original Major Tom exists in some form."

"On this moon?" Skye demanded.

"We are not in direct contact."

"You're in indirect contact with a malfunctioning AI?" Herbert asked. "Is that a good thing?"

"I am not programmed for ethical evaluations."

"Look, do you or do you not know where the original AI is?" Skye asked, her attention totally focused on gleaning information.

"I am not at liberty to convey that information."

Free thought Skye looked obsessive, and wondered what was going on with her. He felt he had to step in and sort this out before all hell broke loose.

"MT, listen to me," Free said. "I want a clear answer. Is the original MT part of your programming?"

"I do not know which parts of my programming were copied from which sources."

"Does the original AI act in any way as an agent in terms of what is happening here with this part of the camp, either the life support, or in any other basic capacity?"

"No."

"Does it act in any capacity on this moon?"

"As far as I know, it does."

"Does its functioning have to do with the Military Complex? The prison?"

"Yes."

"Can the malfunctioning AI hinder our project in any way?"

"At this time, the original Major Tom functions only at the Military Complex."

"I'm not sure I feel reassured," Lynda said.

"Okay," Free turned to the others, "I think we have a relatively clear answer. The original was not completely dismantled and is functioning in some capacity at the Military Complex. Likely it controls the prison environment."

"Is the Military Complex empty of human beings, other than the prison?" Free asked.

"I do not know. I am not in charge of the Military Complex."

"I think we're safe," Free told them. "The original AI has a function. Likely they couldn't completely dismantle it so they set it a specific task. It should not infringe on our work in any way."

"How do we know that?" Lynda said. "We don't know what it did, how or why it malfunctioned, or what it's capable of."

"MT says it won't interfere, so whatever its problem, it's in the past and won't affect us."

"And how do we know this AI taking care of our environment is telling the truth?" Skye asked.

"That's a good question," Herbert said, more adamant than Free had ever seen him.

"I am," the AI said, "programmed not to lie."

"Which could be a lie," Anyar suggested.

"Highly perceptive of you, Ms Singh, and an interesting philosophical paradox," chimed the AI.

"Look, we're all getting stressed out about nothing," Free said reasonably. "Computer programs malfunction all the time. We all know that. Whoever came here and reprogrammed it and set up Major Tom Two here likely used a clean backup program."

"I'd like to know just how the original AI malfunctioned. Do you have any info on that?" Lynda asked.

"Regrettably, Ms Barnes, my chips are limited mostly to the present and functioning normally in that capacity. I would also like to know the answer to that question. It would help to forestall a malfunction in my own system, although I suspect that the reprogrammers have guarded against that."

"Do you know who created you? Who made a copy of the original AI?" Anyar asked.

"No. I do not have that information."

Suddenly Skye leapt to her feet. She snatched a binder of papers at her work station and headed for the door.

"Wait!" Free said. "This meeting isn't over."

She turned, fire in her eyes. "I just worked the night shift, if you recall, before you placed a moratorium on work. I'm tired."

Free had forgotten that. "Uh, okay. Why don't you go get some rest? We'll carry on and MT can brief you on anything relevant to the project."

Without a word, Skye left the building.

Lynda raised an eyebrow. "How come she gets special treatment?"

"It's not special," Free said, feeling his face redden. "She said she was tired."

"So am I! I had to face that… thing. And by the way, AI, what was that thing I saw at the Military Complex?"

"To what do you refer?" MT asked.

"That… thing in the basement. The giant!"

"I'm afraid, Ms Barnes, that I have no idea to whom or what you are referring. To my knowledge, there are no giants in residence at the Military Complex."

"Oh, forget it!" Lynda said, jumping to her feet. "Even the damned computer doesn't believe me!"

"I believe you, darling," Brad said, but Lynda gave him a nasty look. Sometimes she felt like Brad was just humoring her.

"I'm tired too," she said, "so why don't we postpone the rest of this meeting?"

Without waiting for an answer she headed out the door, slamming it behind her. Let them all go to hell! How did she ever get stuck in this stupid place with a bunch of losers like this? If she had any other job offers she would be out of here on the next shuttle.

Even as she thought that she heard the AI say, "The next shuttle is due to land here by Earth II time in approximately thirty days, three hours, thirty-three minutes and three seconds."

"Oh, shut up!" she snapped, heading to her quarters.

With two of the team of six gone, Free had little choice but to tell those who were left that the meeting would resume tomorrow morning, same time, same place, and that they would get started on formulating the details of the individual aspects of the project then.

Anyar and Herbert stayed to examine the equipment in the biolab. Brad left, presumably to join Lynda. Free stood for a minute staring around him at the empty Lab, wondering just how he would be able to control these people.

He left the Lab with no clear direction in mind and found himself walking toward the cabins. Instead of turning left to go to his own, he turned right, heading down the row. As he passed the cabin Lynda and Brad shared he heard them arguing. Or rather, he heard Lynda yelling and Brad placating her.

Before he knew it, Free was standing in front of Skye's cabin, walking up the walkway to her door, and was about to knock when he heard her voice through the door.

"No, mother, it's not dangerous here. Not at all."

Skye was recording responses to what must have been an audio letter she brought with her. Presumably she would send the reply back to Earth II via MT. If only the gases weren't so concentrated on Elysium, they could have brought personal comm links to Earth II. As it was, only specialized links could get through via Major Tom, and apparently it was to be used once a month or for emergencies only. Jackson had impressed upon Free just how expensive every transmission was, and had asked Free to use the link only as needed.

"Of course not. I told you, it's a job. Just a job."

Skye paused before speaking once more. "Why not here? There's nothing horrendous going on at all."

Another pause. "Yes, everyone's very nice."

"No, there's no one I'm interested in." Skye's tone sounded exasperated.

Pause. "I know, and I said I'm sorry. I should have told you. But it was very short notice. I got the job and had to leave right away. And I knew you'd worry."

A pause for what sounded like a very long statement by her mother.

"Mom, I'm not my sisters. I'll be careful."

Free strained hopelessly to hear Skye's mom.

"I'm sorry. I know, I loved them too."

Free could hear the pounding of his heart clearly through his chest.

"Yes, I promise to try to keep in touch, but there's something wrong with the atmosphere so we don't have regular comm links, and we have to send messages through the AI, and I'm not sure how often it's sending them. Please, don't worry about me. Everything will be all right.

There was another pause before Skye stated brusquely, "No, of course I'm not. Nothing to do with his work. I'm here for something entirely different."

Skye's mother obviously said something that she did not want to listen to.

"I really do need to go. I'm not sure how long a message I can send, and I wanted to make sure you heard back from me. I'll try to send another message soon, okay? Love you. Take care, mom. Bye."

For some reason, Free hadn't imagined Skye having a family. Of course she would have. Everyone has a family, even if they don't know who or where they are.

Suddenly he felt silly standing on her step before her door. He didn't even know why he was here. Maybe it was the sense that something was troubling her, and that he should try to talk with her. But now that he thought about it, there wasn't anything he could say that wouldn't just irritate her.

He turned and started back down the path. Behind him, the door opened.

"What are you doing here?"

Free turned at the shrill and accusatory tone. "I just wanted to see how you were."

"Why?"

"You seemed, I don't know, upset at the meeting."

"I said I was tired." Her voice hardened again and she came outside and shut the door behind her. "Were you eavesdropping?"

"I was about to knock when I heard you recording, so I decided not to. Sorry. I was just concerned, that's all."

She walked to the end of the path until she stood before him. This close, he could smell a sweet floral fragrance coming from her. She had swept up her midnight hair into a loose ponytail, wisps flying here and there; the hair was so long that it had been knotted to form its own band. Soulful eyes stared into his as if they were a pale cool ocean calling him to dive in.

"I'm headed to the lake, since that's about as far as we can go these days. We can go to the other side, can't we, or is that forbidden too?" Skye asked.

"It's only for a few days, until they get the prisoners out of here. The other side of the lake is probably safe."

They started walking side by side. He was so aware of her next to him and that made him feel both elated and shy. He wanted to say, "Didn't you say you were tired?' but knew that that would tick her off. He was just feeling shy, anxious, not wanting the contact with her to end. Suddenly he knew he had to be careful of every word he said so as not to scare this exotic bird away.

Once they had passed the cabins, and he could feel the warmth of the day seeping into him—thank you, MT, for raising the temp, he thought—Free said what he hoped would be safe enough. "So, what do you think of Lynda's monster?"

"She's a pea brain! Wouldn't know reality if it walked up and bit her on the ass, not that reality could get through all that heavy velvet she wears."

Free laughed. "Hey, speak your mind."

Skye shot him a look.

"I'm not laughing at you. I'm just laughing. It strikes a chord."

She eased down a bit and finally said, "She obviously saw something that frightened her. Maybe she imagined it—she is totally caught up in fantasy in some ways. Maybe it was even a prisoner for all we know. We can check out the place once they take the cons away. I'd like to see it."

"Me too," Free admitted.

"I believe," MT said suddenly as they reached the lake, "your peers have questions for you. Ms Singh and Mr Dearman are in the biolab, trying to decide who will search for you, Free."

Right! Free thought. I get five minutes alone with this woman when she's not ripping my head off and naturally I get called away.

"Guess I gotta go," he said with what he hoped was a disappointed smile.

"The price of power," she said, half turning from him.

"Uh, yeah. Well, see you."

"Later."

He had just reached the Lab, too far to backtrack, and could have kicked himself. He should have asked her to meet him for dinner or something. What a stupid... The first time they'd spoken civilly to one another, and he just let it die...

A small groan slipped from his lips.

MT said, "There will be, my friend, other occasions."

"Maybe," Free said. "I hope so. She's very cute."

"I suppose most life forms take after their parents, though not always."

Free paused at the door of the lab. "What's that mean?"

"Oh, just what I said: like father and mother, like daughter or son."

"Yeah, and how does that relate to Skye?"

"No more than it relates to you, or to me, for that matter, given that I am the offspring of the original Major Tom."

Free raised his eyebrows. "MT, you've got a philosophical streak."

"Hardly. I'm simply stating an axiom regarding genetics. Or in my case, technology." A sound came from MT that could have been wry laughter, but Free figured that no matter how good this AI's programming, no computer could yet duplicate actual laughter.

Free found himself smiling as he made his way back to the Lab, basking in the warmth of the day, artificial though it was, and already forgetting about MT. He was also forgetting about overseeing this project full of cranky workers. In fact, he forgot about pretty much everything for a short while. Everything but Skye, and how her darker than dark hair shone so brilliantly, and framed so beautifully her softly tanned face with eyes the color of pale water. And how those eyes possessed a longing buried deep within her that he hoped he could fill.

FIVE

"We've got this big problem right from the get-go," Anyar said. She held up a piece of cable that attached the biolab computer to the platform onto which the cyborg would be built. It dangled in her hand like a lifeless snake.

Free felt baffled for a moment.

"There's no way to hook it into the computer," Herbert said. "At… at least we can't find it."

"That's because it isn't here," Anyar said.

Free made his way to the computer bank with its manual buttons and levers, and which also accepted audio commands. All of it was designed to run the biometric computer that would assemble the virtual model of the cyborg, around which the team could replicate materials to build the actual being. The cable hooked into the computer but not to the platform in the middle of the glassed-in room.

Free took the transparent cable that contained a dozen or so multicolored wires from Anyar and looked at the end of it. It was a twelve-pronged plug. He then looked at the platform and saw a ten-hole socket.

"There's got to be an adapter," he said.

"Well, if there is, it isn't in this room," Anyar said.

"Hey, Major Tom. We need some help here," Free said.

"At your service."

"We've got a missing adapter. We can't hook the computer cable to the platform. Where's the adapter for this cable?"

"I'm afraid there is no adapter."

"Well, there must have been at one time."

"I'm quite sure you're correct. To my knowledge, though, there is no adapter."

"Great!" Anyar said. "What do we do, phone Earth II and wait for them to ship us something, and lose what, a month of work time?"

"Let's not panic yet," Free said. He checked the male and female connections again, studying them while Herbert voiced every fear in his head.

"This will look bad, very bad, if we don't get the project done on time. Nobody will remember that we didn't have an adapter; they'll just decide that we weren't competent. My mother told me to make sure we get it done on time because if we don't, they will blame us. I just knew it would come down to me being blamed…"

Suddenly Free had an idea. "Hold on, I think we can deal with this."

"How?" Anyar said, sounding unconvinced.

"I'll be right back."

The second he stepped outside the glass room, he saw Skye sitting at her terminal. It brought a smile to his face, thinking that maybe she had come in here because she knew he would be here. At least he hoped so. Better not seem too eager. He didn't want to frighten her off.

"Hi!" he said, passing her desk as if he were busy.

She looked up, obviously preoccupied, and as she stared at him it was as if she'd never seen him before, which Free found totally depressing.

"Hi," she finally managed, and then her eyes went back to the screen.

Free, his mood suddenly deflated, moved across the room to a toolbox located inside a wall panel. Every tech room, he knew, had one of these, right next to the emergency phone and the fire alarm. This lab had a fire alarm but no phone. Well, there was no one to call and no way to make a call anyway.

Inside the panel he found an array of tools which could be used for dealing with all types of modern hardware. The item he picked up had the beak of a pterodactyl or one of those other ancient giants that roamed the original Earth: long, slim, curved at the end, and sharp.

Without another word to Skye, who was completely absorbed by something on her screen, he went back into the biotech room, picked up the male cable and, much to the horror of both Anyar and Herbert, proceeded to snip off two of the prongs.

"Don't!" Anyar cried.

"Y-you can't do that!" Herbert yelled. "The cable will short-circuit. You'll blow the power grid! And we might need those particular wires and..."

But he had already finished his surgery. As he plugged in the cable to the platform, both Anyar and Herbert raced for the door, as if expecting an explosion of some kind.

The newly cropped plug went easily into the outlet. Before their eyes, the platform lit up. Slowly, first Anyar then Herbert moved back into the room when they realized that they would not be vaporized.

"There," Free said. "Good as new."

"H-how did you know to do that?" Herbert asked. "Which prongs to cut?"

"Where I lived, we sometimes had to improvise because we couldn't get supplies easily, like adapters. I learned that if it's not available, you either make what you need, or adapt what you have to your needs. And I've done this before," he laughed. "Not with such a complex cable, but I kind of knew what was essential for the platform and what wasn't."

Anyar was already pressing buttons at the rim of the platform. A transparent casing came up in a spiral motion to surround the platform onto which the cyborg would be built and hopefully activated.

Herbert went to the computer and voice-activated a command that placed a three-dimensional hologram of a humanoid form within the casing.

They seemed to be set, so Free left them, although neither one acknowledged that he had fixed their problem. They were now as absorbed in their work as Skye was at her computer terminal.

Free had a hunch that he should just pass her by, head on out the door and go for a walk to investigate the campground that was currently available to them. In other words, not talk to her. But he ignored his instincts and instead stopped at her desk and waited the excruciating seconds it took for her to look up from her work.

Her face was streaked with annoyance. She pressed a button and the screen went blank, but he thought he'd seen the same holographic humanoid image that Herbert had placed within the circular casing.

Free, now embarrassed as well as humiliated, said, "Hey, you're on the night shift. You don't need to be here now."

Clearly it was the wrong thing to say. "Is there some problem with me being here in the daytime?" Skye snapped. "I'd like to get a bit of a head start on the work, unless, of course, that's against your philosophy."

Her voice was tense, her tone slightly harsh, and instead of just backing off, Free snapped back at her. "No, there's no problem working all day every day if you want to. That's your prerogative, but nothing can move forward until everybody has their work in so we can make a cohesive whole."

"Don't you think I know that? I'm not doing the project alone, just my bit of it, and I'd like to get a feel for things before we get going in a big way."

He knew he should shut up but he just couldn't stop himself. "Do you really think that working around the clock is going to make you efficient?"

"Well, that's my business, isn't it?"

"Not really. I'm team leader. I'm responsible for everything that happens here."

"Fine!" She slammed a button and the computer submerged into the desk. Meanwhile, she scanned her palm print to lock it and then stood.

Skye brushed past him, furious. What was with this guy? One minute he seemed okay, and the next he was stepping all over her territory, being pushy, a real jerk, and for no good reason. He'd said they could use the Lab anytime. She had work to do besides this project, but if he was going to be looking over her shoulder every step of the way...

She was outside, stomping toward her cabin, when she felt a hand on her upper arm and found herself being spun around.

"Stop!" he yelled in her face.

She jerked her arm away but didn't move. "What?"

"I... I didn't mean for any of that to happen. I just wanted to stop by and say hello. We were interrupted before and... and I guess I managed to muck it all up. I'm sorry. That wasn't my intention. Of course you can work anytime you want. I'm sorry," he said again.

The look in his eyes made her realize that he did have a good intention. "I'm sorry too. I shouldn't

have snapped at you. Sometimes when I'm con-
centrating... I mean, being pulled out of my work
at a crucial moment, when I have a thought I'm
trying to purs—"

"I understand. I'm the same way. I should have
known. I'm just so... unused to people."

He shook his head at himself, and his lips
clamped together and twisted as if he couldn't
believe his own actions. She found the look
endearing. "Well, I mean, you grew up on a satellite and everything. That couldn't have been easy.
Were you an only child?"

Somehow, they had started walking together,
heading back toward the lake where their conversation had been interrupted. Skye felt a bit of a tug
toward the Lab, but she could work later. Anytime,
he said. And it was important to get him onside.

"Yeah. Just me and my mom. And Jackson, who
took us in."

"Took you in? How do you mean?"

"Well, my mother was lost out in space. She
worked on a space station, as a geneticist, and
something happened on the station. I'm not sure
what. I think it might have exploded or something,
I don't know. She never liked to talk about it. She
managed to get out in a shuttle, but it was damaged. There was this weird thing onboard from a
couple of centuries ago, a kind of metallic pod, and
she had to use that because the shuttle was
destroyed in an asteroid field."

Skye stopped. "You're kidding, right? That is
such a strange story."

"I know. I heard it all my life."

"How come you don't know what happened to the station?"

"My mother didn't like to talk about any of it. She only did when I gnawed at her sufficiently."

"Didn't you ever do any research? Read historical records, try to check logs?"

"I did, of course. But I could never find much of anything. I don't even think the fact that she lived was recorded anywhere, for all I could tell."

"My life seems tame compared to yours."

"Were you an only too?"

"Actually, I was one of three sisters; triplets."

This time Free stopped and stared at her. "Really? Was it a natural occurrence, or did your mom have the egg split intentionally?"

Skye looked away and said in a soft voice, "My father was the one who wanted three kids from the same egg. He didn't care what gender, as long as there were three of us. He had a thing for threes."

"Uh, gee, I don't mean to be negative, but that sounds pretty weird to me."

Skye turned back and Free saw her features harden until she looked at him. Seeing that he wasn't putting her down, her face softened and they suddenly both laughed. "Yeah, I guess it was a bit weird."

"So where are your sisters? Do they do the same work you do?"

Her face went from soft to sad. "Both of them died about a year ago, in the spring. They were together."

Free realized that that was about the time when they took the intergalactic exams. That must have been the tragedy she was talking about.

He didn't know quite what to say. "Well, it must be nice to grow up with siblings. I was a pretty lonely kid, the only kid on the satellite."

She looked at him and could see the loneliness in him. It made him awkward and appealing at the same time. "So, your mom escaped in this metal toothbrush holder and then what?"

They had reached the lake and walked about halfway around to a small white stone bench of the type he had seen images of from when the original Earth was in what had been called the Victorian era, named after a queen in a country called England. They sat down simultaneously and stared at the water for a moment.

"You know, I don't really know the whole story. She was out of comm range because this old tiny ship had nothing in the way of communications that would work. I think the manned satellite scanners found her. She was pregnant with me at the time. They took her in, or at least Jackson Mansfield did—he happened to be there when they found her. She gave birth to me, and I lived on that satellite most of my childhood before we moved to another satellite, where I spent the rest of my life until now."

"But you got top marks in the exams. I think you got ninety-nine percent, right?"

Free laughed and looked away, both proud and sheepish. "Yeah, I missed one question. The one you got right. The one about genetic probability."

"I know!" she laughed, feeling that it had been forever since she had last laughed. "I checked your exam too. Nothing like keeping tabs on the competition." She smiled a little. "I missed two questions, both on reversible and irreversible trends."

They sat quietly for a few moments. Free looked up at the sky and could now make out the Sling clearly. It seemed to have lowered considerably since the last time he looked at it.

"Mind-blowing, huh?" Skye said, following his gaze, and Free laughed at the antiquated language.

"I can't figure out how it grounds itself."

"I haven't looked into it," she said. "Too busy. But I think it's got some kind of gravitational anchor that keeps it locked into one place in space, using the strongest gravitational pull in the vicinity. In this case that would be Earth II."

"Makes sense."

He looked at her and saw her beauty in profile. Every feature was perfect. Suddenly, on impulse, Free put his arm around her shoulder.

Skye didn't flinch, although she felt like doing so. The contact seemed alien. But eventually, the warmth of his flesh moved through the fabric of her shirt and spoke to her skin in a way that she found comforting. She'd forgotten what it meant to be human. It felt good.

"So," she said. "Have you heard from your mother since you've been here?"

His fingers tensed almost imperceptibly. "My mom died a couple of years ago."

"I'm sorry."

"It's okay. She died peacefully. And Jackson gave her a good life. And she was a good mom. I know she loved me. She did everything for me. I'll always owe her my life."

"Why did she call you Free?"

"I asked her once. She said because once she arrived on the satellite, she felt both of us were free, but she didn't say from what. Maybe just from floating in space."

"That's nice. It's a nice name."

"So's Skye. Who named you?"

"My father." Her voice hardened a bit. "He controlled everything. My sisters were Terra and Luna. He liked to do everything in triplicate. He was a strange and cold man, but a brilliant scientist, and also a tedious bureaucrat. I'm probably like him. You know, genetic probability and all…"

"Was? Is he gone?"

"Yep. He died about twenty years ago."

"Wow." Free didn't know what to say now, but knew he shouldn't say much of anything.

"Yeah, there's just me and my mother. She's an okay woman, kind of weak-willed in a way. I'm not putting her down, just saying how she is. She was his third wife—the other two couldn't give him the triplets he wanted by any method other than artificial insemination and he didn't want that. So now she's alone, fretful all the time; worried about me even when I go into the washroom, afraid I'll fall into the toilet and drown."

Free laughed despite himself, and Skye smiled suddenly. He was okay. *Really* okay. The fact that he didn't know much about his past made him somehow more trustworthy. But she did want to check one thing out. "Do you know who your father is? I mean, your genetic father?"

"Not a clue. Mom would definitely not talk about him. She had a boyfriend on the station, and I've tried to get records of the crew there, but the info seems to be locked tight, like it's some sort of high security file."

"Maybe it's better not to know. I wouldn't have minded not knowing about my father."

"Why?"

Skye stood up and stretched, her long, slim, slightly tanned legs, and her breasts, pressing against the fabric of that satiny top, distracted him a bit. "Come on," she said. "I'm hungry. Let's see what kind of dried lunches we can find."

"Sure, I'm up for that. Do you like wine?"

"Yeah. Some. You?"

"I've never had any. We didn't have things like that on the satellite."

Skye shook her head, smiling. "You didn't have a lot of things on the satellite. You've got a lot to learn, Mr Free. Or do you have a last name?"

"Not sure. My mom's last name was Jefferson. I think her line was descended from one of the presidents of the United States of America on the old Earth. I guess that makes me Free Jefferson. But nobody's ever called me that."

"Well, I won't start."

They both laughed, heading for the store.

Free felt good. Really good. In fact, he'd never felt like this before. He wondered if he should try to put his arm around her again, but then realized they were in sight of the cabins now, and it probably wasn't a good idea. He knew that he shouldn't show any favoritism. He would wait. There were other days coming. They had a good six months on Elysium, barring an extension. He smiled at the thought, at the day, at Skye.

She smiled back. He really was likeable, *and* attractive. She wouldn't mind a fling with him. It would be genuine, and not something put on to manipulate him. But nothing permanent would come of it. Nothing permanent could come of anything with anyone. That thought threw a momentary dark cloud over her mood. She had work to do; work that was crucial. To her understanding. To the universe. Nothing could get in her way, not even a sexy boy with one blue eye and one hazel eye flecked with green. But she realized that she wouldn't mind staring into those multicolored eyes on somewhat of a regular basis, at least for a while.

SIX

"This is not going to work," Lynda stated flatly. "I can't believe we have this crappy equipment and we're supposed to produce results."

Free blinked twice but decided to say nothing and just let her rant.

"I haven't seen a system this old since school."

"Then you must have just graduated last week," Anyar told her as she passed by and entered the biolab. "The model on your desk just came out a month ago."

Before Lynda had a chance to respond, Anyar closed the glass door.

Brad, ever the diplomat regarding Lynda, said, "Sweetie, we knew we'd be roughing it here. It's likely that this experiment isn't top priority for the big wigs."

Free felt he had to jump in, if only to defend Jackson. "The project is top priority, but it is an experiment, and I know that Jackson Mansfield got the best equipment he could find for the price he paid, and I also know that the price was considerable. We're here to test a hypothesis. It may not work. We might end up with a Major Tom brain and a chunky body that looks humanoid but can't function. Or we might get the opposite. Realistically speaking, we'll be lucky if we can instill even one emotion into this creature."

"Wow, great pep talk," Lynda said. "I really feel like working now. Nobody thinks we'll succeed."

"That's not true. We wouldn't be here, being paid, if there was no hope. One thing I know about Jackson Mansfield is that he doesn't waste a second of his time or energy on what he believes will fail. If he didn't think we could succeed in full or in part we wouldn't be here, and he'd be using Elysium as a giant warehouse for storage or something."

"Well I, for one, don't see how we can replicate human thinking. Thought patterns, sure. We've got the AI already doing tha—"

"He does a lot mo—"

"But that's not the same as how a person thinks. Our best shot is my initial idea: to transfer data from the university computers, a kind of 'history from the beginning' of time on Earth and Earth II, and to let the new AI we're building sort it all out."

"That would take forever and a day," Skye said. "We couldn't load all that into a system here. We'd need expansion cubes, millions of them, and we'd have to find a way for it to run quickly, which means not only more memory but a processor that's faster than anything we can now build."

"They've got a twenty-seven-squared processor where we went to school," Brad offered.

"Yeah, and?" Skye said. "I've used those. That just means if we loaded in one hundred libraries we could run it at top speed. But you're talking about data from a million or more libraries."

"We could fragment the memory," Lynda offered. "Each expansion cube could handle what it can handle and we'd have one for each segment of human history."

"And it would take us five years to make this happen," Free said.

"Well, what's your solution?" Lynda demanded.

Free felt frustrated. "I have no solution. That's what we're here for, to brainstorm and find solutions to this problem."

"I have a better idea," Skye said.

"Oh? And what would that be?" Lynda asked, her voice laced with skepticism.

"We load in our personal and collective memories to the new AI by direct brain to computer hookup," Skye said.

"Are you serious?" Brad snapped. "Give over the privacy of our thoughts to a fucking computer for everyone in the entire universe to see?"

Skye ignored his outburst, which impressed Free considerably. "Look," she said. "If we did it anonymously, nothing would be attributed to any of us.

There are six of us here, and we'd be mixing experiences; emotional, physical and mental reactions; and our ability to analyze situations. What we'd end up with would be an amalgam of the six of us," Skye said.

"The totality would be greater than the sum of the parts," Free said.

"Won't the AI be confused?" Herbert said, sticking his head out the door to also say, "Uh, Anyar and I have come up with a simulation, if you'd like to take a look."

"In a minute," Free said. "We need to sort this out first."

"Even if we decide to go with your plan, and I'm not sure it would work," Lynda said reluctantly, clearly trying to keep her tongue civil, "how are we going to do a direct transfer? That's experimental. As far as I know, nobody has managed it and come up with anything different than a standard input of data."

"Well, one person did," replied Skye.

"And who might that be?"

"Dr Castillo."

"The guy who worked on the Moon Complex for the military, right?"

"Well, great. Do we have his records?" Brad asked.

"Yes," Skye said.

"What?" Free's head snapped around. "Where are these records?"

Skye looked away. "I saw them, or what was available. A long time ago. Before the effort to extinguish them."

"What do you mean extinguished?" Free wanted to know. "I searched and couldn't find anything. Not even a record that there were records."

"That's because they were secret."

"Then how did you see them?"

"I read them as a child."

No one said anything for a few seconds, not fully understanding the implications of what Skye had just said.

"Why don't you guys come see the sim," Anyar eventually said. She stood in the doorway next to Herbert.

The others, for lack of anything better to do, stood up one by one and followed Anyar and Herbert into the biotech room. "Hold on a second," Anyar said. She pressed a button on the wall which locked the door and also set in motion the air vacuum system that sucked out all the dust and other small particles from the room.

Herbert manipulated the computer and a holographic image appeared in the air, standing on the platform.

"Wow, he's huge!" Brad said.

"What makes you think it's a he?" Anyar wanted to know.

"Well, the lack of what's obvious," Brad said.

"What, breasts? There's a lack of what's obvious for the male gender too."

"How come he's so large?" Free asked. "I mean, why do we need a giant? We can use nanotechnology."

"We're trying to build something that can contain all the programs we want to input, right?" Anyar explained. "This is a prototype, remember? Herbert and I think we need to make the form huge, and full to the max with everything we can stuff in there. Once we see what works and what doesn't, then we can refine this model, including reducing the size and shape of the form, as well as reducing the data to nano-programming."

The six stared in awed silence as the hologram began to rotate slowly. The arms and shoulders of the simulated body were massive; the musculature of the back, chest and thighs gargantuan even compared to bodybuilder proportions. The head seemed a trifle square shaped, which Brad pointed out.

"Uh, we, uh needed to make sure the cubes have someplace to go where it's easy to insert them and take them out, as needed."

"I don't like it," Lynda remarked. Her arms were crossed over her chest, her face set, and her eyes rounded with a look that Free could only interpret as barely repressed terror.

"Why don't you like it?" he asked her gently.

She turned to face him, about to say something, when Skye said, "I think this image makes sense. Herbert is right: we need a form large enough to work with. Refinement comes later."

Lynda turned on her like a rabid animal. "No! This isn't going to work! I won't work with a monster."

Skye raised an eyebrow. "A monster? You mean like the one you saw at the Military Complex?" A slight smile played on her lips and Free knew that she had entered dangerous territory. He was not wrong.

"Yes, it's exactly like what I saw! Same shape, same size, everything. Maybe there's a reason this design is used." She turned to Anyar and Herbert who seemed to both lean in to each other, as if for protection. "That sim. Did you make it yourselves?"

"It was in the computer," Anyar said. "We played with the basic model."

"There!" Lynda said, yelling at everyone in the room, and to Free she appeared deranged. "It was already there because it has been used before. To make the… the thing I saw at the Military Complex."

"That's not possible," Free said. "These computers just arrived a few weeks before we did."

"All of them?" Lynda cried out.

"Major Tom?" Free nearly shouted out.

"Here," said the modulated voice.

"When did the biolab's equipment arrive on Elysium?"

"Thirty-two days, six hours, forty-seven minutes and eight seconds ago, by Earth II time. Now ten seconds."

"Did it come with basic programs?" Free continued.

"As far as I know, yes," MT replied civilly.

"Were any programs added?"

"Not to my knowledge."

"There," Free said, turning to Lynda. He wanted to place a soothing hand on her shoulder but was afraid of how she'd react. He had so little experience dealing with people, with women, with emotions in general.

"Sweets, I think this equipment couldn't have been used here before," Brad said, his voice soft, comforting, and reassuring.

Lynda turned to him, and Free watched her face soften a bit while her shoulders lowered, which is when he realized just how tense she had been.

"Do you think that could be true? That the AI is telling the truth?" she asked Brad.

"I think so," Brad said. "There's no reason for it to lie."

"And I have the communication from Jackson that I received on Earth II before we left, with details about supplies and equipment, so I know the date it was shipped here," Free said.

"Then why does this image look so much like what I saw?" Lynda asked, staring at the hologram as it spun mindlessly on the wheel of the platform as if it would any second come to life and attack her.

"I think it's a pretty standard model," Anyar said. "We used one just like this at school."

Suddenly Lynda tensed up again. "I bet the AI did this."

"Huh?" Herbert said.

"You mean Major Tom?" Free asked, incredulous.

"Yes, that AI. It's been here all along. It programmed a form into the computer that matches the one I saw at the Military Complex."

"Sweetie, that's a bit far-fetched," Brad started, but Lynda now turned on him too.

"Don't be a fool! Something went wrong here. That's why there's nobody on this Moon Complex but prisoners. An experiment went wrong. An AI is left that says it's a replica of the original AI but with the malfunctioning chips cleaned out. I say this AI hasn't been cleaned up enough. I think it still has some of Dr Castillo's experiment still imbedded in it, and it reprogrammed our system."

"Hold on," Free said. "That sounds crazy. You have no proof of that."

"I may not have proof, but I'm not crazy. I'm cautious. Everything here is set up to work on a project that might have been the same project that Castillo experimented with. Skye saw the notes. He was recreating life, wasn't he?"

Skye looked down. "In a manner of speaking, yes. He was trying to infuse an artificial form with something resembling human life. His technique used a bitmapping process to create the virtual image first."

Lynda looked as if her worst fears had been confirmed. "His experiment failed. So much so that almost all trace of it was wiped out and this place abandoned. And there you have an image of something I saw at the complex and I know it's the thing Castillo created."

"Maybe what you saw at the complex was a virtual image," Anyar said.

"It didn't look virtual to me!"

"Wait," Free said. "MT, did you program any of the equipment that was sent to this moon by Jackson Mansfield?"

"Certainly not. It is not part of my mandate to program any new additions to Moon Complex. And before you ask, I only reprogram systems as required, for instance, to maintain a safe atmosphere breathable by humanoids, to reconstitute enough moisture to sustain the non-virtual part of the biodome, to cleanse the—"

"Okay," Free said. "So the AI didn't program our biolab or any of our other computers and equipment, and Anyar says that the program image is standard. Even if what you saw or thought you saw—"

"I saw it!"

"What you saw is something from the experiment, that doesn't mean it has anything to do with us. This AI is not the original AI. It has no program that allows it to function unilaterally. I think what we have is a coincidence. This hologram, a standard hologram, looks the same as the standard hologram that Dr Castillo must have used..."

"What, twenty years ago?" Lynda asked incredulously.

"I don't see that they've changed much in centuries," Anyar said. "This is the human form."

"All right," Lynda said. "Let's just say for the sake of argument that what you're saying is so, it's the same hologram or similar, the new Major Tom can't program it, the thing I saw at the Military Complex is some remnant of the experiment—"

"Which is, by the way, trapped inside the building," Brad pointed out. "And we are outside."

"But here we are, about to create life, just as Castillo did, based on his ideas." Lynda looked at Skye with a mixture of scorn and eyes that pleaded for understanding. "And by the way, where did you see these notes on his experiments?"

Everyone turned to stare at Skye. She said carefully, "Castillo knew my family. He left some of his research notes with my mother, and she kept them for several years after his death. I've always been interested in science and I read them when I was eight years-old, barely understanding them, but over time they started to make sense. They probably were the basis for my cybernetic studies."

"Where are the notes now?" Free asked.

"They're no longer available."

"Meaning?"

"Meaning I don't have them on me, if that's what you're asking."

"So," Lynda started again, "you read notes that tell how to directly infuse the totality of human experience into an AI, presumably by direct transfer. Obviously the experiment failed. Why should we pursue it again?"

"I think," Skye said, "because he had a master plan that might have had some bugs but also might have been sound in many ways. Castillo was a renowned scientist, an innovator, so we have to assume that his experiment was not only funded by the military because they thought it would work, but also because he was a genius and had grants coming out of his ears."

"How do you know that?" Free asked.

"I don't know for sure, but from what I read about him, little as it was, and from what my mother said about him, also very little, I got the feeling he was the Einstein of his day."

"Then how come there's no information available about him?" Anyar asked. "If he was such a genius, then there should be records of his work."

"I don't know. I only know that from what I read he had some success. And since we have no other way of infusing our being with humanoid life, I think this is worth a shot."

"I'm inclined to go along with this," Anyar said.

"Me too," Herbert agreed.

"Brad, what do you think?" Free asked. He could see that Brad was intentionally avoiding looking at Lynda.

"Makes sense to me."

From the shocked look on Lynda's face, Free as well as Brad could see that this was not the answer she expected.

"I disagree," she said. "Strongly. I think we should use the library databases. Give the creature some history, and not just the brain cells of six post-pubescent Earth II babies working at their first job."

"I think we can also include some of the library cubes," Free said, trying to mollify her. But he realized that she had a point about history. He knew his own limitations regarding his missing history, as well as that of his species, which he would have learned in a more expansive fashion if he'd been educated anywhere but privately on a satellite at the edge of the galaxy. The cyborg should have a better chance. "I'm with the majority. You with us, Lynda?"

She looked angry and after a pause said, "Well, I guess I have to be, don't I?"

"I don't think you have to put your experiences in if you don't want to. No one does."

"Now that's a relief," she snarled. "But you know, who I am should be in the cyborg. Someone needs to infuse it with caution and skepticism, and apparently none of you can."

"Good point," Free said, hoping that agreeing with her would ease down her paranoia.

Lynda took that as agreement and nodded imperceptibly.

"So," Brad asked, "how and when do we go about giving ourselves to the cyborg?"

"We already have," Skye said. "Wait here." She left them and returned to her console, keying some info into her computer and returning within a minute.

"You can start inputting from computer station one," she said.

Herbert turned to the control panel along the wall and pressed a button and flipped two switches. One of the colored wires inside the transparent cable lit up.

"I've done a quickie download," Skye said.

The input took less than three seconds.

"Activate the input, we should see a result. At least I hope so." Skye said the last under her breath.

Anyar gave a verbal signal which rebooted the system. Lights flashed for three seconds. When the holographic image began to spin again, it appeared slightly different.

"Wow, it looks a bit like you," Brad said to Skye.

"Not much, but then there wasn't time for much transfer. What's your name?" she asked the hologram.

"Skye Fellows."

"How old are you?"

"I'll be twenty-five in one month."

"Where are you located at the moment?"

"I'm working with a group of six cyberspecialists on Elysium, a moon of Earth II. We're trying to build an artificial intelligence that replicates and imitates a human being in all aspects."

"How are you doing on the project?"

"We're at the initial stages, but things look promising."

"I have a question," Lynda said. "What do you think of your coworkers?"

"I respect the credentials of everyone I'm working with."

"And their personalities?"

"Some are easier to get along with than others."

"How diplomatic. Who is not easy to get along with?"

"You."

Suddenly Lynda laughed, and the others joined in.

"One more question," Free said, and Skye looked at him, her eyes fearful that he might ask something embarrassing. "That Space Sling, the UUSA, what do you think of it?"

The hologram paused in its spinning for a moment. The mouth turned up in a simulation of a smile as it said, "Mind-blowing!"

SEVEN

Skye spent the next two hours downloading the thoughts and feelings of every member of the team except Free, at least an initial short download from each of them which would give the group enough to work with. She used one of the new micro laser scanners through a probe, inserting it up the supra orbital above the eye, a painless procedure that took all of one second. The probe captured DNA from each of them, taking it from the cerebral cortex. Those strands were automatically refined by the probe and synthesized, then fed into the computer. Now she had not just their strands of life, but also scanned their neurons, and recorded the patterns of their brain waves. She could do a full-blown download from all six of them later, once they made sure this worked.

As the meeting had wound down, with the shift of mood in the up direction, Free told Skye to work with the others. He would volunteer his DNA and everything else later. So much had happened in such a short space of time that he needed to be alone to think about what had occurred, the implications of it all, and what he should do. He decided to take a walk around the lake to think. As the artificial sun beat down on him, and the virtual birds chirped, and as the unnatural squirrels ran up trees and ate their nuts, suddenly, an idea struck Free, one that might provide some cohesiveness to this disparate group. It was so obvious he had missed it all along.

When he returned to the Lab he said in the most relaxed way he knew how, "Let's all head to the gazebo by the water and share some food and drink." Even Lynda and Brad thought it was a good idea, and the group made a stop at the store.

Anyar grabbed a couple of bags of cereal, and the rest selected some of their favorite foods. Free lagged behind, picking up three bottles of wine, a small case of wine goblets, and some fruit juice for those who didn't indulge in the fermented grape.

He was the last to arrive at the lake and by the time he did, Brad and Herbert were busy setting up the table for the group under the directions of Lynda who shouted orders at them.

"The forks go on the left, the knives on the right," she said in exasperation to Herbert, who in his nervousness managed to drop the knives, making Lynda groan.

"No!" she snapped at Brad. "Chopsticks over the plate!"

Finally they sat down to eat, everyone having a taste of everyone else's food. All the choices were a hit but Anyar's, but they all were gracious about her cereal nonetheless.

The warmth of the air, the laughter drifting around him, the clinking glasses and the clatter of utensils on real plates for once as they relaxed and ate and talked and joked; all of it infused Free with a connection he had never experienced before. Suddenly, in the midst of the meal, a feeling overwhelmed him and his fork paused in midair. Until this moment, he had not realized exactly what he had been missing for most of his life. He had been sheltered, loved and protected by his mom and by Jackson. He had been offered every advantage in terms of education and lifestyle, or as much as was possible living on a satellite. But he lacked the company of people. This type of normal interaction was like an exotic pleasure to him. Chatting about nothing. Teasing one another. Laughing. Not talking sometimes, just being together.

"Anything wrong?" Skye asked quietly, seated next to him at the hexagonal table.

He turned to stare into her beautiful water-blue eyes and felt completely at peace. "Nothing at all," he said with a smile. "Nothing is wrong, everything is so right."

Those serious, soulful eyes flicked over his face for a moment like a caress, and then she smiled too, and it was as if the artificial sun had become a real sun and his world brightened.

In the next moment the ground beneath their feet trembled violently. Anyar, who had stood to pour herself another drink, fell onto her side. Herbert toppled off his seat onto his back. Lynda teetered on the edge of her part of the bench but grasped onto Brad who held onto the seat to steady them both. By instinct, Free's arm went protectively around Skye, and his hand grabbed the table edge. The fingers of his other hand hooked into the lattice of the gazebo.

Glasses, plates, cutlery, all of it shook and spilled off the table and much of it broke. Food and drink slopped onto the table's surface and ran over the edges in a confused soup, hitting the ground in great plops.

The quaking seemed to go on forever but it couldn't have lasted more than fifteen seconds.

"What the hell was that?" Brad yelled when it stopped.

By now they were all on their feet. "Everybody okay?" Free asked, looking around.

Nods and yeses. "It's like something slammed into the surface of this moon," Lynda said.

"MT, what happened?" Free called.

"The UUSA has malfunctioned."

"What? The Sling? How?"

"I am assessing the situation and will have a report as soon as possible."

Free was already looking up, trying to see through the dome; all of them were. "Dim the lighting," he ordered.

Major Tom instantly complied.

As darkness fell over the interior of the Moon Complex, the blackness beyond lit up with stars. Earth II became visible in the distance, as well as its small, dark moon Thanos.

"There!" Brad pointed.

It looked as if it had stopped in midair, somewhere between where they stood and the direction they knew the Military Complex to be in.

"It's an upside-down antique cherry picker," Herbert said. And although no one was watching him, he looked around and muttered, "I-I grew up on a farm."

The enormous object had an enclosed and transparent basket at the bottom, and from it extended a long arm that seemed to stop dead somewhere out in space.

"That's the amazing part," Skye mumbled. "That it doesn't connect to anything, it's just pinioned by gravity from the strongest source."

"Damage report yet?" Free asked the AI.

"I am still analyzing the data but it appears that the UUSA hit the dome."

"How the hell could that happen?" Anyar asked. "Aren't the coordinates set?"

"Perhaps the gravitational pull of Earth II shifted slightly," Free said. "Maybe something happened there."

"Like what?" Herbert asked, his voice fearful.

"A tsunami," Major Tom reported. "Magnitude eleven point seven. From all that I can gather it appears that the tsunami, while causing no human casualties on Earth II, did manage to distort the gravitational pull of the planet, altering the anchor of the UUSA which in turn altered its trajectory by only millimeters—"

"But if you multiply that by the distance from Earth II's outer layer to the position of the Sling in space, it makes quite a big difference," Skye said.

"It threw the Sling off course badly enough that it bashed into the dome. Are we okay in here?" Free asked what was on everyone's mind.

"The dome has been pierced at the outer layer. That does not affect the life support within," MT said. "I will undertake repairs on the dome but first the UUSA must move toward its destination."

"The Military Complex," Lynda said, her voice dismal.

"Yes. The distance is approximately two hundred meters. I must now shatter the dome's exterior layer completely between the UUSA and the complex docking point in order for the UUSA to move along. As it proceeds to its designated docking spot, I can repair the dome behind it."

"You can do that?" Anyar asked, her voice awed.

"Can and will."

"Sounds like a plan," Brad said.

"A good plan," Free added. "Make it happen."

"The procedure is already underway," MT advised them. "I am programmed to support life at all costs."

"That's good to know," Anyar said.

They all stared up, watching through the night sky as the outer edge of the dome cracked open before their eyes, creating a sort of pathway that led to about where the Military Complex stood. As the splintering occurred in the dome's outer surface, the UUSA, no longer jammed in the dome, was free to slide along, and it did. Free could see that behind the Sling MT was already repairing the initial collision site.

"Way to go, MT!" he said, turning toward Skye. But she was no longer beside him. He spun all the way around. She was no longer with the group.

He wanted to go find her, but also felt he had to stay here and make sure the repairs proceeded and that the catastrophe did not escalate. He also should keep morale up, reassure everyone. Lynda and Brad were already turning negative.

"It's a sign," Lynda said knowingly.

"I think you're right, lovely," Brad told her. "Things like this just don't happen for no reason."

"We've already had several signs and this is another one. We ignore them at our peril. This place is evil. I can feel it in my bones."

"Hold on," Free snapped. "The tsunami on Earth II is responsible for the Sling going off course. Shit happens, as they used to say on the original Earth."

"Yes, but so much shit in such a short space of time?" Lynda asked, hands on hips, looking not just adamant but also somewhat possessed.

"Nothing else has happened, just this, and you're making a huge issue out of an accident. MT is already repairing the collision site. Hell," he pointed up, "the Sling is probably over the Military Complex at this moment because we can't see it any longer."

"It is," Major Tom acknowledged.

"And look," Free continued. "MT has repaired not just the impact site but has already started on the path the UUSA took, where he cracked the dome so it could continue."

"I have, indeed," MT said.

Lynda gathered her skirts in her hands. "You can say whatever you like but I know this is a poisonous atmosphere. This place reeks of bad energy. We should leave as quickly as we can, before something terrible happens. And whether or not any of you leave, I will. Call for a shuttle to pick me up!" she demanded of Free.

Free just stared at her, his mouth gaping. Finally, he said, "You want to quit the project? Before we even begin?"

"Not want to, *am* quitting. This is not a project I'm interested in any longer, and besides, I don't feel safe here."

"Sweetie, this has been very upsetting—" Brad began.

"Don't try to talk me out of it!" Her voice rose with hysteria.

"I'm not doing that. I'm just suggesting that we should go back to our cabin and try to relax. This was a shocking incident. All of us are shocked."

As he spoke, Brad moved his arm around her waist and was turning her toward the cabins. "Come," he said, "let's go back. That six-dimensional puzzle of the medieval village awaits us! We both need to calm down."

Lynda looked terrified and at the same time looked like she could conceivably kill anyone in her path. But amazingly enough, she allowed Brad to lead her away, all the while saying, "But I want him to contact Earth II. I want to get out of here. Now!"

Once they were out of earshot, Free sat on the bench and held his head up with his hands. His gaze was focused downward and the ground was littered with the food that had been tossed everywhere, the wine pooling. The water from the lake splashed up onto the shore and soaked some of the shirts and shoes that had been discarded in an effort to relax. He glanced around at the mess, stunned, then up at the sky. It didn't seem to matter that MT had pretty well repaired everything. Somehow, this project was falling apart and it had barely begun. He didn't know if they could do much without Lynda's expertise. She was crucial to the development of the emotional reactions in the cyborg they were building.

Anyar came and sat next to him. She patted his arm. "Don't worry, Mistress of the Universe will likely calm down. And you should cheer up. It could have been worse. The good news is the damned Sling didn't crash through every layer of the dome and suck us all out into space and vaporize us."

"That's the good news?" Free said, turning his head to look at her.

"I… I think I'll just clear some of this up," Herbert said. He carefully picked up the cutlery and broken pieces of dishes off the ground and tossed them and everything else he could scoop up with his hands into the large ice bucket that had held the three bottles of wine that Free had brought along.

"I'll help you," Anyar said, standing, gathering things herself. "Hang in there, bossman," she said to Free.

Free couldn't move. He sat long after they'd left, still holding his head, wondering what to do. If Lynda was serious about quitting, the project was doomed. Maybe he could find a replacement, but who? Few people went into emotional responses these days, and to his knowledge, none possessed her qualifications. Pain in the ass that she was, they had been lucky to get her. And if she quit, would Brad go too? A small groan slipped from between his lips.

"I believe Ms Singh is correct. You should not worry," MT said.

"Yeah, but I am worried. We have to give this a shot. I want to. It's everything I want to be doing, working on this project. How could I screw it up so quickly?"

"I don't see that you are responsible," MT said.

"Thanks. But I think if somebody with more experience with managing people had been in charge, we wouldn't be on the edge of chaos."

MT wisely said nothing.

"How are the repairs going?" Free asked dismally.

"Completed. The dome is repaired. The UUSA is positioned at the Military Complex loading dock. It will begin loading prisoners in less than one hour."

"What about its trajectory?"

"I believe, from the data I have, that its course is being altered from Earth II. Its continuous motion has been breached, but its course will be corrected and it will be set in motion again from the command center on Earth II when all of the prisoners are loaded and ready for transport. It will resume operations in approximately eighteen hours, give or take, Earth II time. The revised codes will likely allow the Sling to move faster in order to compensate for the diminished trajectory."

"Good to know," Free said.

He sighed heavily and stood. He should go see about... something. Maybe Skye. Try to find out why she fled. Hopefully the Sling's crash didn't upset her so much that she, too, wanted to abandon ship.

He started his search at the Lab, but it was empty.

As he walked toward her cabin, he hoped she was okay. He needed her, and not just for the project. He didn't understand the feeling of connection he had but he did know enough that he realized he should respect it.

Her door was ajar when he knocked. No answer, so he pushed it open a bit and called, "Hello? Skye? Are you here?"

Still no answer, so he asked MT, "Do you know where Skye is?"

"Whereabouts unknown," MT said, "which means she has directed me not to say."

"Great!" Free said, about to close the door when a flash of movement caught his eye. He peered inside and what he saw caused him to step into the cabin.

Skye had set up her cabin as both a bedroom and an office. She had brought an extra terminal from the Lab and it sat on a makeshift desk, along with a few pieces of equipment he vaguely recognized as transfer devices; she must have brought these with her from Earth II, but he didn't have a clue why. The equipment Jackson had sent them was more modern and more powerful than this antiquated stuff.

The movement was a holographic image, similar to the one Anyar and Herbert had created in the Lab. This image was not life-sized, but one-tenth the size; what was commonly called a working dimension. It rotated in the air at a speed slightly faster than the one in the Lab. Still, whenever it came face to face with Free, he found himself chilled.

The body was the same, but instead of being made entirely of flesh, or a facsimile of flesh, this form seemed to be partly metallic. But that was not what was unnerving Free. The face was a mask of cold silver metal that had been slipped over and fitted to the features, as if to hide them, creating an angular face, violent-looking. The only human features that came through loud and clear were the eyes—eyes that spoke of blood and torture and... murder! And it absolutely resembled what Lynda claimed to have seen at the Military Complex.

EIGHT

"What the hell are you doing here?"

Free spun around to face Skye, who had entered her cabin without him being aware of her.

Furious, she snarled at him, "How dare you enter my private quarters!"

"I knocked, the door was op—"

"Get the hell out!"

Free turned toward the door but stopped suddenly. "Before I leave, I want to know what this is." He gestured at the spinning hologram.

"I don't have to tell you anything about my private business."

"You do if you want to stay working on this project. That looks suspiciously like the image Anyar and Herbert brought up, but altered. It's almost soldier-like in design. Correct me if my guess is wrong, but I get the strong feeling that this might be an image very similar to the one Lynda saw at the Military Complex."

Skye brushed past him and snapped off the computer. The image in the air vanished. She crossed her arms over her chest and stared at him with a face that hid all emotion.

"You want to work all day and all night. You don't want to really tell us how you got Castillo's notes. You're secretive about everything. Why are you really here?" Free demanded.

"Like you, I'm here to work on the project." Skye looked for a moment as if she would explode, she was so furious.

"And what's the other reason?"

Her lips clamped shut.

"That's Castillo's creation, isn't it?" he said, making an instant connection. "Don't deny it."

"I'm not denying it."

"How did you get it?"

She exhaled as if it had been a while since she'd taken a breath. Her body slumped slightly and she walked over and sat on the bed, looking down at her hands.

Free went and sat beside her. His tone softened, and he knew he should probably be tough but he just couldn't be. "Tell me. I promise I won't kick you out of the project, unless you're out to sabotage it."

She looked at him, her eyes flashing in anger. But soon they softened to match his, because she could tell he wasn't out to get her. Maybe telling him would relieve her anxiety about all this.

Maybe it was a bad idea. Maybe she didn't know anymore what she was doing.

"Look, it's not what you think." She reached under her bed and brought out a rectangular metal box, which she placed on her lap.

When she opened it, Free saw a stack of memory cubes within. She took one out and pressed a button that opened the holographic image. It was Dr Castillo.

Free watched in awe as the holo-image of an exceptionally tall, lean and intense man with half a face discussed the intricacies of how to splice DNA and meld cerebral cortex waves with bitmaps to create an entirely new life form. Dr Castillo was talking to the recording device as if to a colleague, as if this information was precious and to be imparted only upon his death.

The hologram went on for forty-five minutes. Free watched, spellbound. Skye wondered what he was thinking, of the information, and of her.

Finally, it was over. She clicked the cube off and said, "I have another thirty-one of these."

Free looked at her. "This is his work, isn't it? These are his notes."

"Yes."

"The work that went on here, twenty years ago…" He stared at her as if seeing her for the first time. "How did you get these?"

"I told you, he left them with my mother."

"But you said they were destroyed."

"No, I said there was an attempt to destroy them. You all just assumed that meant they *were* destroyed. My mother kept them for several years after his death and intended to destroy them, but I found them and rescued them. I knew this information was important and should be preserved. It's science. Pure science. At it's best."

"You've seen all the cubes."

"Many times."

"And what do you think?"

"I think he was on the right track, but I think his motives were twisted. He worked for the military, and from what I can ascertain, he was trying to create a kind of super soldier. I don't believe in that sort of thing."

Free nodded. At least her values were good. "But why are you trying to hide this info? I don't get it. If it's good, why keep it to yourself."

"Because at the end of his life, Castillo was vilified. He was probably crazy. Mad with power. I think to make this public would have been impossible then, and now. The powerful people that deleted almost every scrap of information about him would confiscate this material and at worst it would be destroyed. At the very least it will be lost to humanity forever. Worst case scenario, these cubes could fall into the wrong hands."

"But why? He tried a technique that worked to some extent, or it wouldn't be controversial. A process can have more than one application. Whatever his intentions, that's not ours."

Skye felt the old familiar pain in her throat, as if she couldn't or shouldn't speak about this. As if it were a secret she should carry with her to her grave.

She must have shaken her head imperceptibly. Suddenly she felt Free's arm around her shoulder. Without understanding how she got there, she found her head resting against that strong shoulder, an act so simple, and one she never thought she would engage in. Her nostrils picked up the scent of him, her cheek the heat from his body. She felt lulled into a warm and comforting place, one where she could open up like a flower to the sun.

They stayed silent for a few moments, Free stroking her upper arm with his thumb.

"The thing Lynda said she saw. It's Castillo's creature, isn't it? Imprisoned at the Military Complex?" Free asked quietly.

"His 'creature' was destroyed."

"Then what is it?"

"I don't know for sure. I want to go have a look."

"We'll go together. Once the prisoners are taken off the moon."

Skye's head jerked up. "I can't wait for that. What if it's taken with them? I have to go see it, to know for myself if this is something he made."

Free looked at her. She was taking this personally. Way too personally for someone who's supposed to be interested in the science of it all.

"How well did your mother know Castillo?" he asked.

She shifted away from him slightly. "As well as anyone could, I guess."

Suddenly it all clicked into place: her fascination with Castillo's experiment, the doctor leaving the material to her mother…

"Is he—?"

"Yes, yes, yes! He was my father."

"I'm… I don't know what to say," he told her.

Now her shoulders fully slumped and her voice cracked, as if she were about to cry. "He married my mother for some reason, maybe because she was pregnant, I don't know. I'm not even sure he liked women. Or men. I think he was just an egomaniac, from all the cubes I've watched. I know he saw me and my sisters when we were babies. After all, he'd created us, didn't he? But he just saw us three times. I was too young to remember, of course.

"I rarely heard about him from mom, and I don't think she saw him, just got the odd note, or just heard things about him on the news. And then, suddenly, about a week before he died, this box of cubes arrived with a note that they should be passed on to the three of us girls. My mother kept them for a while. I don't know if she opened them or not. She seemed ambivalent about them, so I didn't think she opened them. I got the feeling she felt that whatever they contained, it wasn't something that should necessarily be passed on."

Free found his arm surrounding her again. This time he was not tentative. He pulled her close. She curled in under the crook of his arm, against his chest, sobbing softly.

He couldn't imagine it. His own life had been a piece of candy compared to hers. But at least she knew who her dad was. Having a father who conducted experiments for the military was a bit bizarre, but not mysterious.

"How did he die?" Free wanted to know.

Skye wiped tears from the corner of one eye. She felt completely drained; revealing all that had been stored inside her for so long had left her empty. And yet she knew there was more to tell.

"He was murdered. Twenty years ago this month. His work focused on trying to reconstitute a being called Jason, a serial killer that had died, or was thought to be dead. He managed it. And like that fictional story *Frankenstein*, his creature turned on him and killed him."

She faced him with total vulnerability. "I think you should see the cubes. And then come with me to the Military Complex. We have to confront this Jason being for ourselves. It's important to me. I have to see my father's work. He was reviled, his experiment discredited, but I know from the cubes that there's something there, that the formula was right, the interpretation wrong. If there's something salvageable, I have to find it."

Free nodded. He stood and went to lock the door. "MT?"

"Here."

"Do not transmit the coordinates of myself or Skye Fellows. For all intents and purposes we are *incommunicado* until you are advised otherwise. We don't want to be disturbed."

"All right."

"That goes for you, too," Skye said. "You're to tune us and everything happening in this room out until we call you."

Reluctantly MT said, "As you wish."

"We'll call you when we want to re-establish contact," Free said, as if to assure the AI, which seemed silly, but somehow blocking it out seemed a bit extreme.

After a pause he asked Skye, "Why did *you* want MT out of here?"

"Because my father programmed the original AI, the original Major Tom. That system ran Jason. And frankly, I'm not sure how much of that original intelligence, and memories, are in this AI."

Skye pulled all of the cubes out of the metal box and lined up the thirty-two by order of date.

While she worked, Free said, "You didn't take your father's name?"

"My mother didn't want that. And I'm just as glad. I would have had a much harder time of it with the name Castillo."

Once she'd set up the cubes she clicked on the last one.

"Why start at the end?"

"Because I want you to see what the end result was. We can work our way back to the beginning. How it all began is overshadowed by what you'll see first. But in a way it's a reverse buildup. Trust me."

They crawled up to the head of the bed and sat arms around one another watching an extremely egotistical Dr Castillo who had emerged in the middle of the room. Behind him was a laboratory setting. He began manically telling them that the replica was at large, and that when his "biological offspring" as he called Skye and her sisters, came upon these cubes, they should find the replica and preserve it for the future. It was, he said, "My greatest work. And my work is sacred!"

That cube consisted of almost an hour of his rantings. The next one they watched showed what must have been the interior of the Military Complex; an enormous space, large enough to hold a space ship. Massive destruction was taking place around him.

As they watched, everything Castillo said was lost by the images behind him.

A giant being, made of metal and flesh, heads taller than anyone in the space, stumbled through the lab. Clutched in his hand they saw a long knife, and here and there as light glinted off the edge, Free realized just how sharp it must be.

People ran for their lives, screaming, knocking over equipment, tables, jars and glass breaking, computers sputtering as they flew through the air and crashed into walls in the wake of this animated being, tearing through the room like a human storm.

One small woman fell flat on her back. The monster Jason jumped onto her body with both feet, the tip of his massive blade stabbing her in the middle of the forehead. Blood spurted out from her head, flying in every direction.

He stepped along his victim and snatched at a white-coated lab worker, grabbing him by the back of the neck. The blade lifted high and came down across the middle of the body, severing the man at the waist. His screams almost drowned out Castillo.

There seemed to be hundreds of people in the background, some clearly scientists or technicians, others military personnel, and Free and Skye watched as Jason took on all of them. They seemed to be in a sealed room with no means of escape.

The breaking equipment, the bodies and body parts littering the floor... It was all so surreal. And all the while Castillo looked completely calm, as if this were normal. He talked about how he had to end the life of his creation, but not yet.

"Do you think he did?" Free asked.

"Probably not, if what Lynda saw was Jason. And look at the guy, he doesn't look as if he could be killed."

"But your father created him, or at least reanimated him. Surely he knew the weaknesses and could pull the plug if and when he wanted."

"Yes, but did he? He was killed and I'm pretty sure Jason was his murderer. That means Jason might still be alive."

Skye and Free proceeded to watch cube after cube. Most were five or ten minutes, but a few were longer. As they climbed back in time, the cubes got shorter and the information more precise, as if Castillo was preparing to use the information for an academic paper. Each cube seemed to be a section of a larger work, like a chapter of a long essay.

They watched the cubes continuously through the night and into the next day, stopping only to eat some of the supplies that Skye had hoarded in her cabin, and to nap.

Skye had a dream.

Jason—and she knows it is him—stands before her. He speaks with the voice of her father. "You must bring me to life, Skye. I am depending on you. The universe is depending on you. What exists must be destroyed in order that a rebuilding can take place and great minds like yours can rule at last!'

As Jason speaks with her father's voice, his lips do not move. Nothing moves but his eyes, which glance to the left and to the right, back and forth, like a predator searching for prey. Suddenly he seems to notice her for the first time.

"He's going to kill me," Skye realizes. She turns and runs. Suddenly she is running down a corridor. "No!" she cries out. This is wrong! It will not lead to a good place. But she cannot stop herself.

The corridor narrows. The fissure in the floor appears before her and glancing behind her she sees it coming toward her from the rear as well.

"Don't worry," a familiar voice says. "I'm not going to leave you alone."

She sees Free before her, offering her his hand, and she runs toward him as fast as her exhausted legs can move her. Then, suddenly, between them is Jason; enormous, muscles of steel, eyes of death, feet planted in the darkness, machete—how does she know what this is called?—raised above his furious face.

Behind him she hears Free say again, "Don't worry. I'm here." But Free is no longer there, just Jason, and it is Free's voice that is talking through Jason's sealed lips.

She begins to fall, knowing she has fallen here before, the sharpness of the blade sliding without her knowing, her eyes watching as she falls past her decapitated body, her blood, her life, shooting into the air like a fountain of death. And she screams "Nooooo!"

"Wake up!" Free said, shaking her harder. "You've been dreaming."

Her eyes were tear-filled, haunted. "He's going to kill us both," she said. "That... that thing will destroy us before we've even lived."

Free pulled back and his face filled with anger. He shook his head and gave her a little shake too. "No. Not if I can help it." Suddenly he pulled her to him and held her as close as he could, and Skye pulled in closer, entwining her legs around him, her arms, touching him as if flesh-starved.

His lips found hers and her mouth was hungry. Free had never touched anyone like this before. His hands on her skin, lifting up clothing, touching flesh, all of it inspired him to a passion he did not realize he possessed. The dynamic tension soaring through him felt delicious and charged him with a directed energy.

Skye was more knowledgeable than him, but that was to be expected. She took the lead, telling him without words, showing him in the darkness her most sensitive parts, and guiding him in how to worship them.

When they finally made love, Free felt his body focusing in, everything reduced to an intensity that allowed him to understand that his entire body was one piece of flesh, and that Skye, too, was the opposite of him; an opposite that called to him for a connection so natural a small cry escaped his lips at the beauty and intensity and familiarity of what seemed so right, so perfect.

Afterwards, they lay in sweaty silence, breathing, alone and together. Touching. Kissing. Looking into one another's eyes as if searching for a reflection.

"There are just two more cubes," Skye finally said. "Do you want to see them? It's the beginning."

"Sure. Let's do it. Then maybe we can go outside, get some air. Walk."

"To the Military Complex?"

"All right," he said. He would do anything for her now.

Skye clicked on cube number one first. In it, Castillo looked much younger. While he still possessed a fanatical quality, he seemed far less crazy than he did in the last cube. Skye had said that about two years had transpired between the first and the last tape. Castillo had aged considerably over that time, his hair going almost white, and his lean face turning haggard. But in this first cube, he looked like the quintessential scientist with a brilliant idea and the means to actualize it. Even his artificial eye looked less threatening.

Castillo discussed his project, work plan, resources, and his time frame, all in a dispassionate and logical manner. The cube lasted all of ten minutes. Generally the earlier cubes were shorter. Toward the end the cubes had gone on and on, as if he needed to talk to someone, anyone. But Castillo had become almost deranged and made little sense by the end. For him, facing the reality of what he had done must have been a very grim business.

When the cube finished, Skye picked up the only cube left and turned to Free. "This is the second cube. In it he discusses the being he wants to recreate." Her brow creased and she looked worried; she hesitated clicking it on.

"What's wrong?" Free asked, stroking her neck and pulling her long and lush dark hair behind her shoulder.

"I... I just hope..." She stopped and looked away.

Free didn't know what she was worried about. Maybe he should reassure her. Whatever Castillo did or didn't do, it had nothing to do with Skye. She wasn't responsible for her father's actions. No child was.

But before he could voice this, Skye said, "Okay, here we go," and she opened the cube.

Castillo emerged in the air, standing before a map of space. He held a pointer as if he were about to lecture a university class. Presumably he had done just that at one time, and had written papers that must have been published. Free still could not get over the fact that almost every scrap of information about this mad doctor and his work had been destroyed. It made no sense.

"The marvelous Jason came to us via a circuitous route," he began happily, as only a giddy scientist could be.

"I must take you back in time, not far back, only a few years. Earth II has, in the past, funded space stations, laboratories actually, dotting the reachable universe, positioned near planets that for one reason or another were deemed important in terms of research. One station in particular, *G7*—"

"That's the station my mother was assigned to!" Free blurted out, sitting up abruptly and taking a fresh interest in this cube.

"It was assigned to orbit planet number 666." Castillo used the pointer to indicate approximately where in the solar system that planet lay.

"From the research retrieved, which involved plant cloning, it seems Planet 666 was unable to sustain human life. It did, however, possess one important discovery. Jason, who previously had been propelled into space, ultimately ended up on this planet. From the station's logs, which I somehow managed to get my hands on, I learned that Jason's body had been retrieved by the ship Black Star 13, brought aboard, and that ship and her crew destroyed. Apparently, the derelict ship and another attempting to rescue it were forced into 666's gravitational pull; both vessels then crashed onto the planet's surface. No one survived. No one but Jason!"

The look on Castillo's face was priceless. Free thought of the stereotypical mad geniuses in old cinema images. He almost laughed.

"This is pretty amazing stuff," Free said. "I know my mother was on that station. She mentioned it. I can't believe I'm hearing the history."

Castillo proceeded to talk about how Dr Claude Bardox, a brilliant geneticist and cloning expert on *G7* and "an esteemed colleague" managed to not only retrieve the remains of Jason, but to "reanimate him, using the nanotechnology previously implanted into his body."

As Free listened, his emotions vacillated between elation and nervousness, the source of which he could not identify. When Castillo explained how everyone on *G7* had died, his body involuntarily twitched. "Or so it was thought," Castillo said. "Apparently there was one survivor, a woman named London Jefferson…"

"That's my mother!" Free yelled, jumping to his feet. He stared at Skye whose eyes stayed on the holographic. She placed her hand on his back as if to comfort him. "Wait!" he said, "Play that last bit back!"

"…named London Jefferson, who managed to escape in a damaged shuttle. Records exist of her transmissions which were received on Earth II. Apparently she could not receive transmissions, only send them. Ultimately the out-of-control shuttle entered an asteroid field where it was pulverized."

"Pause it."

Skye stopped the cube and Castillo stood frozen before them, mouth open, pointer raised.

"That can't be. My mother survived that asteroid field. I know she did. I'm here, aren't I? She said she had a one-man pod on board, an antique someone on *G7* had owned, and maneuvered her way through the space boulders. The pod was light and at some point she was sucked into a space vacuum but managed to do something to fling her pod out again."

Skye looked as if she wanted to say something, but wasn't sure what. Or maybe she was worried about how to say it. Free didn't know, but he felt even more troubled.

"Why don't we watch the rest," she said in a voice struggling for calm. "It's almost over."

"Yeah. Sure." Free felt completely unnerved now.

He sat on the bed, his body rigid, as if preparing for a blow of some kind. Skye restarted the cube and Castillo said, "Records show that the pod was sucked into a vortex of some sort, and we know this for a fact because Jason was sucked into the same vortex. This information was gleaned by an analysis of his memory in detail. Through some space anomaly, Ms Jefferson, who had entered the vortex first in her vessel, was attacked by a spontaneous regurgitation of some sort, a hiccup from negative space. The force of this reaction thrust her back the way she'd come and out of the vortex. En route, her pod bumped Jason who was also then forced out of the vortex."

Castillo went on to explain how Jason had gotten to Elysium; not half as mysterious as what had come before. The doctor talked about connections through the military that had managed to secure what remained of Jason.

"The biological elements were crucial to my experiment," he said. "I was able to clone the DNA, extract trace elements of mental processes, and use this material as the foundation of the bitmapping process."

The cube that followed, which Free had already seen, explained the process of reanimation using the DNA that remained of Jason into a bitmapped image. Castillo had been able to infuse the image with Jason's memories, emotions, reactions, and imbedded this into a new physical form; all the things that Free and his group were trying to do. The main difference was that Castillo was attempting to build a weapon. Free wanted to build a humanoid cyborg, plain and simple; one that could be used for the good of humanity.

The third cube finished, and Free lay back on the bed, stunned. "No wonder my mom didn't want to talk about her experiences. All she said was that a catastrophe hit *G7*. She didn't say what. Now I know. It was Jason."

He turned his head toward Skye. "What, exactly, is Jason? Where did he come from? He sounds like he was already a serial killer before Castillo got hold of his remains."

"As far as I can tell from watching the cubes over and over, and from the little bit that was published that I read in a scientific journal before it was banned, Jason was just a regular guy on earth…"

"Earth? You mean Earth I?"

"That's the one. They say he suffered a lot of trauma in his childhood and became deranged. And then people kept trying to kill him. But he kept surviving. I think he must have been the subject of a lot of experimentation because by the time he reached *G7* he was several hundred years old, and partly bionic, with self-repairing nano-ants inside him that wouldn't let him die. And now he's part virtual too."

"What do you mean 'now?'" Is that Jason at the Military Complex?"

"I don't know for sure, but I think so. You saw the last few cubes first. This is why I wanted you to see the end before the beginning—I didn't want you to lose it. Or that's one of the reasons."

"Holy shit!" Free said. "Castillo's project might still exist. It's hard to believe."

"There's more," Skye said.

"More cubes?"

"In a sense. Like I said, I opened the cubes when I was a kid. After I saw them—which my mother didn't know about because she would have never let me open these cubes—she stored them in this metal box for a long while. I didn't even know where they were. Then one day I overheard her telling her sister, my aunt, that she was going to destroy them. I panicked. I watched her closely until I saw where she hid the box. She removed it from under the floorboards in the attic where she'd hidden it and then stored it in her bedside table, preparing to get rid of it. That night, I snuck into her room while she slept and replaced the cubes with blank ones.

"The very next day I saw her carry the box out and knew she was going to an incinerator to dispose of it. When she came home she had the metal box, but it was empty. I asked her point blank if that's what she had done. She was a bit upset that I knew about them, but acknowledged that she'd taken the cubes to the incinerator. I asked her if I could have the box, since it belonged to my father, and I guess she felt guilty and let me keep it, thinking there was no harm to that."

"Okay, so the cubes you removed and hid were the original cubes?"

"No, not all of them. When I first found the cubes as a child and watched them, I remember there were thirty-three. Like I said, my father did everything in triplicate. Three sisters, thirty-three cubes... When I stole them before they were to be destroyed, there were only thirty-two."

"There were thirty-three cubes but when you rescued them there were only thirty-two. Maybe one of your sisters took it."

"No, they didn't know about the cubes, and I didn't share the information. And I had a good hiding place so they wouldn't have found them."

"Do you think you accidentally left one in the box?"

"That could have happened. I was in a real hurry, working in the dark to grab the cubes while my mom slept, shoving them in my sweater pockets, and replacing them with blank cubes. Maybe I missed one."

Free had a hard time thinking that the woman in front of him, who was so precise and complete in her actions, could have been careless at one time in her life.

As if reading his mind, Skye said, "But I don't think so. I've thought about it a lot and I believe now that my mother had watched the cubes and that she'd destroyed one of them a long time before. I think she found that what was on that one cube was so much more horrific to her than what was on the other cubes that she had to get rid of it immediately."

"Do you remember that cube? What was in there?"

"I do." Skye turned her face to his, her eyes like blue moons. She rubbed his back gently, and he wasn't sure if she was trying to comfort him or herself.

Inexplicably, a feeling of dread washed over him as he asked, "What was in that cube?"

Skye sighed heavily. Her eyes blinked rapidly as if she were standing in a harsh glare. She eventually lowered her head, and he wondered if he would have to pry the information out of her.

"It was the third cube in the series. I remember it came right after the information about *G7* and your mother."

"Does it have to do with my mother?" Free asked, a feeling of alarm building up inside of him.

"Yes."

A kind of soft groan came out of his mouth, as if some part of him knew what was in that cube. But of course he did not, and was forced to ask, "What was in the cube?"

"An analysis of Dr Bardox's experiments."

"The geneticist guy from *G7*?"

Skye nodded. She picked an invisible piece of lint off the bedspread.

"Okay," Free said, "so tell me about it."

She took a large breath and let it out as a painful-sounding sigh.

"What? He was a cloning specialist, right? He took DNA from Jason and tried to make a clone. Are you telling me he succeeded? That there's another one of these guys hanging around?"

"Not exactly."

"What, then? Come on, you're driving me nuts."

"Bardox, my father says, kept logs, as do most scientists. He exchanged information with a select group of peers, three to be exact, and my father was one of them. The other two are dead, and I don't know what happened to whatever logs they received. My father summarized the information and put it onto the missing cube. He didn't elaborate on specifics, and from what he said about these 'exchanges,' I doubt Bardox actually divulged any details. These guys were pretty competitive, and they kept their cards close to their chests, so to speak." Skye paused before continuing.

"The cube was short, I remember. I wish now that I'd paid more attention to it, because I only saw it the once, and I was a kid, so I'm trying to remember it in order of presentation."

"Don't worry about that. Just tell me what you remember."

Skye stared at him again with those big eyes that made him want to melt. But now they were so full of fear he could hardly look at her.

"Bardox wasn't trying to clone Jason, at least not right away. That was his ultimate goal but he planned on breeding the killer and using the off-spring as a kind of livestock, interbreeding them until he had the perfect female that contained the traits he wanted. Then he was going to breed her with Jason."

"Wow, is that ever sick."

"There's more. He managed to revive Jason X, like the other cube said, so he could extract DNA from living tissue. He used a controversial tech-nology to implant the living DNA into the ova of one of the crew members." She paused. "I don't know for sure, because my father didn't say, and I didn't really think about checking the records of the female crew for *G7*, just a cursory exam. I know that there were only six women and one of them was impregnated."

"What?" Free screamed, leaping to his feet again. "That can't be my mother!"

"I didn't say it was. I don't know."

Free paced the room in a panic. Every cell in his body vibrated. "My mother never said who my father was. She mentioned a guy on the station that she had an affair with, but said it wasn't him.

She never said anything else. Just that it was better not to know, and that it didn't matter who he was, that she loved me, and I was nothing like him. I was special, decent, and nothing like him." He looked at Skye. "I guess all mothers say that."

"Look, we can try to do some research. We know that everyone on *G7* died except your mother. There were five other women. Let's see what information we can find on *G7*. Maybe we can eliminate your mother. I'm sure there were up-to-the-minute medical records, and she might not have been the only pregnant woman."

Skye stood and started to dress. Free, though, wandered the room naked, shaking his head, blurting out fragments of sentences. "I don't... I mean, she couldn't have been... Why wouldn't she tell me? Maybe she did when..."

Skye stepped into a bright red miniskirt and slipped on a pair of sandals. As she reached in the closet for a tan T-shirt, she said, "Come on. There's no use wondering and worrying." She tossed his T-shirt at him which he caught and just held in his hands. "We'll check the main computer which should have access to the personnel databases on Earth II. We should be able to hack into secret military files pretty easily with what we know."

"We don't have a password to access that info."

"You don't, I do."

"How?"

"Don't ask, okay? I've spent my life skirting a system that would identify me as my father's daughter. I've had to become tricky. Get dressed."

Free began to dress by rote. His mind was a jumble of worries, fears, half remembered discussions with his mother, a bit of a conversation he'd overheard when he was about ten years old, between his mother and Jackson Mansfield...

"He doesn't have to know," she said.

"London, it's your call. You're his mother. But knowing Free as I do, I think he would handle it well. You're underestimating him," Jackson had said.

"Maybe," his mother said. "But I'm not sure anyone could handle it."

At the time, Free assumed they were lovers and that his mother was worried about telling him. When he'd seen her later, he tried to set her mind at ease.

"Don't worry, mom. If you and Jackson are like, you know, melded or something, that's okay with me." His mother had looked at him strangely, ruffled his hair and laughed.

"You know something Free? You're an okay son!"

Now he wondered if they'd been discussing something else, something sinister, like his parentage.

Skye gathered his runners and pants and ordered him again, "Get dressed." This time he complied.

As they left her cabin and walked to the Lab they saw no one. Once inside the Lab, it was another story.

NINE

Free and Skye entered the Lab to find everyone else there already. Lynda and Brad looked up at once, and Anyar, who was inside the biolab, caught the movement and turned, at which point Herbert followed her gaze.

"Well, now we know you aren't dead," Lynda said. "The stupid AI wouldn't give your whereabouts."

"I was instructed to report their whereabouts as unknown," Major Tom said a bit huffily. "Is that restriction removed?"

"Yes, of course." To the others Free explained, "We were working on something and didn't want to be disturbed."

"Yeah," Brad grinned, eying them suggestively, "that's obvious."

Free felt embarrassed. He was afraid to glance at Skye.

Anyar opened the biolab's door and she and Herbert came out into the main room. "What the hell have you two been doing?"

"What do you think?" Lynda asked. "Fucking."

"You are so childish!" Skye snapped, brushing past Free to get to her console.

She sat down and pressed a button to raise the screen, eager to put something between her and everyone's staring faces.

"So, how's it going?" Free asked, feeling that his face must be bright red.

"Brad and I are working together to get the emotions and physical reactions in sync. We're building a program so we can interact, back and forth," Lynda said.

"Great," he said. "Sounds like a good plan." She didn't seem to be focused on leaving Elysium, at least she hadn't mentioned it yet, and Free didn't bring it up. Apparently Lynda had calmed down, and he saw no reason to stir the cauldron of her oh so volatile moods.

"We've, um, got a slightly refined prototype form," Herbert stuttered. "Anyar thinks we should build a human limb made of plastic and metal, and then replicate human skin cells from the DNA banks for the 'skin.'"

"We've got all our DNA samples in the computer," Anyar said. "Herbert worked in a stem cell lab for one summer, so he knows how to reproduce skin cells."

"We've created skin cells that are an amalgam of the six of us, and hopefully the process has selected the healthiest, most dominant cells. We're replicating the skin cells around the prototype limb right now."

"Great," Free said. "Just stick to the limb first, so we can see how it goes before we do the entire body."

"Uh, yeah, that's the plan," Anyar said.

Free knew from her tone that he'd missed a beat somewhere and struggled to move beyond this awkward moment and get with the program.

"By the way," Anyar said, "we received a message from the prison through Major Tom. They were about to load the prisoners—that came in about two hours ago. You weren't here so he passed it on to us."

"No problem," Free said. He felt totally distracted and more than anything wanted to be looking over Skye's shoulder as she brought up the *G7* records.

"You guys are doing terrific work," he said by way of encouragement, and to get them to stop focusing on him. "Keep it up!" He just wanted them to go back to their stations so he could see what Skye had found.

Free nervously wandered around the Lab like a lost kitten for about twenty minutes, until Brad said to Lynda, "Hey, sweets I'm ready for a break. You?"

"Well, I'd like to finish this transit code first. Should only take another hour."

Free groaned inwardly.

Brad began to rub her shoulders. "You know, they used to say that a rest was as good as a change and vice versa. Let's go lie on the dock and drink some Synerjuice."

The rubbing of her shoulders got her fingers off her keyboard. A smile reached her lips and Free figured that it was Brad, good man, who had eased her down from the panic attack about leaving. Now she trusted him. Within three minutes she had saved her data and they were on their way out the door.

"We'll be back in thirty," Lynda said.

"Make that sixty," Brad said over his shoulder, a knowing grin on his face and a wink aimed at Free.

"Take your time," Free called after them, waving stupidly at the closed door.

He checked through the glass of the biolab. Anyar and Herbert were wrapped up in a discussion. Now was his chance. He went to Skye's console, pulling a chair up next to hers. On screen, he saw the list of *G7* personnel.

"It took a while to break in," Skye admitted. "For some reason, the detailed info is classified."

He pulled back to look at her. "You got in anyway?"

She nodded rapidly.

"A woman of many talents." He laughed, touching her back gently.

"That I am," she said.

He removed his hand from her back as fast as he'd put it there so that the others wouldn't see. He didn't know why he felt he should keep everything between himself and Skye private, but he did.

Now that they were alone, or relatively so, Skye switched from manual to voice instruction for the computer, which would make things move more quickly.

"Female personnel only," Skye said.

A list came up on the screen of six names in alphabetical order:

Renata Henderson
London Jefferson
Felicity Lawrence
Bella Morrison
Akaka Tsunami
Brandy Williams

"Status of all female *G7* personnel," Skye said quickly.

One word appeared on the screen next to each name: "Deceased."

"That can't be," Free said. "My mother was alive."

"But she's dead now. These records are kept up to date."

"Oh, right. Sorry. I'm a little emotional about all this," he said.

"Don't worry. Hang in there until we find something concrete."

To the computer she said, "Date and circumstances of death for each *G7* female team member."

On the screen Free read the dates of death. His mother's information was accurate, and he told Skye, "Yeah. That's right."

As to the rest, he read quietly. "Felicity Lawrence. Death occurred on Planet 666. Apparent cause: exposure to the elements. Brandi

Williams. Death occurred on *G7*. Apparent cause: complications from a genetic heart problem."

The other three were simply listed as "dead or missing in action."

"They probably died when Jason rampaged through the station," Skye said softly.

"Can we get anything else? Like their physical health before they died?"

"Last health checkup for *G7* crew members," Skye said.

The screen lit up with the images of the dozen crew members; thumbnails to be clicked on to retrieve further data. Free was astonished to see his mother, young, vivacious, sensual. Her eyes looked alive, her face relaxed. Free had never seen her relaxed. All his life it was as if she were always on guard, ready for something awful to happen at any moment. He also saw the face of Andre Leblanc, the man who had been his mother's lover. Free realized instantly that while he looked a lot like his mother when she was closer to the age he was now, he didn't look anything like Andre.

The screen also held the image of Dr Claude Bardox a slim, balding man in his forties, a face laced with the same degree of obsession as the holographic images of Dr Arthur J Castillo.

One by one Skye clicked on the images of the six women. Skye and Free both silently scanned the records, and they learned that all of them appeared to have been in perfect health but for Dr Brandi Williams.

The records indicated that she had rejected all offers of a cloned heart.

"Weird," Skye commented. "They could have saved her. And she was a doctor, too."

The records did not indicate that any of the females were pregnant, not even Free's mother.

"That's funny," Skye said. "When I pulled up the general records before and asked if any of the women were pregnant, the response was positive." She paused. "I'll ask it directly. Is there a record of any of the six *G7* female crew being pregnant?"

What came up on the screen surprised them: "Bella Morrison, pregnant at age sixteen years. Duration of pregnancy: two weeks. Result: pregnancy terminated by natural miscarriage."

"What about London Jefferson?" Free asked.

The screen read: "No record of pregnancy."

"Well, that's that," Skye said. She sat back.

Free, feeling tense, leaned forward and manually scrolled through all of the records, as if he could find something that the computer could not.

"Last recorded physical of London Jefferson," Free said suddenly.

The computer screen showed the date.

Suddenly he thought of something and clicked back to read the record of Brandi Williams. Then he asked the computer, "When was the last recorded communication within the station?"

The computer displayed the date and Free fell back against his chair. "That's it. The doctor died two days before the last communication, so there were no medical personnel on board from the date of her death until the ship was abandoned by the lone survivor, my mother."

"Hold it," Skye said. "I just thought of something else." She said to the computer, "Were any messages picked up by the *G7* computer from any ships or shuttles in the vicinity of *G7* after the last onboard communication?"

Free looked over his shoulder to see that Anyar and Herbert were still occupied. "Verbal response please," he said quickly.

"*G7*'s shuttle number two, piloted by London Jefferson, sent three messages to no specific destination. All messages were recorded by the *G7* computer."

"Bring up those messages," Skye said.

"That information is not available."

"Where is it?"

"Unknown."

Free took over with a sudden inspiration, "Did any of the messages from the shuttle have attachments, like medical reports?"

"Yes."

"Her messages would have been standard SOSs or verbal communications," Free explained to Skye. "Her personal medical file and shuttle status reports would have been sent directly from the shuttle's computer system where they were logged, as attachments, anytime a communication was sent. Maybe the communications are classified, but the attachments were overlooked. It's worth a shot." Free turned to the computer screen. "Can you bring up the health reports on screen?"

The screen filled with information. Free sat spell-bound, in awe and fury as he read of his mother's wounds. The information at the end of the file had to do with her pregnancy. London had, apparently, wondered about the father, because the report showed that she checked the DNA of Andre Leblanc, and it was not a match.

"Is there any indication of who the father was of the embryo in the uterus of London Jefferson?" Free knew his voice sounded desperate.

"There is no match to the embryonic DNA related to the sperm."

"Does the sperm DNA match any of the male crew members of *G7*?"

"No."

"Were there any male visitors to *G7* prior to its destruction?"

"The crew of the ship *Revival*."

"Does the DNA of the sperm match that of any crew member of the ship *Revival*?"

"No."

"You're asking the same thing over and over," Skye pointed out.

He paused and Skye took over, asking the questions his emotions kept him from logically pursuing. "Was there anyone else aboard station *G7* within four weeks of its destruction?"

"Yes."

"Who?"

"Unknown."

"Does the sperm DNA match the genetic profile of this unknown on *G7*?"

"Yes."

"Is this unknown who matches the sperm DNA human?"

"Unknown."

"Probability that the unknown on *G7* is genetically the father of London Jefferson's child."

"One hundred percent."

Skye must have taken him from the Lab but he could not remember leaving. Free found himself sitting in the gazebo by the lake, staring at the crystal clear water but not really seeing it, when Skye said, "You can't know for sure who that was."

He looked at her. "I know. It was Jason. He's the only other one who was on the station. Bardox wanted a breeder. My mother must have been the best candidate and he artificially inseminated her with Jason's sperm."

"You can't know for sure," she said again, but he really wasn't listening.

"What a way to find out who your father is," he laughed bitterly. "A serial killer. Hardly even human. Something that comes back to life over and over again through the centuries and slices and dices his way across the universe, leaving a trail of blood and guts. How many people has he killed? There must be hundreds. No, it's been centuries. Thousands. Maybe tens of thousands. Hundreds of thousands."

He turned to Skye and stared at her with horror-filled eyes. "What does that make me?"

"It makes you who you are, that's all," she said, wishing she knew what to say or do to get him beyond this. Finding out your father's identity is a shock. She knew that for a fact.

"You don't know what it's like—" he began, and she cut him short abruptly.

"Oh, but I do know what it's like, remember? Trust me on that."

"Your father wasn't a killer."

"Really? Who do you think was responsible for all the deaths on Elysium?"

"Jason. My father."

"And who brought Jason back, knowing full well what he was capable of? My father. I think we both have a lot of regrets about our lineage. But I've lived with my knowledge longer than you have, and I know that I am not my father. You'd better figure that out too, or you'll be paralyzed with guilt."

Free's hands rose to cover his face. He didn't have a clue how he could ever accept this. His mother was right: some things are best left unknown.

"Look," Skye said, "I'm going to the Military Complex. I want to see that being for myself before they cart it off to Thanos forever, because there's no way anyone will be able to get there. From what I've read they already have a couple of dozen prisoners there, and the moon is locked tight. Only the Sling can get people in and nobody can get out. It's now or never."

She stood and looked down at him. "I'll be back soon."

Free, somehow, roused himself. "No. I'll go with you. You shouldn't go alone." Heavily, he hauled himself to his feet. "If that's my father, or some reanimated version of him, I want to see him with my own eyes. We'll go together. We both have some pieces of the puzzle of our lives to slide into place."

They walked at a good clip to the Military Complex, silent until they reached the dirt path with the sign that warned them against where they were headed.

"Right!" Free said. The sign only served to fuel their shared tension.

Free had no idea what he would find. His father? A replica of his father? A virtual form of papa? In the flesh? A poster? And if this being *was* resurrected from DNA and bitmapped brainwaves, how could it be anything more than a computer-generated being in a false body, even if Castillo had somehow managed to pour it into a flesh and blood clone? This was too bizarre. He couldn't get his head around it. And every cell in his body screamed, "Stop! Your mother was right. Some things are best left unknown…"

Skye climbed the hill with equally troubled thoughts. She knew Free was full of anxiety, she could feel it radiating off him like waves of heat. It worried her, what he would find and how he would react to it. But she had her own worries too. She had viewed those cubes dozens of times and pretty well understood her father's experiment.

And she had a good sense of why it had gone wrong.

Besides the chilling fact that her father had struggled through failure after failure to arrive at success, only to create the ultimate killing machine that the military would use to control everyone and everything in the universe, somehow, Castillo had also brought back the most heinous criminal to have ever lived. She could not believe that she shared the same DNA with this madman. It had taken her years to get past the mixed emotions of being a progeny that had been abandoned almost from birth, and to come to terms with the fact that the science of her father's experiment was sound, but the ethics were corrupt. The ethics went against life. That was the chink in the scientific armor.

But an experiment could be used for good as well as evil. She needed to see with her own eyes the results, so she could see the parameters of his work. It was one thing watching cubes where he discussed it at length, even though he did not reveal all the details—paranoid maniac! Like father like daughter? She had to witness even part of what had come to pass. It surely would help her in her own work, here on Elysium, and whatever else she longed to do in her life. And she just had to know anything about her father that she could find out since there was precious little information available to her.

Somehow, in knowing her father, she would know herself. And in knowing her father she could make up for what he had done. She felt exhausted from a life of hiding her identity, never admitting that she was the offspring of a man so vile that society had tried to expunge all traces of his existence. She had to make the past right, or die trying.

As they neared the top of the hill, the Military Complex came into view.

Skye stopped in her tracks. "Look!" She pointed at the cage-like box at the bottom of the Sling arm resting on top of the dome above the Complex, open at what must be the loading dock. They watched as a transparent elevator rose up from the Military Complex through the sky toward the lowest layer of dome. From there the prisoners would go through the layers of the dome via airlocks, similar to how Free and his crew had entered Elysium. The elevator was crammed with people, all wearing similar black, one-piece outfits. They were too far up for either Free or Skye to distinguish faces.

At the lowest level of the dome, the elevator stopped and the people filed out like drones, moving down a transparent corridor between dome layers toward an airlock, and into another elevator that would take them up further to the loading dock, where they would board the Sling.

Free thought about Thanos. Not much was known about it, other than that it was uninhabitable by humans, which made it a lot like Elysium. But there was a big difference between Elysium and Thanos's dome: Thanos's complex would be in darkness at all times. The prison dome had been built near the north "pole" of the moon, where no light of the sun, or even a reflection of that light was visible. It would be a forbidding environment to be dropped into, with only rudimentary tools and supplies available. If the convicts didn't quickly figure out how to work together and grow their own food, they would be doomed to starvation. If they couldn't learn to live together in a civilized manner, they faced extinction from another angle. It was not an enviable fate.

"I wonder," Free said aloud, "if they have any idea of where they're headed, and what's waiting for them."

"None of us know our destiny," Skye said.

They soon reached the wall of the Military Complex. Nine floors of the pentagon extended upward into the sky, pushing outward, each floor larger than the one under it, top heavy.

"The prisoners are on the upper floors," Free said.

"That's where we're going," Skye said, pointing down at the ramp that ran around the building, presumably lowering with each level that, from Lynda's description, narrowed as the building went below surface level.

"Brad was right," Free said. "This structure *does* look as if it's been screwed in. Maybe it's also screwed up a lot of people..."

They headed down the ramp. There were few windows on the soulless building, and the narrow vertical slits that did exist seemed hardly anything you could describe as a "window." They reminded

Free of slots that coins were slipped into; thin, dark places that one could not see into but whoever was inside could surely see out. He suspected these were not real windows, but more like a translucent substance that was not just shatterproof and unbreakable but also holographic to some extent.

"This is deep." Skye said as they rounded the ramp.

"No kidding. It's like they didn't want anyone who got down this far to get back up easily. How many more levels are there?"

"The cubes said there were nine underground, and Lynda and Brad said they guessed around nine. I don't know if my father's lab was at the bottom—I don't know where it was—or if that lowest level is just some kind of storage floor or something. I guess we'll know what Lynda saw when we get there."

"I think we've walked down around four levels," Free said. The slope was steep, forcing them to keep their feet flat and to lean backwards slightly in order to keep from pitching head over heels.

They suddenly heard a loud *thwack*, and the earth beneath their feet trembled slightly.

"What was that?" Skye asked. Her feet were planted wide for balance and her hand was placed against the side of the building for support.

"No idea. I hope the Sling isn't malfunctioning again. We don't need any more holes in the dome," Free said.

"Yeah, that would truly suck, but I guess the AI would repair it, like before."

They looked around them and above, but from here they couldn't see the Sling because of the way the building fanned out.

Free said to Skye, "Maybe the UUSA is starting to move the prisoners out. I don't know how many prisoners were here, so maybe we saw the last of them being loaded in and the Sling is taking them away.

"Major Tom?" Free called.

The AI didn't answer, which made Free a bit nervous, because theoretically it was supposed to be everywhere.

"Probably busy fixing the new hole," he said to Skye.

She gave him a look. He was trying to reassure her, and she knew that, but they both knew that the AI was a multitasker and should be able to talk to them while doing repairs.

As they continued further down, the air temperature altered, becoming colder. Skye wondered about that. There shouldn't be any change in temperature at all, no matter where you were in the dome. She wondered if the Sling had breeched the dome, and something had happened to the environmental controls. Whatever, she felt cold, especially her arms and legs that were exposed by the skimpy T-shirt and short skirt and sandals. She watched Free, ahead of her, rubbing his exposed arms. At least he had on long pants. She wished she did. She hugged herself to try to warm up a bit.

After what seemed like an eternity, they finally came in sight of the bottom of the building. They walked around the ramp which had leveled out and suddenly came to a dead end.

"Lynda was right, there are no doors," Free said.

"I don't get it. Why have this ramp outside that leads nowhere?"

"Maybe there's a door and we don't know how to find it. Maybe it opens by a remote. Maybe there's some sort of loading dock down here."

"Maybe it's just a holding site where they tortured prisoners, letting them look out at nothing."

"Wow, that's a grim view," Free said. "But, uh, at this point, nothing would surprise me."

On the far side of the ramp where it leveled out at the bottom was the one window Lynda mentioned.

"Wait!" Skye said, grabbing Free's arm to hold him back. She wanted to walk beside him for some reason, so she kept pace, which was slow now, as if neither of them was that eager to get to the window.

They reached the dark window and stopped. Skye moved close to the glass and Free joined her. They pressed their faces against it, two kids peering through a candy shop window, but they weren't looking for a sweet treat. They were looking for their respective pasts. It was dark inside, and if the past was there, it wasn't showing itself.

"I can't see anything at all," Free said. "It's like a black hole in there."

"Lynda saw something," Skye said, struggling to catch any movement in the blackness.

Suddenly something came out of that blackness, lumbering straight toward them. Huge. Monstrous. Half metal, half flesh, shoulders double the width of a normal man's. Its body slammed against the glass, causing it to tremble. One fist that looked the size of Free's head pounded the glass, and another fist held a knife as long as a thigh.

Both Free and Skye instinctively leapt back at the assault. They fell on the ground, staring up at the fiend before them, hell-bent on shattering the barrier, stabbing its way out of confinement. Hell-bent on getting to them and destroying them!

"My god!" screamed Skye. "What is that?"

The inhuman eyes glowing red like death were glaring at Skye and Free, back and forth, as if trying to decide which one to kill first, if it could only get to them. Through the eyeholes of the metallic face the being looked deranged. It slammed its full body weight against the shatter-proof glass over and over, making it tremble violently, as if the glass would burst out of the frame or shatter into a million pieces. And much to Free's horror, and contrary to the claims of zephyr-glass manufacturers, the transparent barrier began to crack.

"Oh my God!" Skye screamed, sliding backwards on the ground toward where the ramp would slope upward. "We've got to get out of here!"

Free was already on his feet, grabbing and yanking her to a standing position.

"Run!" he yelled, pulling her along behind him, but she soon caught up. They ran as fast as they could up the steep ramp, all the while hearing the sounds of the rage below bashing against the glass. It seemed determined to explode out of the complex and get them. Intent on murdering them. And all three of them knew it was only a matter of time.

Halfway up they were both winded. "I... can't..." Skye said, gasping, doubled over.

"Come on! You've got to!" Free yelled, tugging her arm and half pulling, half dragging, almost carrying her, although he too needed to catch his breath.

Suddenly the earth began to quake violently. They were both knocked off their feet and began to roll down the ramp. No! Free would not roll back there to face whatever was trying to get through! He braced his back against the building and jammed the heel of his foot into the ramp floor. The ramp had no crevices, nothing that he could wedge his foot into; still, he hoped to find purchase. He snagged Skye's T-shirt as she started to roll past him. That brought him over the top of her as they continued to roll. His back slammed the wall of the building and that was enough to stop him.

The rumbling seemed to ease up for a moment, and Free jumped to his feet.

"That can't be him, can it?" Skye screamed, as he pulled her up too.

"No. It's something else," Free yelled, relentlessly pulling her up the ramp by her shirt.

Around them dust and dirt began to fall down from above. First sprinkles, then a shower, then a downpour. Free thought they were one level from ground when the soil beneath them shook so much that the ramp split, the fissure racing up the middle of it from above and below.

"My dream!" Skye screamed hysterically, grabbing at Free, paralyzed with fear. "We're going to fall in and be buried alive! He's going to cut off my head!"

Suddenly the sides of the ramp above them began to cave in.

Buried alive! Free thought. Not if I can help it.

He pushed and pulled and clawed and struggled up, finding a burst of renewed energy. Just at the top he sprinted the last five feet, then around and up onto the surface, now dragging Skye behind him as she struggled to stay on her feet on legs that would barely function.

They reached ground level one second before the outer wall of the ramp fell completely, caving in the ramp, which was now one hundred percent impassable. The split in the soil continued, though, and began moving around the building in a circle that was spiraling toward them.

Free didn't know where he found the energy because if anyone had asked him, he would have said he couldn't move a muscle. But he got Skye and himself a dozen meters from the fissure and when the split stopped just a meter from them, a strange sound between a laugh and a cry came out of Skye's mouth.

"We were almost pulled down!" Down, she thought, into a grave with that monster. Just like in her dream.

The tremors stopped abruptly, but not the ones in Skye's body. Her whole being quaked from exhaustion, from the shock of the experience, from the terror of nearly losing her life in a scenario ripped right out of her unconscious. From the horror of seeing… whatever it was below them that they had come face to face with. What she knew in her heart that her father had been responsible for bringing back to life.

Both of them struggled to catch their breath in the dust-filled air. Skye pulled her T-shirt up over her mouth and Free figured that was as good a filter as they'd get and did the same. The ramp had collapsed and was completely gone. Earth had fallen by the ton and engulfed the building so that it did not appear to have any levels below ground. Access to the basement from the outside was no longer a possibility. Somehow, that felt like a blessing.

Free glanced around them. All was quiet, as if this catastrophe had never occurred. He looked above. The Sling sat motionless at the top of the dome. The elevator was nowhere in sight. It must have descended back into the building. He hoped it had not fallen down the shaft with the quake. He wondered if maybe it was the elevator that had caused the quake.

"MT?"

Still nothing.

"MT? Where the hell are you?"

"He's not answering," Skye said. "And that worries me."

"Me too, but right now I don't think there's anything we can do about it."

Skye followed his gaze and must have followed his logic. "Do you think the prisoners plunged to their deaths?"

"I don't know. MT? Are you around?"

Nothing.

"Why doesn't he answer?" Skye asked, her voice quivering like her muscles.

"I don't know that either. All I know for sure is that we've got to get back to camp. We need to talk with the others, figure out what happened, and what, if anything, we can do."

He stood, his legs rubbery, his knees aching. More than anything his body demanded a good long rest. "I know," he said to her as she groaned, "I'm tired too, but we have to get out of here. We don't know what caused this, or how far it extends. Or if that's the end of it."

"You're right." She pushed herself to her feet with a moan, feeling her legs threatening to buckle beneath her. Skye clung to his arm for support. "I can't believe this. Any of it. I can't believe… him."

Free said nothing, but on the way back to camp his brain was littered with images of the monster Jason, and he had no doubt that that was Jason. Jason, his father, or the remnants of him. How could that be? How could he be the child of… that? Was he a monster too? He had had dark thoughts throughout his life, half homicidal, half suicidal, but his mother had assured him that many people did, especially the young; it was normal. Now he wasn't so sure. And in fact he hadn't had those thoughts in a very long time. Somehow, with his mother's death, he had realized he owed it to her to not just go on, but to do well for himself. He owed her his life.

Now, if that thing below had been what his mother had tried to protect him from, what had almost killed her, almost killed both of them, he owed her even more. But he had so many questions, and wasn't sure there would be any answers. Who could he ask?

They were near the end of the dirt path, and the road that led to the cabins was in sight when suddenly two men leapt out of the bushes on either side of them. Both Free and Skye jerked backwards.

"Fuck! A woman!" the big one said.

"Fuck is right!" the wiry one laughed.

Free instantly recognized the black one-piece outfits of the prisoners. He had a split-second moment of confusion as to why they were here and not in the Sling, or dead in the middle of the Military Complex, or still locked up in a cell, when one of the guys grabbed Skye from behind, picking her up and throwing her violently on the ground on her back. The other one jumped on her, struggling to unzip his pants. Free moved forward to stop them when suddenly he was hit on the back of his head. He fell onto his knees. The world spun and yet Skye's screams forced him to try to stand. A fist connected with his cheek and a boot kicked him in the stomach and he went down on his face, her screams now ringing in his ears like a reverberating bell.

Skye kicked and shrieked, trying to jam her knee between the legs of the man on top of her. He obviously expected her to struggle and he easily held her down with one hand as the other moved into his open fly. She would not let him rape her, even if it meant she had to die!

As she struggled, he slapped her hard across the face and then backhanded her. She tasted blood in her mouth and her vision went blurry.

The other one stood above her, also unzipping his pants. So they were going to take turns.

"Over my dead body!" she shrieked. "Bastards! Ugly, motherfucking bastards!"

That earned her a punch to the stomach which forced all the air out of her lungs and brought tears to her eyes and made her want to vomit. It also kept her quiet but still struggling, if minimally.

"Hold her legs down!" the short wiry one on top ordered.

She screamed "No!" when she felt first one ankle grasped and pressed to the ground, and then the other.

She began to sob. Tears gushed out of her eyes at her helplessness. The wiry guy laughed at her viciously.

Then suddenly, as if she were waking up from a horrible nightmare, everything changed. Her ankles were released and the guy on top of her flew up into the air and arced back. She saw the muscular arms that had tossed him onto the road behind him.

Through tears that nearly blinded her she watched a group of black-clad men surround her, and she moaned. This was a worse fate: they had only saved her for a gang rape! She curled into a ball and sobbed.

"What the fuck did I tell you?" an angry male voice snarled.

"We ain't inside now. You ain't the fuck in charge anymore, JJ." That was the wiry one who landed up the road.

"Yeah, Viper? And you are?"

"I'm not sayin' I'm in charge. I'm just sayin' things is different now," said Viper's considerably diminished voice.

"Not that different. Get him up!"

Skye glanced to her right and watched two men walk over to the wiry one called Viper and haul him to his feet, his pants falling around his ankles. A woman rushed to the wiry guy to console him. She shoved the hands of the two men away from him and helped him pull up his pants.

"See about her," the guy in his forties, who seemed to be in charge, said to someone.

Within a second another woman said to Skye, "Sit up. You'll live. They didn't even get it into you, so stop bawling!" The voice was harsh and expected to be obeyed.

Skye opened her eyes to see a woman with a shaved head, most of her scalp tattooed, and muscular arms that implied she worked out regularly. The harsh voice was modified by the eyes, which had a spot of kindness in them that Skye responded to.

"I'm okay," she said, whether to reassure this woman or herself, she didn't know.

"Sure you are, kid. Nothing happened."

Skye didn't feel as if nothing had happened, but she wasn't about to argue.

When she sat up, she saw Free being lifted to his feet. His face was pale as if all the blood had left his body, and he had an oozing cut on a cheek already swelling. He moved one hand to the back of his head, and the other to his stomach, coughing and spitting out blood.

"Oh my God, are you all right?" Skye yelled, rushing to him.

Free looked dazed but said, "Skye? Are you okay?"

As he looked at her, Free's focus became less blurry. His head hurt though, and his stomach felt as if it would force him to double over and barf. Or maybe he was bleeding internally. Either way, he glanced at the black-suited prisoners surrounding him and tried to keep control of himself.

"What are you doing here?" A big olive-skinned man with tattoos and several rings in each ear as well as his nostril said. His suit was open to the naval, and Free could see a ring in each nipple too. "I asked you a question!" The tone was hard, and Free felt if he didn't respond he'd get the crap kicked out of him.

"We... We're from the camp."

"The camp is empty!"

"He's lyin' JJ. Lemme beat it out of him."

"Shut up, Viper. Nobody's beating anything out of anybody until I say so," the one named JJ said. He was obviously in charge of the group.

"He's not lying," Skye said. "We work at the camp. Over there," she pointed.

"How'd you get here?" the woman who had insisted that nothing had happened asked.

"We came here to work on a project," Skye told them.

"Fuck!" the woman screamed, and Skye jumped. "Are you telling me they're starting up Castillo's project again?"

"No," Free said. "We're not working on Castillo's project. We're working for Jackson Mansfield."

"Who the fuck is he?" JJ wanted to know.

"He owns Elysium."

"What the fuck are you talking about, kid?" the woman asked. "Nobody owns the fucking moon!"

"Yes, he does. The government of Earth II sold it to him. That's why they're moving you guys. How come you didn't get moved?" Free asked.

"I'm asking the questions," JJ said. "How many more of you are here?"

Skye said, "There are six of us altogether." If you count Jason, she thought to herself, then there are seven, but she decided not to mention him. Maybe they knew about him. Maybe Jason was one of them. What a horrible thought.

"Amanda," JJ said, "you and Blister bring these two. The rest of us are going ahead to check things out."

The woman named Amanda grabbed Skye's

arm. "I'm not going to run away," Skye said. "Where would I go?"

The other woman, Blister, who had rushed to help the one named Viper, was skinny with a brush cut and even more tattoos. She strode over to Free and shoved him backwards just for the hell of it, snarling like an animal, her face twisted with rage. Free almost fell.

JJ, Viper and the six other men had gone ahead to the camp. Now Free and Skye were led that way too by the two female prisoners.

"What happened? How come you're not on the Sling?" Skye asked.

"Shut the fuck up!" Blister snapped, raising a hand as if she were about to hit Skye. "You're lucky we don't kill you!"

Skye did shut up, as did Free. Briefly they had a chance to glance at one another and see the fear they shared.

Free wondered just how many prisoners were loose on Elysium, and how they got that way, and if they were free, did that mean that Jason was free too?

TEN

Free and Skye were led into the camp, prisoners themselves now. They watched the half dozen male convicts rampaging through the grounds. They broke into every cabin, beginning with Skye's, and all the way up the line.

Anyar heard the commotion and came out to see what was going on. As she tried to retreat, one of the men dragged her out. Herbert was also dragged out of his cabin by his hair, kicking and screaming.

The Store was attacked, and the prisoners hauled out into the open bins and pails of food, eating some of what should be cooked uncooked in their haste to "Party!" as Viper yelled over and over. They'd found the cases of wine and had the bottles open and the liquid pouring down their throats even before Free and Skye and their guards made it to the center of the campgrounds.

Lynda and Brad had been in the Lab, which was invaded quickly. Free heard Lynda screaming, and didn't want to imagine what was happening to her.

Once everyone in the project had been dragged onto the road, Free and Skye were tossed into the ring with the others, surrounded by the men eating, drinking, yelling, shoving, laughing, tearing at the velvet dress Lynda wore, touching both Anyar and Herbert in inappropriate places. And Skye. Beautiful Skye was the focus of so much loutish attention, and Free tried to protect her by shoving hands away from her. For his efforts he was punched in the eye, knocking him on his ass.

Finally, a blast filled the air, then another, ear splitting, and Free looked up to see the one named JJ holding something metallic that had a puff of smoke coming from one end. "Listen up, assholes!" he said.

Skye crouched next to Free, holding onto him for protection he couldn't provide. "What is that?" she whispered in a trembling voice.

"It's a, uh, gun…" Herbert said in his own quivering voice. "A relic from, um, a thousand years ago."

"What does it do?" Skye asked fearfully. "Besides deafen you?"

"It… kills people with metal bits."

"We're free!" JJ said, and made the long metal weapon fire again, shooting something into the air. The sound caused Skye to put her hands over her ears and when she took them away her ears rang.

The male and female prisoners yelled and screamed and jumped into the air. Some of the men, including Viper, kicked over anything nearby and threw things around.

Free and his team members cowered and quivered. None of them, in all their young lives, had encountered anything so base and crude as what was happening to them now.

"We're free, and I'm still your leader!" JJ announced, firing that damned weapon yet again.

All of the convicts cheered, although Free noticed that Viper didn't cheer quite as loudly, nor did the woman named Blister. He saw them glance at one another.

"That means I make the rules," JJ said.

"Yeah! You done good by us so far," one of the men yelled, and the others shouted approval.

"Right now, we got ourselves some hostages."

More screaming, throwing of things, and the weapon firing again.

"We got a chip to play to get us off this fucking dead moon and back into the land of the living."

While they cheered him on, Skye said to Free, "We've got to escape. They'll kill us."

"I know," he whispered.

"Let's make a run for it," Lynda said from behind them.

"No," Skye said. "They'll just capture us and—"

But it was too late. Lynda, in a panic, tried to run from the circle. One of the men grabbed her and began ripping off her clothes while she screamed at the top of her lungs.

Brad jumped up to help her and instantly was beaten up by two men until he lay on the ground not moving.

"Hold it! Hold it!" JJ shouted. "I want them alive and well and living in hell, but not yet. I need to question all of them first. You'll get your chance with the ladies," he leered, "and the men." And the prisoners grinned and laughed and punched each other and Free felt his fear escalate.

JJ motioned to Amanda who quickly joined him. "Get them into that big cabin," he told her, "and you and Blister keep watch on them."

She nodded and came to the six hostages from one side while Blister approached from the other. "Stand up!" she ordered, and they did but for Brad who was barely propping himself up with his elbows. Blister kicked Brad in the side with a metallic-toed boot and Brad groaned.

"Gee, that will help him stand up," Skye said.

"Watch your mouth, bitch!" Blister said, and raised her hand to punch Skye.

"You two, get him up!" Amanda said, catching Blister's fist. Skye and Free reached down to help Brad stand.

"Get movin'," Blister ordered. She picked up a metal rod on the ground and slapped it against her palm in a threatening gesture, swatting Herbert on the butt, making him yowl and trot along ahead of the others.

En route, they picked up a sobbing, half naked Lynda. Anyar helped her on one side, Herbert, reluctantly, on the other, when Blister snapped the rod in the air and said, "Get her up! We ain't got all day!"

As they left for the cabin that had belonged to Lynda and Brad, Free heard JJ say, "I want everything in these cabins brought out here and dumped into the middle so we can see what's what. Viper, take Jake and go into the store and see what all's in there. We're gonna need provisions and we don't know for how long. And find their comm system. I want to know how they're in contact with Earth II. I'm headed into that Lab to see what these guys have been up to."

JJ entered the building that was the laboratory, a building he was somewhat familiar with. A building on this very spot used to function in another capacity, a kind of office where camp instructors would come to chill out. The exterior of the building looked different, although it was a similar size. The interior was filled with the latest tech equipment. He moved from console to console, letting his mind flash back a couple of decades, wondering if he would be able to use any of this stuff.

What a place this camp had been... There was nothing like it in the galaxy. He and Amanda had come here, run things in a way that made sense to them, as far as he could reason, they had saved the damned universe. And what thanks did they receive for it. A very royal thanks. Up the ass.

As if things weren't bad enough in the past, the idiots in charge were trying it again. Maybe,

maybe not. He wasn't sure what they were here to do, but he'd find out pretty damned quick.

He entered the glassed-in room and went to the bank of buttons and knobs. Not much of it made sense to him. He noticed the pause button was lit so he pressed it to see what they had been doing. Just behind him a holographic image lit up and spun on a round platform. An image that looked remarkably and frighteningly familiar. Jason.

"What the fuck?" he muttered. "They can't be bringing him back!"

Just then, Viper came through the Lab door. He saw the image but didn't know what or who it was.

"Can't find no comm system. No linkups neither. Checked all the cabins, the store, couple of the other buildings." Viper looked around. "Don't seem to be nothin' here neither."

"We'll find it," JJ said, turning his back on the virtual image as if that would make it vanish from his mind. "They've got to have a way to communicate with Earth II."

"I say we kick it outta those punks. Why we keepin' them around anyways? We only need one to exchange."

"We don't know what we need yet. What if the government wants one for one?"

"Then we don't got enough anyway. There's nine of us here and six of them."

JJ shook his head. "Yeah, and then we negotiate. Easier to go from six for nine than one for nine."

Viper reluctantly saw the logic of it, but he didn't like it, and JJ knew that. Viper was one of those guys you could trust only so far. He'd always backed JJ up but he didn't always want to. They'd gotten into it a few times over the years and so far JJ had always pounded the crap out of him, and once cut him bad. If he hadn't have done that, Viper would have stuck him in the heart and he'd be gone.

Viper was in his thirties, and JJ was forty-two. JJ was getting tired of being tough; tired of having to be king of the shit heap. It hadn't come naturally to him, he'd had to learn damned fast. And it couldn't last forever. One day, Viper would get the best of him, and he knew that. But so far, most of the other guys didn't want to follow Viper. He was mean, cruel0 and reactive. He couldn't think things through, and that meant he would go down the wrong path, fast. Most of the guys understood that, but not all. Every leader and potential leader had his followers.

"Come on. We'll head outside," JJ said, clasping Viper on the shoulder, partly as a friendly gesture, partly to show who was boss. "Being outdoors, even in this shitty environment, will do us good. Been a long time…"

"You got that right!" Viper said, grinning.

"Let's see what the guys have found. Maybe there's something useful."

They found the others in the road running around a bonfire they'd built, throwing furniture and papers and everything they could gather in two hands into it.

"Jesus!" JJ muttered under his breath. What idiots, he thought. "Hold it, guys. Lemme see stuff before it gets blazed. We might need it.

"It's just papers and shit, JJ, all of it," said Odin, a big lug of a guy that had the physical power of three men and the brain of a child. At least he was loyal to JJ.

"You're probably right, but maybe there's something we could use. We wouldn't want to burn the comm system by accident," which made all the men pause.

"Get outta here, you morons!" Viper yelled, pushing men away from the blaze, some of whom pushed back.

"Whatcha got, Sam?" JJ asked a man of medium height and medium build. Sam had been a model prisoner over the years, and had somehow survived the chaos without going insane, and accumulating only a handful of scars on his body. It was all relative, of course, his sanity. In actual fact, Sam was a sociopath and had no feelings for anyone or anything.

Sam held a tin box. "Got a buncha cubes in here. I'd guess they're holos. Wanna see one if I can figure how to get it to work? Maybe it needs a machine to run it."

He picked up one of the cubes and looked it over from all sides. "Hold on. There's a button here." He pressed it and an image appeared with the flames as a background.

"Hey, what do you know?" somebody shouted. "They're like the old ones, from when I was a kid."

JJ was astonished to see Arthur J Castillo floating in the air. His mouth dropped open when he heard Castillo say, "We will, of course, with Jason, have the most advanced soldier ever created. He will be virtually indestructible."

While Castillo ranted on, JJ felt his fury build. So they were trying to replicate Castillo's experiments!

He watched the cube for only a few more seconds before yelling, "Shut that damn thing off!" When the cube stopped, he spun on his heels and said to Viper, "Look for comm equipment. I'll be back."

He stalked his way to the cabin where Amanda and Blister kept guard over the hostages. When he stormed in, the six kids looked up at him as one unit, twelve frightened eyes.

"There's a bonfire, Blister," he said to the pyromaniac. She constantly rubbed the tips of her fingers which were always blistered from setting fires, hence the name. "I think Viper could use your help."

"Sure," she said, almost flying out the door.

"What's up?" the woman named Amanda said. She looked at JJ with concern, clearly aware of his anger.

"Who's in charge of this little group?" he asked the six.

Free raised his hand. "That would be me."

In two long strides, JJ was on him, grabbing him by the throat, lifting him to his feet, off his feet even, while the others yelled and screamed to let him go.

"So, you're here to do Castillo's work after all."

"N-no!" Free gasped, feeling terrified, trying to pry the fingers away from his larynx so he could breath, fearing he was about to have his lights punched out.

"Don't bullshit me!"

"I'm not! We're here to build a cyborg—"

"Yeah, I know. One by the name of Jason."

"What are you talking about?" Brad jumped to his feet.

"Down!" JJ ordered, pointing, and the bruised and battered Brad fell to his knees like a puppy with a bashed-in nose.

"JJ, they're just kids," Amanda said.

"Mandy, I saw Castillo, at least a holographic image of him. They've got all his notes on cubes. And I saw the image of Jason in the Lab."

"That's just a stock image," Anyar said. "We were working with the computer's basic form, trying to build something that could house the large number of programs we want to insert."

"Yeah, and let me guess. Some of those programs have to do with the ability to kill."

"Not at all!" Lynda said, starting to her feet, holding the top of her torn dress against her chest. But instantly she saw the look in JJ's eyes and stayed seated. "We're putting together a cyborg that can replicate human thinking, feeling and reactions. It's got nothing to do with the military."

"Yeah, and who's financing this? The Mansfield guy you mentioned?" He stared hard at Free who was now back on his feet. The fingers around his throat had loosened, but not much.

It took all the courage Free had to answer. "Yes, he's the one. And his aims are not destructive. He's an honest businessman, and a philanthropist… and a humanitarian. Look, you've got the wrong idea. We know about Castillo, but we're not replicating what he did."

"Then where'd you get the cubes?"

"They're mine," Skye admitted. "I brought them along when we came here last week. The others didn't know about them until yesterday, when Free found out I had them and we watched them together."

"That's where you were!" Anyar said.

"You had his notes?" Lynda added.

Skye ignored them. "Look, we were hired for a simple cyborg project, to replicate life, not to create the ultimate soldier. We don't want to create anything like what we saw at the Military Complex, we just want to learn how to—"

"Hold on!" Amanda's hand went up like a stop sign. "Like what you saw at the Military Complex?"

Skye paused and Free took over. "We went to the Military Complex because Lynda here," he nodded at her, "saw something when she and Brad went over there for a picnic the other day. It scared her. When Skye and I watched the cubes, we realized that what Lynda saw may have been this Jason that Castillo had resurrected, so we went there. We were on our way back when you found us."

"And?" JJ said, his face a mask of repressed violence.

"And, we saw... something. We think it was Jason."

Amanda said angrily, "Jason was destroyed."

"Maybe there was a copy, a backup," Free argued. "Maybe that's what we saw."

"The backup isn't there," Amanda said.

"What?" Free said. "So there was a backup! But we saw something. It had to be Jason. He's huge, right? With a metal mask for a face, red glowing eyes, burning like the fires of hell. And this long knife or some—"

"It's a machete," Amanda said, her voice low.

"How did you get the cubes?" JJ turned to Skye.

She didn't want it known, didn't want to say it, but she didn't know how she could avoid it now. "I got them from my mother. My father sent them to her before he died."

"You're his kid?" Amanda said in a stunned voice. "The bastard had a wife and a kid?"

"Three kids. I'm the only surviving child."

"Jesus!"

Just then Viper came through the door. "We can't find no comm system that goes off Moon Complex," he said. Then to Free, who was the only one standing, he demanded, "Where is it, fucker?"

"There's no communications system," Free said. "That was decided before the project began. It would have been too expensive to have a comm system here because of the gases, so we opted to not have one so we could get some better computer equipment instead."

"What are you talking about?" Amanda snapped. "We had a communications system here twenty years ago. We didn't have any trouble with gases then."

Free just stared at her, then at the others in the room, feeling confused. "I don't know. I'm just telling you what Jackson told me. The gases preclude easy communication. We're alone here."

"What exactly did Jackson tell you, Free?" Skye asked.

Free tried to remember clearly. "He said we couldn't contact Earth II, that we should use the AI."

"Couldn't, or shouldn't?"

"I... I'm not sure." Free thought for a second, then his brain suddenly cleared. "It just occurs to me now that Jackson was trying to place us here to be self-sufficient. It may be that communication is possible but he wanted us to try to go it alone and see how we fared. I mean, this is a first job for pretty well all of us. Our first time away from home..."

"What if you had an emergency?" Amanda asked.

"Jackson said that any time we needed to send a message to Earth II we should use Major Tom."

"What?" Amanda screamed. "He's fucking still around? That demon!"

Free, Skye and the others shrank back, staring at one another in confusion.

Finally Free said, "He's our AI. We rely on him for life support, supplies and to send messages to and from Earth II. He's not the original Major Tom, he's a copy that's been reprogrammed by Jackson Mansfield. His bad chips have been removed. We haven't had any trouble with him."

"Call him," JJ said.

"Major Tom?" Free said.

No answer.

"MT? Where are you?"

Nothing.

Free turned to the others in the project. "You guys been in touch with the AI in the last day?"

"Not since you and Skye left the camp," Brad said. "We didn't need him for anything."

"We couldn't reach him at the Military Complex but thought we were out of range. Or the earthquake had him busy repairing the dome or something."

"What earthquake?" Viper said. "There was no fucking earthquake. This is such shit! Lemme get the truth outta them!" He started toward Free, fists raised.

JJ blocked him with a muscled arm. Viper, behind the barricade of flesh, glared at Free.

"Why do you think there's been an earthquake?" Amanda asked.

It was Skye who answered. "Because when we were at the Military Complex looking to see if it was really Jason that Lynda saw, down at the lowest level, level nine, the ground rumbled and then the earth started falling in on us and we could hardly get up the ramp. Every floor below ground was completely filled with earth. We just assumed it was a seismic disturbance."

Amanda nodded a bit. "That wasn't the ground, it was from the sky."

Free put it together. "The Sling! It malfunctioned! We thought that it was a quake and that the elevator plunged back into the Military Complex."

"The Sling took the next load of prisoners up and then the elevator moved back down into the complex for the next group when the Sling started moving. It pulled away, then bashed the dome again and stalled. Everybody up there's stuck," Amanda explained.

"Hopefully no one was hurt," Lynda said.

"Like you give a fuck!" Blister snarled, coming in the door. "Hey, they got the fire going real good and hot and high!"

"Burn your butt baby!" Viper said, pinching her arm.

She pulled away, saying, "Ouch!"

"We were still in the prison but the cell doors were open because we were being loaded. We made it out," Amanda said to Anyar. "The rest are coming."

Free felt despair settle over him. The rest! These guys were barely human, and now there would be more? Herbert asked the question he wanted to ask.

"How... how many more?"

"Enough to rip your insides out with their cocks!" Viper said.

"There's probably a hundred or more of us who didn't get to the Sling," Amanda said.

"Why the fuck you telling them anything?" Blister snapped.

"You two, outside!" Amanda said.

Viper laughed at her. Blister yelled, "When the fuck did you become leader?"

Amanda looked at JJ who, for all intents and purposes, didn't return her look. But he did say, "Viper, get a barrier built around this camp. Fire if you have to. And we're gonna need some weapons. See what you can find. I don't think there'll be much, but maybe we can build some stuff. When the rest of them get here, there'll be some power plays. Which one of you works the bio builder?"

"Bio builder?" Anyar said. "You mean the biolab equipment? That can build actual forms?"

"Yeah."

"Me and Herbert."

"Okay, Viper, take the guy with you."

"Yeah!" Viper said, licking his thin lips and rubbing his hands together in anticipation.

"No!" Herbert screamed, digging his heels into the floor, clinging to Anyar and to a chair. Suddenly he wet his pants and began to cry.

"I'll go," Anyar volunteered. "I know the equipment better than him anyway."

"Sure, pretty pussy, come along," Viper said, licking those lips even more. Blister scowled at him, then at the girl.

"She's ugly. You blind?" Blister said to Viper.

"*I'm* blind," Anyar said.

"Very funny!"

"But I can 'see' the equipment, and I'm good at working it. I'll help you build what you need."

"Come on," Viper said, grabbing her by the arm, shoving her in front of him, slapping her on the ass with his other hand and laughing.

"Shit!" Blister said, shaking her head, but followed them out.

JJ turned to Free and the others. "All of you, sit. We got some talking to do."

Once Free had explained more of what their project was about in detail, and who Jackson Mansfield was, and what they knew about the Sling, and the prison colony to be formed on Thanos, and everything they understood about Jason, Amanda said, "JJ, I think we should tell them about us."

He nodded, and Amanda started. "JJ and me, we were here twenty years ago, when this place was a camp. We were counselors, can you believe it? Castillo was in charge of the Military Complex, where he was conducting experiments. He was building a new and improved Jason out of his remaining DNA, to be run by the original AI called Major Tom, but you know all that. What you don't know is that everybody on Moon Complex was killed, including Castillo. Everybody but us."

Skye wanted to know everything. But she wanted to see if they were making this up as they went along. "Who killed Jason?" Skye asked. "Castillo? He said on a cube he was going to do that."

Amanda looked at her blankly. "It was the other way around. Jason did him in. Stabbed him in his techno eye with three pieces of glass from a mirror."

Skye gasped and Free slipped an arm around her shoulders, wanting to comfort her. But Skye was horrified for another reason: that image of how Castillo had died had repeatedly appeared in her dreams, only it was she who was stabbed in the eye with three sharp objects. Her stomach roiled. Despite feeling nauseous, Skye also felt merciless, with herself, with everyone. The truth had to be known.

"You said Jason was killed. Do you know who did it?"

Amanda paused. "We thought we did."

"Look," JJ said, "here's what happened. Castillo created a virtual Jason and at the same time managed to get his hands on the real Jason, or what was left of him. He was bitmapping the virtual Jason from the DNA of the original Jason, and from everything he could use, feeding the thing with a few victims he had stored in his lab. The rich camp girls."

"Oh no!" Skye said, her hand over her mouth, and Free pulled her close.

"Things got out of control real fast. Castillo was killed by Jason, and so was just about everybody else on the Moon Complex. Mandy and me tried to get help from a ship but in the end it was up to us and we managed to use Castillo's equipment to ship the physical Jason and just about all the madman's equipment out into space, into a black hole, if all the calculations were right. And that's where he is. Or was."

"But you guys saw him at the complex. JJ, what do you think?" Amanda asked, her voice filled with terror.

"I think this is fucked. I know we got rid of him. Castillo likely made a copy."

"He intended to make a copy." Everyone looked at Skye. "It was in one of the cubes."

JJ said, "As far as we know, if there was a copy, it must have been strictly virtual, and in a rudimentary form. And it should have been eliminated when the prison was opened because the entire Military Complex was cleaned out by the military, and they supposedly reprogrammed the AI to run the prison."

"Which is what Major Tom told us," Lynda said. "He was a copy from the reprogrammed AI. And then Jackson came here and added some further programs."

"Then what's at the Military Complex now?" Free asked.

"I'm betting either the original Major Tom, or your AI had something to do with that," JJ said.

"I'm thinking that too," Free said. "Our Major Tom is a copy of the original Major Tom, with all the bad programming supposedly eliminated, the corrupted chips removed. It couldn't have been him. And our AI told us that the original Major Tom still exists and is in charge of the Military Complex. That's its only function."

"Then there are two Major Toms," Amanda said.

"Okay, this is getting crazy," JJ said. "So where's your AI now?"

"I wish I knew," Free said glumly.

"If you guys were like camp counselors, why were you put in jail?" Lynda wanted to know. "I mean, if you got rid of this killer, isn't that a good thing? Shouldn't you have been rewarded?"

"The military didn't see it that way," Amanda said. "Jason was their baby, and even if the baby was a demon, it was their demon. We knew too much about what went on here, about Castillo, and about all the deaths. We were dangerous, so they tossed us into prison on a basically uninhabitable moon where nobody would ever find us. We've been rotting away for twenty years, growing gray and tired and bitter. Now, suddenly, they want to send us to an even worse place. What's that about?"

"Are you the only ones here from the original camp?"

"Yeah. Just the two of us. All the other cons came within a year of us being incarcerated."

"You were wrongly imprisoned," Free said, suddenly getting it.

JJ just nodded, and Amanda looked distressed.

"You killed the physical Jason, or at least got rid of him. And got rid of Castillo's equipment. You did the universe a good turn. But here you are, in jail?" Free said.

"Tell us about it," JJ said.

"The other guys," Amanda continued, "they don't know the whole of it. They know we killed somebody, but not who or why. We never told them. Figured it was better to keep a lid on it, just in case there are spies. There are always spies. We didn't want any information about Jason to get out. We didn't want to risk that somebody else would pay the price if the military found out. Or worse, that somebody else would try to recreate him. Hell, we thought that by sending Castillo's equipment and notes into the black hole with the physical Jason we got rid of everything. Yeah, the virtual Jason still existed, controlled by Major Tom, but it was ineffective without the body. And besides, the AI was reprogrammed. Or so we were told."

"You probably did get rid of everything," Skye said. "There were only the cubes, and a handful of notes to my mother which said almost nothing about Castillo's work." She didn't mention the missing cube, the one that talked about Free's past; they were in a bad enough situation with the convicts knowing that Castillo was her father. If they knew that Free was the son of Jason...

Amanda said to Free, "Look, are you sure this guy Mansfield didn't have a master plan to replicate Castillo's project? Are you sure he wasn't interested in creating another Jason?"

"I don't see how," Free said. "I hired everybody here, and it's just a fluke that I selected Skye. Jackson didn't have anything to do with it. Both Skye and I tried to do research on the history of Moon Complex and there was nothing available, and we're both very good at researching. I found one small reference to Castillo, and it was innocuous. And Skye found a paragraph. It's like he and his project were erased, as if he and Jason had never existed."

"Still, maybe this Jackson got hold of information you couldn't get."

"I've known him all my life," Free said. "He raised me, helped my mother. I saw all his business dealings. He's a fair and honest man, and his work involves helping humanity, not hurting it. He only bought Elysium because it was cheap and a good place to do research. The government of Earth II wanted to get rid of it and offered it to him. Nobody was interested in Elysium because of the catastrophe that happened here, which nobody really knew anything about anyway because there was no information available."

"Look," Brad said, "we've never completely trusted the AI. At least Lynda and me."

"And me," Herbert said in a small, frightened voice.

"I'm thinking it knows what happened here twenty years ago. Who did what to whom? It knew every in and out of Castillo's work."

Amanda said, "The original AI ran the resurrected Jason. What you saw could have been a virtual Jason."

"No!" Lynda snapped. "It was real. Flesh and blood."

"I'm not sure," Skye said, "but the Jason Free and I saw looked pretty real too."

"Okay," Brad said. "How about this? The original Major Tom had control of the virtual Jason. Maybe he built a body to store it in, the one Lynda saw, and you guys. That's why it's in the prison. The original AI is trapped there so the virtual Jason, now embodied, is trapped there as well."

"And do you think that our Major Tom, because it's a copy of the original, knew about it?" Free asked.

"It's hard to say," Skye said. "We don't know what he did or didn't know, and now he's not around, which is pretty creepy when you think about it."

"Wow," Lynda said. "The original AI made a body for the virtual Jason all by itself, without direction. That's amazing!"

"Probably some crucial instructions were left in the original AI's programming," Brad said. "Or just maybe, even as it was being reprogrammed, it rebuilt its original chips."

"Holy shit!" Lynda said. "It's designed to repair itself. It replicated the parts that were removed or reprogrammed!"

"Then why didn't it take over the entire Moon Complex?" Free wondered. "Why was Jason imprisoned in the Military Complex?"

"Maybe because the original AI didn't need to move him out. Or couldn't," Skye said.

"And just maybe," JJ said, "this Jason was scheduled to end up on Thanos too."

"I still don't get how the AI made a body on its own," Lynda said. Nobody had an answer for that. Finally she sighed. "Well, what does it matter now anyway? The Sling is broken, so nobody is leaving here on it. And the below ground floors of the complex are buried, so the virtual, embodied Jason is buried. Jason II is dead."

"I doubt it," JJ said.

"Why?"

"Because it took a hell of a lot to get rid of the first one Castillo built. And I'm pretty sure it will take a hell of a lot more to kill the second one because knowing the original Major Tom as I do, or did, he'd have learned from his mistakes and made this Jason a lot stronger. I'm betting that what's under the Military Complex is even more powerful than the first one. Nope. We haven't seen the last of him."

"God!" Free said. He could barely incorporate everything he was hearing. If all this was true, they were in grave danger, and not just from the other prisoners. The main threat was Jason himself. "We've got to get off this moon!" he said.

"Great idea," Amanda said. "Any ideas how we can do that?"

"Maybe we can repair the Sling—"

"And end up on the prison colony? That *is* the Sling's destination. Where there are no guards, just prisoners. Nobody to hear you screaming."

"And," JJ said, "risk Jason ending up there too?"

"We can reprogram the Sling, change its course," Free announced.

"Kid, are you out of your gourd? From what I saw, that Sling must have been built by a team of technical geniuses. By the time you figured out its components and software, we'd all be dead. Our grandchildren will be dead!" JJ said loudly.

"There has to be some way off this moon," Amanda said. "How were you all to get off when your project was over?"

"There's a shuttle scheduled to pick us up six months from now."

"Great. Nobody will be alive by then," JJ said.

"In case of an emergency, we were to send a message through Major Tom, and then Jackson would send a shuttle," Free mumbled.

"Wonderful!" Lynda said. "And now the stupid AI won't answer us. Why? Because it's in league with the original AI. Or maybe it *is* the original AI for all we know."

"Look, okay," Free said in a determined voice. "There are the other prisoners that are coming. And there's Jason. JJ, you've commanded these guys for a while, it looks like. And you killed Jason before, or at least gotten rid of him. We can survive this."

JJ looked Free square in the eye for a long time, too long; his irises brown agates that spoke of something so fixed in the universe that it became impossible to keep staring, and yet Free couldn't do anything else. Those eyes made Free nervous beyond what he thought made any sense.

Abruptly, the convict leader stood up. "Let's go," he said to Amanda who turned with him and headed out the door.

"Are we still under guard?" Lynda asked tentatively.

JJ glanced back at her. "What's the point? You'll be dead soon. We'll all be dead. You might as well enjoy yourselves before Jason gets here."

ELEVEN

Blister had been eavesdropping at the window while that asshole JJ and that bitch Amanda talked with the camp babies. She knew Viper would want to hear all about it. Just as they were finishing up, and before anyone could get a glimpse of her, she bolted over to the Lab.

What she found there did not please her at all. Viper had his hands all over that blind girl while she worked at a bunch of controls in the biolab.

"Hey!" she called as she opened the transparent door, just to let him know she was coming.

Viper pulled back only a bit and stretched out an arm, motioning with his fingers. "Babe! Come 'ere. We'll go three ways."

Blister forced a smile. "Yeah, sure, but I got somethin' to tell ya that'll make you more excited than any pussy could."

He turned away from her to run his tongue up Anyar's neck. The blind girl ignored him as if she felt nothing, as if he didn't exist. Blister knew that nothing made him hotter than being ignored. He slid a hand far down inside the back of her pants while she worked, pressing his hard self up against her butt. Still, she kept working.

Blister couldn't stand it. "Viper! This is serious!"

He turned and hissed at her, which is how he got the nickname. That sound she used to find so sexy, and still did, when it wasn't turned on her. That sound plus the one massive snake tattoo that slithered up and around his body starting at the big toe of his left foot, up to the top of the foot and around the ankle, up the back of his leg and spiraling around to his butthole, then up his spinal column to the back of his neck, further, onto his scalp...

"Can't you see I'm fuckin' busy, bitch? Fuck off!"

"Yeah, you're busy fuckin' a blind girl while this whole thing is fallin' around your stupid ears!"

He jumped away from Anyar and got to Blister in two strides, which was quite a feat for such a short guy. His energy always amazed her. Blister, though frightened of his violence, which she'd been the recipient of before, stood her ground.

"Wha'd you call me?" he snarled in her face, his breath hot and stinking of onions, his hands balled into fists at his sides.

She forced herself to talk calmly. "I'm just sayin' that things are goin' down you need to know about. Big things. Things that'll let you be the boss instead of dickhead."

"What things?"

She whispered, "Not in front of her."

"She's nothin'!" he snapped.

"Trust me," Blister said. She jerked her head and he followed her out of the glass room.

As she closed the glass door behind them he said, "This better be good or you're lookin' for a whoopin'!"

Quickly she explained everything she'd heard as best she could understand it. The bottom line, she told him, was that, "There's a guy JJ's scared shitless of, who can help you."

"I don't need no fuckin' help!"

Blister sighed. "I don't mean 'help,' I mean HELP!"

She stared at Viper, giving him a quirky nod.

He scratched his scalp, still not getting it. "You're telling me there's some kinda super soldier up there at the Military Complex?"

"Yeah. JJ knows about him, and Amanda. They seen him or one like him twenty years ago and he wiped out everybody on Moon Complex but them."

"And? What's this gotta do with me?"

"With us, Viper, with us," she said, pressing her body into his.

He grabbed her arms so hard she felt a bruise forming, and then jerked her back. "You interrupted me for this shit? Why I oughta—"

"That Jason? We can use him to fight for us. You could command him to do what you want and he could take out JJ and some of the others and you'd be the boss."

That stopped him. A dozen possibilities flashed in his eyes like laser images at the speed of light. "Yeah, you got a point." Then he looked worried for a moment. "If this Jason guy is as tough as they say he is, why'll he listen to me? He'll wanna be boss himself."

"No he won't, 'cause he ain't human, or not enough of him or somethin'. And that's why he'll listen to you, too. He's like a computer shaped like a guy. You're good with machines. You can figure out how to control him, and then this place'll be yours."

Blister watched Viper thinking some more.

"So where is he?"

"They said he's in the basement of the Military Complex. Nine floors down from the ground. We just gotta go in there and get him."

"Okay, so we'll do it later. There's no rush."

"There is, Viper!" she said, sensing she was losing him to thrills the of the flesh that beckoned. "If we don't go get him now, JJ will. You gotta go now, while you got the edge, and a chance of havin' some guys on your side. If you wait, it'll be too late. And don't forget, the other guys from the prison'll be here as soon as they can claw their way outta the Military Complex."

Viper thought about all this some more. Maybe the bitch was right. Maybe he should go now. He glanced into the glass room at the little blind chick with the fleshy butt and thought about how nice it would be to slip it in her.

"You gotta go now," Blister was saying.

"All right, all right! Get off my back!"

"Let's go find Frank. He always liked you. He'd side with you against JJ, Sam and Odin."

"Yeah, Frank's okay."

"Let's go talk to him now. Come on, Viper. Here's your chance to be leader."

They left the Lab together and saw JJ and Amanda at the bonfire. The babies must still be in the cabin. Unguarded. Viper sneered. Just like JJ, giving them the chance to get away.

Blister looked at the flames longingly. God, she wanted to get close to that red-yellow flicker! She felt like peeling off her clothes and standing buck naked, getting herself hot all over, spinning like meat roasting on a spit, so close that the hairs on her naval would singe as the flames licked her body like a hot hand. Just touching it a few minutes ago had made bubbles on the fingertips of her right hand. She wanted that fire near her.

But there was no time. She had Viper interested, and she had to get him moving. He had to be top dog in this pack of curs so she could be top bitch and give it to that bitch Amanda and any of the other bitches that thought they were so hot. And Viper'd be so grateful to her for getting him to be king he'd fuck her whenever she wanted it, and give her everything she wanted when she wanted it and not be mean to her, and he wouldn't belt her around no more. She knew he only hit her because he was frustrated at having to bend over for JJ who was just a punk but had somehow gotten control of the whole prison. Well, that would change. And soon.

Viper had a word with Frank who was tossing papers into the fire. Then he gave Blister the palm-in-her-direction signal to remain at the camp. He and Frank walked off together, casual like, between two of the cabins. JJ noticed but it looked like he didn't think it mattered. Or maybe he just didn't care.

Blister really wanted to go with them, but she also wanted to stare at the fire. What to do? There'd be other fires, she guessed. She'd better go and make sure they did this right. A lot was riding on it.

When she knew that JJ and Amanda and the others were not watching, she ran behind one of the cabins and followed Viper and Frank at a distance. She had to make sure he did this, but she didn't want him knowing she was following or there'd be hell to pay. Once they got Jason on their side, things would be damned near perfect around here!

As Viper and Frank reached the path to the Military Complex, they ran into Crully and his bad-assed gang. "Hey, asshole! Or you still got one?" Crully called, and the nine guys with him laughed.

Viper and Crully had been rivals inside, twin dog number twos, and this wasn't a good place to meet, just Viper and Frank against ten of them.

Viper wanted to shove it to him but that wasn't going to work out right now. Not if he wanted to come out of this with a jaw intact and no knife wounds in his chest. He had an idea.

Viper laughed, turning Crully's challenge into a joke. "Listen, Crully, I got a proposition for you," he said, smiling what he hoped was an ingratiating grin, although he wanted to cream the bastard.

"Hey, guys, hear that! The fucker propositioned me. I should beat the crap outta you for that," Crully threatened.

"Don't lose your cool, Crully. I got a big gig on the roll here, and I'm offerin' you a piece."

"Offerin' me a piece!" Crully laughed. "Your ass or Blister's? Now she's a nice piece of ass…"

The other guys laughed and Frank whispered, "Stay chilled, Viper. We got business interests."

Viper was barely restraining himself. He gave it a quick thought, then grinned. "Yeah, she's an okay piece. Likes it every which way. Boring, though. I've had it with her, so she's up for grabs."

Blister, watching from the bushes, was royally pissed off. Maybe he was just saying that to save his own butt, but she resented being taken for granted.

"So what's this gig?" one of Crully's guys asked, a sneer on his face, like Viper wouldn't know a good score if he tripped on one.

Viper pulled himself up to his full height of hard muscle, as short as that actually was. "I'm about to take over."

"Over JJ's dead body," somebody laughed.

"Yeah. Probably."

"You and Frank and your twat gonna make that happen?" another of Crully's dudes wanted to know, and they all laughed.

"Me, Frank and Jason."

"Who the hell is Jason?" Crully asked.

And Viper explained it to him. "Just the biggest, baddest mutherfucking killing machine that exists, that's all. He was designed to take out anybody and everybody, got the strength of ten men, and he don't give a shit about nothing. Even JJ's scared shitless of 'im."

"If he's such a bad mofo," Crully said, curled fists on his hips, "what's to say he won't take you out?"

"'Cause I got a heads-up on how to control him," Viper said. It wasn't true, but he had to convince them somehow. He knew he'd need help getting rid of JJ.

He told them a few more things that Blister had told him and ended with, "So, we get this guy outta the basement, program him to do what we tell him, and the first thing we tell him is to terminate JJ. You in for fifty percent, Crully? Your boys, my boys; we share the rule?"

Crully thought about it for barely a second. "Sure, I'm game for half."

Viper knew this was total bullshit on Crully's part. The dumb ass probably figured that once they found Jason, Crully would start by having him take out Viper. Or maybe Crully and his boys would do that. But Viper had his own plans, and they involved getting rid of Crully at just about the same time he got rid of JJ.

"Then let's hit it," Viper said good-naturedly, waving them to follow as he started up the path.

They continued toward the Military Complex, meeting more of the cons en route, until they had a party of close to forty men. Once they arrived at the complex, Viper saw that what Blister had said was true; the ground had caved in around the structure and the floors beneath the ground floor were buried. When Viper had fled from the Military Complex earlier, he had no idea that there were floors below ground. Viper had figured that the ground floor was it, the piles of dirt around it a mess because nobody took care of anything but the prison. The freed convicts saw that the dirt looked weird, kind of newly filled in, but Frank or somebody figured it was from when the Sling hit the biosphere. Now that they knew about the cave-in, the look of the ground surrounding the Military Complex made sense. Total sense.

"Okay, we shovel," Viper said. "You guys go in there and get whatever you can that'll work to clear out this dirt."

"Why don't we pull this Jason guy out from the inside instead of trying to dig him up from the outside?" someone asked from behind Viper.

"'Cause who knows how to get down there from inside? Anybody here know? When we broke out, the elevator only went to the ground. Any of you guys see anything different?" he asked Crully's men specifically.

A few head shook, and Viper heard a couple "Noes" and "Nopes" and "Un-uhs."

Then Crully said, "Yeah, well, there must be a way down from inside, even if we didn't see it."

Viper sighed. "'Member that time Andy and Osler was sent down to get a prisoner when the elevator took the wrong direction? They got down to ground from the top, hit metal, and discovered there was no way down from there. Well, why would it be different now?"

Crully thought about that for a minute. They had all gotten down to ground level from the elevator but it didn't seem to go any further. "Maybe when the damned Sling hit it broke through the building," Crully said, as if Viper was brain dead.

Viper figured it was Crully who had a few missing brain cells. "Okay, we'll send a couple guys in to see if there's a way down through the inside," Viper said. "The rest of us'll dig here. Between all of us, we'll find him."

"I'll go in," Frank volunteered.

"Me, I got a bad back. I'll go too," said Prat, one of Crully's men with a pockmarked face.

"Okay," Viper told them. "You two find a way down, you go get 'im, and you bring 'im back out here with you fast, *and* in one piece! Got it? And if you run into any of the other guys, send them out here with buckets and shovels or whatever the hell else they can find to help us dig."

Several of the men were already returning with pails and scoops they'd found, and two guys had shovels. They started in right away, Viper directing them to the side of the Military Complex where the windows lined up from the top floor to the main floor. He figured the below-ground floors followed suit. Jason had been seen in a window once

before. He thought it might be easier to find him
that way now.

Frank and Prat headed past the others who were
searching for tools and went right to the main
elevator which stood open. They stepped inside.

"Might go down from here, but you probably
need a key or a code or somethin'," Prat said,
pointing at the slot for a key card and the print
scan beside it. "You any good at hot-wiring?"

"Nope," Frank told him. "Let's look for some
stairs. There's gotta be stairs."

Prat kicked the back wall of the elevator as if to
punish it for not accommodating them.

They wandered around the massive ground
floor, although it was not nearly as large as the
top floor which held the prison. Against a far
wall they found a door—almost invisible, it was
so flush with the wall—and up close they could
see that the door was not meant to be conspic-
uous.

The door *did* have a knob, but it was locked,
and a panel waiting for a code or print was
placed near it on the wall.

"Now what the fuck do we do?" Prat said.

Frank looked at the panel for a moment, and
then said, "Fuck it!" Out of the piles of debris littering the ground floor that had fallen when the
Sling hit, he grabbed a metal bar that had broken
from the ceiling and used it as a crowbar. Quickly
he broke through the wall to find metal behind it,
and used the bar to pull the door away from the

wall. The door opened after a few pulls of the crowbar, revealing a way down the complex.

Inside, the stairwell was completely dark. "Could use a light," Prat said. He glanced around the room, not finding anything of use.

"Yeah, well, there ain't any I can see," Frank said, "unless you've got one up your sleeve."

They headed into the darkness. Frank spread his arms and felt the walls with both hands, which told him that the stairwell wasn't that wide. They moved slowly down into the black mouth, going forever. There seemed to be a good hundred steps down to the next level, maybe more, and Frank was wondering about what they were doing: heading down to find some super soldier in the dark, when suddenly Prat said, "Man, it's like we're goin' to ice-hell," and only then did Frank realize just how much the temperature had dropped.

It was quiet, too, and he didn't like that. He wished he was with anybody but Prat, who he'd never cared for, and didn't trust to watch his back. He only trusted him to stab him in that same place.

When they finally reached a landing, Frank felt around with his hands and feet.

"There's no more steps," he said. But he thought he felt a door. "Help me kick this fucker in."

The combined force of two muscled men managed to push the metal inward after a dozen fierce kicks. The door finally fell off its hinges, falling to the ground with a loud crash.

Frank stepped into the completely dark room carefully, not knowing what he would find inside, holding the metal pipe that he now would use as a weapon if he had to.

"There's gotta be a solar panel somewhere," Frank said. He felt along the walls on both sides of the doorway, his right hand touching what he knew was the scanner, which started to beep because his print wasn't an authorized one. "Shit!" he yelled in frustration. "Where's the damn light?"

Suddenly the room lit up from all directions.

"Holy shit," Prat said. "We just hadda ask, that's all."

Frank was so annoyed he spit on the floor. The beeping noise was driving him crazy and he took the metal bar to it, pulverizing the latest scanning technology with brute force behind his weapon. The beeping stopped as suddenly as it started.

His fury somewhat spent, Frank glanced around the room. White walls, high ceiling, fake wood floor, one tall slit of a window that was blacked out from the outside; dirt he figured. This level was large but not as spacious as the floor above. Every floor seemed to diminish in size and he thought that was a really weird way to build a building, since usually you wanted what was below ground to hold up what was above.

This room had been some sort of lounge area at one time. There were a couple of bars, lots of tables and chairs, all the comforts of a place to relax. Frank saw another door against the far wall, likely leading to more stairs. They had this place pretty tight, he thought. You couldn't get anywhere easily.

Prat had headed straight to one of the bars and was searching behind it to the sound of breaking glass and a continuous monologue along the lines of: "Man, there's gotta be some booze here. They couldn't have drunk it all and we know they didn't take it with 'em."

What an idiot! Frank thought. He glanced behind the other bar just to make sure nobody was hiding back there, or under the tables. Frank spied a couple bottles of liquor and found himself wetting his lips. It took an effort to force himself away, but he had a job to do and he wanted to get it over with.

"Looky here, bro!" Prat suddenly yelled from across the room. He held up four bottles of booze by the necks, two in each hand. "Fuckin' brandy!" he screamed, tearing at the seal of one bottle with his teeth to get at the cork.

"There's nobody here," Frank said. "Come on."

"Hey, let's have a drink first. We got time. Those guys are diggin' outside, we got the inside covered. Ain't had anything but prison hooch in… well, since I been in this sewer pit."

Prat had the sense to put down three of the bottles so he could dig out the cork of one and now he had that bottle upended to his lips, swallowing down as much as he could, stopping only to breathe. He then took another deep swig, and then he coughed and sputtered liquid into the air and puked up a bit of the booze and spit it out, and on

and on he went until Frank wondered if Prat's fat
gut would empty out.

"Come on, man, help me with this fucking
door," Frank called, struggling to get it open by
himself. The metal rod worked pretty good getting
down to the metal underneath, but he needed
Prat's muscle to back him up in order to open the
door completely.

Prat took his time joining Frank, and only put
down the bottle of brandy reluctantly. Together
they managed to get the door open and in the next
second, Prat grabbed up his bottle, offering it to
Frank, his face full of glee like a kid with a new
toy.

Frank stared at the bottle of brandy. It had been
years since he'd had a real drink. The shit they
bootlegged in prison was so vile that he thought
he'd lost a taste for real liquor, and he figured his
liver was shot by now. As Prat waved the bottle at
him, the rich, woody scent wafted up from the
bottle and entered his nostrils like a snake, curling
its way to his brain cells that instantly recognized
it from all the years he'd boozed and drugged and
had gotten himself into such a bad place that he
did stupid things and ended up in this fucking hole
on Elysium for a dozen homicides. But the
thoughts of his crimes left him fast as that smell
brought back other memories: good times, fine
women, nights being high and gambling and partying until he couldn't party anymore.

Before he knew it, he grabbed the bottle from
Prat's hands and had himself a good long swallow,

the fiery alcohol burning its way down his parched throat. He stopped briefly and looked at the bottle long enough to read the large print on the label, then had another big drink. Prat laughed, trying to snatch the bottle back from him, and eventually succeeded. But not before Frank had polished off over half of it.

"Fucker!" Prat said, staring at the bottle. He then took another drink himself.

Frank grabbed it back from him, and Prat said, "Okay, there's more. I'll go and get some."

Frank still had his wits about him and said, "Not now. On the way back. We'll bring it all back up with us."

"What? For the rest of them pigs?"

"Hell, we're the only ones who know it's here," Frank said. "We can hide what we want for ourselves and take up a couple bottles and those guys will be grateful that we found anything at all."

The idea made its way into Prat's brain slowly. He tilted the bottle to his lips again, drinking slower this time, staring at Frank as he swallowed. Then he passed the bottle to Frank like they were buddies. And while Frank let the liquid slide down his throat, erasing years in prison and filling his mind with all the good times he'd had and would now have again, Prat said, "Yeah, man, we'll sell it. You and me. We're partners. We'll make a fortune."

They hit their fists together, partners in crime, and had another drink each, finishing the bottle, to seal their partnership.

"Okay," Frank said, "we got to go down and get this guy and get him back up to the ground floor. Then you and me, we'll sneak back here and stockpile what's left."

"Got it," Prat agreed.

They headed down the new stairwell. Suddenly Frank remembered and said "Turn on the lights," and the stairwell came to life with white light. "Must be on automatic," he told Prat who nodded stupidly, licking his lips, not one to know about such things and was most likely thinking about the bottles of booze awaiting them.

The next level down, once they'd broken in, was a repeat performance in terms of walls, ceiling, floor and window. This room functioned as a dormitory of some kind, full of beds and night tables and little glass refrigerators full of things that had probably been sitting there for the last twenty years since the prison had opened. Prat was already in there, finding food, stuffing his fat face, while Frank headed toward the door on the far wall of the room.

They traveled further down, level by level, passing two medical laboratories, and a room that held weapons of all types. Frank and Prat spent some time going through the stock, outfitting themselves with assault lasers, pulsar rifles, napalm torches, grenades, laser handguns; everything and anything they could pack onto their bodies that the weight of the weapons would allow in terms of letting them move. As they armed themselves they decided to hoard this military equipment too, although Frank knew that Prat would tell Crully just as he would let Viper know about the munitions.

"Man, how many more levels are there?" Prat whined.

"I think we've gone eight," Frank said. "According to what Blister found out, there are nine below, just like above."

"Fuck, man," Prat said, looking tuckered out. Frank figured it was all the crap food he piled into his system, clogging his arteries. The booze probably didn't help much either. "I can't go many more," Prat whined again.

"Just one more," Frank said, although he didn't know that for sure. He just hoped it was so because he was getting pretty sick of this himself.

At the bottom of the next stairwell, which was narrower than the others, they reached a door that he hoped would be the last.

"Damn, it's cold. You think we're at the bottom?" Prat asked.

Frank didn't answer him. He had noticed the temperature lowering as they went down and now it seemed to be close to freezing, if not below. He, too, wanted to get this over with. "Help me kick this fucker in."

They put their all into this door, kicking until the fucker fell into the room with a huge crash. Even colder air rushed out to greet them.

"Lights," Frank said. But this time the lights didn't come on. "Lights!" he demanded. "Goddamn you, bring up the fucking lights!"

Prat moved close to him and his voice trembled a little when he said, "I don't like this."

Frank felt his own resolve fading. But something in him compelled him to say, "We gotta check it out. Hey! Anybody in here?"

He was met with silence.

"Nah. There's nobody here," Prat said. "Anyways, there're supposed to be nine levels and we ain't gone that many. There's gotta be more steps somewhere."

"You go along the wall that way, I'll go this way," Frank said. "Let's see if there's another door."

They parted at the doorway, Frank going left, Prat right, moving along the wall as fast as they could with only the light of the corridor. It was so dark Frank couldn't see his hand in front of his face.

"You finding anything?" he called out.

"Nope. Nothing," Prat said, his voice even more laced with what Frank suspected was fear.

Frank called out again. "Anything?"

The voice coming back to him was almost in his face. "Nothing." In a second they both stepped into the light that came through the doorway and shone on the far wall, bumping into one another.

"This is it, then," Frank said, and turned toward the doorway. "Looks like this is just a small, empty room. Nothing in here. Nobody."

"Yeah," Prat said, clearly eager to get going. "Let's go back up and hide some of the guns and the booze."

That sounded good to Frank.

They had both taken only one step when something came between them and the light from the doorway. Something big that blocked most of it. It had a head and, when it raised them, Frank could see arms.

"What the fuck?" Prat said.

"Hold on," Frank said, grabbing Prat's arm to keep him from saying or doing anything stupid. "Looks like our lucky day."

"You!" Frank said, using the voice he used in prison to get in the face of anybody who tried to fuck with him. "You the guy called Jason?"

Silence met his demand, and Prat said, "Hey buddy, we come to let you outta this hole."

Still, nothing. The man before them stood not only quietly but immobile, and if he hadn't moved his arms Frank would have thought he wasn't real.

"Hey!" Frank yelled, upping the ante. "We're talkin' to you!"

"This guy's creepin' me out," Prat said in a loud whisper, annoying Frank.

Frank felt the need for action. That was more his style than talking, which was obviously Prat's thing.

He moved quickly toward the hulk blocking the light. He got within a couple steps of him when suddenly the guy's arm shot out as fast as anything he'd ever seen. A hand hard and tight as a metal clamp grabbed him by the throat and squeezed.

Frank barely noticed that his feet left the floor when Jason lifted him; he only knew that he couldn't get air into his lungs, and that the fist clutching him was crushing his windpipe.

He flailed, struggling to pull the fingers away, and when that failed and his energy was giving out and the world was going black, he remembered the laser gun jammed into the waistband of his prison suit and pulled it out, aiming at what he thought was the face of this demon.

Jason squeezed even harder and Frank's aim went far and wide as his vision blurred. The heavy laser fell from his grip and all he could do was ball his fists and weakly punch at the face of his attacker.

Frank's fists hit metal. He didn't feel the pain. He didn't feel much of anything. There was no air coming in or going out. His lungs were about to burst. His head felt like it would explode. But out of the corner of his eye, with fading vision, he saw two things: Prat, the wimp, rushing out the door, and Jason's other arm, raised high above his head. From the light that shone out of the doorway, Frank could see the arm dropping fast. At the end of it he held a huge blade, the biggest Frank had ever seen. And he wasn't surprised to feel it slice him in half at the waist.

Prat ran for his life, huffing and puffing his way up the stairs, taking them two and three at a time. When he reached the next level up he slammed the door behind him, knowing it wouldn't hold since they'd broken through it. Sure enough the door fell down on the ground as soon as Prat stepped away from it.

He raced across the room and was about to go out into the lighted stairway and up another level when suddenly he realized that this was the ammo room and that he was well packed with weapons.

"Okay, okay," he said to himself, panting, sweating, about to pee his pants, trying to calm himself. Every cell in his body wanted to run up and get out of here, but he knew in his heart he wouldn't make it. He just didn't have the stamina.

His head swam. His stomach roiled and he bent over to vomit out the brandy he had consumed not too long ago. "I gotta take a stand here," he gasped, looking around him. He pulled out the flame thrower that he'd slung across his back in front of him. "This is the best place. I got all I need here. I'll blow the fucker away!" he screamed. "Yeah! Come and get it, mofo!"

But his words sounded weak in his ears. The hands that held the flame thrower trembled. He felt his legs go rubbery beneath him. He couldn't bear the tension of waiting and stalked to the open door, yelling down the stairs.

"I'm up here, fuckhead! Come and see what I got for you!"

All his life Prat knew he had been a coward. He got through life bullshitting everybody, and he even knew that most of them knew it. But he just never had the courage to fight. Bottom line, he was too afraid. But now, he knew he had to do something. The only way he'd get out of here alive was to take this guy out, right here, right now.

While he was thinking all this he heard a sound below him, like something hitting the wall or the ground, hard.

"Frank. Frank! You there?" he yelled.

Maybe this wasn't a good idea, waiting here like this. Sure there was ammo. But he had plenty on him. He could maybe fight better from up higher. The rooms were bigger and he wouldn't feel so claustrophobic. Yeah, waiting here was real stupid.

He turned and ran to the door leading up. It wasn't easy hauling himself up one hundred steps, and his legs were giving out half way. It's the damned weapons, he thought. He had too much ammo on him. What kind of stupid fucker packed himself with so much firepower? One laser, one flamer, that's all he needed. That's enough to take any fucker down!

Prat quickly discarded everything else, letting the weapons drop down the stairs behind him. "Yeah!" he yelled, moving easier. When he got to the next level, a lab, he felt winded but told himself that that was natural and he was lighter and almost there. "Just six more to go," he told himself.

He struggled up the next two levels, past the dorms and the other lab. By the time he got to the lounge his body was dripping with sweat and he had discarded his clothing and the laser gun, leaving him with just the shoes on his feet and the flame thrower clutched in one hand. It was heavier than the laser but he was old school and liked a heavy weapon. Heavy equaled dangerous in his brain. Lasers were for sissies, like Frank.

Frank. What the fuck happened to him? Prat didn't know, and didn't want to know. Last he remembered, the fucker Jason had lifted Frank up into the air by his neck, and Prat figured it was time to get the hell out of there.

Sweat dripped into his eyes. "You're almost there," he gasped, barely able to catch his breath, reminding himself as he entered the lounge that he was just one floor away from his buddies.

He looked around, his eyes focusing on the bar. It was like he'd reached heaven…

"Fuck, I'm thirsty," he gasped, knowing he didn't have much time, but staggering to the bar nonetheless where he'd left a couple bottles. He didn't have the patience to tear at the paper and get the cork out of the bottle, so he just bashed the nub at the top of the neck against the bar like he'd done as a kid and poured the hot liquid down his throat like there was no tomorrow.

He coughed and sputtered from the burning brew but drank more, his head swimming, his body about to pool at his feet. "Okay, I'm outta here," he gasped again, his voice only a whisper, and he took a final swig. "Just one more," he said, thinking about the levels, knowing he was one from the top. The "one more" had to do with the bottle, too, and although every instinct told him to stop swilling and get the fuck out of there, Prat found himself lifting the bottom of the bottle to the sky and finishing the sweet brandy off.

The booze helped calm his nerves, and when he heard a sound and turned and saw Jason's head as he reached the top of the stairs from below, Prat, courage renewed, figured he could take him. Until, that is, Jason stepped into the room.

Prat's automatic response was to raise the flame thrower, but his finger hesitated on the trigger just as Jason stopped inside the doorway. Prat had never seen anyone like this before, and he'd seen some pretty bad mofos in his life.

"Hold it right there!" he said, lifting the flame thrower to shoulder height. "I'm taking you to the top, so you just move on over to that doorway ahead of me and we'll go up and you'll meet the guys and see what's what." His voice sounded weak to his own ears, but there was nothing he could do about it. More than anything, he wanted another drink. But even though there were two more bottles right on top of the bar, he didn't dare lower the thrower to reach for one. Prat then thought that he could perhaps soften Jason with a drink or two, making it easier to persuade him up the stairs...

He moved the flame thrower down to chest height and, not taking his eyes off Jason, reached a hand out to try to grab one of the bottles sitting on the bar. The back of his hand hit the bottle and too late, he quickly turned his head and watched as it crashed to the floor.

"Damn! Fuck!" Prat spat out. And when he looked back up he was shocked to see Jason striding across the large room toward him.

"Stay back!" he yelled.

Prat hesitated. He was supposed to bring this guy up alive. "Fuuuuuck!" he screamed, and disengaged the lock on the trigger before pulling it.

A line of bright yellow and blue flame shot into the air before him, hitting Jason in the chest. The

metallic breastplate he wore heated to red. Jason
staggered back a few steps, his huge arms dangling
at his sides, one holding a huge knife.

Something in Prat registered that the blade was
bloody and Frank's face flashed in his mind for a
split second, but he couldn't worry about that
now.

The thrower was an older model, one he was
familiar with. It was designed to shoot flames for
five seconds, and then automatically turn off for
ten. You had to pull the trigger for another round.
He guessed that this particular model, if it was full
of fuel, might have six rounds in it.

Prat was no fool. He backed up toward the
doorway to the stairs leading to the top floor. As he
did so, Jason started toward him, the breast plate
cooling back to its natural color.

Prat pulled the trigger and nothing happened. He
waited and then tried again. Another blast of fire
shot out from the weapon, hitting Jason at about
crotch level. Again, the monster stumbled backwards. All the while, Prat backed up to the stairs.

When the fire died, Prat turned and ran, reaching
the bottom step before he figured he'd better turn
and blast this sucker again. He pulled the trigger.
Again and again. Nothing happened. Or, rather,
something did happen, but not what he wanted to
happen: Jason was heading toward him at a
furious pace and had considerably bridged the gap
between them.

Prat did not want to be trapped in the stairwell.
He knew he couldn't get up fast enough to escape.

He just needed this damned machine to send another blast out to give him some time.

Finally the damned gun shot out flames, and Prat noticed right off that it was a weaker jet than before. During the five seconds that the flames spurted out, he backed up the steps, and Jason moved forward. Even before the fire died, Prat turned and ran.

He got up about seven steps before he felt himself being caught by his hair and hauled backwards. He was yanked so hard that his neck could have broken, and he realized a few seconds later just how unfortunate it was that it had not. He still had the flame thrower in his hand so he frantically pulled the trigger, but there was no fire coming to his rescue.

Jason hauled him down the steps and back into the lounge. He dragged Prat across the floor like they were in the Stone Age and Prat was the bitch being hauled back to the cave to get fucked—something Prat had seen plenty of in jail.

"Fuuuuck!" he screamed, hoping to hell that someone would hear him and come down to help. He started to babble in abject fear.

"Listen man, there's booze here. We can go halves. Sixty-forty, your favor. I got the contacts. We'll make a killing. You need me, bro!"

It was only when they'd reached the center of the room that Jason stopped, dropping Prat onto the floor as if he were a dirty shirt or something. Prat looked up at him, staring into eyes so soulless, glowing red like death. Eyes that said "Nothing

Lives Here." And while Prat focused on the eyes, part of him watched the massive arm lift, and that knife—where the fuck did he get such a big fucking knife?—rise over his head. A knife blade so red, the red dripping, splattering onto Prat's face as it came down fast and split Prat's body from skull to crotch in two. Prat saw blood spurt into the air, then felt pain, then there was no more face, no more sound, no more Prat.

Jason looked from the doorway of the steps going down to the doorway of the steps leading up, back and forth, until he heard a noise. Then, by instinct, he turned toward one of those doorways.

Several of the men were already returning with portable speed diggers they'd found that ran off micro waves. They started in right away, Viper directing them to the side of the Military Complex where the windows were lined up from top floor to the main floor, the current bottom, figuring the below-ground floors likely continued the straight line. Jason X had been seen in a window before. He figured it might be easier to find him that way now.

"Okay, guys, we're down at the bottom," Crully said from the pit where almost all the guys were. Viper and a couple others had stayed at the top. Crully had pretty much taken over as boss of this project. Viper didn't mind letting him do the organizing for the Joe jobs. Viper wasn't interested in being a foreman, lording it over the laborers. He wanted the crown, where he would lord over everybody, including Crully...

Under Crully's direction, the men dug further, creating a trench along one wall which had a long vertical window that became more exposed as the soil was removed.

"Damn, never thought we'd get down here," someone said.

"Fuck, if I'm not tired!"

"Who's got some water?"

The fifty or so men doing the digging were just about at the end of their tether, even though they'd taken shifts, so Viper was pretty glad they'd reached their goal because he sure didn't want to be here much longer.

"Crack that window," he ordered before Crully could get a command in.

Two of the guys who had shovels began bashing the spade end against the glass. Viper knew it was the type of window that wasn't supposed to shatter, but this one had, somehow, and it looked like it had done so from the inside. A web of fine lines ran through the window, and it didn't take the guys long to start prying out chunks. Once the hole was big enough for a smallish man to climb through, they sent Tiny, the littlest guy in the prison, who only came up to about Viper's chest. He got through, carrying a low-level solar light, and ran into the room.

Crully called into the darkness that swallowed Tiny. "Find him?"

"Not yet, boss," Tiny said, and the "boss" part rankled Viper. He was losing control and he hadn't even gained it yet.

They waited for a bit before Tiny yelled, "It's too fucking dark. I can't see anything!"

Finally Crully sent in another guy, who didn't fit as easily through the opening. Another five minutes went by and Tiny appeared in the broken window.

"Nothin' in here, and nobody either," Tiny said.

"What?" Viper yelled from up above.

Crully looked up and around, giving Viper a murderous look, one that said if he'd been had, Viper shouldn't expect to make it to the next morning.

"He's in there!" Viper said with more confidence in his voice than he felt.

"Well, we can't see nothing, just where the light comes in from the hallway. Gét us a light, will ya?" Tiny said.

The second guy came to the window, too, and somebody tossed down a solar lightbox which was handed in to Tiny, who flipped it on and turned.

"Holy shit!" he cried out.

"What?" Crully asked. "What the fuck are you lookin' at?" He bent his head to peer into the window. Then he said, "Damn!"

Instantly, he pulled his face out and turned to the men who fell silent, including Viper.

Finally, Viper got it together and said, "What the fuck is it?"

Crully, for once, couldn't speak.

One of his guys asked, "Boss? What's in there?"

"Looks like Frank's in there."

"Yeah, and?" Viper asked.

Crully stared up at him with stunned eyes. "I think he's dead. Not just dead, but it's like there's two of him now."

"What the fuck you talkin' about?" Viper said, feeling a chill run up his spine.

"Somethin'—somebody cut him in two."

"That... that ain't possible," Viper said. "He went down with Prat and Prat ain't that strong."

Tiny said in a frightened voice, "There's some other stuff in the room, you know, like a guy might've been livin' down here."

"Maybe he went up through the building, trying to get out," Viper said.

"Then how come Frank's dead and Prat ain't brought him to us?" Crully said, his voice hard, his eyes focused up on Viper.

"Maybe they're on their way. Hey, Tiny. See if you can get upstairs from there," Viper called down to him.

Tiny, his head still poking out the window, said, "Yeah, there's a door and some steps. You want we should go up?"

"Yeah," both Viper and Crully said at the same time. The two glared at each other, and Viper felt dozens of pairs of eyes from tired men in the pit below also staring at him.

Crully assumed command again. "Tiny, you wait there. Send the other guy up."

"Look, they're comin' up through the building," Viper said like he knew for sure, making his voice stay steady and commanding. "That's what's happening. Prat's bringing Jason up here. I'm gonna go meet them and bring this Jason guy out here."

"Yeah, and if he's not there?" Crully said. "How do we know he even exists?"

"Because JJ knows about him. You can ask him yourself. Look, we're wasting time. Tiny, you go on up and I'm coming through the main entrance and comin' down. When we meet we'll find him, and we'll bring him out. You guys can wait here," he said to the others.

But Viper had no intention of going inside the Military Complex. He had a bad feeling about this. And he didn't want to be around if Jason had left the building.

As he headed away from the top of the mound, he heard Crully speak. "Tiny, stay put."

Fuck! Viper had already lost these guys. How the fuck did that happen? The first thing he'd have to do was have Jason take out Crully. That would be the only way he could be in charge.

Once he'd made his way around to the entrance, he found only a couple of stragglers there, and he sent them to join the others. Part of him thought he'd see Prat, but he was nowhere within sight. He knew that if he was going to get out of this alive, and not be beaten to a pulp by half a hundred angry, tired, sweaty cons who were in a foul mood, he had to get the hell out of there right now.

Viper looked inside the entrance, which was empty, and when he thought that there was nobody around outside, he headed for the dirt road. He trotted along it, checking over his shoulder from time to time. All the way back to the camp he thought about how jammed up he was, thanks to Blister. Blister. He couldn't get his hands around her throat fast enough!

Crully stood with his fists on his hips, royally pissed off. Viper, as usual, proved to be a fanatical fuckup. But Crully was also pissed at himself. He'd leapt into this without knowing all the facts. And Crully didn't give a flying fuck about facts. What enraged him was that Viper had, this time, sucked him in. How in hell did he get blindsided like this? His guys would think he was some kind of royal ass. A real fucking fool. It was hard enough to keep control of these dead-heads without falling into stupid schemes dreamed up by scum like Viper, a loser if ever there was one.

Crully wasn't about to forgive or forget. He was about to crawl out of the fucking pit, find Viper, and use him as an asswipe.

"Hey! Get me out! Help me outta here!"

Crully turned to see Tiny at the window, trying to jam his legs and arms through at the same time, his face a mask of terror. A couple of the guys nearby were laughing their heads off at him. Finally he got through and fell into the gully they'd dug. Now that he was out, Crully could see that his shirt and pants had been ripped and torn, and he was covered in blood.

"Wha'd you do?" Crully asked. "Cut yourself? And where's the other guy I sent in there?"

"Don't know, don't care!" Tiny panted, out of breath as if he'd been running, already on his feet, trying to claw his way up the mound of dirt that stretched nine levels. The guy was a wreck, shaking like a girl, just about crying. "Hey! You guys up there! Toss me a rope or something!"

"What the fuck's the matter with you? You think you can get up from here? Go through the building!" somebody said.

"I ain't goin' back in there," Tiny said.

"What the fuck?" somebody snapped. "What'd you see?"

"It's Frank."

"Yeah, and I told you he was dead. Cut in two," Crully snapped.

"Yeah. Yeah you did. But that ain't all of 'im."

"What's that supposed to mean?" Crully asked.

Most of the guys in the ditch had gathered around a jittery Tiny as he told them what he saw. "There's blood everywhere. Coverin' everything. When we got the light we could see it. And there was body parts, like a guy's been cut in pieces. We didn't know what to make of it and then the other guy, he knows Frank pretty good and says that's his hand, 'cause of the ring he always wears. Then I see Frank's face lying under this table, just his face, like it's been ripped off the front of his head or something."

"Holy shit!" Crully said.

"Whoever did this," Tiny said, "he ain't no normal guy. He's some kind of devil. Man, I'm getting outta here! Throw down that damned rope!"

Tiny started to crawl up the mound again, but the other guys down there with him were pushing and shoving and struggling to get out themselves, and it was impossible from such a depth. Tools and fabric dangled down from the few guys at the top to help, and guys boosted other guys making a human ladder that went up rather high. A couple guys from above held the legs of other guys who were dangling down the pit, and were able to reach Tiny who was at the top of the human ladder for one second, before the whole fleshy chain collapsed.

Tiny hit the ground with a thud. He ran into the waiting crowd of a dozen men flapping his arms like a beheaded chicken, and the group parted like a sea opening to let Moses through. It was as if they all thought that Tiny could lead them away from this strange situation they'd found themselves in.

The men who remained at the bottom surrounding Crully were tense as they saw Tiny finally get to the top. Then the guys at the top disappeared and word quickly spread that "They're getting out!"

Many of the guys at the bottom of the pit then tried to climb up the dirt mountain, clawing with their hands which was worse than useless.

Going through the inside of the building to get back up had been the original plan, and it made more sense than trying to get all these guys back up the dirt mound, but Crully didn't have the heart to try to stop them. Something was really wrong about all this. Real wrong. He felt it intuitively. He'd spent a long time in the joint, here, and on Earth II before that, and the air always felt weird and electric before the shit hit the fan.

Crully turned and headed inside the narrow window, barely fitting his bulky body through, packed as it was with muscles that had been worked on over the years.

Once he got inside, Crully realized that a few other guys had joined him. At least a dozen. They all stopped as one unit, stunned by the blood everywhere: the walls, the floor, even splattered on the high ceiling. And just like Tiny said, there was half a torso here and the other half there, and the face of Frank under the table like a mask. But it was his face, that was for sure. Whoever had done this was pretty damned sick! And strong.

"Fuck man, this ain't right!" one guy said, and the others agreed. More men from outside crawled in through the window, knowing this was their only way out.

No kidding, Crully thought, but didn't say anything.

The men—close to sixty of them—were getting out of hand, jammed into this small, stinking room, and he had to control them. They'd go up through the building, try to hook up with this

Jason dude, and then hunt down Viper and string up his ass!

"We're goin' up!" he said. "You guys wait here," he said to two of them. "I want to make sure nobody goes in or out by that window. The rest of you assholes, follow me."

They started up and the first floor they hit was pay dirt. Weapons. Everything from military to civilian and back again. Big mothers that took a couple guys to load and shoot; flame throwers and lasers for the individual killer.

"Hey!" one of the guys shouted. "I used to have this baby when I was a kid." He held up a kind of spear-throwing projectile missile, and one of the cons laughed.

"Yeah, Billy, we all had 'em in the nursery!" Most of the guys laughed, and that was good, Crully figured. He had the feeling that humor would be in short supply soon. Whoever had covered the lower floor with blood was somebody they had to watch out for.

"Okay, load yourselves up so we can get to the surface."

They grabbed just about everything they could wear or carry in their hands, and still there was a veritable arsenal leftover, as if whoever had stocked it had expected an invading army.

The next two levels up were laboratories. Most of the equipment looked damaged, smashed on the floor, partitions and monitors broken, connectors ripped out and flung every which way, like some madman had been through there.

A few more levels and they hit a lounge. Guys ran in all directions, pulling bottles out from behind bars, and cupboards over the bars, yelling and screaming like they were at a party. Crully wouldn't have minded but for the blood. And the butchered body that he recognized as Prat. Fuck, the guy was cut to ribbons! When they first entered the lounge and saw it, several seconds of eerie quiet settled over all of them. They were spooked. Crully was pretty wildly spooked himself. Now, those guys were going nuts.

"We got another two floors," Danny said to him.

"Yeah, well, let these bozos have a few belts, then we head up. I want to find this Jason, if he exists. And I sure as hell want to find Viper!"

Danny grinned, the gaping hole from a tooth he'd lost in a fight a constant reminder that these guys were nothing if they weren't wildcards. Booze would loosen them up. But it would also make them crazy. Crully didn't mind either one, or both. He wanted their loose, crazy energy available. Whoever or whatever responsible for all this blood and these body parts needed taking out, and to do that, his guys had to be half loaded.

Crully headed for one of the bars and snagged himself a bottle of Jack Daniels. The whiskey scorched his throat, but it was a good fire, one he'd missed. He drank like a man parched, until he had downed half the bottle, then wiped his mouth with the back of his hand.

"Okay, guys, we're heading up," he called, turning to the door.

Standing in the doorway was one big mutherfucker. The guy was a giant, mostly covered in metal. If the shape of the metal was any indication of the muscles underneath… fuck!

The men slowly became quiet as they turned, sizing up the intruder, mainly to assess if they could take him out. Crully glanced around him and from the looks on the guys' faces, he gauged that no one thought they could.

He slammed his bottle onto the bar to get the big guy's attention. Hell, to get the attention of all of them. This would be his show. He wanted to make sure it went his way.

"You the fucker made this mess?" he asked, his tone as threatening as he could make it, and there wasn't a guy in this room that didn't tremble a little. Crully knew he was capable of anything, and so did everybody else.

When the guy didn't answer, Crully lifted the assault laser he had snagged down below loaded with ten clips. Each clip held one atomic pellet that would lodge inside whoever it struck, burst open, and clean out those insides like a nuclear explosion limited to one.

Every guy in the room raised one of the weapons he had snatched at the same time, so it became a face-off, roughly fifty to one. The asshole in the doorway didn't have any weapons on him, but he didn't even flinch.

"Get your ass in here, mutherfucker!"

Still no response. Then, suddenly, this Jason guy stomped into the room. Crully and everybody else saw the big knife or whatever in his hand, and some of the guys laughed. Firepower! That's where it was at, not old-fashioned metal. At least the guy had the sense to know that and was obeying Crully.

Jason kept moving directly toward Crully, who said, "That's far enough!" but the guy kept coming. "Stop, or you're a dead fucker!" He kept coming.

Crully pulled the trigger and blasted him with one round that hit the metal chest plate and bounced off. The atom bullets were not as hard as other bullets because they had to be eroded from within the shell—that was one of their drawbacks—but once they lodged inside a victim they were a hundred times as powerful as anything else.

The bullet bounced onto the floor. It started to glow red. "Fuck!" somebody yelled, and the guys began to scatter, some running to the stairs that went down, others running to the ones that headed up.

Crully would have run too, but when he turned, Jason had him. The big fucker swung that knife like a crazy man, the blade hacking at guys as they raced past, lopping off heads, arms, cutting through the middle, down the middle, up from the middle, cross ways and catty-corner.

Blood began spurting through the air in all directions, and the room filled with the sound of guys screaming. Crully's back was to Jason because he'd turned to run back to the stairs going down, but that massive paw had caught him by the seat of his pants and hauled him backwards.

He struggled to get another weapon out, one that would fire fast and repeatedly, not like the damned atom assault laser that needed too much time to reload, and which he dropped to the floor as useless.

His movements got his arm chopped off at the elbow. Blood gushed out of him as he struggled to get away, and he clamped his other hand over the wound, but the iron grip the guy had on him couldn't be loosened.

Crully let go of his wounded elbow so he could pull out a small handheld laser with his left hand, his only hand, but he couldn't get turned around enough to fire, so he shot under his severed arm. His body twisted at the last second and he hit his own armpit, sending a blast of searing laser from his underarm to his back, and he screamed.

Most of the guys had scattered, and the three who remained to "help" him suddenly ran for their lives. Jason caught them, sticking them through the chest, the groin, the eyeball; everywhere he could stick them with that impossibly sharp quadruple-size knife.

Despite the excruciating pain, Crully tried again, with a shaking hand, to shoot the laser behind him, but the beam went wild around the room.

Danny, still standing, his eyes wild with fear, fired a direct hit at Jason at about face level. Surely some of that firepower would hit the eyes behind the mask, Crully thought. It should stop the bastard. It should lessen his grip.

And it did. For about two seconds. It was enough time for Crully to spin himself around to face this demon. As he spun, he pointed the laser at where he hoped the eyes would be, and was immediately mesmerized by the sight of something very strange. It was like there was some kind of mechanism inside Jason that was repairing the damage to his eyes even as Crully watched.

But he didn't watch for long. He pointed to fire.

The blade, as if by instinct, chopped off his other arm. With his finger on the trigger, the laser beam flashed around the room as it fell to the ground.

Out of the corner of his eye, Crully watched Danny flee down the stairs, and now Crully was alone with Jason and the atom bullet that was already seeping material that would blow this place sky high because it was on a floor and not inside someone's body!

When Crully turned his head back up, Jason was staring at him, his eyes pure evil and full of hate. Crully was bleeding out at both arms, and suddenly Jason dropped him onto the floor, on top of the fucking atom bullet, and stood for another moment as if watching the vitae gush from Crully's arms. It was like he was waiting to see what would happen next.

Crully was weak, but he knew he had to get off that bullet. He tried to move himself with the short stumps that remained of his arms, and then tried to dig the toes of his boots into the floor to shove himself away and turn himself over, but he didn't have the strength, and the pain became his entire focus but for one thought: move off the damned bullet!

Suddenly, he was alone in the room. Even Jason was gone. He heard screams, though, and knew the mother of all killers had gone up or down and had found some of Crully's guys and was taking them out in the most gruesome ways.

But Crully had his own problems. The bullet was moving toward his flesh and blood, what it had been built to do. This was why it was such a desirable weapon, limited though it was in other ways. If it got near your body it would enter like an iron filing drawn into a fleshy magnet, and Crully could feel it inside his chest already. His body trembled in terror.

The atomic stew burned its way through him and he would soon become a little nuclear explosion of one.

Suddenly the burning intensified. He ignited from within, like a spontaneous combustion. As his body burst into a zillion pieces, he stupidly could only think about the walls of this lounge: what a paint job!

Jason stomped down into the bowels of the Military Complex. He overtook the men he found as if they were ants, crushing them underfoot, pounding the life out of them with his fists. His machete arm flailed in every direction, and he cut to bits all in his path. Blood sprayed and gushed and spattered and coated everything. Body parts flew into the air, or crunched under his feet, making the floor slippery for the men still running away, but not for Jason.

Methodically he went through each room, taking the men as he came to them. Whether or not they resisted mattered not at all to him.

As the rooms became smaller, and the men had nowhere to hide, they pleaded, and charged, and ran like crazy and did all the things they usually did when he raised his machete. His vision coated in red blinded him to all but the necessity of stopping everything that stepped in his path.

Finally he reached the place that had been his home for so long, that had kept him imprisoned. It was empty of living beings. Just the dead now. He crashed through the window to get to the pathetic insects struggling to climb up the hill of dirt and avoid his machete, but they could not.

He sliced and stabbed and cut one after the other, filling the mound with bodies and parts, soaking the soil in blood. And when all of them were gone, he stopped a moment to listen at the window. He heard nothing up through the building. No one. But he could hear them up above, at ground level.

Stepping on the slippery bodies, he climbed the mound of them as if they were a fleshy ladder. And then he used the building wall, creating a ladder as his fingers pushed through technology's most advanced materials, making finger and toe holds. He hauled himself up until he was high enough, and then he leapt to the surface.

Men ran, screaming in all directions, some yelling, "We gotta stick together!"

Another said, "Fuck that!"

Jason went after them. Those who had followed the advice of the first, he found together, and used the blade to bind them in twos and threes to the earth, cutting off two or three heads at once, and slicing several bodies at the middle, until they were all dead.

Then he went after the others, one by one. The first he sliced from behind, up the middle, parting him into two. His machete hit the back of the head of the next guy, going through the skull and then lopping it away from the body horizontally, until the guy toppled forward and stopped moving. The third victim fell forward as Jason hit him on the legs.

The screaming never bothered him. In fact, it made no impression. Nothing did. He would not stop until he had killed every last one of them. Until the last breath of life was gone gone gone. That was his goal, his only goal. And he hacked and sliced and diced all living, breathing beings in his path, sensing them by instinct, until the ground was red, the air putrid and the bodies lay rotting about him.

And then he headed down the dirt path to follow the scent of those still living.

TWELVE

Viper got back to the camp to find the bonfire burning low and the place deserted. At least it seemed empty at first glance. He checked a couple of the cabins, including the one where the geeks had been held. He also tried the store and the Lab. Nobody. Following the breadcrumbs, so to speak, he saw footprints in the dirt that told him every-body had gone in the same direction.

He strode quickly up the path toward the lake, calling as he went.

"Hey! Anybody here?" he yelled, for maybe the tenth time.

Nothing, not even the AI that was supposed to answer. He stopped for a minute and listened. He could hear talking, and saw smoke drifting up in the distance on the other side of the lake, and headed around the large body of water.

Damned artificial world, Viper thought as he trudged around the lake. This whole damned place annoyed him. He didn't mind a session in a virtual reality lab. Back when he'd been a free man he used to hit the arcades regularly. Some of those virtual babes had three tits! And their flesh felt pretty damned real to him. But this place, it was all false. He didn't know if he was stepping on real ground or imaginary ground or what. He did know that everything he was seeing, except maybe the cabins and a couple other buildings, was just an image, some of it floating in the air.

Some of it was pretty good: the trees, the lake. If you looked close enough, you could see through to the other side. It all just made him mad; this and that jackpot at the Military Complex. Man, was he in trouble! Whoever this Jason guy was, he'd either left the Military Complex already, or he'd been killed when the soil covered up the bottom half of the building. Either way, Viper didn't deliver to Crully, and he knew the price he'd pay for that. And it was all that bitch Blister's fault!

When he got to where everybody was sitting, he was astonished. It was like some damned campfire, everybody sitting around it all cosy and everything. What the hell? The guys were there, and those fucking kids, including the hot little blind one. And Blister, looking all smug and comfortable… Well, he'd fix that real fast.

JJ noticed him and said, "Viper, where you been?"

"Around. Took a walk."

"Sit."

Viper thought it might look suspicious if he dragged Blister away first thing, but he did toss her a look that said, "You're Gonna Get It." He grinned at the fear in her eyes.

He took a seat next to the blind girl. She moved away from him like he was poison. He was just reaching out for her when that bitch Amanda said, "Don't!"

"Fuck off!" he said, shaking his head and looked at the water. What in hell was going on here?

"I'm telling them about this place," JJ said. "Listen up."

"It was set up by Castillo, in conjunction with the military. This lake is a holo replica of a lake on the original Earth that existed around the year 1980. They named this one after the original: Crystal Lake. This lake has a lot to do with Jason. He was born near it, and some bad shit happened to him near and in this lake."

"So there is a Jason!" Viper said.

"That's right." JJ gave him a look as if to ask, "How did you know about him, since you just got here?" Viper watched him glance at Blister, too, and could tell from the stupid way she sucked on her fingertips that JJ knew something was fishy, but he didn't say anything.

"The lake on the original Earth is connected to Jason. When he was mortal—"

"What do you mean 'when?'" Brad asked.

"Look, if the guy was alive in 1980 and he's still around, then he's not exactly human anymore, is he?" JJ said.

"Point taken," Brad said.

"Back on original Earth when Jason was mortal, he had a lot of bad shit happen to him, and around him. From what we found out after Castillo died, this Jason led a pretty twisted life. He had a mother from hell, and started killing people from a young age. And the number of attempts on his life, well, let's just say it's about equal to the number on mine. But at least those close to me haven't tried to take me out." He looked at Amanda, who smiled, and then turned to Viper, who did not smile.

"Anyway, when they set up Moon Complex it was totally around the project Castillo was working on, to create the perfect killing machine. None of us who were hired on at the camp knew about that, of course. Amanda and me were young, full of enthusiasm and energy, in charge of a lot of the camp including the girls who were here as campers, and by the time we found out there was something else going on, it was too late.

"Castillo was able to resurrect Jason with the help of the AI Major Tom which became the brain that ran the body, if you want to think of it that way. Then, when everything went to hell, Jason killed Castillo. I think what you guys said today makes sense," he nodded at Free and the others. "You haven't heard from your AI because it's still communicating with the original AI, which, it looks like, created another Jason. Even if AI number one's programming was cleaned out and chips were removed like your guy Jackson told you, there's still Jason number two, and somebody or something is running his program. My guess is that it's your AI."

"But I keep saying, and nobody is listening," Lynda said, her voice tight with fear. "The one I saw was in the basement. You guys saw it," she said to Free and Skye.

"Yeah, we did," Free said.

"And if the basement is buried, we don't have anything to worry about, do we?"

"If it's still buried," JJ said, "then there's nothing to worry about, except for the AI. At the very least, the AI is, or was, our link out of here."

"Hey!"

They all turned at the intrusion. About twenty men made their way toward the circle. They all wore prison garb but were very dirty, as if they'd been digging in soil. All of them looked angry, and some held tools as if they were weapons.

The guy at the front that JJ knew as Tiny started running forward and yelling, "Viper, you're gonna get skewered, you sonofabitch! Making us dig out that fucking building with Frank and maybe Prat inside, or what was left of 'em!"

Viper was on his feet running with Tiny close behind. Maybe six of the twenty or so guys accompanying Tiny went after Viper. The rest of them reached the campsite and jumped on whoever was there, yelling and screaming at the top their lungs. It was worse than any prison riot, JJ thought, because there were civilians here.

Some of the men went for the women first. Lynda had started running and was brought down like a gazelle by a lion. Anyar sat frozen in terror and soon one of them was on her, pawing at her body and face.

Resistance, she thought, is futile, seeing in shadow form the crowd surrounding them, and hearing the screams and grunts and curses and watching them fight like animals. She crawled into her own world, one that was safe, and the external world dimmed.

Free pulled Skye to him and covered her with his body and for a moment they seemed to be ignored, as if they were encased in a bubble. Or dead. Then, suddenly, he was kicked in his lower back so hard that the wind was knocked out of him. He fell into Skye, groaning, falling on top of her and pinning her underneath him. Skye reached out from under Free's body and grabbed the foot of the kicker as he struck again. She pulled and then pushed and threw the guy off balance and brought him down. Before he could move, she shoved Free off her, and her hand found a non-virtual rock which she used to bash the convict until he stopped moving.

JJ took on a couple of them, guys he knew he could beat down fast, to level the odds. His men went one on one with the others. Amanda struggled, as did Blister. They were used to these guys: how they were, how they acted, what to do to help themselves when attacked. It flashed into JJ's mind that if these kids had been fighters, they might have been evenly matched with the fifteen or so still standing, but they weren't. They just served as temporary distractions.

JJ hit one guy in the face while another jumped on his back, punching him in the side. He flipped that dude and stomped on his head.

Brad was caught: help Lynda or escape. He didn't know what to do. Finally, her screams got to him. He found a log and used it on the back of the gorilla attacking Lynda, whose skirts were up and whose underwear was down. Brad had to hit the guy half a dozen times before he fell.

He grabbed Lynda's hand and pulled her to her feet. She sobbed uncontrollably but he pulled her along, out of the fray. As they ran around the lake he said, "We'll get stuff from our cabin, some food, and hide." It was all he could think to do.

Herbert was or wasn't as lucky as the others. He had taken a step, paralyzed with fear, and had been knocked off his feet instantly by a guy running past. His body flew a couple meters before he fell. His head hit a rock and he went unconscious.

Anyar endured the brutality of being raped. Her mind went to her family's gardens back home, and the place she loved to sit under the flowering lilac tree. It was as if she didn't notice what was happening to her body. It was, she thought, one of the advantages of being blind. Her imagination had soared at an early age out of necessity, and now it came to the rescue of her soul.

While Amanda and Blister fought off two guys, JJ staggered around the camp, throwing men to the ground and kicking the shit out of them. He had learned early in prison to take your best shot first, because you might not get a second. Three of his five guys were on the ground and bloody and looked like they might be dead, or close to it. His other two guys were still standing, still fighting, and he figured they were doing okay on their own, so he looked for Amanda to help her. Just as he turned he saw a moron named Guy, who always carried a weapon, slit her throat.

JJ was not aware of how he got from here to there. He found himself jumping on Guy, throwing punches with all the force in him. The big guy with the braids went down, finally, to his knees, and then JJ kicked him over and over in the solar plexus and the stomach and the face. JJ didn't stop there. He lost track of himself, of time. A red haze covered his eyes until he had beaten the guy to death.

By the time he reached Amanda, she had bled out. Everything around him disappeared. He picked up the woman he had loved for twenty years and held her in his arms. He turned her face, her throat still seeping blood. Her sightless eyes stared at nothing. JJ, hardened from all he had been through over the years of brutal living, had not suffered any brutality equal to this. He bent his head over her body and sobbed.

Viper ran for his life. He knew that he was no match for six guys, but he could take Tiny easy. So as he ran, he laid a trap.

He reached a clearing that forked four ways, including the way he'd come. Viper tore off a shred of fabric from his con suit and hooked it to a tree heading along a path away from him. Then he hid behind a virtual boulder, curling tight so if anybody looked through the translucent rock they wouldn't necessarily pick him out—he hoped it looked like the rock had a pattern. Then he watched.

The six men hit the clearing at a run, brandishing weapons. "Which way?" one of them wondered.

"Fuck if I know," Tiny said.

"Look! He went that way. His suit got ripped." One of the guys held up the scrap of black fabric.

"No, it's a trick. I know Viper. Fucker'll snake his way around this somehow," Tiny said.

"I'm goin' this way," the guy with the fabric said. "It's where he went. And I wanna make that asshole eat as much dirt as he made me shovel!" He headed down the predesignated path, joined by all but Tiny and one other guy.

"I'm tellin' you, Eddie, this Viper's tricky. I think he's somewhere else."

"Yeah, I'm with you."

"Look, we'll fan out. You go down there, I'll go this way. He ain't along the road we came, and the guys went that way, so between us we got all directions covered."

"Yeah," the square-jawed Eddie said, heading at once away from the clearing.

Viper wondered if he should follow Eddie and take him out first. But that was risky. And he knew that if he got Tiny first, it would rattle the others.

Yeah, he'd stalk Tiny. And when the little dude was far enough away that nobody'd be able to get to him fast, he'd do him good. Real good. Yeah!

Viper felt renewed. He loved to fight, as long as he was winning, and this would be a good one. It was one fight he was sure to win.

Blister had succumbed to the charms of Bailey and Mohammed, two of the guys from cell block seven. What… ever… She'd been fucked before. Gang fucked even. This was nothing. It would be over soon, and then she could get out of here.

While Bailey and Mohammed went about their business, out of the corner of her eye Blister had seen Amanda getting her throat slit. Shit! She'd never liked the bitch, but hell, what a way to go.

The place was chaos, guys lying, bleeding, some never getting up again. The nerdiest of the geeks didn't look too healthy either, lying on his back, pale, lookin' like he wouldn't make it to daylight. The blind girl was a mirror image to Blister, except she didn't look like she cared much what the two guys were doing to her for an entirely different reason, like she was somewhere else. All the rest were outta here. She'd be outta here soon, too.

And then she saw him, and gasped.

"Yeah, it's good, ain't it, bitch? I'll make you holler too," Bailey snarled.

She tried to use her hand to point but Bailey slapped her arm to the ground and clamped a paw around her wrist, as if she were struggling, which she wanted to do, but not for the reason he thought.

The giant she saw came from the road that they had all traveled on from the campgrounds. He stood for a moment staring, but not at any of them. It looked like he was staring at the lake.

Blister had never seen a guy so big. She wondered if his cock was big too. And what he'd be like. Out of the corner of her eye she watched him as he made his way to where Anyar was getting screwed.

Anyar smelled the lilacs in her mind. Such beautiful flowers. She loved the color, the scent of the blooms. Every spring they came early and as a child she felt they had come especially for her, although her mother said that the flowers came early because they had to catch the sun before all the other flowers, so they could spread their sweetness and awaken blossoms everywhere. It was their job.

Dimly, Anyar heard something. Then, right in her ear, a yelp of pain. One of the men abusing her suddenly left her completely. Then, more slowly, the other moved away and said, "Jesus H Christ!"

She turned her head and saw, as she saw most things, a vague shimmering shadow. This was a large one, and beside it a smaller one, one that she thought must be a prisoner. The large image couldn't be a man. It was too big. Yet it was moving like a man. She watched these silhouettes, and it was as if they were dancing together. The large one moved one of the smaller one's arms up and down. One of them was screaming. Suddenly the smaller one's arm seemed to come off in the hand of the larger one. At the same instant, hot liquid flicked across Anyar's naked body. She reached down and touched it with her fingertip and brought that to her nose and smelled it. Blood. Something or someone had bled.

The small image moved away fast, the larger one stalking him, capturing him quickly from the scream she heard. She wasn't certain what she was seeing, wasn't certain she wanted to know for sure. It seemed like the other limbs were being torn from the body of the smaller one, but that couldn't be. No one was that strong. She only knew the one guy screamed and screamed, long and loud, and then suddenly it was as if he was bent over the knee of the big one and broken in two. The screaming stopped abruptly.

Anyar watched impassively, knowing that what she envisioned couldn't have really happened, although she was aware that her heart pounded hard, and she heard a roar in her ears that almost obliterated the sounds of violence around her. The enormous shadow moved toward her. What looked like an arm on one side seemed to be very, very long; much longer than his arm should be. Within seconds he was standing before her, and she feared she would be raped again.

In terror that suddenly zipped up her spine from out of nowhere as if her soul had split open, she longed to run screaming. But she knew that she could not and must not move. She looked up, hoping this giant would not hurt her too much. He did not move, and it seemed that what she hoped for would come to pass.

"Thank you," she said softly, almost a prayer.

His long arm raised high into the air, as if he were bestowing some sort of blessing. She barely felt the pain of the sharp cut at her neck. For a second she was aware of flying through the air, but it was as if she were light as a feather, and did not have her body along with her. Spinning, spinning, like a ball, growing weak, watching the scene behind her, the shadow bodies littering the ground, the big guy, and the shadow he walked away from, what looked like a kneeling girl, without a head. Then a miracle happened. For the first time in her life she could see! Just like anyone else. And while it only lasted a fraction of a second, like a flash of lightning, what she saw did not make sense to her. A girl, kneeling, without a head, the naked body with blood spurting from the neck, falling, pitching to the earth.

Blister wanted to scream. She struggled, trying to shove these guys off. For her trouble, Bailey just locked her body down, and Mohammed locked her head. She could only watch as what must be Jason cut one guy up the middle and tore the arms and legs and head off another. Then he lopped off that blind girl's head and threw it through the trees. And now he was coming toward the three of them.

Bailey got it first, that knife used from behind. It stabbed up and into him around butt level and lifted him into the air, off Blister, and he howled like an animal.

Mohammed didn't click in for several seconds and kept doing what he was doing. But Blister's hands were free now, and she shoved him away from her with her hands and feet, yelling, "Run!"

But he still didn't get it. He grabbed her and threw her onto her stomach and fell on top of her before she could get away. Blister was trapped once again.

She turned her head and saw Bailey up in the air, his body slowly sliding down the long, long knife, his face twisted in pain. Blister, who didn't usually scream or cry, did this time, and her scream echoed in her ears. She didn't feel sorry for Bailey. Why should she? But she sure felt sorry for herself and what she anticipated would happen.

Once Bailey had slid to the bottom of the knife, blood gushing out of him like water from a waterfall, washing over Mohammed and Blister, finally Mohammed realized something was really off.

Jason shoved Bailey forward and the blade cut through Bailey's back from chest level. Jason pushed him completely off the knife and Bailey split in two at his back end.

He fell on each side of Mohammed. The second he saw Bailey's bisected body, his lust faded.

Blister used the opportunity to easy out from under him.

She jumped to her feet and ran naked, glancing back briefly to watch Jason. The guy was a never-ending source of torture. He made his hands into fists and punched both of Mohammed's ears at the same time. The fists smashed through flesh and bone and brain, and blood and gray matter burst out of the sides of Mohammed's head, his eyes popping out.

Just as Blister entered the woods, she realized that there was no one left alive around Crystal Lake, or alive enough for Jason. Maybe that's why when she glanced back again she saw him focus on her. He started running, big, long strides, and she knew she couldn't outrace him. And there was no point screaming. There'd never been anybody to help her. There was nobody now.

All she could think to do was trick him. She saw a big tree and ran behind it. She was skinny enough that standing sideways behind the virtual tree made her look like a stick and hid her completely from view.

Jason was no more than thirty feet away but he passed her by, not sensing she was there. She held her breath and kept as still as the dead.

Once he seemed out of earshot, she headed back to Crystal Lake at a good clip.

The place was a disaster area. A dozen or more bodies littered the ground. Some had been killed by cons, but at least five had been done in by Jason. The ground was saturated with so much blood that the soil looked red. The blood had also reached the water and dripped down the virtual bank. One guy who had been gutted hung over the bank dripping blood out of his mouth like a cadaverous gargoyle.

Even the fire that Blister had built, that was still flaming low, stank of burning blood that had gushed onto the logs, and the stench was a new one to her. One she wasn't sure she liked much.

She paused to look at the flames: yellow, red, orange, all the colors that got her hot. Fire. That element that spoke to her, that she loved so much. She hated to see a fire go out. She absolutely hated it when that happened. Especially one she built herself. She took the time to place a few logs on the low flames, and as she picked them up she could feel they were dry enough to catch almost instantly. It would make a little inferno! One that soared and roared and fast! No matter how bad life got, there was always fire. It scorched away all impurities and sins in its path. Changing everything...

She took a step closer, feeling the heat warming her naked body.

Suddenly a sharp pain sliced through her back. She looked down to see the point of a huge metal blade sticking out of her chest, just under her ribs between her breasts. Then she was lifted up into the air by that blade, the honed edge cutting her up like a wire through a block of cheese as her weight pulled her down. Then she watched herself pitching forward, face first, onto the fire. She crashed onto the newly blazing logs, landing on top of those delicious flames as the blade stabbed through them, past the ashes and into the soil below. A foot clamped onto the back of her neck and she lay across the fire like a hot dog being cooked. Soon the flames began to eat into her stomach and chest and thighs, burning her deep, like acid. It was a searing, burning pain. Hotter than anything she knew. She had always liked it hot, and she liked the blisters the heat created on her fingertips when she lit fires, even as a kid, when she set buildings aflame and watched them burn just for the hell of it. But this was too much!

Blister struggled and screamed. Her body flipped around like a fish out of water, pinioned as she was through the chest where the stab wound ached and ached. Jason's heavy foot crushed into her neck, threatening to snap her spinal cord. She couldn't move away from the burning, and could only flap her arms and legs. And scream. She liked to burn a little, and then move away, but now she couldn't. She was stuck, cooking through and through, smelling her flesh toasting as fire changed her, making her skin swell and crackle like the skin of a chicken, and the muscles beneath roasting like a side of beef. The heat finally reached bone, baking in the fire that felt so hot it would annihilate her, making her organs melt and wiping her existence from the face of the universe. Cremating her alive...

Blister screamed and screamed, but no one heard. No one had ever heard her screaming. No one but Jason, whose big foot was like a vice insisting that this was a fate she had always wanted, and whose knife pierced her like a giant skewer that told her that she was doomed. He was the holder of her fiery destiny. She had always suspected that something horrible awaited her, but not anything quite as horrible as this!

Viper heard a bloodcurdling scream in the distance, one that sounded like Blister. Maybe it was one of the other chicks. Well, fuck them! Or he would, but later. Right now he had business to take care of.

Tiny made his way through the forest, angrily bashing back virtual bush. "Hey, Viper! I know you're in here. Show your ugly face, you pussy!"

When Viper was sure the other guys were far enough away, he stepped out in front of Tiny. "You lookin' for me?"

"Yeah," Tiny said, reaching around behind him for the knife he had stashed in his back pocket.

Viper laughed. "You think that's gonna make a difference? Who's the bigger man here? Much bigger…"

Tiny blinked once. Apparently in his fury he hadn't remembered that. "Just words," he said, as if to himself. "Anybody can take anybody at any time. We all know that."

"Yeah, anybody with the balls."

"You sayin' I ain't got any?"

"You said it, not me."

Tiny lunged with the knife out in front, like Viper knew he would and had baited him to. He'd seen Tiny fight before. Most guys who'd gone up against him never really had a chance.

Viper sidestepped the knife and at the same time twisted Tiny's other arm behind the little guy and got it behind his back.

Tiny tried to swipe behind him and it only took a second for Viper to catch that arm too. He bent it back hard and at an angle, dislocating the elbow, and watched the knife fall to the ground. Just to be on the safe side, he kicked his leg up between Tiny's legs, making the littler man howl in agony and double over. Viper let him fall forward almost gently and bent to pick up the knife. It was a shafter, the kind guys made in the joint outta whatever was handy, and this one was made from old metal that had been shaved and pounded to a fine edge.

Tiny's cry brought the other guys running. They stood at the path watching, not venturing forward, because Viper had the knife, and they all knew he was good with one.

He jammed a foot in the small of Tiny's back. "You guys, you dug real good. And guess what? There is a Jason, and he got out all by himself. He's gonna help us get control of these dirtbags. How many of you are with me; how many not?"

Square-jawed Eddie was the first one to make a commitment. The redhead was pragmatic, always had been, and knew that he should stick with the stronger side, not the weaker. He stepped forward and said, "Yeah, I'm with you." It didn't take long for the others to agree.

"Pussies!" Tiny screamed at them.

"Okay," Viper said, his foot still on Tiny's back. "Here's how I see it. We head back to the camp, snag whoever's left, and get ourselves a few hostages while we're at it. At least the chicks.

Then we wait. This Jason, he'll find us. Then we can negotiate."

Viper looked at the knife blade, touching the edge with his finger, seeing a layer of skin open but not enough to bleed. "Yeah, negotiate," he whispered.

"Sounds good," Eddie said. One or two other grunted in agreement.

"But first we gotta take care of business." Viper looked down at Tiny, still groaning from the dislocated joint. "No room for any weak links here."

Before the others could respond, Viper bent down and made a cut at the back of Tiny's neck. The smaller man cried out in pain. Instantly he stopped moving.

"You paralyzed him!" Eddie said, his voice an awed whisper laced with terror. His square jaw had dropped open like a box.

"And? Fucker had it comin'! Anybody disagree?"

The guys looked fearful, as if they were facing a deranged animal and had to be careful about what moves they made.

"We'll leave Tiny here. Maybe come back for him tomorrow." But Viper had no intention of coming back for him. Ever. He knew that Tiny would starve to death or die of thirst, whichever the devils of hell deemed appropriate.

"Okay," he said, walking away, "we're outta here."

He led the motley crew back to the clearing, only to find no living men. Or women.

"Holy shit!" one of the guys said as they all looked around. The scene before them was one of mayhem, utter and complete. The known world had been painted red and littered with corpses.

The little blind girl was there, or at least her headless body was. Too bad. Viper felt cheated. He should have fucked her sooner. And on the fire, all charred like overcooked meat, lay Blister, or what remained of her. Viper had a fleeting thought that her skin had all popped up like one big blister, and that was probably how she'd have wanted to end it. For a moment he felt… something… and understood it to be the closest he had ever come to a sentiment, and likely ever would.

Around them were others, some the victim of fights, clearly bashed and brutalized. But there were a few that had been cut and torn in ways that only a butcher could manage, and then only a butcher who was a giant with a knife like a machete. Viper soon realized that only Jason could have created the cut-up mess before him.

One body that didn't have many wounds was one of the geeky kids; the tall, lanky one that had practically shit his pants when he thought he'd have to go somewhere with Viper. Now he had shat and pissed in them too.

"See if that one's still got breath," Viper ordered.

Eddie turned the body over with his foot saying, "He stinks!" He then bent down and listened at the chest and held a finger under the nose while with his other hand he pinched his own nostrils.

"Don't hear nothing," Eddie mumbled.

"Bring 'im anyway. At least he looks alive. The rest of these guys don't. Maybe he can tell us how it went down."

"Who the fuck did this?" Eddie asked, taking for himself the position of second in command by gesturing at two guys to pick up Herbert. The two men begrudgingly lifted Herbert up by the wrists and ankles, both bitching about the smell.

"This here, gentlemen, is the work of Jason," Viper said proudly, although he had no idea what Jason even looked like. "Now you know why we need to get him onside fast. We want this guy workin' with us, not against us. Then the universe is ours!"

"You got that right!" Eddie said.

The group trudged back around the lake to the road that led to the cabins. There was no one in sight.

"Maybe they're all dead," Eddie said.

"Nah. They was at the lake and they couldn't've got away. They're hidin'," Viper figured. "Fuckin' afraid of us."

The others laughed as they strutted through the little village of cabins, chests puffed out, as if they'd done something big when none of them had managed to do much but get out of jail. All but Viper. Viper had just killed a man.

Viper searched the ground as they walked, looking for drops of blood, and he found them. "Follow me," he said, waving the others toward him.

The drops of blood led them to the door of a large cabin. Viper made a motion to the others to keep quiet by putting his finger to his lips. He pointed at the two guys carrying Herbert to put him down and to go to their left. He motioned two others to go right. That left him and Eddie and one other. He positioned the last two beside the door, out of sight, and then knocked and entered like he was on the run.

Viper opened the door and peered in. "Fuck, am I glad I found you guys!" he said, rushing in like he was fleeing from someone, or something.

Inside he found JJ, a dead Amanda, and two of the geeks: the one who ran the place and, he guessed, his girlfriend. Viper would run the place now, he thought.

"Anybody else get away?" Viper asked, as if he cared. Well, he did, but not for the reason they thought.

"Nobody's here with us if that's what you mean," JJ said. He looked beaten down. Viper figured that's what happens to a guy who falls for a woman.

Viper relaxed. His stance changed from one of a fugitive to that of a confident leader, and the tone of his voice matched. "Well, that's a shame, JJ. A damned shame. Seems I got a few people with me, though. Come on in, boys!" he called, and Eddie and the other guy out front entered. The four who had gone completely around the cabin to check it out came in behind them.

JJ figured it out real fast. Viper had survived. Maybe nobody else, for all he knew. There were another bunch of guys who should have gotten out of the Military Complex by now, and maybe they'd show up at any minute. Maybe he still had a friend

or two. But right now, he knew he was vastly out-
numbered.

"So, JJ, looks like your days of runnin' the show
are over. Looks like I'm in charge now."

"For now," JJ said.

Viper laughed. He strode up to JJ who stood up
for a face-off, but Viper had a knife, and he was
good with a knife. JJ was good with his fists. It was
no match.

"Sit down, JJ."

JJ sat.

"Here's how it'll be," Viper said. "We're gonna
find Jason and get him onside."

The girl called Skye laughed. "Good luck."

"It don't take luck, sweetie. It takes knowin' how
to negotiate."

The young guy said, "You can't negotiate with
him. He's not completely human."

"And don't you think I know that?"

"Then how are you going to make any deals?"
the girl said. "He won't listen to reason. He's a
killer. It's all he knows."

Viper laughed. "Everybody's got their price,
missy."

The girl shook her head as if he were stupid. He
didn't like that. He walked over to her and slapped
her good. The young guy jumped to his feet to
defend her and Viper slapped him too, so hard he
fell on his ass. His men laughed.

"While we're waitin' for Jason, we're gonna
keep you guys here. At least you two," he said to
the young couple.

He turned to JJ. "And you, well, I ain't sure how much use you are anymore. Maybe we'll keep you alive for now, just in case."

Viper was silent for a few seconds, obviously thinking about something.

"Once we get old Jason onside, we'll use the AI to call Earth II. Then we'll negotiate. So yeah, we'll keep JJ around. Maybe they'll find some value in puttin' him in the package, since they kinda wanted to keep tabs on you, right?"

The men laughed for no reason. Free and Skye looked as somber as they felt. JJ was just depressed, not having anything left to fight for.

"Eddie, put a guy outside the door. The rest of us'll have some supper and wait for the other guys. Maybe they'll have Jason with 'em. Oh, and we got a present for you." He nodded and two of the guys went outside. They came right back in and hurled Herbert into the room. He hit the floor with a thud.

Viper left the cabin followed by his small crew of cons, laughing. The door closed behind them. Free and Skye looked at one another in shell-shocked horror. JJ stared at the dead Amanda.

THIRTEEN

The second they were alone, Free said to JJ, "Look, we've got to get out of here. Now!"

"And go where?" JJ asked.

"Anywhere. But we can't stay here. You said there are other prisoners and they will be coming too. Not to mention Jason." Free stood, agitated. He went to the window to look out. Viper and his gang weren't outside, just the one guy at the door.

Skye had moved over to Herbert. "He's awfully cold. I don't know if he's in shock or what."

JJ said dully, "Lift his eyes lids. Are his pupils dilated?"

Skye did as she was told. "Yes, they are."

"Check his pulse. Best one's in the neck, the big artery."

Skye put her index finger to Herbert's throat and felt around for a bit. "I can't feel anything."

With a sigh, JJ got up and squatted down beside Herbert. With practiced movements, he placed his fingers on the artery. Then he placed a hand at Herbert's nostrils and his ear to the chest.

"If he's not dead, he's in a coma," he said, checking the wound on his head. He sat back on his heels. "Maybe we'll have two dead bodies to bury."

"Bury?" Skye said, suddenly angry with him. "Are you crazy? They'll be burying us, the living, soon enough. Free is right, we have to get out. Sure, they'll try to use us to cut a deal but—"

"There won't be any deal," JJ said, as if explaining to a child that Santa doesn't exist. "Nobody on Earth II will cut a deal. They don't care about me, or any of the other cons, and I'm betting they won't care about you two, and anybody else from your project that's left, if anybody *is* left.

"Secondly, the AI isn't around, in case you forgot. It, or the original AI, or both, won't be sending any messages to Earth II or anywhere else on our behalf. The machines won't be helping us; they're helping Jason."

Skye tried to speak but JJ held up a hand.

"And last but not least, Viper is going to kill us all. The only reason he's keeping us alive is because he thinks he can cut a deal, which he can't. When he realizes that he *can't* contact Earth II, or that they don't give a shit about what he has to offer, we are history."

"He has one thing to offer," Free said. "Jason."

"Why would they want him on Earth II?"

"They wanted him before. They'll want him again. Somebody on that planet will see the desirability of a super soldier. Somebody will think he can be controlled. Maybe the military... *Especially* the military."

The thought was sobering.

"Look," Free said, trying to sound both calm and reasonable when he didn't feel either one, "Jackson Mansfield will cut a deal to get me out. I know he will. And that means Skye and you will get out, too, I'll make sure of it."

JJ gave a sharp laugh: a short, abrupt sound that came off as gruff and cynical and laced with finality. "You know kid, you remind me of myself at your age. Full of hope and optimism. Did it ever occur to you that this Mansfield guy might be part of the problem?"

"No, that couldn't be. I've known him all my life. I don't believe that for a minute."

"Even if he isn't in league with the enemy, he might not get your message. There are people out there that just want all this hushed up, and if that means, say, blaming the AI for screwing up life support and gee, ain't it a shame that those six kids died down there with all those cons because the AI still had some corrupted chips, well... Don't be surprised when you're taking your last breath."

"Okay," Free said angrily. "Maybe I'm a wide-eyed innocent, not jaded enough, always hoping for the best, but it beats the hell out of being a depressed pessimist. All I know is that Jason is somewhere around here, there are more cons out there, this guy Viper does not have our best interests at heart, and we have to get out of here and hide and hope that we can find Major Tom and that he's not in league with the original Major Tom and/or Jason, and hope he'll help us send a message to Earth II. Because otherwise, we might as well commit suicide."

JJ just stared at him, as if that last suggestion was the most viable option presented.

"You know," Skye said softly, "I didn't know Amanda very well, but she was pretty okay to me and Free."

JJ turned away, and his voice softened. "Yeah, she liked you both. I could tell. I guess you two reminded her of us when we were young."

"She seemed like a fighter."

"She was. If it wasn't for her, I'd have given up in that stinking hole long ago. She kept me alive, kept me going. She helped me keep my faith intact in a pretty much hopeless situation. She stuck by me."

"Would she have wanted you to give up? Wouldn't she have wanted you to fight?"

"She would have. I know it."

"Then you should do it for her. Isn't that what love's about?"

Both Free and JJ turned to look at Skye for entirely different reasons.

JJ nodded silently.

Free could only stare at her, finally drawing her eyes to him. In that moment he knew she loved him. And he loved her. And he would do anything for her. That's what love was about.

"All right," JJ said with a sigh, as if giving in to the idea of fighting was taking the path of least resistance. "We have one guard. He won't be hard to take out. Where we're gonna go from there, I don't have a clue."

"I… I don't know either," Skye said. "The whole place is virtual except for these cabins. You can see through practically everything if you look hard enough."

"There's one other place that's not virtual," Free said. "The Military Complex."

"Yeah," JJ agreed, "and that's about the only place we can go."

"Maybe we can get the Sling working," Free said.

JJ stood, shook his head and raised his eyebrows. "And get catapulted to Thanos? I think I'd rather take my chances here for the rest of my natural life, with Viper and fifty cons and Jason."

JJ walked around the room, looking out of each window. "Nobody's around. They're all likely stuffing their faces, except for our guard. I think we need to get him in here. Skye, that's your job."

"Why me?" she said. "Uh, never mind. Got it."

She walked to the door, opened it and said, "Hey!"

The guy outside turned slightly and eyed her from head to toe. She took a suggestive pose so that her miniskirt hiked up on one side, and smiled. "Listen, I'm kinda bored. My boyfriend's sleeping, and the other guy's depressed over his dead wife. Wanna talk?" She grinned.

The guy licked his lips like a puppy dog.

"Sure," he said, "we can talk."

"Should I come out there, or you wanna come in and sit on the bed with me?"

The guy didn't look like the brightest laser ever constructed, and he glanced briefly at the store, where Skye figured the others had gone. Lust got the better of him and he followed her inside.

Free pretended to be asleep, curled into a ball on the floor. JJ stared forlornly at Amanda's body, his shoulders collapsed, head bowed, and little sounds coming out of him like sobs.

"Jeez, what a putz!" the con said, staring at JJ.

Skye sat on a bed across the room and patted the mattress. "Come on over here and sit with me."

The guy started over to the bed, but before he even got there, JJ, with the stealth and silence of a natural predator, snuck up behind him with hands clasped together for a two-fisted punch to the back of the neck. As the guy fell forward, JJ caught his head between his hands.

"Don't kill him!" Skye said in a panic.

But JJ did a quick head-snap and then let go. The guy slid to the floor, lifeless.

Skye's hand was at her mouth, and Free said, "Couldn't we have just knocked him out?"

JJ looked at both of them with disgust. "We need fewer enemies. Trust me. If you don't do them, they'll do you. I don't know how you two will survive the night."

He went to the door. It was still silent outside. "I wonder where the rest of the guys are. There's at least fifty more, and they should have gotten out of the Military Complex by now. Let's just hope we don't run into them on the way there 'cause I'm betting they'll be hungry, horny and hell-bent on trouble."

They hurried out the door. "What about Herbert?" Free said.

"We can't help him, and we can't take him with us," JJ said. "We'll come back for him later."

Free and Skye shared a glance. They both knew there might not be a later, and the chances of coming back for Herbert were close to zero. And Herbert might be dead by then anyway. They both also understood that if they tried to carry Herbert it would slow them down so much that they would all likely be discovered and murdered. Neither of them could see a way around it.

JJ led them behind the cabins and they walked parallel with the road that led to the dirt path, seeking what cover they could in the translucent virtual world. Hoping for the best. Fearing the worst.

Viper figured it was time to go visit that chick Skye. Far as he knew, she was the only pussy left, though he hadn't seen the body of that other girl who wore the funny clothes. He guessed she was probably dead like the others.

He headed out of the store, leaving the guys to further gorge themselves. He had just turned toward the large cabin when he saw that nobody stood guard outside the door, that the door was open, and he could imagine the rest.

Viper, angry as hell, opened his mouth to call the guys out here so they could hunt down the hostages, when he felt someone come up behind him. Before he could turn around he was knocked off his feet and was hurtling through the air, landing two cabin lengths down the road. He fell onto his shins, bruising them and his knees, and skittered along stunned for a couple of meters. When he turned, he knew what he would find, but hadn't really been prepared for what Jason would look like.

Before him stood an enormous being, massive in height, legs more muscled than any he'd seen, even on weight lifters. The guy wore a chest plate, forearm guards and a mask that covered his face, and none of that metal had even a dent in it. He had feet and hands more than twice as large as Viper's, and eyes that may never have reflected an emotion other than fury nurtured by hate.

Viper felt his sphincter muscle start to go slack, but pulled himself together as best he could so he didn't shit his pants. He held up a hand and tried to get a friendly smile onto his face.

"Hey! Jason, right? We been hearing a lot about you, dude. Waitin' for ya. You are the man!"

His monologue produced no reaction, no apparent response. It was as if he hadn't been heard. Jason just stood there, staring him down; no, glaring down at him, like Viper was some

insect that didn't have a right to exist and was in
need of crushing.

"Bro, we got an arrangement we wanna make
with you. I mean, a deal. We can get you just
about anything you want, even transport back to
Earth II. Anything. We got a plan."

Still, nothing. Yet it was as if Jason were listening, not to Viper's words, but for other sounds.

Viper could feel the weakness in his bowels
intensifying, as if he'd lose control at any second
and make a mess like he did as a kid. He got his
ass whipped hard by his mother just about every
day for that. He recognized that feeling for what it
was: stark fear, but he didn't know what to do
about it.

Reverting to childhood, he felt he needed the
support of guys around him who were tough and
could form a gang. He yelled in a loud voice, "Hey
guys, get out here! Meet Jason!"

He wasn't sure they had heard him. His voice
sounded thin to his own ears, as if it wouldn't
carry. But then Eddie appeared at the door swilling
back a bottle of vino, and absurdly, Viper felt
relief, just as he had when his father appeared and
stopped his mother from beating the crap out of
him.

Eddie's eyes almost popped out of his head when
he saw the giant, and the bottle lowered from his
lips. He stepped out onto the road and yelled,
"Fuckers, get the fuck out here!" over his shoulder,
and the rest of the guys ran out of the store duti-
fully.

"Hey," Viper said, "meet Jason. He's one of us, guys."

Eddie had moved forward, coming up behind Jason, who, by his relaxed body stance, didn't appear to have heard him. But Viper could see that the big guy was aware of everything, every sound, and all of them.

When he came up beside him, Eddie slapped Jason on the back, and offered the bottle of wine. "Good to meet you, man. Here you go!"

Jason turned his head slowly to stare at Eddie, who still held out the wine bottle. As Eddie looked up into those glowing red eyes that could not have been more inhuman than they were, the con took a small step back. Suddenly, Jason reached out to take the bottle.

"Yeah, that's it!" Viper said, trying to sound encouraging. A wave of mild relief washed through him, although his voice did not reflect that as much as he would have liked it to. "Drink up, man. You're among friends, and we got lots of work ahead of us. Work and partying! Yeah!" He punched the air above his head with his fist.

As Jason grasped the bottle, his eyes never leaving Eddie's face, Eddie wanted to take yet another step back; a big one. And then a bunch more steps back. He wanted to turn and run and get the hell away from this guy. The vibes coming off Jason were enough to make Eddie, who himself was a pretty big guy, break out into a cold sweat. But he wasn't gonna act stupid or like a pussy or a fag in front of the other guys—he had his image to maintain—so he held his ground and plastered what he hoped was a solid grin full of confidence on his face.

Jason lifted the bottle up as if to drink, and Eddie stared up, mesmerized by the giant's every move. But the big guy didn't put the bottle to his lips. Instead, he raised it higher than his lips, higher than his head, higher, like he was going to pour the wine on top of his head. With lightning speed Jason brought down the bottom of the bottle onto the top of Eddie's head. The bottle shattered at impact, and it was just a nanosecond before the fist holding the bottle slammed Eddie's crown, forcing his brain downward against the brainstem that pierced through the spongy gray matter.

Blood shot up and around Eddie's head like a fountain, splashing down to his shoulders, leaving only shreds where Eddie's head should have been. Blood spurted out his nose and mouth, out of his bulging eyes. Eddie's body stood rigid for a few moments before the former prize fighter went down for the last time.

Viper blinked rapidly several times. He couldn't believe his eyes. Eddie was about as tough as they came, and Viper had once watched him take out half a dozen fuckers when they ganged up on him.

The guys behind Eddie reacted by charging Jason, but Viper felt rooted to the spot. He knew he should join in, but this didn't look like good odds to him. Running; *that* was good odds, but his knees were locked, and his feet stuck to the soil, all because of the horror of what he was seeing, which he could not tear his eyes away from.

The four guys who rushed Jason jumped on his back, tackled his legs, hit him with whatever they had in their hands; basically pounded the shit out of him. And Viper stared in amazement as the giant's body began to wobble and buckle, falling to one knee.

Seeing this allowed Viper's heart to unfreeze, and he raced to join in as they pummeled the shit out of the guy, jump-kicking him in the head, in the sides, trying to stomp him to death. And while the giant wouldn't go down, he didn't get up, either. Jason's eyes stared straight ahead, like he was dazed, or like he was hearing voices inside his head or something.

When the five of them fell back from exhaustion, they started to laugh like hyenas, stomping the ground. Even Viper lost it for a minute. One guy opened his pants and took a piss on Jason's chest, and Viper was the first one laughing and calling out with the others. "We kicked his ass good!"

"Fucker, you ain't gonna cause nobody no more trouble!"

"Deserved what you got!"

"Asshole ain't so tough!"

"See how tough you are now!"

All the yelling was laced with madness, and the men leapt up and down, still sending the occasional kick at Jason, one guy jumping on his back. Suddenly staring into those fiery eyeholes, Viper thought he saw them flicker once or twice, and instantly he became completely sober, feeling alienated from the celebratory mood surrounding him.

Still, he tried to tell himself he should feel pretty good about it all. Yeah, Jason was beat. Beat good. Fuck, if they could hurt him so easy, he wasn't that fucking tough anyway, so it was all bullshit! They didn't need Jason. They had Viper!

But even as he thought this, something registered as being not right. He didn't know what it could be until one of the guys voiced what had been hovering in the back of his own brain.

"Wonder how come there ain't no blood?"

Even as the words were spoken, Viper felt as if his bowels had fallen.

"Internal injuries," one guy ventured.

Viper thought that there was no way that Jason wouldn't be bleeding. Unless, of course, he wasn't human. Maybe they hadn't even hurt him at all. And then in a flash he remembered what he'd heard about this guy, and how there was something inside him that repaired itself even as he was being injured.

As if synchronized to Viper's thoughts, the red eyes of the not-so-gentle giant shifted and locked onto Viper's. It was not the hesitant, blinking look of somebody coming to consciousness. Not the tentative glance of a guy who had been brutalized. No, this was a ferociously confident glare from the big guy, one that said he wasn't afraid of anybody or anything, and he sure as fuck wasn't hurt! Jason, in one smooth motion, leapt to his feet, like nothing had happened to him.

His machete had not been knocked out of his hand, and now that Viper looked at it he realized that Jason clutched it like it was a part of his fist; a deadly, sharp extension of his arm that might even be the strongest part of him.

Viper watched the other guys, still recovering from their extremely violent workout, slowly get a grip. They took up positions surrounding Jason: north, south, east and west. They were going to try and distract him, Viper knew. He'd seen this setup a hundred times in prison when a gang attacked a lone prisoner. The two in the victim's view would half lunge, and when Jason backed up, the guys behind would bring him down backwards. Then he would be dead meat.

"You're goin' down this time, fuckhead!" one of the guys in front snarled. He and the other guy in front stepped in toward Jason, each brandishing a makeshift weapon of some kind that had been lying on the ground.

What happened next was a blur, but in slow motion. And without being aware of what he was doing, Viper had already begun to back away.

Instead of backing up as the guys in front advanced, Jason stood his ground. He swung the machete behind him, and the guys behind jumped back. When he brought his arm back around, he did it fast, the momentum of the machete pulling Jason forward. Jason spun once, fast, in a complete circle. During that little "pirouette," as Blister would have called it, the deadly blade managed to slice every one of those four guys. The ones in front got it across the chest. The machete lowered as it continued around, and the two behind Jason were sliced in the stomach and the crotch, respectively.

The wounds were not superficial, but they weren't that deep either. They were, however, bad enough to show those guys that they were quite badly hurt. All of them. And that their best shots weren't worth shit anymore.

But like the lugheads they were, instead of scattering to the wind, Viper watched them react by heading toward Jason, even as Viper himself edged away.

Jason moved faster than Viper had ever seen any guy move, faster than seemed humanly possible. Still, he noticed that what looked like a tear on Jason's arm was bleeding, and that gave him some misguided comfort. The guy was human after all, or at least partly human. He probably had internal injuries, like one of the guys said. Maybe the armor protected him. But he could be killed. Yet even as Viper thought that, he watched the cut on Jason's arm closing, like something inside the guy was repairing him.

He saw all that just before one of the guys leapt forward, flying at Jason through the air feet first, putting his full body weight into it, making contact with his heavy prison boots. It was a move that should have brought Jason down, and he did stumble, but not much. The guy must have thought he was on the right track, because he ran back and took another flying leap. This time he got a bigger response, but not one he expected. This time that damned machete flicked through the air, cutting fast and furious, lopping off both of his feet. The guy screamed as he fell to the ground, blood pumping out of the ragged meat stumps at the end of his legs.

Nobody helped him. His friends were too busy. One grabbed at the arm that held the machete and instantly the arm lifted and the guy rose into the air. Another one of the guys tried to get Jason into a headlock from behind. Meanwhile, the last guy standing besides Viper went in for deadly punches to the stomach and groin, hitting with his fists, kicking with his feet, not fighting pretty, but knowing he probably had just one chance at such close contact.

Jason reached behind him with his free hand, grabbed the guy chokeholding him in his fist, hurled him over his head and sent him through the air. He hit the ground a hundred feet away. The machete arm still held the guy clinging to it like it was a tree branch over a cliff. That arm swooped down, the murderous weapon it held stabbing the puncher from one side of his body to the other, just below the ribs, about the same area where the guy was punching Jason.

The puncher paused for a heartbeat, staggering back a couple steps. The machete pulled out. The guy had turned slightly and the machete went in for another hit and stuck him lower this time, groin

level. In. Out. Then the blade sliced through the
lower body, chopping off both thighs at hip level,
taking with it some of the guy's privates. All the
while not one sound had come out of the con's
mouth. Suddenly, as he dropped to the ground leg-
less, a howl like a fatally wounded animal filled
the air.

Blood spurted from the arteries, mixing with the
slippery puddles that had already formed on the
ground. Viper stared at the pools of red, horrified,
frozen with fear.

The last guy was the one hanging onto Jason's
tree limb arm. He looked, to Viper's eyes, terrified,
so much so that he couldn't figure out whether he
was safer holding on, or safer letting go. Viper
could almost read his thoughts as they settled on
the idea that if he dropped to the ground he could
run.

Viper also could read the thoughts of Jason, and
he knew the killer knew what the dope was
thinking even before he did.

When the con let go, he hit the ground on his
feet and turned to run behind Jason. But that
machete was too fast for him. The sharp heavy
metal stabbed through his back, about heart level,
all the way through his chest, pulled out, then
back in, out, in, until the guy's heart was forced
out of his chest at the front. Pierced by the tip of
the blade, it pulsed in the air for a moment until
Jason withdrew the blade back through the body,
knocking the heart to the ground where the vital
muscle pulsed, leaving the shell of the human it

had so recently inhabited behind to drop like a leaf before the massive oak that had felled it.

Viper saw all this and more. By now he had backed himself away and was almost at the end of the cabins, ready to take the road to the Military Complex. Suddenly, Jason looked up and their eyes met. Viper felt like a mouse being mesmerized by a snake, and before he was consumed, Viper broke eye contact and turned to run for his life.

If he could just get to the Military Complex; if he could just get there... He knew the place like the back of his hand, at least the upper floors. He could hide. He could be safe. But his knees had been damaged when Jason had hurled him through the air and he landed on them. Maybe the kneecaps were even broken; they hurt like hell! He could not run. He couldn't even move forward, just backwards. He wanted to run. He willed himself to. But his knees refused to function, and instead of racing as his mind was doing, his body could barely hobble like he was an old lady.

Behind him he heard feet pounding hard on the ground, the sound drawing closer and closer.

And then stop.

Close behind him, he heard breathing. The guy was breathing. He was human. Why wasn't that reassuring?

Viper didn't know what to do. The only weapons he had were words, and he used them now, like he always had, to talk his way out of beatings, and usually it worked. Once he had learned speech, his

life got better. It became easier. And he let himself
believe for a moment that his words could work
their magic now.

"Okay, man, I give up!" He forced himself to
laugh, and raised his hands, like this was a
holdup. "You win. You're the toughest dude I seen.
Ever!"

He struggled with his knees, willing them to let
him turn and face Jason. When he did face the
giant, he lowered his eyes, not making direct eye
contact. He knew how to play the submissive role.
Roll over and play dead. Tail between your legs. He
knew how to offer up his ass for… whatever… He
knew how to survive.

"Lemme do stuff for you, man. Whatever you
need. You gotta have somebody to do the grunt
work. That's me. I'm your man. Your boy. Your
bitch," he corrected. "Lemme give you what you
need."

Viper tried to lower himself to the ground, but
his damaged knees wouldn't cooperate. Instead, he
bent over at the waist, like he was bowing to
the guy, thinking maybe he'd give him some pleasure or something, get him to chill out. Maybe he
should just offer himself up. Yeah, that was more
like it. He turned around again, dropped his pants
and bent over. It's what he'd seen hundreds of
guys do in the jail. What he'd done once or twice
before in his life, when he needed to. Just until he
got enough power to turn the tables.

Well, if the big guy used him, he'd still be alive,
wouldn't he? And then he could get the hell outta

here, get off this damned moon, couldn't he? Survival was the thing. Always had been, always would be.

He felt the cold metal of the machete against his skin and figured it was the flat side. Maybe the guy wanted to torture him a little. Shit! He might be cut to ribbons, even with the flat side. Well, Viper'd survived that too. He could survive anything. While he awaited his fate, he let his mind drift to more pleasant subjects.

Yeah, that little blind girl was a cute! He remembered his hands all over her. If that damned Blister hadn't interrupted him, he woulda had the chick half a dozen ways. She'd have been his bitch, or he'd have sold her to one of the other guys for something or somebody else he wanted...

Suddenly the cool metal left his skin, and Viper braced himself. Next thing he felt was a blinding pain that caused him to gasp and double over further, grabbing his ankles to keep himself from falling onto his head.

Looking through his knees he saw the machete blade had cut through his stomach and intestines, and had stopped inches from his face.

The pain stunned him. He watched in shock as blood flowed down his legs, coating them red. He didn't know how he could stand at all now. Any movement would make the pain that much worse. Suddenly the blade pulled back, out of him, and the wound at his stomach opened up like lips parting. From it, what looked like a long sausage emerged and dimly he realized that his intestines were spilling out, all over the place, down his trembling legs, onto the ground, gathering at his feet. In the midst of it all, his sphincter had unlocked completely and the intestines and blood were joined by shit, loose stinking shit that poured out of him. All he could think was he'd gotten the beating of his life. And this time it came from daddy.

Words left him completely. It was too late for words. All Viper could do was scream.

FOURTEEN

Like terrified lambs, Lynda and Brad had dug a
hole and crawled in. They were under their cabin,
and had been listening to every word, every grunt,
every scream; watching and seeing men being
stabbed, blood gushing, limbs cut off and flying
through the air. They had witnessed all that had
transpired around them. They had heard Free and
Skye and JJ, and Viper's threats. They had
watched through the latticed wood that covered
the opening from the ground to the small porch of
the cabin as Free, Skye and JJ escaped. After all the
violence that they had seen at Crystal Lake, and
then again watching Jason destroy Viper and his
crew in front of the cabin, they were left trembling,
holding each other, too terrified to cry or to make
any other sound. Their eyes were glued to the
monster that stalked down the road toward the

path that led to the Military Complex, leaving a dead Viper in his wake.

Time went by before either of them could stop shaking and make an effort to speak.

"We have to do something," Brad whispered.

"Why bother. We're going to die," Lynda said bleakly, softly, her voice hardly a whisper and laced with terror.

Brad tried to sound calming, yet he felt anything but. They had seen Jason eviscerate several men without expending hardly any effort at all. It didn't seem that a single thought went through his head. He looked purely reactive, as if the very sight of a human being set him off. Brad thought he must be like a dragon of old, whose job was merely to ravage everyone in its path by spewing fire that destroyed anything and everything.

"He's following them to the Military Complex. We can get out now, get ourselves some food—"

"I can't eat anything. I'll never eat again."

"You'll need food to survive. We have to get some food and water to sustain us while we figure out what to do."

"There's nothing we can do! Didn't you hear them above us? We'll be lucky if the camp isn't overrun with more of those escaped cons. And nothing is going to save us from Jason!" Lynda sobbed hysterically.

Brad was getting annoyed with her; really annoyed for the first time. "Look, Lynda, like they said upstairs, it's better to have hope than to not have hope. We don't know if we'll survive, but we have to try. And the first step is to get provisions because we might be hiding down here for a while. If we can keep a low profile, maybe we can eventually reach the Sling and see if there's a way to get it moving again."

Lynda shoved him away. "Are you crazy? We don't know anything about hardware! And the software isn't here, it's on Earth II. We can't fix it. Nobody on the Moon Complex can."

"Then maybe we can find the AI, get it working, reprogram it, I don't know, just do something, instead of whining about how it all won't work and there's nothing we can do. Get a grip, Lynda. Since you don't have a plan, you can just get with my program for once, or consider yourself on your own."

The look of horror that spread across her face actually pleased him. He was glad she was finally coming to her senses. All she did was bitch, and this wasn't a situation where bitching helped.

Suddenly, without a word, Lynda went to the lattice and forced it out and began to crawl up from the hole they had made under the cabin's porch. Brad went after her, relieved that she had realized that his way was pretty much the only way.

But when he got to his feet outside, he saw that instead of heading to the store—which would have meant stepping over dismembered bodies and dancing around the pools of blood—Lynda was walking the other way, toward the Military Complex.

"Hey! Where are you going? We're getting supplies."

"Not me."

"What are you doing? That's the way Jason went."

"I know."

Brad hurried to catch up with her. He grabbed her by the shoulders and turned her to face him. Her features were set in anger and bitterness that spoke of a control that would not be released, not for him, not for anyone. He stared at her, not sure if he was really seeing her, or maybe seeing her for the first time ever.

Lynda was sure Brad was out of his mind. There was no use hiding under the cabin with the virtual bugs for God knew how long. "I'm going to the Military Complex," she said. "I'll hook up with Free and Skye and JJ, and if there's a way out of here, we'll find it together. You're welcome to join me."

"But, Jason went that way!"

"Yes, he did. But the Military Complex is a huge building. I'll be careful, trust me." She turned to go.

"You're just going to leave me here? You fucking bitch!"

Lynda snapped around to face him, ready to explode with fury. "Listen, Brad, I said you should come along, but I can't force you to. If you want to hide under the cabin for the rest of your natural life, go for it. Me, I'll take my chances with the others. There's some safety in numbers, even small numbers. I don't want to be here when the rest of the cons arrive, because if they find us, it will be me who gets gang raped."

"You think they won't rape a guy?"

She sighed in an annoyed way. "Stay or go, it's up to you. I'm going to the Military Complex."

Brad felt whatever shreds of manhood he had gathered together dissipating like clouds in the wind. He had no way of forcing her to stay, or even arguing with her. Sure, he could let her go, but then he'd be alone and that notion terrified him. With both Jason and the cons coming at any second, he had second thoughts about hiding. Maybe it wasn't the best idea. What if they burned the cabins down? As he'd seen with his own eyes, those guys were out of control at the lake, and the rest of them would most likely be the same, or worse. They were capable of anything. He ran to catch up with Lynda as she strode down the road.

"Uh, shouldn't we take a less obvious route?" he asked.

"We can go through the bush when we get to the path that leads to the Military Complex. Right now, we know Jason is ahead of us. And if the cons are coming, we'll no doubt hear them."

She was right, of course. She was always right. Something about that bothered him tremendously. She had an answer for every problem and he wished that just once in a while she had the wrong answer so his would be the right one and she would depend on him.

"What about Herbert?" he said bitterly, just wanting to piss her off, to find a chink in her armor.

"We can't help him. No one can."

"That's pretty heartless," he snapped.

She just gave him a look that said: "If you care so much about Herbert, you go help him!"

The second they turned onto the dirt road they saw Jason ahead of them crashing through the bush, like he had been checking everything on both sides of the path. Strewn along this dirt path were bodies in black outfits, at least a dozen, cut to bits.

Lynda and Brad stopped abruptly and Lynda put a finger to her lips and quietly and slowly pulled Brad back into the brush that Jason had obviously already checked. Both of them squatted down.

"He can see through the virtual foliage, just as we can," Brad whispered to Lynda.

Lynda held her finger up to his lips this time.

They watched Jason stop and look in every direction as if hearing a sound on the wind. He paused a moment staring straight at where they crouched, but then his head turned and his body followed and the huge knife came up and sliced at more bush and he proceeded on his way.

Lynda motioned with her finger and carefully and quietly moved backwards, watching where Jason had gone, no longer seeing him.

Brad did as she did, and when she had reached the road to the cabins, she pulled him back onto it with her.

"Let's go," she said softly, running up the road toward their cabin. Once there, she pulled away the lattice and Brad followed her as she dived under the cabin. Once the lattice was secure, they both fell back against the soil, panting.

"God, that was close," she said.

Brad wanted to say "I told you so" but he needed to calm down first. He did notice that Lynda was sitting up against him, and he could feel her body trembling, no doubt out of both exhaustion and fear.

He felt that now was the moment to take charge again, while she was vulnerable. He also knew that him being "right" and her being "wrong" would only get on her bad side. Instead, he spoke in a reassuring voice.

"Once we're sure we're alone here, we'll get some supplies and come back. We need to dig out a better spot for ourselves, too, because we don't know how long we'll be hiding here and we should be comfortable. We'll get some blankets and—"

"No, we've got to get to the Military Complex!"

"What? Are you insane? Did you not just see Jason headed that way? Did you miss the dead cons on the road?"

"I saw all that," she said in exasperation, "but we can't hide here forever. We've got to find the others. They don't even know we're alive, so if they find a way off this forsaken moon, we won't be included. We've got to find them and—"

Suddenly Brad slammed a hand over her mouth and pointed. He had been looking through the lattice and saw giant metal-covered legs, not on the path, but coming toward the cabin.

They hardly breathed as they heard heavy footsteps going up the stairs and then walking across the floor above their heads.

To keep her from making even the smallest of sounds, even a soft whimper, Brad pulled her closer and put her head against his chest. He covered her head with his arms and buried his face in her shoulder. They trembled against one another like frightened children as the heavy thuds moved around the room.

Herbert, Lynda thought, is lucky. He's comatose. He can't feel this terror that threatened to cause her heart to beat beyond its capacity, or to just stop dead in terror. It pounded in her ears, pumping blood through her body at a terrifying pace. Never in her life had she trusted anyone else, and now her fate was in the hands of Brad. It had to be. She had no more ideas. Every instinct in her said to break through the lattice, crawl out of here and just run as fast and as far as her legs would carry her. To the Military Complex. Join the others. Safety in numbers... But her brain told her that that would be suicidal. Jason would hear her, and catch her, and... She didn't want to think about it.

As they listened, Brad wondered why Jason was up there walking around the room, in ever smaller circles, as if he were zeroing in. Herbert was still up there, maybe alive, and Jason probably wanted to do him in. Poor bastard, that Herbert. Brad hadn't liked him much, and thought him dull and pedantic and wimpy, but nobody deserved the fate that had befallen everyone who crossed Jason's path.

Suddenly the footsteps stopped just above their heads. Lynda began to tremble violently, so hard she feared her bones were rattling together and giving her away. Brad could not stop himself from trembling either. They were lost children, alone, frightened, with no adult to help them, no one to come to their aid. They just had to hang on and wait out the monster, until they could get away.

Jason took a step away. Then another. Brad was about to breathe a sigh of relief when suddenly the floor above their heads crashed down on them. Lynda screamed. Brad screamed. Hands the size of both their heads combined reached down and grabbed them, one in each hand, and hauled them up into the cabin.

Lynda kicked and screamed, hysterical. Brad only noticed peripherally because he was doing pretty much the same thing.

Jason tossed Lynda so hard the air was knocked out of her lungs. She hit the bed on her back, and part of her brain screamed, "He's going to rape me!"

Suddenly Brad fell on top of her at full force, breaking her clavicle as his shoulder bashed into her, taking her wind again.

Brad tried to move, but his shoulder was dislocated, sending shooting pains through his arm and chest. He screamed out as Lynda tried to push him off her.

But soon he screamed for another reason. Lynda, her face beneath him, turned into a mask of stark terror. Her eyes widened, her mouth dropped open to scream, and her skin turned the color of pale cheese as she looked over his shoulder. He knew, of course, what was behind him.

Suddenly a pain worse than he could ever imagine hit from his back to his chest, and he stupidly remembered something that his mother always told him. "Let a greater pain distract you from the lesser pain."

Lynda watched the machete come down onto Brad's back. Her arms struggled to push him off her, to escape, but the blade didn't stop at Brad. It went further down, into her chest, through her heart, out her back, staking them together to the bed.

Brad felt his life force ebbing away, and he saw the same thing in Lynda's face. Jason had hit the mark with both of them, right into the heart.

Two hearts, Lynda thought, tears leaking from her eyes. Two hearts beating as one. But not for long.

On the way to the Military Complex, JJ, Free and Skye understood why none of the other cons had come to the camp. Along the dirt path and now all around the Military Complex lay bodies, close to a hundred of them, in stages of dismemberment and decomposition. The air reeked of the noxious iron odor of blood decaying, and skin and muscle turning rancid in the heat. Free put his arm around Skye to shield her as they walked through the killing field.

JJ steeled himself. He had seen death before, in the prison, and death just like this, two decades ago. "From the look of the bodies and how they're spread out, I'd say that Jason escaped the Military

Complex, took out these guys, and then headed for the camp. We know the rest."

"Then how come we didn't see him on the way?" Skye asked.

"Because he was there in the camp earlier, while we were at Crystal Lake. He might still be at the lake, or in the camp, but he's not here."

"But how do you know that?" Free asked.

"Because if he was, he'd be all over us."

"Okay, we're here. It looks like we're alone. That's probably a good thing," Skye said.

"Yeah," JJ said, looking around at the dead guys, some of whom he liked, some he didn't like, and none of whom deserved this fate. "All right, what I figure we need to do is get to the control room and see if we can figure out the AI, either of them, if there are two, which we're not certain of. We've got to see if we can reprogram or deprogram it— whatever needs doing so that we can get a message out of here."

"Makes sense," Free said. "Do you know where the AI's memory banks are stored?"

"I can only tell you where they were twenty years ago. Chances are they're somewhere else now, but we might as well start with what we know and work our way into the unknown only when necessary."

JJ led them into the Military Complex. Free had never seen anything like this massive structure before, which seemed even larger inside than outside. Whatever Castillo had done here, he'd had a grand design, and the environment to execute it.

Carefully, they took the stairs down, finding devastation and bodies at every level of the way. JJ had picked up a sizeable metal pole, just in case, but he knew that would only be effective against a human foe. It would have absolutely no effect on Jason whatsoever.

Skye felt sickened by all the death and destruction surrounding them. "I can't believe my father made this… this place," she said. "He created this building, the program that allowed Jason to exist again. And all of that led to this. It's horrible."

Free pulled her close. "And gee, my father, look what he did. All of this."

"What the fuck are you talking about?" JJ asked, stopping to stare at Free. "Jackson Mansfield?"

"Not Jackson. It's nothing. I don't want to talk about it right now."

"Yeah? Are you hiding something, kid?"

"Nothing important to what we're doing," Free said, trying hard to keep control of himself. If JJ knew of Free's connection to Jason, he probably wouldn't help them. And he'd likely kill Free.

JJ looked as if he wasn't sure he believed Free. But there were bigger fish to fry, and there would be plenty of time later to find out what the kid was holding back.

They made their way down to the first laboratory, then the second. "It was in one of these labs," JJ said.

"Looks like the controls for the AI have been moved," Skye said, checking all the equipment.

"Yeah. Well, I expected that. Let's go to the bottom and see if there's anything useful."

They entered the lowest level; a small room splattered with blood and body parts, illuminated by a single solar box lying on the floor. No AI. No computer equipment. Just mayhem.

"This is where we saw him, from the outside, through the window," Free said. Now the window was just a hole that led outside, and out the window they could see that the soil had been shoveled out, at least on this side of the building.

"He was here, maybe in some kind of suspended state. Or at least a controlled state. Maybe this room itself was like a virtual chamber that housed him. As long as he was here he was more or less a prisoner, as much as we were in the floors at the other end of this building. Somehow, somebody opened this doorway. My guess is it was the guys whose remains we found on the floor above. Either them, or the guys digging outside smashed the window in and he got out that way."

"If he was locked in here," Free said, "then that means he has vulnerabilities. It also means the AIs are not invincible. If they'd had the power to release him, they would have."

"If only we could find the control center," Skye said.

The three wended their way back up through the munitions floor where JJ picked up a couple of weapons and ammo saying, "This won't touch Jason, but just in case there are some prisoners around." They climbed their way up to the laboratories, the lounge, all the way back to ground where they found the stalled elevator.

"Let's use this," Skye said, and they took it to the second floor above.

They searched the second and third floors thoroughly. The fact that each was larger meant they spent more time at each floor, but Free didn't think there was a way around that.

They took the elevator to level four and that's as far as it would go. The cage was fine, but the walls that encased the elevator shaft above them had obviously caved in.

"I think that when the Sling hit, the elevator knocked out some of the power and destroyed the walls above. Or maybe the AI sabotaged it, and that's why it's only working from level four down to one, but not above," JJ said.

"Even if we could get the Sling going, there's no way we could repair this elevator and get it up and running again to get us up there," Free said. "And aren't there prisoners in the Sling already?"

"Yeah," JJ said. "A couple of elevator loads of them got there before the Sling whacked the dome."

"Look," Skye said reasonably. "We'll have to get off Elysium the same way we got on, and in the same spot, back at the camp."

"Let's not get ahead of ourselves. First things first," JJ said. "We need to find the controls for the AI, or we'll never leave Moon Complex."

They took the stairs and searched every floor to the top of the building, finding here and there a prisoner who had been murdered by mortal hands. "Why do they kill each other?" Free asked.

"You have no idea what life in a place like this is about. What makes us human is ground away, day by day, hour by hour, second by second. Only the animal part of us can survive this, at least for the lucky ones. Higher values are destroyed by the inhumane conditions of the place. People turn on each other when they see 'other' as the enemy."

"You sound like a philosopher," Skye said.

"You learn a lot in jail," JJ told her.

"You also sound like Jason, at least from what we know about him."

"Maybe. But you either go down, or you go up. I choose to go up. So did Amanda. We were in it together."

Skye didn't know what to say. She looked help-lessly at Free, who shook his head. Sometimes it was better to say nothing, and right now was one of those times. JJ had his grief to bear. She couldn't imagine it, loving someone that much for twenty or more years. She looked at Free again and despite how horrible everything seemed at the moment with all the mindless death, the senseless destruction, the hopelessness of their situation, the seeming inevitability of Jason, she smiled at Free, and he smiled back at her, and she felt less hopeless, and very much less alone. Maybe love was, like the poets always said, eternal. And maybe she loved Free.

They passed the high-tech prison cells where the prisoners had ate, slept, exercised, worked to sustain themselves; where they did everything required of them to survive.

"We'll go up to the roof," JJ said.

"Did you guys come out here for R and R?" Free asked.

"Not us," JJ said. "The guards."

Free noticed the different uniforms and realized that most of those killed in the jail by the prisoners were the guards. It was tough luck for them since they were brought in only recently to facilitate the relocation of prisoners to Thanos.

"Oh no!" Skye said.

They had arrived at the roof of the complex, and Skye was looking over the railing to the ground below. She pointed and Free and JJ stepped to the railing, one on each side of her.

There was Jason, coming along the dirt path, stepping on bodies, crunching them underfoot as if they were ants and not formerly living human beings. He couldn't have heard her from down there, but it was as if he had some kind of honing device implanted into his brain because suddenly his head snapped up. He stared up at the roof as he kept walking. Skye, Free and JJ stared back over the railing, leaning as far as they could, watching him entering the Military Complex.

Skye looked terrified. "What are we going to do? Is there another way down?"

"Not that I know of," JJ said.

Free turned to JJ. "Look, you got rid of him before. How did you do it?"

"We shipped him somewhere else. Or thought we did. We used Castillo's equipment to send him back out into space, to the black hole he'd been pulled out of. But of course we had the equipment to do that."

Free fell back against the railing. "Great. That won't work this time. If we had a way to ship him out of here we could ship ourselves out of here. We don't even have a way of getting out of the Military Complex alive!"

"There's always over the side," JJ said.

"Are you kidding?" Skye said, her voice so strained she sounded like a two year-old.

"Guys have gone over before."

"We're nine stories up," Free said. "Did any of them survive?"

"Not many."

"But some did."

"One did. But then he was captured."

"How did he do it?"

"Your basic high-wall break." They didn't understand until he spelled it out.

"We find some rope, some fabric, anything, and tie it together so we get something long and stable enough to hold the weight of a man, then climb down. Come on."

They ran inside to the closest cell block. The prisoners had rioted before they left and most of the bedding had been torn from the mattresses, ripped almost to shreds, and much of it had been set afire. They each grabbed armloads of what was salvageable and ran back to the terrace.

"Better hurry," JJ said. "Jason will be here any second. He moves fast."

Frantic, with fumbling fingers, Skye and Free tied some sheets from end to end. Some of it tore in the process, with shouts of "Damn!' from both of them.

Meanwhile, JJ tied one of his ends around a permanent fixture; a planter that was part of the terrace
itself, molded into the floor, with a curve near the
bottom so that it looked like a big urn. The wide
planter sat in the middle of the terrace, and it took
up a lot of the fabric to run from there to the edge
of the roof, but there didn't seem to be anything else
stable enough that Free could see, and they had to
anchor their home-made rope to something.

Free had just finished tying his sheets and blankets together and was about to attach them to the
fabric tied to the planter when he heard a thud and
looked up.

"Oh no!"

Jason stood in the doorway of the roof, as if
taking all the time in the world, because he had all
the time. His laser red eyes scanned the scene and
locked onto Free's eyes for a moment, as if studying
him, until JJ got between them.

"Start down!" he yelled.

"But, you—"

"Go!"

Free and Skye struggled to tie the ends of their
lines together. They heard a *clank* and another and
Free looked up to see JJ banging the metal pole onto
the floor of the roof. Two bangs. A pause. Two more.
He probably learned that rhythm in this very jail,
Free thought.

Skye tossed the loose end of the fabric chain over
the edge and looked down the wall. "It's not long
enough!" she cried. "It only goes to around the
second level."

"It'll have to do," JJ said. "Here, take this." He tossed Free a knife with a short handle and a long blade. "Get out of here while you can. And if you get a chance, bury Amanda and me together."

Skye felt her heart sink. She wanted to argue with him that he wasn't going to die, but the situation seemed pretty futile. And she didn't have time for a debate anyway because Free was pushing her over the side of the wall. She clung to the fabric for her life, and began to shimmy down it, scraping her bare knees en route against the surface of the Military Complex.

Free had just begun to climb over as well when he heard a terrible scream and looked up. JJ was charging Jason like a warrior of old, holding the metal bar like a spear. He struck a glancing blow off Jason's upper arm. The power of his body moving forward kept him in motion, rocketing past Jason and into the far wall.

Free didn't know what to do, but he knew he couldn't leave JJ to fight alone.

JJ spun around with Jason on his heels. There was no way he'd go hand-to-hand with the guy with the machete. If he and Amanda had learned one thing in the past about Jason, it was that you couldn't take him on directly.

Suddenly JJ ran to the edge of the terrace and jumped onto the ledge.

Jason started running, machete above his head, like he would slice JJ to ribbons once he reached him.

JJ's plan was to fake him out. Once Jason was close enough, JJ would drop down and, with some luck, the giant would go over the ledge himself without JJ suffering a scratch. At least he hoped that's what would happen. He knew from the past that Jason could almost read minds, especially because it was the AI running him back then, and probably now as well. JJ had to convincingly make it look like he was truly about to leap to his death. He had to even *think* that he would jump for real.

"No!" Free screamed from on top of the ledge, and suddenly JJ watched as Jason spun on his heels and headed toward the kid.

"Jesus H Christ!" JJ cried.

There was nothing to do but charge, and so JJ did. He leapt onto the back of the beast. Jason continued forward, just about on top of Free—and the kid looked horrified—when JJ realized he had to do something drastic. He flipped himself over the top of Jason, falling at his feet, and tripped him using his body as the block.

Jason fell flat onto his face, two steps from Free.

"Get the fuck out of here!" JJ yelled at Free who stared at him with dazed eyes. "Get down!"

Free managed to lower himself so that he was no longer visible. But two seconds later he popped his head up again.

Jason leapt to his feet with an agility that any gymnast would have envied. JJ couldn't do much more than run, yelling, trying to get his attention. Maybe he could do the edge of the roof thing again, give it a try. But he didn't get far before Jason had him by the scruff of the neck. JJ felt himself being lifted high into the air. As the machete came down and cut him in two lengthwise, he thought of Mandy, and smiled. At least for him this would have a happy ending.

Free watched Jason hurl JJ's severed body off the roof.

Suddenly, Jason snapped his head around in Free's direction. Free loosened his grip with both his hands and legs and slid down the fabric rope fast, burning his skin as he went. The knots that held the fabric together barely slowed him down, and he slid at a pace he wouldn't have thought possible.

He glanced up in time to see that Jason was about to climb over the railing. He looked down. Skye was at the very bottom of the chain.

"Jump, Skye, jump!" he yelled. "And run!"

She looked up, seeing him sliding her way, and then saw Jason above him and instantly realized what was happening. She gave a quick scan of the ground and found a spot that might not break a bone when she fell.

"Jump!" Free yelled again, as if she had to be reminded.

Skye did. She fell through the air briefly and landed in the mound of earth that had been dug up, saving herself from injury. Immediately she climbed to her feet and while brushing herself off she looked up.

Free clutched onto the fabric to stop the out-of-control slide. Now he shimmied down. But Jason was on the rope, too, coming down behind him.

When Free reached the seventh floor, he pulled out of his waistband the knife that JJ had given him. With a quick sawing motion he cut the fabric just above a knot. The fabric began to rip from his weight.

"No!" Skye yelled. "You can't jump from there!"

Suddenly Free loosened his hands and feet and let himself fall all the way, grabbing onto the bottom of the fabric just as he reached the end of it.

"Jump into the dirt!" Skye called to him. "I made it—so you can."

Instead, Free looked up. Jason was just at the spot where Free had cut the fabric. The rope below could barely hold Free's weight, so it wouldn't hold Jason.

Free used his feet to push himself away from the wall hard. The sheet rope swung outward and he heard it rip more. Jason stopped climbing down for a moment. The second they swung back, Free used his feet again, this time slamming his boot soles into the edifice and jarring the fabric chain so that at the tear, its weakest point, it severed completely.

Suddenly he was falling, falling, and Skye was screaming. Free had a flash memory of a martial arts class he had taken as a kid: relax into the fall! And that's what he did. Next thing he knew, he hit the dirt, dazed but unharmed.

Skye was by his side instantly, helping him up. Above them, Jason swung from the short chain at level seven of the nine storey building, too high for him to jump, or at least they hoped so.

"He's at the end of his rope," Free said. With nothing beneath him but a lot of air, self-preservation kicked in and they watched as Jason climbed back up to the roof to go down through the building.

Time did not matter to Jason. He understood that no one on this Moon Complex lived but the two running from him. He knew he would get them in the end.

Free and Skye ran for their lives.

FIFTEEN

With nowhere else to go in this mainly virtual world, Free and Skye headed back to the camp. They did not talk as they ran because neither had a plan. At the moment they were operating purely on the instinct to flee.

As they hit the main road, still running, Free said, "We have to be careful. Viper isn't Jason, but he's dangerous in his own way."

Skye, puffing, pointed ahead. "I don't think he'll be a danger to us."

They saw his remains and those of his gang. As they reached the cabins, Skye doubled over and held her stomach. "I'd vomit," she gasped, "if I had anything in my stomach today."

"Let's head to the Lab. At least we have equipment there. Maybe we can think of something."

"All right, but wait just a second," she said, seeing the open door to the cabin where they'd been held captive. "I want to check on Herbert." But when Skye looked in the doorway, instead of entering, she backed out. This time she got the dry heaves.

"Come on," Free said, pulling her away, catching a glimpse of who and what was inside that cabin. "We can't waste any time. He'll be here soon."

Inside the Lab they found that somehow, most of the equipment was still intact. "I guess they didn't know what to do with it, or even how to destroy it," Free said.

"Major Tom. Come in Major Tom!"

Nothing.

"Damn! Where is he?"

"Let's just hope he's not controlling Jason," Skye said. "But it sure looks like he is, or the original AI is, or maybe both of them are. I wish we knew for sure."

They looked through the glass door of the biolab at the same time and saw the same thing, and jolted.

"What the hell?" Free said.

The holographic image that Herbert and Anyar created was now a body, covered with skin and beneath that muscle and bone. It was a very familiar body; the body of Jason.

Tentatively Free went inside first. He walked around the platform. Skye went to her computer, typing away madly.

"I think I've got it," she said. "Anyar and Herbert were supposed to program a bio arm from DNA from the bank. It looks like they did the whole body."

"But they weren't supposed to," Free said, remembering that he had instructed them to stick to the arm.

"Remember when Anyar came in here with that Viper guy? Maybe she saw a chance to do something that might help."

"By building another Jason?"

"She likely didn't know that this model was based on Jason. It was the computer model, remember? Only you and I knew it resembled my father's model. And only a few of us had seen Jason face-to-face. Look, she probably figured that if she could complete the biological part of the cyborg, maybe it could be animated to help us."

"How do we do that?" Free said. "That's our project. It's supposed to take us six months, not six days, let alone six minutes!"

Skye left her console and entered the biolab.

"I wish I knew more about this equipment," Free said.

"Here, let me at those panels. I studied this stuff."

"Finish him off," Free said. "Can you do that? Is he close enough to being finished?"

"I think so. The body looks complete. Hold on... I've got my father's program in the computer. Well, not his, but one I created based on everything he said on the cubes. I haven't tested it yet but—"

"Can we program the cyborg to fight for us?" Free asked, cutting to the chase.

"Can and will, if I can help it."

"Just do it. See if you can bring this creature to life."

Skye spent several minutes keying in the codes she had created that would infuse the form in the biolab with life.

The minute she hit "send," the being on the platform began to alter. Its face took on features, and its body definition became more detailed. It looked more and more like Jason with every passing second. And then a most astonishing thing happened...

"You've done a marvelous job. I'm very happy with this version."

Free and Skye looked at each other and Free said, "Major Tom?"

"It is I."

"Where... have you been?" Free asked tentatively.

"Free, don't be so distrustful," the AI chided him. "Why, I've been waiting here for you to finish the cyborg."

Skye and Free looked at each other.

"Oh, it's all very simple, really. I was programmed to participate in your project by Mr Mansfield. The project reached the stage where the cyborg was about to be infused with life. This is where I come in."

"So you've been waiting here until we reached a certain stage of the project, yes?" Free asked slowly and carefully.

"That's correct."

"And now that we've reached it, you can direct the cyborg?"

"Yes."

"Wait!" Skye said. "Who's running Jason?"

"No one is running Jason. He runs himself."

"But your original AI program, the first Major Tom, wasn't that program running Jason?"

"I suppose so. And perhaps some fragments of programming are still within Jason from my predecessor. I have no way of knowing that. I have my own mission. I am the new, improved Major Tom. My programming takes precedence."

"But if there are fragments of programming in Jason from the original Major Tom," Free said, "then that must mean that Jason is the one that was sent off this moon by JJ and Amanda twenty years ago. Into a black hole, they said."

"Well, as far as my understanding goes, yes, that was their intention. And I believe Jason did manage to leave here for a time and go elsewhere."

"What do you mean 'leave here for a time?'" Skye asked. "Are you saying he was brought back?"

"Of course! He and my predecessor were inseparable. I believe he was brought back here before the original Major Tom was reprogrammed by the military. Part of his new program was to keep Jason in storage, as it were, until needed."

Skye and Free just stared at each other. "Okay, this is too weird," Skye said to Free.

"I agree," he said. "And we don't have the luxury of time to explore this existential dilemma right now. Knowing that Jason is controlled by the original AI and that he was brought back is enough to know. And it doesn't really matter, does it? We've got to get this cyborg fully functional. Maybe with your father's program… Can you get the cyborg fully functional, MT?"

"I can. I will complete the program that the late Ms Barnes and Mr Simpson began and amalgamate it with Dr Castillo's reanimation program. I do need a bit of help, though. I require a verbal or manual command to incorporate the program. The password is 'Medieval.' I fear the voice recognition software will not accept my voice, nor the voice patterns of anyone else, although, of course, you are the only two living beings left."

Free and Skye looked at each other again.

"Just the two of us? Nobody else?" Skye said.

"Well, there is Jason. And with a little help, there will be another Jason, a superior version. The program 'Medieval' will recognize your voice, Free. You are, after all, the project leader, and have the authority to supersede any program."

"Another Jason," Skye said. "I hope we're doing the right thing."

Free said aloud, "Open program 'Medieval' and incorporate the software into the cyborg!"

"Done!"

Skye and Free looked at the being they had created. "I cannot believe it, but he looks exactly like Jason," Skye said.

Suddenly, she looked down. "I hope this isn't a mistake. My father did everything in triplicate,

including splitting my mother's egg into three parts
so she would give birth to triplets. He reanimated
Jason when he pulled him out of the black hole.
And he built the software that built the Jason that
was thrust off this moon, the one who was buried
under the Military Complex. This might be the
third Jason to come out of Moon Complex. And if
I read my father's words correctly, each one should
be an improvement. This one will be the most
powerful."

"Jason to the third power," Free said somberly.
He looked at Skye. "We have no choice. Let's just
hope we can control this one." To the cyborg he
said, "Step off!"

Jason the third turned its head and said in Major
Tom's voice, "I'd be delighted to, Mr Jefferson."

"God!" Skye said. "This one even talks!"

"Not exactly, Ms Fellows. You might notice his
lips do not move. I could correct that, with time,
but I gather that right now there are other priori-
ties."

With that, the cyborg Jason took a step off the
platform onto the floor. The being didn't have the
refinement of movement that it should. Nor did it
have the ease and rapidity of response. But Free
knew that it was all they were going to get right
now. And if this was a more powerful Jason, they
would need to control it.

As if reading his mind, Major Tom said, "I can
iron out the bugs as we go. And of course your
wish is our command."

"Our?" Skye said.

"MT," Free asked, "are you able to operate outside the cyborg?"

"For short periods, yes, as needed. I can still maintain the basic operations of the Moon Complex automatically, such as supporting life, sending and receiving communications to and from—"

"Okay, that's what we want. We need to send a communication."

"To whom?"

"To Jackson Mansfield."

"But he's so far away," Skye said. "Why not to Earth II?"

"I think JJ was right. They're not going to help us. Remember what happened to Joe, the shuttle pilot?"

"Yes, but that was an acci—"

"Skye, wake up. This is a bigger problem than just a shuttle accident, and a computer malfunction, and a serial killer that wants to destroy the entire universe. We're dealing with things that the government on Earth II is at best trying to repress, and at worst trying to revive. And we're in the way of that repression or reconstruction. I've been thinking about it and I get the feeling that it wasn't just chance that Earth II sold Jackson this moon. And I'm wondering if all this was set up."

"How do you mean?"

"I mean they had the records from the pod my mother escaped in, including her medical records. If we could get them, so could they. They knew she had a child, and they likely knew where she ended up. And as for you, I can't believe they wouldn't have known who your father was."

Skye paused a second before looking up at Free. "You think they put us together? Manipulated us in some way to work on this project together? Maybe even adjusted our test scores?"

"It sounds paranoid, but I'm beginning to get really paranoid. I think we have to consider it."

"Do you trust that Jackson wasn't part of this?"

"Skye, I've known him all my life—"

"And maybe he's known all about you. And me. He's a powerful man. Maybe he had something to do with this."

Free was mortified by the idea, but he had to consider it. "I can't say anything for sure, Skye. But I know that Jackson was there for my mother, and for me. I believe he'll help me. Us. I say it's our best shot."

She was silent, just staring at him, looking as frightened and confused as he felt himself. Free wasn't sure if she understood all that was going on inside of him. But from all that Free had seen and heard, it appeared to him right now as if his entire life had been lived to reach this point. He didn't know if Jackson had been part of a large conspiracy which had to do with recouping Castillo's work, but of everyone in the universe, it was Jackson Mansfield he trusted. And they had to trust somebody.

"MT, send an SOS to Jackson Mansfield."

"Done."

"Can you sense Jason II on this godforsaken moon?"

"I can."

"Where is he now?"

"Jason II is entering the road leading to the camp."

"Good God!" Skye cried.

"Okay, we're going out the back door. All three of us," Free said. "Let's go!"

"But what's the plan?" Skye asked.

Free didn't answer her, just gave her a warning with his eyes.

As they headed out the back with Free in the lead, Skye rushed to catch up to him. The cyborg that was Jason X the third controlled by the AI Major Tom the second was several steps behind, its motor skills improving by the second.

"Why won't you say what you've got in mind?" Skye said softly.

Free put his arm around her and pulled her close, kissing her ear so he could whisper, "Because I'm not sure if or how MT is linked with the original MT. We've got to be careful."

He led them around the back of the cabins and down a path that would get them back to the dirt road quickly.

"We're headed to the Military Complex," the AI said.

Free said nothing. Skye also said nothing. The cyborg that was Jason III said nothing, but Major Tom started to sing softly.

SIXTEEN

"Where is Jason II now?" Free asked MT.

"Following. Approximately half a kilometer behind us."

"Oh my God!" Skye cried. "We can't move fast enough."

"Just keep going," Free said. "We're almost there."

"I assume we are headed to the Military Complex," the AI said again, but Free didn't take the bait. He did notice, though, that the kinks had been worked out of Jason the third's body. His movements were easier, and he now kept pace with Free and Skye.

The five-sided building came into view and Free put on a burst of speed. He raced around the structure to the edge of the huge dirt mound.

"Stop!" he called behind him.

Skye doubled over, gasping where she stood. Jason III was of course not winded, simply waiting for instructions. From here, Free was unnerved by the eerie resemblance to Jason II. Even the red eyes were the same.

"MT, come with me. Skye, wait here until you hear from me."

Skye watched Free move around the building further, past the start of the mound which he climbed. Then he was out of sight. Jason III followed him until he, too, was out of sight.

She looked around in a panic. She didn't know what Free's plan was. She saw the sense in keeping info from the AI, but why from her? Why did he want her here, as bait? Jason II didn't care about girls. He didn't care about anything, just the blood and guts he produced as he murdered everyone in his path.

Suddenly she saw Jason II appearing along the path, over the rise. The monster her father had been responsible for creating was coming along the path. Coming toward her.

Every cell in her body screamed "Run!"

From behind her, somewhere, she heard Free yell, "Wait, Skye. Don't move yet. Just stay there."

She glanced behind her but couldn't see him. He must not realize how close Jason was to her or he wouldn't be saying that. He was close enough that she could see the light glinting off the blue-gray metal of his machete, the ripple of muscles like steel where his skin was exposed, the burning hatred in those impossibly laser-red eyes. As she stared into them she felt that he knew who she was; that he knew, if not by intellect then by instinct, that she was the daughter of the man who had manipulated him, who he had killed. Just as he would kill her.

Skye tried to calm herself. Tried to be logical. She struggled to think clearly, even though she had begun to hyperventilate. That couldn't be. It made no sense that he could know who she was. But then she realized that Jason II was run by the original AI, wasn't he? Or maybe not. Maybe he's run by the duplicate AI. Maybe it's a setup. But either way he has a memory, and was maybe sophisticated enough to identify DNA.

He knows who my father was, she realized. The original Major Tom most likely had Castillo's DNA, and probably passed it onto the new AI. And Jason II knew her father was the man he had murdered by driving three mirror fragments into his artificial eye, slicing open his brain mass. And now he wanted to kill Skye. Not even because she was Castillo's daughter. Just because she existed!

Panic swelled up in her like a river overrunning its banks. She couldn't control herself. Skye turned and ran.

"No, Skye, wait!" she heard Free yelling, but she could not. Her body would not allow her to stand there as this demon stalked her, just like in her nightmares. But this was real. Not imaginary. Not virtual. That huge knife had her name on the blade!

She ran in the direction Free had gone and could feel Jason closing in on her. Panicked, she twisted her head around to look behind, to make sure he wasn't about to snatch her, and lost her footing just as she reached the mound. Her body tumbled and fell down nine storeys into the corpse-ridden gully below. Surrounding her were bodies, many bodies, cut and bloody and stinking, and she cried out in fear and disgust. Dirt fell in with her, causing a mini landslide. Skye quickly became covered in earth like a quick burial with the already dead, drowning out her screams.

Bloody mud clotted her eyes, filling her nose and mouth, her ears, cutting off the outside world. Now she shrieked, the sound low in her throat, having no way to get out, and nowhere to go. Hysterically she clawed her way up through the soil, fighting for air, her hands touching cold-as-marble body parts slick with blood that make her shriek all the more, and when her head finally surfaced she gasped in air. She rubbed the dirt out of her eyes, off her face, coughed it out of her lungs and breathed it out from her nostrils. She saw a corpse lying close by, its dead eyes staring into hers as if it were saying, "Hello! Glad you could join me." She tore her eyes away and looked up.

Nine levels above, malevolence stared down at her. He crouched down, preparing to leap into the hole, anything to get at her and to tear her apart! The scream coming out of her was long and loud and she could not for anything have stopped it.

* * *

"Now, MT! Get out there and distract him!"

Free ran ahead even as he gave the order, hoping that he himself could distract Jason II while waiting for the newer version to get in there and help him out.

All this had gone so wrong! He should have told Skye what he wanted to do. But he was so used to them being in sync mentally, and he hadn't wanted to spill his plan to MT, just to be on the safe side, and now it was all screwed up.

Skye was supposed to have stayed there until he called her. Then she would have run around the building, avoiding the hole, and the two of them would have been behind Jason III which he would have sent into battle with number two, with instructions to shove him into the hole. They could have buried him and gotten the hell out of here!

But now it was all a mess. Now, he didn't know what to do. The only thing he was sure of was that he had to get Skye out of that grave she had fallen into, and get Jason II into it!

"Over here!" he yelled, waving his arms until Jason II looked his way.

Jason III finally caught up and stepped out into the open where Jason II could see his mirror image, as well as see Free.

The two Jasons stared at each other with hate-streaked eyes. Then Jason II snapped his head to look at Free, who wondered briefly about this three-way DNA triangle, and how odd it was for all of them.

"Keep him away from the hole!" Free said.

Jason III advanced. Meanwhile, Free yelled down at Skye, "Try to climb up!"

"I'm trying!" she yelled back. "The soil is too loose, too slippery. I need a rope!"

"A rope, a rope..." Free searched for the makeshift rope they had used to get down from the top floor.

He saw it, then suddenly remembered that it hadn't been long enough to begin with, and that he'd cut it so the rope was even shorter than before. Even if he ripped the shirt off his back, and used his pants to extend it, the rope would not be long enough.

"You have to go through the inside!" he yelled. "I'll come and get you as you come up."

Skye trudged through the loose dirt and reached the window. She climbed in as fast as she could and hurried to the stairway.

Free's intention was to head around the building to the entrance but he quickly realized that he was still between the two Jasons. He realized something else as well: they were not facing off against each other, but were both staring at him. And he didn't like the way they were looking. It was like irrational rage in duplicate. Free kept staring back and forth between them—one had a machete, one did not, otherwise they were identical—until suddenly, as one unit, they both began running in his direction.

"What the hell is going on?" he screamed. "MT! Major Tom! Get Jason III to attack Jason II," Free said, running as fast as he could.

"Oh, but I can't do that," MT said.

"Why the hell not?" Free ran away from the mound of dirt, widening the distance a bit between himself and each of the Jasons.

"Isn't it obvious? They share the same DNA. They can't turn on one another; it would be like attacking one's self. It's the DNA, you see. I'm programmed with the DNA, programmed toward the DNA, programmed to support the strongest DNA, and they are equally matched."

"What the hell are you talking about?" Free yelled. He was in a full run now, both giants close on his heels. He had to do something to escape. But he couldn't leave Skye!

He didn't know whether to run back to the camp and lead them away from Skye, or to enter the building and get her. If these two decided to split up and one headed for Skye, she was finished.

Instinct took over and he raced into the entrance of the building and headed for the stairwell and down. He remembered the weapons floor. JJ had said that weapons wouldn't kill Jason, but they might slow them down, and that would give him and Skye some time.

He tore down the steps, slamming the few doors that remained on hinges behind him, even though he knew they would not hold them back but for a second. But a second here, another there, it could add up to survival.

At the lounge, he was confronted with bodies littering the floor and the walls painted with blood. He tried not to focus on the horror of it. Mixed with the stench of blood and decay was another smell: alcohol, and when he noticed the bottles of booze he got an idea. He grabbed a few bottles and the flame thrower, and raced to the next doorway. The two Jasons were already in the lounge.

As Free reached the doorway he lifted his arms above his head and threw all the bottles a couple of steps ahead of him. As he leapt over the broken glass, he ignited the alcohol. It caught instantly and spread quickly. The flames weren't that high, and it wouldn't last long once the alcohol burned off, but it might be high enough to keep the two Jasons from passing. He didn't wait to find out. He was already down the next flight and slamming that door behind him too.

Free and Skye met at the second laboratory down, one floor up from the munitions floor. "There are bodies everywhere!" she cried.

Without a word he grabbed her arm and turned her around, pulling her across the slippery floor to the next doorway.

Only when they reached the floor with the weapons did they dare to speak to one another.

"What happened?" Skye gasped.

"They're the same," Free said. "The two of them are identical and the two MTs are running them, I think."

"But that can't be! The one we built has the DNA, the memories of all of us, all but you."

"And I think that doesn't matter much. I think what we put into the cyborg didn't make a dent because frankly, it was already programmed in some way."

"By who?"

"I can't tell you that. I don't know. All I know for sure is that those two are identical. I see it and I can feel it in every cell of my body." Free grabbed up a couple of laser guns, and what he thought were laser clips, plus a long gun that might pack a wallop, shoving as much ammo as he could into the pockets and waistband of his pants. He didn't even know if he could figure out how to reload.

"Here, take these," he said, handing her a dozen weapons, and she stored them the same way as he had.

"These guys had guns," she said, nodding at the bodies surrounding them. "It didn't help them."

Free knew she was right, but he had to do something.

"It's my fault!" Skye cried, holding her head. "I shouldn't have used my father's programs. I'm just like him. I created another Jason!"

They heard movement on the stairs.

"They're coming!" Free said. And with hand gestures, he indicated to Skye that she should stay on one side of the room and he would be on the other. He wanted to split up the two Jasons. He hoped that with the weapons they could force them down into the basement floor, and he hoped he conveyed some of that to Skye. The fire in the lounge had slowed them. That was a good sign. Something to remember.

Jason II and Jason III entered the doorway almost side by side. The only way Free could tell the difference was that one had a machete and the other did not.

Free caught Skye's eye. He grabbed his own arm and slapped the skin there, and at his neck, indicating that she should aim for flesh.

Skye felt almost paralyzed with fear. She did not know if she could even fire a laser. Every part of her wanted to run screaming down to the next level, but her dreams came to mind at that moment, and she knew that if she ran away, she would not survive.

The two Jasons split up, one going for Free, one for Skye. Free fired lasers with both hands, and Skye did the same. The power of the beams stopped both Jasons. They stood quivering as the lasers cut into the armor and seared flesh.

Free began moving along the wall to the doorway that led up and on the other side of the room Skye did the same. As one laser died, he grabbed another, training it on Jason II. Skye did the same with Jason III, not stopping to reload, and just going to the next gun.

They reached the doorway and Free nodded for her to go first. She turned and ran with Free on her heels. But Jason III was on *his* heels, followed by Jason II.

They managed to make their way across the laboratory, using up another full laser each.

"We're gonna have to reload!" Skye cried.

"On the way up!" Free yelled back.

Free noticed that both Jasons were not stunned as long as they had been the first time. He wondered if

they were adapting as they went, if the programming was altering.

Up they went through the other lab, the sleeping
quarters, and continued on until they reached the
lounge.

"Oh my God!" Skye screamed at the carnage
before her. She was bent over, trying to catch her
breath, and Free was breathing hard, too.

"Give me all your weapons. I'll hold them off!"
Free cried. "Get all the booze bottles you can and
break them at the other stairwell. Do it fast!"
While he yelled he fired down into the descending
stairwell they had just come up, hitting Jason II
who was now in the lead. His massive presence
kept the other Jason from passing him.

"I've got at least three dozen," Skye called to
him.

Free heard her breaking the glass. He knew that
while the two Jasons didn't seem to have broken
out in a sweat, his own stamina was waning and
he suspected Skye was more than exhausted.

He snatched the flame thrower, turned and ran
across the room, the two Jasons pounding up the
rest of the steps and across the floor after him.

Once more he leapt over the bottles, igniting
them on the way. The alcohol caught instantly, like
a small blast. But this time a massive hand
grabbed Free's shirt and he felt himself being
pulled back.

"Look out!" Skye called, reaching for him at the
same moment, pulling him forward as the shirt
ripped off his back. The fire licked at his legs,

searing the fabric of his pants as it rose. The fire somehow caused Jason's grip to loosen, allowing Free to dash toward Skye and the stairway.

They ran up the last flight of stairs, through the main floor and out the door into the air. Suddenly the earth trembled beneath them.

They stopped for a second, instinctively glancing up.

"Oh my God, the Sling is moving," Skye said.

The Sling was scraping along the dome, creating new fissures at the outermost layer.

"Come on!" Free said, pulling her toward the road.

With the last of their energy, they managed to get to the camp, and reading each other's minds, they silently headed to the Lab.

SEVENTEEN

"Where can we go?" Skye asked as they entered the Lab. She slammed and bolted the door behind them, although she knew no lock could keep out either Jason. "There's nowhere! It's over." She doubled over from a stomach cramp.

"It's not over until either we're dead, or they are. I'm not giving up!"

Free paced the room for two seconds. "How can we alter the programming of Jason III?" Free asked.

Skye, gasping, shook her head. "I don't know."

They stood stymied for a moment. Suddenly, Free snapped his fingers. "I've got it! Remember when you did a brain transfer from everybody in the program? Everybody but me? What if you put my DNA, brain patterns—all of it—into the Jason X III program? That would make him very different than Jason II."

"Why would it? He has the material from the rest of us already, and it hasn't made him different."

"But none of you share DNA with Jason X. I do."

Skye shook her head. "I think at best it would be a waste of time, at worst it would put you at a disadvantage."

Free went to her and took her in his arms. "Skye, there's no waste of time now. We have to do something. This just might be the key. And if it's not, well, like you said, there's nowhere to go."

"Maybe the Sling? We could try to get there. Maybe if it moves far enough we can board before it takes off for Thanos." Even as she said it, she knew it was a long shot. More likely, one of the Jasons would get them when they were trying to get on the Sling. And if the best-case scenario was going to Thanos with a cage full of convicts... She no longer knew which alternative was the worst anymore.

"Skye, we have to try it. MT can change the programming with my authorization, and I don't know what would make a difference in the program of Jason III, but he's the only one we can alter."

"Might not help, but can't hurt," she mumbled into his chest and sighed. "Okay, we don't have much time before they get here. Let's do it and hope for the best."

Skye inserted the probe above Free's eye. She had the other end of the micro laser scanner hooked up to her computer and had the data transferred in seconds to the program in the bio lab.

Free had already called up Major Tom that second. There was no use avoiding the AI. It knew where they were, and told the Jasons where they were, and it also knew their plan. It knew everything. And Free suspected that it had a pre-ordained agenda, which included running the Jason X they had created. He did not know who was behind all this, whether it was the government of Earth II, if this was some remnant of Castillo's reign on Elysium, or—and he prayed that it wasn't so—Jackson Mansfield had something to do with all this. But, none of that mattered. They had little time, and not many options. Part of Major Tom the second's mission was to obey orders, and that included an order to input data into the newly-created cyborg, which is what Free commanded it to do. "But only when I tell you to activate the data."

"Certainly," MT said. Free and Skye just looked at each other.

"Tell us the whereabouts of the Jasons," Free demanded.

"Approaching the camp," the AI told them.

Skye jerked visibly.

"Are we almost done?" Free asked.

Skye nodded. "Just a couple of seconds to go... there! At least we've got your DNA in there, and some of your brain patterns. I didn't have time to do a full transfer."

"Let's hope it's enough," Free said, helping Skye remove the suction cups from his scalp and along the top of his spinal cord. He jumped to his feet and said, "Wait here."

"What are you going to do?"

"Just stay here." He kissed her lips. "I'll be back."

"Free!" she screamed as she watched him run out the door.

The two Jasons were almost at the Lab. Both of them spotted Free at the same time. The one without the machete was in the lead slightly, which would be Jason III, and Free figured that should be so, since he was the more advanced version.

He tried to catch the eye of Jason III. Looking into those hellish orbs made Free feel weak and quite sick, engendering the feeling that death was imminent. But Free stared on. He stared into the eyes of what he knew now was his father. A father that now had some knowledge of his son.

Jason III slowed and Jason II picked up speed. Free ran out to greet them, then bolted to the left, and then feigned right, then ran in a large circle around them, causing the two Jasons to separate in order to trap him. This is what Free thought they would do.

His intention was to separate them, to delay them. And he sure hoped this would work. If not, he'd be torn apart or cut to ribbons, and that would be the end of that.

"Major Tom, activate the new data you input into Jason III."

It was as if the AI sighed. "As you wish."

Activation took two seconds. Before Free's eyes, everything changed. Jason III and Jason II stopped simultaneously. Their eyes left Free and went to each other. They were no longer identical. One of them had inside him additional DNA; DNA he recognized as familiar. And while that did not breed familial unity, it made him different from the other Jason. Different enough that now they both wanted to battle the strongest being in the vicinity. And the strongest on this moon was the other Jason.

Jason II was three meters to the left of Free, and Jason III three meters to the right of him. Carefully and slowly Free backed away, leaving just the two of them in what was like a virtual ring.

Suddenly, number two lunged. A split second later number three leapt toward him. Free couldn't believe this. It was all he had hoped for and more. They were attacking each other. Free knew full well that neither daddy had made the move to save his son. This was pure murderous rage at work.

With the honed instinct of an A-1 predator, Jason II had that machete lifted above his head. But he wasn't quite fast enough. Jason III ducked out of the way and plowed into the other's legs, knocking him off his feet.

The two killer giants wrestled on the ground, fists pounding, hands choking, the machete struggling to find a mark, and when it did it stabbed number three in the back.

Free was amazed to see that that did not slow number three down at all.

The two beings leapt to their feet, facing off like hockey players, the machete between them like a hockey stick. Free could not tear his eyes away.

Jason II had the machete, but number three had the advantage of being all that Jason II was, and then some. Number two swung the machete again. This time number three caught his opponent's wrist in the air. He bashed the arm against the skull of number two and the machete went flying into the air. Now they were hand-to-hand, and it wasn't going to be pretty.

To Free's eyes, they were two deranged entities battling it out. Each anticipated the other's moves. Jason III punched Jason II in the face and at the same time two kicked three hard in the stomach. Both went flying in opposite directions. Their speed was not a normal human's speed, but the pace of something or someone superhuman.

Free got the sense, somehow, that Jason II knew number three for the superior creation that it was, possibly the most powerful being in the vicinity, and that's why he waited for it.

Free knew that they both realized that he and Skye weren't going anywhere. Both Jasons were convinced they could get at them any time. It must be like a macabre game to them, Free thought. A very simple game: you exist, I kill you. But I kill the strongest first. Then I kill you two. It was a game Jason never really lost. And now there were two of them playing at it.

As the two got into the fight more heavily, Free used the opportunity to dart past them, heading toward the Lab. He felt the earth rumble again, nearly knocking him off his feet, and looked up. The Sling had edged slowly toward the camp, tearing more of the outer layer of the dome as it went. It would be directly over the camp soon; their one chance to escape.

Once in the Lab, Skye ran to him sobbing. "What happened out there?"

"No time to talk. Come on."

He pulled her out the back door of the Lab and they raced toward the spot where the elevator had dropped them on arrival.

"MT, send down the elevator!" Free ordered.

The AI did not respond, and Free hoped it could still multitask. They had so little time.

Suddenly the earth trembled again, and both Free and Skye clung to one another to keep from falling as they looked up to see the Sling move more toward the point where they had entered the dome.

"We need that elevator!" Free screamed. How the hell could they get the elevator down without the help of Major Tom? Or maybe, Free thought gloomily, it didn't matter anymore.

"MT!"

"At your service."

"Are you still controlling Jason III?"

"Jason III is no more."

Free and Skye looked at one another.

"So… Jason II won the fight?"

"He did not."

"What are you saying? Both of them are dead?"

"In a manner of speaking, yes."

"God!" Skye cried, her body trembling. "Can they really be dead?"

"We've got to get out of here," Free said. "MT! You told me that the bottom line is that you are programmed to provide life support for human beings, no matter what, is that right?"

"Yes, that is correct."

"And that's still the case?"

"Correct again."

"Life support includes escape mechanisms, should the human inhabitants feel that this environment cannot sustain their life."

"That is correct also."

"The two remaining human inhabitants believe that this environment can no longer sustain human life. Bring the elevator above the camp down to ground level."

"As you wish."

Skye looked amazed. "We could have done this before. All along! Why didn't any of us think of this before?"

"We could have, but I know I didn't make the connection that life support is not just air, water, food, but it also includes escape mechanisms, because the idea is to sustain life at all costs. But whether we realized it then or now, we've got the same problem. The elevator has nowhere to take us but up. And there's no shuttle waiting for us up there, just the Sling, which we might miss. Or which we might not be able to enter. And which is filled with dangerous convicts headed to a moon they might not survive on."

"Yeah. We might be killed in any number of ways. And if we miss the Sling we could starve to death waiting for your friend Jackson to send help. If he gets the message at all... And if he sends help."

"Good point. The elevator took about half a minute to get us down when we arrived. Should be the same now."

"The elevator," the AI said, "was powered up for your arrival. It has sat dormant and now will take approximately ten of your Earth II minutes to power up, then about thirty seconds to descend."

"Great!" Free said, exasperated. Then, to Skye, "Look, let's gather as many lightweight supplies as we can carry like nutrition capsules and crystallized water, so we don't have to lug anything heavy. If we miss the Sling, we might be up there a long time."

They both ran toward the store. "We'll grab a couple of blankets," he told her, "though I think we can get MT to control the temperature up there."

Just as they rounded the corner of the store, Skye held him back: Jason stood in the clearing at the center of the camp, machete in his hand, standing amidst the bodies.

"Forget the supplies," she whispered.

Free just stared. "Jason still exists, doesn't he?"

"Yes," MT said.

"Which one?"

"Both."

As he and Skye turned and raced back toward the descending elevator, Free demanded, "Explain!"

"Quite simply, they battled. The survivor, who was as you called him, Jason III, absorbed all that was Jason II. Now there is one. You've done a remarkable job. I commend you."

Free couldn't believe it. Jason was alive and well and headed in their direction. No need to even confirm it. He could sense that Jason had sensed them. They were the last two human beings who would die on Elysium.

"You told us they died!" Skye gasped, staggering along, every bone in her body exhausted, her voice filled with hopelessness like a child that had discovered she'd been lied to.

"I believe I said they died in a manner of speaking. There is no 'they,' simply 'he.'"

"The one I made? He's the new Jason? The strongest Jason ever?" Her voice lowered, as if she had given up all remaining hope.

"That is correct," MT said. "And my mission and my programming are virtually complete, if you will excuse the pun."

Free grabbed Skye who had stopped and pulled her beyond where the elevator was descending at a snail's pace, and headed toward Crystal Lake.

"Free, we're not going to make it!" she gasped.

"Come on!" he yelled. "There's safety on top of the dome from Jason. He can't get to us if we're up there. But we've got to dodge him until the elevator makes it down to ground level."

The second after he said this, Skye was wrenched from his grasp.

It took Free a moment to realize that she was gone. He spun around to see Skye in the clutches of Jason, being lifted into the air, her feet dangling, her arms flailing. "No!" he screamed, charging the giant, hell-bent on freeing her.

Jason backhanded him in the face, instantly splitting Free's lower lip and snapping his head to the side as his body went flying. He only stopped his flight when his head hit the elevator, which had just about descended and was coming to rest on the ground. The elevator was the last thing Free was aware of before he passed out.

Skye screamed, punching and kicking, just as she had seen others do when Jason had them, but it was as if she were a child in the grasp of a giant. Despite how active her body was, her mind and emotions were shutting down. She did not feel her body move, or hear her voice. It was as though she were dreaming that awful recurring dream, locked in the paralysis of the nightmare world. In her mind she was in a dark corridor, the ground splitting in front and behind her, and when she looked down she saw that in fact the ground was splitting, all around them, as the moon rumbled and quaked and Jason struggled to keep his footing.

Then, suddenly, the tremors stopped. In that moment, Skye watched, coolly, calmly, knowing the outcome could not be other than she always envisioned it would be. What she had always known would happen would come to pass. A part of her felt that in some way this was her reward for resurrecting her father's work. Her life did not flash before her eyes, but a synchronistic connection did: if she had not found the cubes; if she had not studied engineering; if she had not taken this job... She would not be here now, living out what should be images from the trash can of her psyche. And at the end of these thoughts she realized that if she had not done these things, she would not have met Free, and felt, for a brief period of her short life, love.

The machete sliced across her neck as if she were made of soft cheese. There was no physical pain, only emotional. She realized as her head flew straight up into the air, just as it had over and over in her dreams, she realized that she and her body were no longer connected, and she understood the entirety of everything, all of it in the fragment of the second when she realized that she was dead. It was a state beyond emotions. Her pain was spiritual.

With fading consciousness as her head plummeted after her body, she watched the darkness below open up to engulf her, her body and Jason. And she only stopped falling when something sharp entered her left eye and pierced her brain, and brought with it a light so bright it broke open and permeated everything that she had ever been. Finally, Skye slept peacefully.

EIGHTEEN

Free came to consciousness slowly, his head spinning. He felt like puking, and it took all his control to not do that. Besides being dizzy, he had trouble focusing, and sucked in some deep breaths, letting them out slowly, waiting for his vision to clear and his stomach to settle down before he attempted to stand.

His head hurt all over, but especially at the back, and he touched the back of his scalp gingerly to feel a tender lump. He also felt a wet stickiness that, when he pulled his hand back before his eyes, he knew was blood. It was then he remembered that he had been knocked into the air and hit his head, and probably suffered a minor concussion.

Once he was on his feet he began to look around—the elevator, the camp and a large split in the soil that had created a kind of wide pit that he didn't remember seeing before. There was nobody in sight.

"Skye?" he called tentatively. "Skye? Where are you?"

Silence greeted him. What was happening? Sure, he'd been knocked out, but that didn't mean he was dreaming, did it? Why was he the only one here?

"Hey," he called.

His vision finally returned and he was able to see with clarity. To the right, he saw Crystal Lake. To the left, in the distance, he saw the main part of the camp: the cabins, the Lab, the store and bodies, many, many bodies, mostly in parts, all strewn around the grounds like life-sized toy soldiers that had died in battle.

Memories began to surface, and while the concussion kept him from putting them together into a cohesive whole, he saw flashes of murders being committed. And a clear mental picture of the murderer.

"Jason," he said aloud.

He looked up. The Sling was just about at the spot where he and the others on the team had entered the dome. He had a plan. To get up there, with Skye. He remembered now. But where was she?

"Skye!" he yelled, and heard a faint echo of his voice. Panic began to edge up his spine. He couldn't recall where he had last seen her.

"Perhaps I can come to your aid," a familiar voice said.

"MT! What happened?"

"I believe you are concussed."

"Tell me what I don't know," Free said, rubbing his head, trying to ease the pain so that the headache that was subsiding would diminish faster. "I could use an aspirin."

"I would suggest that you take—"

"What happened? I can't remember it all..."

"Where would you like me to begin?"

Free thought for a moment about what he did remember. He recalled being with Skye, waiting impatiently for the elevator to drop down. They were going to the store, to gather supplies. They wanted to flee here, to get away from..."

"Jason," the AI said. "You were hoping to escape Jason."

Free shook his head. "But, weren't there two of them, or did I imagine that?"

Even as the AI explained again how they had amalgamated, Free's memory of that returned. He remembered, too, when he and Skye had seen the survivor, the union of everything every Jason of the past had been, Jason to the third power rounding the corner. Then he and Skye ran to the elevator, but it wasn't there yet. Then, suddenly—

In a blinding flash, Free remembered Skye being torn away from him, as if it were happening all over again. He had charged Jason to help her. That's when he had been backhanded, and cata- pulted through the air, and struck his head, and...

"Where's Skye?" he asked, his voice rising with fear, sinking with impending despair.

"Perhaps you should look in the fissure."

Free walked slowly to the wide gap in the soil, his steps heavy, his heart heavier. As he neared, he saw that the split was not just wide but deep, growing deeper in his vision the closer he got. Soon he stood at the edge, peering down into blackness.

"Illumination," he said, and MT complied instantly.

The chasm must have been twenty-five meters deep and stretched into infinity in both directions. With the light MT provided, he could see to the bottom. Twisted and curled in on itself was Skye's body, arms and legs at impossible angles. She would have broken her back, he thought, and many other bones. He knew he was being too logical, aware that he felt too calm and analytical. Aware that the most grotesque aspect of what he saw was not the positioning of her body but the fact that her head was not attached to it.

His eyes scanned the cavern until he saw her head five meters further along, her long beautiful hair surrounding it like a dark halo. Her eyes stared blankly, dead eyes, he thought, or at least the one, since the other was bashed in by pieces of something that might have been zephyrglass.

Just like her father, he thought: three pieces of glass in the eye, everything in threes, death at the hands of Jason. What a horribly ironic end. And still he felt anesthetized.

Out of the blue a sudden pain hit him at chest level. He knew it was his heart. It felt more like a fierce ache that intensified with every breath. On each exhale tears leaked from his eyes and low moans from his throat until finally he was yelling "No! No, no, no!!!"

He fell to his knees, holding his head with his hands, kneeling at the grave of his beloved, sobbing out of control, suffering an agony he did not know until this moment that he was capable of feeling.

Free could not take it in. Skye, the woman he loved, lying in a grave at his feet, dead. His head suddenly felt both heavy and empty, as if every thought he had or would ever possess dropped down into his gut and rolled around in a cauldron of instant despair. Then the pain inside his chest began burning him with laser intensity, searing away parts of him that he wanted, needed, longed for. What would give his existence meaning amidst all the horror that had overshadowed his life? And suddenly, irrevocably, he knew he would never be the same again.

As if responding to a question, the AI said, "Yes, I believe if you intend to get to the Sling, now would be the appropriate time to board the elevator. By my calculations, you have exactly seven minutes until…"

But Free tuned MT out. He tuned the AI out because he saw something else in the chasm. The body of Jason, lying face down.

The burning pain that had been in his heart exploded like a fire bomb, turning into a rage that boiled through him. Free wanted to jump down there, grab the machete and stab and cut the remains until there was nothing left, no flesh intact, no veins and arteries unsevered, no organs not punctured, no limbs not sliced off from the torso, no bones not cut from one another. He wanted to gouge out the eyes, stab up through the nostrils, into the mouth and ears, cut off the genitals, cut off his head, burn out his heart...

"In order to align yourself with the Sling, you now have exactly five minutes, fifty-two seconds. Fifty-one seconds..."

Free dragged his eyes from the fissure. The AI, as if sensing that he needed to stop looking, dimmed the lighting in the chasm, and the hole became dark, even more like a grave.

Free's mind raged. He did not want his beloved buried in the same place as Jason! But a more rational part of him was surfacing. He could come back here. Exhume her later. Rebury her. Or better still, cremate her remains and scatter them throughout the universe. All but for a small glass vial he would fill and seal and wear close to his shattered heart for the rest of his life. He knew he would never love another. Never.

"You now have exactly four minutes, twenty-nine seconds, twenty-eight..."

Free rose and walked to the elevator. He entered the glassed-in cage and said to MT, "Take me up. I want to get the hell off of Elysium."

The elevator began to rise. It was no more than two feet from ground level when out of the chasm Free saw a blur of movement.

Jason! He was not dead. He didn't even look harmed. His body, covered with soil that he shook off like a dog, had leapt out of the hole and landed on the ground as if twenty-five meters were only twenty-five centimeters. And now he was running, fast, and Free stared in horror as the monster that shared his DNA hurled himself into the air and caught the lower edge of the elevator and hung onto it with both hands as it rose rapidly into the sky.

Okay, Free thought, this is bad. Really bad. He knew that taking Jason with him did not just endanger his own life, but that of the prisoners as well. How the hell could he just hang on like that? Surely the air thinned as the elevator ascended, but maybe not. Elysium was so artificial that maybe it was consistent all the way up.

But what could he do about Jason hanging on? Could he fight pop and survive? A barking laugh of despair came out of Free. Jason was probably triple Free's weight, had a muscle mass that Free couldn't even guestimate, had no spare fat to speak of, plus abilities like super speed that belied his weight and height, and a pure killer instinct that nothing could penetrate. Free figured no, a physical fight with his biological old man who had survived centuries and was only partly human was definitely out of the question.

He glanced down through the glass floor of the elevator at the malevolent face turned upward, and those hellfire eyes bore into Free's. Already Jason was hauling himself up higher so that his head came to the side of the elevator, to the height of Free's ankles.

Free could feel his body covered with the cold sweat of fear. He tore his eyes away and looked up. The elevator would enter the first layer of the dome, fitting into a kind of box or shaft that was designed just for it. Free hoped that Jason would not be able to get to that level which held the corridor. The elevator had arrived and the doors were opening at an agonizingly slow pace. He would know soon.

Free looked down quickly. Jason had lowered himself again, so that he was under the elevator's glass floor, but for his finger tips. Free thought longingly of how, if there was any justice in the universe, those fingers would have been severed, and Jason would be plummeting to his death. But the shaft and the elevator were not a perfect fit, and the gap was just big enough for the massive fingers to retain their grip and to allow Jason to cling to the elevator. To life. Couldn't anything kill him? Free wondered.

The second the elevator doors opened wide enough, Free slipped out and raced along the corridor toward the airlock which would take him to the narrow platform. He hoped to hell the Sling's cage stopped there, or at least paused long enough for him to get into it.

He had to get into the cage. Because if he didn't... Already Jason had broken through the floor of the elevator, hauled himself up and was rushing down the corridor at a speed Free found astonishing.

The airlock had closed, and Free started up the steep ladder. The Sling looked just about in place but for a couple of inches. Even if it was not perfect, he thought he could get to the top of the airlock, get the airlock sealed around the cage's door, and then figure out how to get inside. Once he got the door open, he had no idea what or who would be waiting there, but it didn't matter. Whatever was inside was better than what was coming up the ladder after him.

"MT, surround the Sling's cage with the airlock."

He was near the top and saw the seal automatically begin to surround the cage's door. He stepped onto the narrow platform and searched quickly for some way to enter, but ended up just pounding on the door in desperation. Below him, Jason was about halfway up the ladder.

"MT? Crack the top of the dome so that the Sling basket can move out of here, but wait for my signal."

Free knew that even if he got inside the basket, unless the Sling started moving fast, Jason X would also get in. And unlike Free, Jason X would smash his way through the metal, shattering the door, which, as the Sling moved away from Elysium, would expose those inside to the vacuum of space. They would all be sucked out, and everything inside their bodies would be sucked out of them too as they would become instant shells. Survival hinged on that Sling moving fast, with Free inside, Jason X outside, and the integrity of the basket intact.

"Wait for my voice signal," Free said again.

As he pounded on the door he yelled, "Help! Let me in! Open the door from inside!"

Finally, a voice came from inside the basket. "Who the fuck's out there?"

"My name is Free. Please. Let me in. It's a matter of life and death."

"Why the fuck should we?"

"Who the fuck is Free?" another voice said. "Ain't no Free in the prison. Maybe he's a screw!"

"We fuckin' killed all the guards, you idiot!"

"I'm not a guard," Free explained, trying to sound logical and also trying to keep the massive hysteria out of his voice, but he failed. "In a minute, I'll get sucked into space. Let me in. I want to go with you!"

A harsh laugh from the other side of the door. "Who the fuck cares?"

And another said, "Why the fuck would anybody want to go to Thanos?"

"Please. Just open the door. I can help you people."

Jason was three-quarters of the way to the landing when the door to the cage opened.

A huge bearded muscular man who looked like evil incarnate stood in the doorway staring at Free, whose body was blocking the view of the ladder and Jason steadily climbing up it. "It's a kid," the man said. "Hey! We can get outta here and back down to Elysium!"

"Yeah! Let's do it!" another behind him yelled.
A new grisly face appeared in the doorway with
the big con as a crowd formed behind them both.

"No, wait, you don't understand!" Free said.

"Yeah, we do. We ain't going to no fuckin'
Thanos for the rest of our lives!"

The big guy kicked out, knocking Free back and
down. He fell against the ladder and bounced as
he went, past Jason, all the way down to the floor
of the airlock. Jason was now visible to the cons
inside.

"Well, what the fuck!?" one of them said.

As Jason climbed to the top of the ladder,
placing one foot on the platform, he and the
meaty guy locked eyes, challenging one another.

Free had fallen on his back, hurting his tail-
bone, but not so much that he couldn't sit up.

"Now MT," he said, hoping that the Sling would
move away, that the prisoners would close the
door, and that at least they would be free of
Jason, even if Free would never be. His best hope
was that Jason would be sucked into space.

The Sling began to inch forward as the dome
cracked in front of it, creating a path. The insta-
airlock began to shrink around the door. But the
guy in the doorway just stood there yelling, "Hey,
fucker, you want a piece of this? Come and get
it!"

Free crawled out of the airlock at the base and
fell into the corridor. "MT, seal this airlock at the
bottom and the top. And close the door of that
Sling basket."

"Unable to close the door of the basket, but I can comply with the rest."

Free watched as the airlock seal shrunk further. It seemed to be enough for the prisoner, stupid as he was, to realize that they couldn't enter the dome now, and that they would be sucked into space if he didn't close that damned door, and that Jason was about to leap out of the airlock and inside the basket.

"Shut the door, shut the door!" Free said under his breath.

He watched as the Sling basket moved forward into the fissure that MT created. The guy in the doorway took it all in, finally. From where he was, Free couldn't hear him, but the door suddenly closed as the basket moved further into the crack, and Jason lunged for the door that slammed shut in his face just as the airlock sealed shut.

Free hobbled along the corridor, back to the elevator that would take him back down to the surface of the moon Elysium. He did not have much hope that Jason would be sucked out into space. Likely the airlock seal at the top would prevent that. All Free could do was get down to the surface and see if he could keep the elevator down there so that Jason couldn't follow him, at least not until he found another way off the moon, and Free was sure he would find a way. And he had at least one AI helping him, though in actual fact, there was probably only one AI left anyway, now.

Free glanced up. Jason was nothing if not resourceful. And determined. As if reading his mind, MT said, "It's in the genes."

TO THE THIRD POWER

"Is that supposed to make me feel better?" Free mumbled, but the AI did not respond.

The elevator floor was damaged and Free figured that it would not be good for him to drop such a great distance to the surface. "MT, can you repair the damage to this elevator?"

"Already in progress."

The breaks and ragged cracks were being sealed, and Free pressed his palms to the walls so he could balance around the repairs, holding on despite the pain in his back. He felt disheartened. He would end up on Elysium alone. Not alone, but with Jason. The AI had an agenda; to aid Free's survival. But it had another agenda, and that was to help the being that it controlled. Here was MT controlling Jason and helping Free at the same time. It was totally insane. But Free knew who MT was rooting for. And Free also knew he had nowhere to hide. Maybe it would be best to just kill himself. At least he could be with Skye.

As the elevator began to descend, he looked up, terrified of what he would see. The Sling's basket was just at the edge of leaving the dome completely for its journey through space to the moon Thanos.

In the blink of an eye, Jason turned his head and looked down. It was as if even from this distance Free could feel the burning of those eyes boring through his soul. What was the monster thinking?

Suddenly Jason turned his attention back to the cage. He crouched low, and then propelled himself like an athlete into the air. The machete broke

through the top of the airlock and the fist of his
other hand smashed through the opening.

Free watched in awe as Jason seemed to be
pulled into space, and a spark of hope revived in
him. Maybe the universe was benevolent after all!
The vortex was forcing him out of the airlock. He
would be sucked to his doom!

At that moment, the basket moved away from
the dome. Jason lunged. And reached for it. And
grabbed on. He pulled himself up and out of the
airlock and clung to the bottom of the basket as it
now freely fell forward into space.

Free, amazed, watched as Jason crawled the
length of the basket and clutched onto the arm that
held it.

He should be dead. How can he breathe up
there? The nano-ants that Castillo talked about,
that had been implanted into Jason many years
before Castillo even got his hands on the killer,
they must have been revived as well when he
brought Jason back.

"The nano-ants are in the programming," MT
said, as if reading Free's mind. "And of course
when the two Jasons amalgamated…"

"So, we revived the ants, and even if we hadn't,
they were transferred from two to three," Free said,
not really a question, because he knew the answer.
He was just really thinking out loud. It explained
why the Jasons never really got hurt and why he
revived almost instantly. Why he had the power of
ten men. Why he could survive in airless space,
even though he was still human, or partially so.

"Yes," the AI confirmed, although Free had no need of confirmation.

The elevator reached the surface and Free dragged himself out. He looked around at the camp, the destruction and the bodies. As the only living being on this moon he felt despair settle over him. Above him, the Sling moved away rapidly on its course through dark space toward an even darker point in the sky; Thanos.

"He'll survive it, won't he?" he asked MT.

"Quite likely."

"And he'll kill all the prisoners?"

"If he can. Of course."

"Why?" Free asked, as any son would ask about the actions of a father that were inexplicable; in this case the actions of a mass murderer. And the "why" had so many connotations. Too many.

"That's who he is," MT said.

Free felt deflated. More than depressed. He wondered if Jackson got the message. And when he would get here. Worse-case scenario, Free had another five plus months to survive here, with the ghosts, until the first shuttle was scheduled to arrive. Yes, he had escaped with his life, but what was his life now? He was alone. Now. Always. And he was the son of Jason. Could he ever lead anything resembling a normal life, knowing what he had been through, knowing who his father was? Free wondered what his life was about. Why he was born. Why he alone had survived. How could he be the only one with strength enough to survive? Or was he just lucky?

Suddenly he said, "MT, am I like him? Am I like him in any way?"

MT paused. "I suppose you will need to find that out for yourself."

"Did you... Did you help me survive?"

"I am programmed to aid in the survival of human beings."

"And the survival of Jason. Especially Jason, right?"

"Yes, especially Jason."

"And he and I share DNA, so you helped me."

The AI did not respond.

"Why? Why was I the only one saved?"

"But Free, you aren't the only one. There are the prisoners headed to Thanos. And, in case you ever forget, Jason has survived. He will always survive. It is in his nature."